The Blackbird Conspiracy

The Blackbird Conspiracy

a novel

Ted Bolerjack

First Paperback published in 2023
by Ingram Content Group

ISBN 979-8-218-39916-0

Cover design by Nick Venables

For Danielle
Without your love and support this book
would not be possible

This book is dedicated to the British Secret
Service agents of Special Operations Executive
(SOE) who put their lives in danger to support
and stimulate resistance efforts in occupied
countries of Europe during World War Two.

Chapter One

THERE WAS NO DOUBT in his mind, someone was following him, and when they caught up to him, someone was going to die.

The river Meuse passed before Richard Thorne, and except for the trickle of water around the supporting piers of the Saint Servatius Bridge—the oldest bridge in Holland—a hush had fallen over the rain-dampened city of Maastricht. A cool mist rose up from its dark surface, wrapped around the bridge's seven arches, and eventually overtook everything in its grasp. He paused at the water's edge while his senses reached into the still night seeking a target which would not reveal itself.

A rain drop fell from a broken street lamp, landed on the back of his neck like the touch of a steel finger, and soaked into his collar. Standing rigid with a quickening pulse, he held his breath; a sudden motion had caught his eye. A cadaverous man materialized from out of the fog no more than four or five strides away. Thorne instinctively tightened his grip on a Fairbairn-Sikes double-edged, commando knife concealed within the folds of his heavy overcoat; it was the only thing he had to bolster his courage.

The skeletal man looked back and forth in indecision, ignoring Thorne at first. A tiny amber glow pulsed as he inhaled and exhaled on a cigarette. Before Thorne had a chance to react, the man coughed, flicked the still-lit cigarette away into the shadows, and called out across the path between them, "What miserable dog's weather."

Thorne relaxed his grip. "You can say thunder to that. Rain again tomorrow I suppose."

"*Ja,* and cooler too," the man said looking skyward as if to read a forecast from the starless night sky.

Thorne knew a true Dutchman loved to discuss the weather and had often used such a challenge-response phrase with his resistance counterparts. The man closed in on Thorne, his features barely visible in the poor light, hand extended in a friendly gesture. Thorne could make out bright eyes, mere pinpoints of light hidden beneath the brow of a western-style fedora, as he accepted the man's clammy handshake.

"What have you got for me?" He released the boney grip of his companion and searched the surrounding fog.

"I counted seventeen tanks, a mix of Tigers and older *Sturmgeschutz* tank destroyers. Do you know them?" Seeing Thorne nod, he continued. "They moved into position on the road outside of Eindhoven before the sun went down yesterday." He handed Thorne a folded piece of paper. "I marked their location for you there."

"Part of the 9th Panzers no doubt." Thorne imagined the tanks plotted as little boxes on a large map, with crisscrossing red and blue arrows showing their progress. Some British general, perhaps Monty himself he thought, would use this information in planning the forthcoming assault on the Siegfried Line.

"What about men? I need to know how many men, where they are located, who their commanders are. Do you think you can get that?"

The Dutchman shifted on his feet before nodding. Thorne slipped a wad of folded papers—food ration coupons for butter and milk—to the Dutchman.

"Tomorrow my children eat well." The man grinned.

"Let's hope by Christmas, they eat well every day thereafter."

"Brussels has been liberated." The man anxiously tucked the ration papers into his vest.

"With any luck, Holland shall also be free soon!" Thorne looked back in the direction from where the Dutchman had emerged. "Did you see anyone back there?"

"I was not followed, if that is what you mean."

"What about *Polizei*?"

"No. Only a few soldiers near the tavern by the river, but they did not see me."

"Very well then."

"Until next time my friend." The Dutchman smiled before vanishing into the fog.

Thorne crept to the edge of a stone wall, and leaned against its rough surface in an effort to blend into the shadows. He waited nearly a full minute after the Dutchman had gone, staring into the murky night, and contemplated his next move.

Seemed a bit sheepish.

The information about the Panzers was a tidbit at best, nothing substantial, but enough to confirm the Germans were still moving—withdrawing from the western front and licking their wounds after brutal fighting all summer with the Allies in Northern France. Thorne had seen the thin man once before, hovering around resistance headquarters. While not a direct member of the underground faction operating in Maastricht, Thorne assumed he must be one of dozens of informants looking for a handout in exchange for information about their occupiers.

Convinced it was safe to move on, he stepped out from concealment. But in the next brief second, something alerted his ever-keen senses—a shadow, a shade, a shape—no, nothing but a trick of his mind; it was something else.

A stone skittered into view along the path just in front of him announcing the arrival of another stranger. With no time to react, Thorne moved as if to pass the stranger, but as he did so, a hoarse voice came from the shadowed figure, "Miserable weather, no?"

In the instant it took to decipher the words, Thorne detected danger in the stranger's voice. There was something in the man's dialect—a hint of an unusual accent, an uncommon phrasing, not so much a question, but a stoic account of fact. Out of the corner of his eye, he'd seen the man stop in mid-stride with hands tucked deep into the pockets of a dark overcoat.

The enigmatic words still hung in the air when, as if on cue, search lights appeared along the river. Whether from a patrol boat or other vehicle on the opposite bank, Thorne could not tell, but he knew he had been betrayed.

Richard Thorne was a veteran agent of Special Operations Executive, the British intelligence service—he was a spy. Although practiced in the art of gathering intelligence on the movement and strength of the German war machine in Northern Europe, he was no assassin. Nonetheless, SOE had trained him to defend himself, even if that meant having to kill. Armed only with the seven-inch commando blade and his bare hands, there were only two options at hand: flee or fight. He turned slightly to face the stranger and judged the distance between them. "Yes, a wet night no doubt," he replied.

The stranger seemingly took no notice of the search lights which probed the foggy river bank several meters down the path from where they stood. Thorne anxiously awaited something further from the man, but it did not come. Without warning, in a single swift motion, he lunged cat-like toward the spot where the featureless black form stood. In a moment of panic, the man turned attempting to put distance between himself and Thorne, and that was all he needed. Rushing his victim from behind, Thorne cupped his left hand over the man's mouth and jabbed the point of his knife into the side of the man's neck, scarcely penetrating the skin; the man did not resist and willingly stepped backwards.

Thorne pulled him from the pathway keeping his back from the river as he moved.

A beam of light inched its way toward them, combing the shadows along the shoreline.

"Why are you following me?" Thorne whispered as he slipped his hand downward from the man's mouth keeping grasp of the man's chin. He waited for a response and when it did not immediately come, he tightened his grip on his captive. "Easy now mate," he shifted to English momentarily. "Who are you working for?"

A ragged circle of light crept closer, only seconds before they would be seen.

The man stuttered—his words unintelligible to Thorne—and squirmed in an effort to break away. Thorne misjudged the dexterity of his opponent, and although he held the man firmly in check against his own body with his left arm, the man clutched at his knife hand, keeping it at bay. With great effort, he managed to free his right hand and promptly slammed the butt of the knife into the man's temple. The man dropped like a bag of wet stones. Thorne followed suit and lay motionless in the damp earth next to his victim—their forms indistinguishable from the jagged rocks and thick gorse that lined the river bank. The searchlight skimmed across their prone position and doubled back.

Thorne slipped the knife back into his jacket and dragged the limp body further off the pathway into the shadowed bracken near the base of the Saint Servatius Bridge. Rummaging through the man's pockets turned up a pistol and a wallet with identification papers he could not make out in the darkness. He stuffed these into his pockets and took up a crouched position just paces from his unconscious victim.

The headlights of a vehicle materialized a considerable distance from the bridge, but there was no doubt of their bearing. They grew in intensity making for Thorne's position. The fog thinned as a cool rain began to fall along the river front. Thorne jogged southward along the causeway, parallel to the river, and slipped into the shadows of the city, making his way back to his den where he would hole up for the remainder of the night.

IT WAS TWO HOURS LATER, in a safe house located in the village of Gronsveld, just southeast of the capital city of Maastricht, where in the security of a cramped and sparsely furnished room, Thorne reflected upon the fallen man—most definitely a German agent, or local detective. Identification papers showed the man as Albert Boels, a resident of the province of Limburg, carpenter by trade. The other papers in his possession matched those of an average citizen, but Thorne knew it was all a cover of course; the giveaway was the Luger 7.65mm pistol the man carried. If he wasn't a Nazi, he was most definitely working for them.

I should've killed him.

Seated in the middle of his room, Thorne flipped his

commando knife from hand to hand while a cigarette dangled from the corner of his mouth. The bastard would have a hell of a headache in the morning, he decided, but he would live. Thorne despised killing. He'd done it before, only when necessary, and only just now swallowed hard and let out a deep breath.

It's all part of the job; God forgive me when this ordeal is over.

He threw the knife at a dark spot in the back of the door to his room. Its blade stuck with a loud thud, resting within a tight cluster of notches from previous throws, and hovered there, ready and waiting, for an unexpected visitor who might knock in the middle of the night. He checked his watch; just enough time for a couple hours of sleep before relaying the information about the Panzers to London. He snubbed out his cigarette in a small tray that held a single candle, and extinguished its flame before he crawled into bed. His hand slid beneath his pillow and reassuringly found the pistol he kept hidden there. It was once said that a certain peace comes to a man from sleeping with a gun, and on a night like this, he knew why.

If they come for me tonight, someone will die.

In the early years of the War, more than fifty of his fellow operatives in Belgium and Holland had ended up in the hands of the Nazis. It was all part of *Das Englandspiel*—the English Game—orchestrated by Major Hermann Giskes, then head of German Intelligence who oversaw counter-espionage in the Netherlands. With the capture of several agents, the Nazis were able to dupe the SOE by continuing to send encoded messages back to England that appeared to originate from the English spies previously inserted into occupied territory. This subterfuge went on for two years before SOE learned of the ploy.

Thorne thought back to his last meeting with his SOE chief Thomas Beecher in the weeks after the discovery of the *Englandspiel* ruse. Beecher had handed him two hardback, pocket-sized copies of Shakespeare's *The Merchant of Venice*.

"We're going to try something different. We'll be using a book cipher on a go forward basis," Beecher said.

Thorne was familiar with the coding system from his SOE training; the book cipher was based on replacing individual words in a message with numbers signifying their location in the book being used as the key. He was also aware that SOE had all but abandoned the practice and now promoted other means of coding their messages; he assumed Beecher must have a good reason for sticking with this cipher.

"But why the extra copy?" He thumbed through the two books and noticed that both were exact copies—the same 1915 edition by Purcell and Somers.

"One will serve as your key, the other is for your counterpart in the resistance. You'll be working with a new set of contacts in Maastricht this go around." Beecher slid a manila folder across his desk.

Thorne looked through the paperwork. Beecher had arranged for everyone involved in the upcoming mission to use codenames from *The Merchant*. He recognized the name of his friend Stefan Visser, Dutch resistance leader in the Maastricht circuit, who would be called *Arragon*. His own codename was to be *Launcelot*. There was also reference to a new underground agent codenamed *Portia*.

Interesting.

"I've retained a copy of *The Merchant* for myself, and have given instructions to the various listening teams to be alert for your messages. You'll find specific times of day and frequencies on which to broadcast there in your orders. They will be relayed directly to me for deciphering. Brilliant, wouldn't you agree?"

Thorne knew this was Beecher's attempt to strengthen the chain of messages from resistance, to SOE operative, back to headquarters, but he thought the entire process overly cumbersome. He'd simply nodded in agreement.

That had been nearly six weeks previous. Now as he lie in bed, time crept through the night while his ever-working brain replayed the day's events over and over in his mind.

A creaky floor overhead told him the venerable Mr. Braam was awake. Footsteps shuffled across the floor to find a chamber pot, curtains were pulled aside for a quick examination of the weather, and after a series of hacking coughs, a loud plop fell upon the rickety bed frame above Thorne's own, signaling the end of the nightly routine. Somewhere at the rear of the house a broken shutter tapped annoyingly in the wind. In the alleyway, Madame Abels' dog barked incessantly at shadows in the night. Thorne's brain sifted through the night sounds discarding them as a regular part of his mundane existence.

He finally pushed up from a sleepless rest and looked at his watch again; it was just before midnight and time to check in with London. He relit the candle and prepared for transmission. The flimsy scrap of cloth that served as a blackout curtain covering his window did not provide enough shade to hide light from within, so he draped a heavy, wool blanket behind it. He recalled a passage he'd read in *The Merchant*, 'How far that little candle throws his beams!' and he smiled to himself. 'So shines a good deed in a naughty world.'

He set about scrawling out a coded message to report his findings to headquarters. Flipping through the pages of his burgundy-colored, hardbound book, he searched for his next piece of code. When he was finished, he pulled a saddle-brown, weather-worn suitcase from under the bed that held the British Type B Mark II radio set, commonly known as the B2. He opened the lid and pulled out the Morse key he would us for transmitting dots and dashes to a radio operator listening somewhere across the English Channel, and after plugging in the key and checking various switches and knobs for the correct settings, he powered on the radio letting it warm up.

Thorne looked back on earlier missions when things had been much simpler. Dropped behind enemy lines without a radio, he'd used his false identity to traverse the country making contact with local resistance members and providing them with specific objectives. After a few days, he'd slip aboard a secret return flight to London and relay his information to his commander in a face-to-face debriefing. But as of late, he found himself stuck in occupied territory for days, or even weeks, on end, and he was now forced to send tidbits of information by radio as he gathered them. Headquarters had warned him of the decreasing likelihood of extraction by plane—there simply wasn't a stretch of flat land in the Low Countries that the Germans didn't occupy, or one they hadn't flooded in anticipation of an Allied offensive.

I'd sure like to get the hell out of here; all this lurking about is wearing me out. Every day brought the threat of discovery and arrest by the *Sicherheitsdienst*—the intelligence arm and secret service of the Nazi regime—or even worse, capture, torture, and death at the hands of the secret state police, the dreaded *Gestapo*.

At half past midnight, he hastily sent his message using Morse code. He momentarily worried that his radio signal might be intercepted by someone besides SOE—including the *Gestapo*, thus revealing his location—but he reassured himself the message itself would be totally undecipherable to anyone except Beecher, who held the exact edition of Shakespeare's *Merchant*.

Chapter Two

AT DAYBREAK, THORNE STARTED his day with a shave, then washed his face using a pitcher of water and bowl on the dresser. He inspected himself in a cracked and faded mirror nailed to the wall while he gnawed on a loaf of hard bread. Dressed in civilian clothing, he carried false identification papers declaring his name as Alexandre Jacobs, thirty-six years old, employed by the state-run railroad. SOE had forged the documents using a black and white photo of him taken nearly two years earlier.

The photograph showed a fair-complexioned, handsome face, chiseled with squared-off jaw, and a high flat forehead topped with smooth black hair parted from left to right. Inquisitive eyes hid beneath a set of thick, straight brows. Thorne was of average height and build, and although physically fit, his frame did not call out his superb physique. He compared the photo to the figure now staring back from the mirror—*a few pounds lighter perhaps*—and set his ID card on top of his other papers as he finished dressing.

He also carried a medical release exempting him from military service. A tobacco certificate and food ration stamps rounded out the stack of documents he took with him everywhere he went. He snatched up the papers, tucked them inside his coat, and left his room, destined for an abandoned, garment factory in the center of Maastricht where he would meet Stefan Visser.

When Thorne had first arrived in Maastricht several weeks earlier, Visser had immediately arranged a meeting with a man named Van Buren. Situated on the outskirts of the city, Van Buren's safe house in Gronsveld provided an ideal location for Thorne. The quiet town had fewer German patrols than Maastricht itself, yet sat close enough to the city for him to meet resistance operatives in short time.

Visser had put things in motion by opening up his network of informants and resistance spies to Thorne, thus allowing access to the information London sought on the whereabouts of the German army in and around the ancient city.

As he plodded along Station Street in Gronsveld, Thorne blended into his surroundings like a lifelong citizen of Holland. His mother, a native of England, had an elderly aunt that lived in a village named Neerhespen in the Dutch province of Flemish Brabant. In the wonderful days before the Great War, he'd accompanied her to Holland for long visits during the summer while she nursed his great aunt. Summertime in Holland was overwhelmingly joyful in those days; he recalled countless windmills dotting the landscape, flanked by canals that crisscrossed flat fields full of brightly colored tulips. And everywhere he went there were children, running and playing, absolutely carefree.

Now, nearly forty years later, he paused under a gloomy sky looking across the river at rows of buildings turned to rubble. The breeze held a pervasive odor of charred wood that hung about the war-torn city. Many of the trees along the river were stripped bare, many were no longer alive. The grass in a once glorious park near the river was unkempt and grew wildly in places, and while there were children about, they had no bicycles, no toys, nor playgrounds for amusement.

A melancholy weight had set upon him in recent weeks. He longed for a quiet life somewhere far away from the desolation, despair, and death that had taken hold of Europe. The War dragged on and on, and the return of magnificent days slipped further and further into an uncertain future, and he was tired of it all. He took a deep breath, inhaling through his nose and exhaling out his mouth. With feet planted firmly in a wide stance, he pushed his shoulders back and decided then and there that he would do something about it. If harvesting morsels of information for SOE—no matter how insignificant—contributed in any way to bringing an end to the War, then that was what he had to do.

He pressed on, moving more or less parallel to the river, and arrived at the garment factory through a long-forgotten sewer tunnel that opened upon a rocky ledge along the river front. After confirming his identity, he was escorted by two members of the Dutch resistance to a secluded room in the basement where he found Stefan Visser sitting at a table under a dimly lit bulb.

"Please sit down," Visser said, looking up from a map he studied.

Thorne noted dark circles under the eyes of the man's wearied face. When they had first met three years earlier, during Thorne's first foray into Maastricht's resistance underworld, he had at first sized up Visser as a Lothario, a libertine, and someone overly attractive for such clandestine work. The stress of running the underground movement in Maastricht had weighed heavily upon the man before him, and Thorne now saw his friend in a new light. Obviously pleased at Thorne's arrival, he stood up with hand outstretched toward Thorne. "I trust you are doing well."

"Not as well as I'd prefer," Thorne replied bitterly. He emptied his pockets onto Visser's table, laying the Luger pistol atop the papers from the man named Boels.

"What is all of this?"

"It's what I took from a man who followed me last night. I met with your man, the one from Eindhoven. As soon as he left me, this other fellow showed up." Thorne spun the identification documents to face Visser. "Do you know him?"

Visser examined the documents momentarily. "He does look familiar but his identity here is probably false. And you think De Vries—", he instantly corrected himself, "*our friend from Eindhoven* is acquainted with this man?"

"I was hoping you could tell me. I didn't like either

of them. De Vries, or whatever his name is, seemed on edge when I spoke with him. Then this chap appeared out of the fog right after De Vries left, followed by a German patrol boat on the river and a car that I didn't wait around to identify."

"I take it you are unharmed?" He looked Thorne up and down with concern, and when Thorne nodded, he continued, "And what about this man?"

"He'll be lucky if he remembers what hit him. But now I have to wonder about the validity of the information De Vries gave me. I've already transmitted it to London, so I hope it is accurate."

"I'll have someone look into both of them." Visser rose from the table and pulled a bottle of port from a wooden crate in the corner of the room.

"Yes, you do that, no more amateurs. When do I meet Portia?"

"As I told you before, there will be no direct contact." He poured the ruby port into two glasses and offered one to Thorne. "I prefer to keep a veil between SOE and the members of my organization."

"And why is that?"

"I find it makes things *simpler* with Baker Street."

Thorne savored the warmth of the port as it trickled down his esophagus. He cleared his throat, "I prefer to know who I'm working with, no veils."

"Richard my friend, we have worked together for a very long time. Please trust me on this."

Thorne finished his port. "Very well, what have you got in mind?"

"She will leave messages for you, coded with the

book you gave me. There is a park, here in the southern part of the city." He pointed to his map as Thorne closed in for a better look. "She has personally chosen this spot as a safe place to exchange information."

"Then why not meet me in person?"

"It is far too risky. The Nazis have many eyes in this city. A man and woman conversing openly and sharing information would surely be spotted by someone. Instead, she has picked this location near the fountain to leave messages for you."

Thorne studied the map. The park was a short distance from Gronsveld.

Convenient—he'd retrieve her messages, append them to his own, and then relay them to London at a later time—*seems simple enough.*

"You should arrive precisely at nine o' clock on every Tuesday morning, and there you will find a packet waiting for you. As your boss has ordered, she will be the go-between with a man on the German border who will supply information from along the Western Wall."

Thorne reluctantly agreed. With Visser's plan, he felt he'd been reduced to nothing more than a link in a twisted chain between the Dutch resistance and SOE. The two men finally shook hands after the details were wrapped up, and Thorne was escorted out the tunnel, and back to the edge of the river.

He made his was to his safe house, all the while brooding over his current assignment. He'd lost count of the number of missions he'd served for SOE, but hoped this one would be short-lived. He preferred working on his own, setting his own schedule, and hated relying on others for completing a task. The next several weeks would present an unforeseen challenge, and with a sudden vengeance, he took out his frustrations on a piece of rubbish that met the toe of his boot.

ON AN OVERCAST TUESDAY, three weeks after meeting with Stefan Visser, Thorne made his way to the park. He arrived just before nine, and sat for several minutes surveying the area for any sign of his contact. Having failed on previous attempts to catch her in the act, he was determined she in fact must arrive at some other time than what had been agreed upon. Regardless of her method, he could tell she was definitely an ingenious woman who patterned her arrival in a manner that neither he nor anyone else could catch on to.

Today was no different. He'd seen no one in the area, and approached the drop-off location expecting to find something waiting there for him. The 'packet' he was to retrieve was a discarded cigarette—its tip burnt and scrunched as if hastily put out after two puffs. When he got back to his room, he'd dismantle it to find a handwritten note scrawled on a piece of tobacco paper wrapped around a needle that had been stuffed back into the cigarette.

Thorne considered himself fortunate; having supplied a copy of *The Merchant* to Portia, would save him the time of decoding her messages. The information he received would already be written in their established format, he simply had to add it to the end of his own messages or transmit it by itself if he had none to add.

Perhaps there is something to be said for Beecher's plan after all.

But today, there was nothing waiting for him. He had agreed on a contingency plan with Visser—if there were any threat of observation, Portia would avert the drop and try again the next day. Both Visser and Beecher had reassured him that Portia was experienced and could be trusted. In this game, Thorne knew that no one could truly be trusted, but having lost his previous resistance contact to the *Gestapo*, he had to rely on their faith in the woman. It was all he had.

He tied his boot lace while he perched there in front of the drop spot contemplating his next move. Even now there was a chance he might be under observation. Had he missed something she had seen? He glanced skyward as a duo of ME-109's flew southward. In that glimpse, he also scanned the fenced boundaries of the park. Pedestrians passed beyond a rusted, wrought-iron gate framed by ivy covered, stone walls, but no one else was within its perimeter besides himself. With hands thrust deeply in his coat pockets, he hunched his shoulders and bowed his head as he left the park.

On the avenue just to the east of the gate, he paused indecisively. One block away to his left, a couple of German soldiers harassed two women on the opposite street corner. One of the soldiers questioned the older of the two, shouting *Juden* threateningly to her. At the same time, the other closed in on her younger teen-aged daughter. Thorne used the distraction to move parallel to the soldiers keeping to his side of the street. He wove between citizens on a cobbled sidewalk, most of whom like himself, tried to ignore the soldiers. When he was directly across from the commotion, he noticed one of the soldiers yank a handkerchief from the younger girl's head, revealing curly locks of auburn hair that fell upon her shoulders. The soldier pressed her against the stone wall of a three-story building.

Thorne halted in his tracks with fists clinched tightly in his pockets. His fingernails dug into his palms as he took a deep breath and exhaled loudly.

Bloody hell!

With no other soldiers in sight, he fleetly crossed the road, weaving around a horse-drawn cart, and approached the soldiers from behind. Before they had taken notice, he grabbed a rifle slung across the shoulder of the man to his left, jerking hard and spinning the surprised German to face him. Before the soldier had time to react, Thorne's fist smashed into his nose sending a spray of blood and snot across his face. The soldier fell backwards landing on his rear, and his already clouding eyes stared blankly toward the sky, as his head fell to the side dragging his limp body with it to the pavement.

The other soldier released his grip on the older woman's coat and turned to see his unconscious comrade. He took a step forward in a slight lurch toward Thorne, but Thorne was quick to counter. Thorne drove his right foot into the man's knee, and with a sickening pop, the soldier's leg buckled from under him. As the German let out a startled cry and fell forward, Thorne grabbed the back of the man's helmeted head driving it into his knee. The older woman and her daughter panicked in that moment and dashed away from Thorne before he could confirm their well-being.

Thorne ducked his head from gawking onlookers and moved into a side street that curved away from the avenue. Tucking his floppy hat into his coat, he moved swiftly through a maze of back streets and alleys before he finally found himself back on the same avenue where he'd started. He was three blocks down from the corner where the two soldiers lie unconscious, and with their discovery imminent from other Germans undoubtedly in the area, he took no chances at loitering in the vicinity. He jumped alongside the driver of a passing cart, the driver looked at Thorne seemingly without surprise. Thorne smiled in return as the driver snapped his reins thrusting his pony forward.

"Can you take me to Gronsveld?" he asked in Dutch.

"No, but I will take you as far as Kobbe's Way."

"That will do just fine." Thorne grinned as he scrunched his floppy hat low over his brow and unfurled his collar to help conceal his face.

Chapter Three

NEARLY TWO HOURS LATER, Thorne walked along the cobbled stones of Kobbe's Way back to Van Buren's. He talked to himself taking note of people he saw, vehicles that crossed his path, buildings that were used and disused, and stored precise details of everything he observed in the file bank within his mind. He constantly watched for German police or soldiers, and diverted from his route at the slightest hint of danger.

He'd been alone for so long that he didn't think much about walking alone, nor holding a conversation with himself about his agenda for the day. Nor did he take into account the lack of interaction with another soul for weeks on end as anything awkward. He'd settled into a perfectly complacent life as a loner, a solitary man. Was it his comfort with solitude that made him an excellent candidate for SOE service or was it the years of operating in secrecy and isolation that had left him alone in the world? He no longer contemplated which had come first, but deep down inside the recesses of his soul, he desperately wished for a friend—someone to talk to, someone to spend time with, *someone to help forget this bloody war.*

A light rain had moved in the previous night ahead of a weather front, bringing with it a damp and chill wind off the North Sea. Raindrops clattered on broken roof tiles and water trickled in refuse strewn gutters. It reminded him momentarily of London and he suddenly longed for a heavy wool overcoat and a wide-brimmed fedora instead of the lightweight coat he wore. He unconsciously let out a heavy sigh; he'd fallen into a monotonous routine, gathering information by day and sending it by night, with very little in the way of activity or social interaction in between. He constantly reminded himself that the bits of intelligence he supplied to London somehow served a greater purpose, but at the same time, he increasingly felt like he was merely a cog in some giant machine. All of these thoughts, his reclusiveness and detachment from society, his desire for companionship, and any thoughts beyond tomorrow, were all tucked away in the back of his mind allowing him to focus on the minute details within his immediate sight.

He rounded a familiar corner; Van Buren's safe house was just up ahead. *Interesting, that horse cart was not there earlier. Empty.* He counted the number of windows that were shaded and unshaded in neighboring buildings—*seven and nine, same as this morning*—and took inventory of every person on the street and what they were doing; *nothing extraordinary.* He ducked into a book shop intending to use an interior stairwell to gain access to his second-floor room in the adjoining building, but when he entered the store, he found a familiar man there waiting for him.

"Hello Stefan," he said.

"Ah, Mr. Launcelot, how are you this fine day?"

Thorne started, "What's so fine about it—", he paused when a middle-aged woman appeared from the back room. "Good morning, Madame Abels. Please do excuse us." Thorne pointed toward a side door and escorted Stefan up a flight of steps to his apartment.

Once the door to his room was secured and the curtains drawn, Stefan continued, "You look upset again; I do hope you haven't run into strangers following you once more."

"No, but I just came from the park. There was nothing there for me."

"Hmmm." Stefan scratched at his head. "Portia is a smart girl; something must have alarmed her. You should try again tomorrow."

"Yes, of course. But I have to wonder about her choice for a drop location." As he talked, he set up his radio to receive messages from London. Beecher had arranged a twice daily schedule for communications whereby Thorne would transmit in the middle of the night beginning any time after midnight, and would subsequently listen for incoming messages during the middle of the day starting at noon. By splitting the sending and receiving times, they hoped to minimize the amount of time he spent on air, and thus limit his chances for detection by the Nazis. He also moved frequently, using different locations for transmitting his radio messages back to England, but this required carrying the bulky suitcase with his B2, and increased the likelihood of discovery during the daytime. The *SD*, and more recently the *Gestapo*, had become increasingly proficient at finding wireless operators. When tipped off about a possible spy in the area, they would drive around the vicinity with specially designed radio-detection trucks listening on various frequencies until they found a signal, then it was simply a matter of using triangulation to determine the location of the wireless operator.

"Keep an eye on the window there." Thorne opened his suitcase and prepared for reception from London. He squatted in the middle of his room, headphones over his ears, while Visser kept an apprehensive view on the street below. Within minutes, he heard the familiar sounds acknowledging his sender was on the air. The first word came across in a series of encoded numbers—he recognized them as the codename *Morocco* that his boss Thomas Beecher used. Thorne doubted that Beecher actually sent the messages himself, but presumed he had given orders to a staff member to transmit the code on his specific frequency.

He recognized the sender's signature—the subtle pattern used with the Morse key—and was able to instantly scrawl out the message. As soon as he received the last of a series of dashes and dots, he powered down his radio and packed it away. He tucked the case safely under the bed and covered it with the wool blanket he kept with him as he moved from location to location. He waited in the shade just beyond the window for several moments while Visser eyed the street below.

Convinced there were no radio trucks in the area, nor *Gestapo* officers rapidly descending upon their location, Visser nodded and Thorne opened *The Merchant of Venice* and began decoding the message from London.

Visser watched in fascination as Thorne flipped back and forth between pages, jotted words on his note pad, and searched for others in the book. While there are variations on how a book cipher is precisely coded—some rely on finding the first instance of a particular word and numbering that specific word, other methodologies number specific letters from individual words—the approach Beecher and Thorne had agreed upon used a three-digit number to identify a word based on its unique location in *The Merchant*. Separated by colons, each number referred to its page number, sentence number, and word position in a given sentence. It was a tedious process. He often struggled to find certain words in his coding scheme that described contemporary military classifications, nonetheless he was able to cleverly substitute words of similar meanings and still convey the overall intention of his messages.

Decoding Beecher's messages was much simpler; he drew a hash mark after every third number received by Morse code, and then looked up each number in the key. He finished writing out the last word of the message and read it aloud with deliberate slowness for Visser's benefit. "Increase frequency of information exchange to every other day STOP Significant action comes to Low Countries in six weeks STOP Need more on strength of Second Army along Aachen front STOP."

Both men looked at each other in jubilation. "Finally! It must be the invasion. "While Thorne himself was not aware of the name *Operation Market Garden*, nor was he privy to any details about the invasion plans or dates, he knew—as well as everyone else in Northern Europe—that it was only a matter of time before the Allies launched an assault on Germany using Denmark, Holland, and Belgium as the gateway into the Third Reich. The Normandy invasion earlier that summer had sent a shock wave of rumors and stories throughout Europe, the most common being that the War would be wrapped up by Christmas. Beecher's missive now provided a glimmer of hope that Hitler's war had an end in the not-too-distant future, an end that would take him back to England where he vowed to remain for several years until Europe was whole once again.

"What is the best way to contact this girl Portia? We need her to step up our exchange schedule."

"I will take of everything. Go back to the park tomorrow, you will have your information."

THE NEXT MORNING, THORNE shuffled through a newspaper, never obscuring his view of the secret location just beyond the decaying water fountain. He thought it amusing how the Nazi-published paper downplayed the impact of a recent Allied bomb strike—simply mentioning that a few cattle were killed during a raid—when in reality, he had seen first-hand an entire city block annihilated by the accuracy of British and American bombers.

What a load of rubbish! He looked again at his watch; it was now a quarter past nine. *Let's get this business over with.* After two passes at the drop sight, he'd found nothing this morning, nor had he seen anyone in the vicinity. *Something must have gone astray yet again.*

He folded his paper and made ready to leave when just across the clearing from the fountain, a woman caught his eye. She had short, blond hair that shimmered even in the faint overcast morning light, and graceful, supple hands that brushed a fallen lock of it from her face. She was not dressed outlandishly to attract attention; in fact, her wardrobe lacked any color at all and hung baggily against her lithe frame.

Something unusual here; might this be her?

In fact, it was the manner in which she walked with purpose, as if trying to hurry while trying not to look like she was hurrying, that first caught his attention. She feigned an intentional pause, looking for something in her pockets while adjusting her floppy blouse; to his well-trained eye, Thorne knew she was putting on a ruse.

There was an intensity of movement just then in her clear, bright eyes that he could see even at this distance which alerted him to a well-dressed man entering the park, following her in a leisurely gait that drew no attention, except that of herself and Thorne.

The man was about his own age, clean-shaven with close-cropped hair that was likely as blond as hers if allowed to grow out. He stalked the woman with a deliberately slow fleetness, always keeping his distance, yet staying well within sight of her. His suit was of newly made fabric and stood out as peculiar, much like a solitary flower growing out of a crack in a broken sidewalk. There was something in his rigid frame and Nordic features—ice blue eyes, long head with a straight nose and tall stature—that some would say exemplified the perfect model of Aryan race.

Unmistakably German.

Whether this woman was his resistance colleague or not, Thorne decided to intervene. He rose from his bench and walked parallel to her on an adjacent path next to the grass clearing that separated them. His trajectory converged with hers where both sidewalks angled toward each other intersecting in a fancy, diamond shape. As he neared the intersection, he deliberately unfurled his newspaper, reading and walking simultaneously. A well-timed collision with the woman sent his papers flying in the air and pushed her gently aside.

"Run," he said in perfect Dutch. The woman, momentarily startled, looked puzzled as he gathered his papers. He noticed the German stop in his tracks and look away from the commotion pretending he hadn't noticed.

"Run," he urged her.

She did not hesitate this time and took off at a brisk pace, breaking into a jog as she exited the park onto the outer walkway. Thorne gathered his papers as the German fell into quick pursuit after her. He knelt to grab a final piece of paper and as the man neared, he guilefully spun on his heels and sprang up to collide full on with him. Both men went down in a cloud of floating papers and curses, but Thorne dexterously rolled to his feet and was already running after the woman before the German got to his feet.

In that brief contact, Thorne learned two things. First, the German weighed a full stone or more less than himself. Second, a sharp sting in his shoulder—a twinge of pain from having hit a hard object—told him the German was wearing a gun beneath his coat.

Must be an undercover bob.

Thorne rapidly caught up to the woman who weaved around people on a busy walkway. He caught her elbow and shouted, "This way!" and pulled her into the street. They dodged two bicyclists and dashed across the street into an alleyway. He tugged her by the arm and forced himself to slow to her pace. "Hurry!"

He looked back over his shoulder to see if the German followed and in that brief moment noticed her calm face; instead of a panic-stricken expression, she wore a mask of tranquility that said she was not afraid. They came to the end of the alley which opened onto a side street, deserted except for a parked car to their left. Thorne stepped into a recessed alcove and tried a door. Locked. Over his shoulder, he saw the woman rush across the street and disappear into a narrow doorway. He darted into the opening just behind her as their pursuer shouted from a distance, ordering them in Dutch to stop.

Thorne slammed the door behind him but could not work the locking mechanism. He haphazardly jammed a table and chair in front of the door to impede his chaser, and from across the room, saw her slip out another doorway.

"Who's there?" a man's voice cried out from upstairs.

Ignoring the man's ranting, he maneuvered through the room knocking over chairs and a small table to create additional obstacles for his pursuer, and barely managed to get out the side exit at the same moment the front door burst inwards on the furniture piled at its back.

He caught up to her on a quiet street as they picked up their pace, and pointed out another cross street to their left. Diverging onto its cobbled surface, they heard footsteps gaining on them.

"You, stop!"

He noticed frightened faces looking out from dirtied windows in his periphery, ducking into interior shadows when he passed them by. He tried another locked door on his right and kept moving.

I've got to do something or he's going to catch us.

The cobbled road narrowed, the walls closed within arm's reach, and Thorne nudged the girl toward an abutting stairwell. They frantically descended into a claustrophobic passageway that led off at a right angle from the street and tunneled below a building. In the murky space, they were hit with the stench of raw sewage. A square patch of light in the distance showed the passage ended some fifty paces away. They raced toward the daylight, splashing in puddles of unseen filth as echoed shouts, now in German, came from behind them.

The narrow tunnel ended in the rummage of a disused courtyard. Broken bricks and stones littered their path, along with objects of wood and glass. Thorne made for a pile of brick that used to be part of a wall but now rose up to a gaping hole in the second floor of a building. He momentarily forgot the woman while he scaled the loose mound making his way toward the ragged opening. He stopped when he heard her let out a muffled cry and saw her topple to the ground.

Just then, the German exited the tunnel, gun drawn, and advanced guardedly toward the fallen woman who clutched her ankle. He looked around the courtyard but failed to notice Thorne perched atop the rubble. He heedfully walked over to her; pistol held firm.

In perfect Dutch he said, "Madam Larsen, we finally meet."

Thorne leaned against the building, attempting to mask his gasps for air by burying his mouth in his sleeve. He waited and watched as the German reached out his left hand to help her from the ground. She carried her weight on one leg and leaned into the man who still held the pistol toward her.

"Tch, tch." He shook his head. "Ach, can you walk?"

Thorne's attention was locked onto the scene unfolding before him. Again, he found himself intrigued with her calm demeanor, and although she continued to favor one leg, she showed no signs of fear toward her captor. Having made a practice of not carrying a firearm or knife during daylight for fear of being caught, he wished he'd planned otherwise today as he searched for a simple weapon. His gaze happened upon a shaft of wood—possibly a table leg or stair spindle—protruding from the pile of rubble.

If I can reach it, I might catch him off guard.

He crept forward, carefully placing footholds amongst the loose brick, but it was no good. His third step sent a stream of debris sliding downward that caught the man's attention.

Bollocks!

It was just enough of a distraction for the German to turn his head away from the woman, and that was all she needed. She swiftly brought her left forearm down just above his wrist dislodging the gun from his hand, and with the outer edge of her other hand, she thrust a chopping blow into his throat.

The man doubled over, retching violently. Thorne took advantage of her keen action and slid down the brick pile grabbing the wooden club in the same motion, and swiftly brought it down upon the back of the German's neck. The man fell face down, still coughing and gasping for air. Thorne turned to her briefly, seeking her approval, but she only ignored him, and instead seized the fallen gun. She flipped the release opening its breech and discharged its magazine into her palm. She tossed the magazine amongst the rubbish lining a nearby building and chucked the pistol into a sewer drain before returning a priggish smile at

Thorne who watched with curious fascination. Then she turned and ran.

He took off after her. The proficiency in which she had disarmed the German, coupled with the way in which she handled the weapon, convinced him of her true identity. The German had not followed and when he caught up to her on a busy street, he called out to her, "Portia, wait!"

Chapter Four

BENEATH THE MASSIVE Victorian-era dome—some forty-odd meters in diameter—that spanned the central reading room in the London library, a white-haired man dressed in a herringbone-patterned, fitted suit with matching vest and trousers, clutched a Hamburg style hat behind his back. He looked the archetypal modern man of a previous era.

He stood off to one side of the dome, in front of a row of iron bookshelves, and looked for a specific section of the more than forty kilometers of shelving housed within the building. Having found the intended area, he retrieved a burgundy-colored, hardbound book from the middle shelf and thumbed through its pages.

The elderly man shambled over to an oak reading table and sat alone. He set a worn, leather valise on the floor next to his chair and pulled out a scrap of paper and fountain pen from his jacket. Had anyone been looking over his shoulder—not that he had drawn any attention to himself—they would have seen that he feverishly flipped back and forth through a copy of Shakespeare's *Hamlet*, seemingly at random, scribbling notes to himself. They would also have seen him suddenly pause—almost in shock—after reading a particular passage. He looked again closer at the page in front of him, and reread the words that had caught his attention, 'There is nothing either good or bad, but thinking makes it so,' and he smiled.

His immersion in the text was disturbed when footsteps approached from his left side; he listened for their passing, but instead they stopped directly behind him. A man's voice whispered close to his left ear and confirmed the stranger's proximity.

"As the blackbird flies."

The white-haired man did not take his eyes from the book. He recognized the gin-soaked breath of his nefarious colleague and merely replied in a quiet voice, "So too follows Falconbridge."

He slowly cocked his head to one side to see a smaller man dressed in a grey, double-breasted suit standing over him. In a practiced routine, the white-haired man slid his leather case into the toes of the shorter man. The short man adjusted his fedora, looked once over his shoulder, then back again at the case, and picked it up. He unbuckled one of two straps securing the valise and pried open the edge. Satisfied with its contents, he pulled the buckle tight again.

"Fifty-thousand pounds," the older man said quietly.

The short man nodded, turned, and disappeared from sight beyond another row of tall bookshelves.

The white-haired man momentarily looked again at the copy of *Hamlet* in front of him, and discreetly tore out the page he had just read. He gathered his things and returned to the section of shelves holding various editions and revisions of Shakespeare's works. He pulled another book from the shelf, and in the gap from where it sat, he carefully slid *Hamlet* through the space turning it sideways to rest behind the others on the shelf. He tactfully replaced the book he had removed, pushed it back into place, and satisfied that *Hamlet* was now hidden from prying eyes, he recited another passage to himself, 'Though this be madness, yet there is method in't,' he snickered.

THORNE SAT IN A DIMLY-LIT room, at a makeshift table—nothing more than a wide plank stretched across two empty barrels—and looked into the eyes of the woman named Portia.

They'd found their way through the streets of Maastricht, and convinced the German undercover agent had not tailed them, made their way to a bicycle repair shop where, after sharing a password with one of the workers, they were admitted to a back room.

A female laborer shoved a large crate aside revealing a trap door that opened into a dank and musty cellar used for hiding resistance members—or anyone else fleeing German authorities.

In the confined space illuminated by a single, small lantern, he got a better look at her. Late twenties, he guessed.

She stared back suspiciously across the table.

In fact, they'd hardly spoken during their escape, except for the name Launcelot he'd uttered in response to her inquiries about his identity.

He had not been this close to a woman in quite some time. His mouth felt suddenly dry; he was instantly captivated by her attractiveness and aroused by her delicate features. Her short, blond hair was roughly cropped above her shoulders. She had a smooth and graceful complexion, a small, thin nose perched above delicate, full lips that longed to be kissed, and a smooth alabaster neck which held her head up with confidence. He also noticed that her left cheek was smudged with dirt, and badly scratched from where she had fallen earlier, but neither detracted from her beauty.

She could be magnificent under any other circumstance!

"How did you find me?" She spoke fluent English with a strong accent.

"You were late. I was in the park when I saw that man following you. Who was he?"

She offered him a cigarette from a small box. He took one and lit it with a match, inhaling deeply. She pulled another for herself and set the box aside.

"Gerhard Mueller. Lieutenant-Colonel Mueller to be precise. He is the deputy of the *Abwehr* here in Maastricht."

"*Abwehr*, I knew it." Thorne was all too familiar with the name *Abwehr*—the shortened version of the German *Abwehrspionage*, or spy defense—which referred to the counter-espionage service of the German High Command. Thorne had been in a constant cat and mouse game the past several months, running and hiding from their intelligence officers as he moved about the Low Countries at the direction of Beecher. She lit her cigarette off the end of his and handed it back to him.

"Thank you for following me; I do not think I would have gotten away without your help."

"Why was he after you?"

"He has been searching for me for many weeks, but he is stupid and lazy."

"We should have killed him. Now he's seen your face. Where will you go?"

"I don't know," she said indifferently. Thin streams of smoke wafted from her lips seductively.

"I have a safe house in Gronsveld, not far from here. I could take you there."

"Thank you, but Arragon will hide me somewhere. I will be fine, he will protect me," she added defensively.

Could there be something between her and Visser?

Thorne flicked ashes on the dirt floor as he admired her courage; the morning's ordeal had barely shaken her.

"Why did you miss your drop earlier this week?" he continued.

"I spotted Mueller following me. I tried to confuse him by stopping in a store. The owner helped me leave through the back, but he must have waited for me, because I saw him again. He followed me soon after that." Thorne was intrigued by her accent and phrasing; it suggested that while well-educated in the language, she did not use it often. She slipped a rusty can across the table. After a brief examination, he tilted it on end dumping a hand-written note into his palm.

"Is this what you were going to drop at the park?" He held his cigarette in his lips.

"Yes."

He looked again at the note written in their secret code. "I received a message from London," he said flatly. "We are to increase the frequency of exchanging information to every other day, did Arragon tell you?"

She looked startled at this revelation. "Every other day? That seems very risky."

"Yes, I know. We should find a new drop location— now that Mueller is onto you, the park is no good."

"It is not only the park I am worried about."

"What do you mean?"

"The information I give you, you know that it comes from another agent, the man called Falconbridge."

"Yes, I remember." His cigarette threatened to leap from the side of his mouth, bouncing as he spoke. "Is he also with the resistance?"

"No," she nodded. Her brow crinkled above her eyes and lines formed on her forehead.

"What is it?"

"I do not trust him." She handed him her copy of *The Merchant of Venice*.

"You shouldn't carry this around—if it fell into the hands of Mueller our entire scheme would fall apart."

She nodded apologetically with a knowing look that satisfied his scolding, and handed him a pencil, before she stepped away from the table and paced the confined room.

He pulled the cigarette from his mouth and held it in the V-shaped space between his index and middle fingers. Sensing at what she was getting at, he looked again at the note and searched through the book for corresponding words. He stopped after translating the first string of numbers, and read the message in front of him before looking up at her quizzically.

She nodded in agreement, pointing to the note again. "Does any of that make sense to you?"

He read the note aloud a second time, slowly.

"Falconbridge : enter : love : though : no : season : one : Venice: what : Gold : Shylock : faith."

She crossed her arms while he studied the note further.

He double-checked his work, making sure he had chosen the correct words from the key, and continued where he'd left off.

"Fifth : Jew : who : never : more : infidel : flesh : do : prepare : scene : fire : bond : other."

He lingered at the end of the second string of words, holding his chin with his free hand while he reread the two lines of code.

"It is all nonsense."

"Maybe." He buried his forehead in his free hand as he read the words once again. He waived the note in front of her. "Did he give you this in code or did you encode it?"

"I received it exactly like you see it. He always gives

me the message already coded and I simply pass it on to you. I add my own information at the end."

He had never considered spending time decoding and recoding the messages from his companions. He cursed himself now for the error. He'd done the same thing she had, simply retrieved the coded messages and appended them with his own.

You lazy sod!

He clinched his fists looking up toward the ceiling for inspiration which did not come. *What a mess Baker Street must be having deciphering these messages.* But then he reconsidered. *Only Beecher uses the Shakespeare code.* It was his personal direction to use a unique encryption. *He must think me a bloody fool; providing sets of rambling words all jumbled together.* He paused in rumination; *yet he has never reprimanded me for sending such messages previously; somehow, he must be able to make sense of it all.*

"There's three possibilities," he finally announced. "First, Falconbridge may have a different version of *The Merchant* than we have. While some of the words may be correct, others are out of place. But I doubt that. Beecher took great care to make sure we had the same copies, so if he's working for us, he should have the same edition."

He looked away momentarily rethinking his pronouncement.

"Second, he may be using a different code, every third word for example, or just the first letter of each word. He starts with the codename Falconbridge, which is easily verified in the book, but after that, everything goes astray." He paused considering this option. *But why use a different code? It's virtually unbreakable the way it is without the key.* He looked again at the message to confirm his doubt.

"Or," he looked directly into her eyes and continued building his hypothesis, "He may be using a totally different key." He took a long draw from his cigarette and exhaled through his nostrils with squinted eyes. Extinguishing his cigarette, he leaned back from the table. "What do you think?"

"I do not know."

"Have you met him before, or does he leave the information somewhere for you?"

"I always meet with him face to face."

"Where does this take place?"

"He travels across the border from Germany into Nederland. We have a couple of different meeting places. We vary our times of arrival; it is all coordinated by him. He usually wears a Nazi uniform—an officer—but I do not think he is a Nazi. I don't know what it is, but I can tell."

"But he is German?"

She nodded in affirmation as he leaned forward on his elbows.

"So maybe the Nazis are paying him to deliver false information to you. Could he be a double agent?"

She shrugged her shoulders.

"You said Mueller knows of you; does he also know about our communications?"

"I don't think so. He has been hunting a number of us in our group all summer. We arranged the bombing of a trainload of supplies coming from Germany last spring. One of our men, Peter Houtman, was captured. We think Mueller got our names from him; we never saw Peter again." Her clear, blue eyes shimmered in the pale lantern light with tears threatening to spill down her cheeks.

"So, what inspired you to decipher this message?"

"I don't know, curiosity I suppose." She looked away from him.

"No, it's something else. Think."

If there's a bloody double agent among us, he could wreck everything for the upcoming invasion!

She stared blankly at the stone wall of the cellar. "We met the night before last," she finally continued. "Everything went as planned, he was on time as usual." He saw a twitch in her face as something ran through her mind. "Something was different about him, something dark. I had not seen him like this before." She paused again, searching the shadowed corners of the room for a glimpse of the German agent, but it did not come to her, and she turned back to face Thorne. "Maybe it was nothing. Anyway, after I left, I began wondering what type of information he provided. So, like I said, maybe it was just curiosity."

Thorne considered her explanation. He knew all too well that a secret rendezvous with any stranger, especially one dressed as a Nazi officer, could be quite daunting to even the most experienced agent. *Perhaps it's nothing but nerves.* He also wondered when Falconbridge was first brought into the picture.

He was distracted from his speculations as she

returned to the table. He stared again into her eyes; gold and amber sparkles reflected in the black pools that were her pupils. His pulse quickened as he tried to imagine her before the War: *a librarian, maybe a school teacher? What would she be like sitting across the table in a cozy restaurant sharing a bottle of wine?* And at that moment, he thought of Catherine.

Catherine Brown had been Thorne's fiancée before the War; killed in a German bombing raid on London while he was away in SOE training. Although he had not thought about her for many weeks, maybe even months, her spirit now rose up from the depths of his soul and hovered in the room. Upon joining SOE, he'd been sent to Training School Five in Wanborough, just outside of Guildford, where an Elizabethan manor house had been converted for training new recruits. He was to be there three to four weeks initially as he learned the basics of weapons and firearms, unarmed combat, and sabotage. During a brief three-day layover while he awaited transfer to parachute school, he planned to meet up with Catherine—a surprise visit. Instead, in the last days of his training, he had received the fateful telegram from London explaining her death at the hands of the Luftwaffe.

"What do you think?" Portia asked, disturbing his brooding.

Caught up in her femininity, he blinked rapidly and refocused on her sanguine countenance.

"I'm not sure."

A shaft of light showed through the trapdoor as one of the workers called down from upstairs. It was time for them to leave—she would return to the garment factory, and he to his room in Gronsveld—and suddenly he was quite sad.

Chapter Five

GERHARD MUELLER SAT BEHIND his desk in the office at *Wilhelminasingel* 71, located in central Maastricht. Originally, the house had been owned by a wealthy, Jewish family prior to the War, but shortly after the German occupation, it was confiscated and turned into the headquarters of the *Sicherheitsdienst.* Among the most important tasks of the *SD* in Maastricht was finding and destroying resistance cells, and searching out anti-German conspirators in the Jewish community.

Mueller's ice, blue eyes stared across the room at a German military officer's uniform hanging on a coat hook. The sight sickened him, not so much the uniform itself, but what it stood for. The drab, greenish-grey officer's jacket was neatly pressed. Its collar displayed two patches: the one on the right was solid black, outlined in fine white piping; the left patch was also black and displayed three diamonds. A red, white and black ribbon was affixed to the top button of the jacket and tucked at a forty-five-degree angle into the coat. The shoulder lapels, along with the three diamonds on the collar patch, signified the rank of *Obersturmfuhrer,* which translated loosely as senior assault leader. Assault leader, he shuddered at the name.

On the left sleeve, approximately six inches above the wrist, a black diamond patch was emblazoned with the crisp white letters *SD*; this is what despised Mueller the most. He had come up through the ranks of the *Abwehr*, the original intelligence service for the German army, at least *original* from his point of view, and had enjoyed his role in the *Abwehr* working in Holland's regional headquarters, reporting back to his chief Hermann Giskes. Mueller's responsibilities included the abduction of subversives, including SOE operatives and underground partisans working in Holland. He considered himself a detective, not a soldier.

When the *Abwehr* was disbanded, its functions were absorbed into the *SD* in the summer of 1944. Mueller considered the *SD* to be the intelligence agency of the Nazi Party, *not* the German Army. When he learned his *ast*, or local office, was being absorbed into the *SD*, he'd assumed he would be given a position in the *Kriminalpolizei*, and had even looked forward to working in the *Kripo* as a plain clothes detective in the criminal investigation department. Instead, as a 'reward' for his previous accomplishments in rounding up Dutch resistance members and gathering intelligence from them—before summarily executing his victims—he was bestowed the rank of *Obersturmfuhrer* and moved beneath *Brigadefuhrer* Walter Schellenberg, head of the foreign intelligence agency for the *SD* in Berlin.

Only through a series of negotiations—more like

begging and pleading, he reflected—had Mueller persuaded Schellenberg to allow him to operate undercover in civilian clothing. He'd told his boss, "I am close to ensnaring the leader of the resistance group working out of Maastricht." Nonetheless, he was strongly urged to assign those duties to junior officers in his corps, and don the uniform of the *SD* with pride.

Mueller did not hate the Nazi Party, he simply despised the in-fighting and conniving that went on between its various organizations, particularly those under Heinrich Himmler. The leaders of the *Abwehr*, *Gestapo*, and *SD* had continually tried to undermine each other in an effort to demonstrate to Himmler—and Hitler—that one particular organization was more efficient than another. In the end, the *SD* won out. He reached across his desk and pressed a white button on a wooden call box, summoning his assistant into his office.

"*Jawohl Oberst*," his assistant called out as she entered his office.

"Take this uniform to be cleaned at once."

"But *Oberst*, it has only just come back two days ago and you have yet to wear it."

"Then take it to the other room. I want it out of my sight. It's distracting my concentration!"

Once his assistant had removed the uniform, he heard himself let out an audible sigh. *Now where was I?*

He turned the top page from a stack of papers and read the name: Anna Larsen. He read the other names she had used previously which included Anna Jansen, Anna de Graaf, and Clara Larsen. The file reported her age as approximately twenty-six years old, slim figure, average height.

He studied her file, subconsciously massaging the back of his neck while he read. There were still visible bruises on both the front and back where he had been attacked by Larsen and her accomplice who had helped her escape. Could he be the British spy, he wondered, thinking back on a piece of information that came across his desk a few weeks earlier—an informant had reported a British agent working in and around Maastricht for the past several weeks. He knew nothing about the spy and this irritated him.

He looked at one of the photos of Larsen in the file, and stared into her sober face. "In time, I will learn the identity of your friend too," he said aloud. He set Anna's papers aside and picked up another set his assistant had handed him earlier that day; he'd asked for the military records of SS Major Karl Hartmann. Reading through the service files now, he picked up the black telephone on his desk.

"Get me *Herr* Albertson." While he waited for the connection to go through, he noticed a word someone had scribbled on the corner of one of the pages. *Blackbird.* It conjured up images of the *Bundesadler*— the Federal Eagle—the heraldic bird Hitler and Himmler had chosen as an emblem to rally the spirit of the Germanic people. The bird was familiar to most German citizens from their folklore and the historic coats of arms of Germany, but for Hitler, it was a symbol that harkened back to a more important time;

it was the Roman Eagle Standard used by the First Reich, the Holy Roman Empire.

A voice came on the line disrupting his thoughts.

"Albertson? This is Mueller. I have a new assignment for you. Can you be in my office before three?"

RICHARD THORNE SAT ALONE in his room that night studying the note from Falconbridge. He'd finished decoding the remainder of the message Portia had given him, and despite his best efforts using his well-honed, puzzle-solving skills, he could not arrange the words in a meaningful fashion, nor determine a logical pattern in the letters and words in front of him.

It was nearing on midnight, there was nothing left for him to do except transmit the information back to London. As he prepared his radio for transmission, a thought occurred to him.

If I only send Falconbridge's information, Beecher might suspect something. I've always appended his messages to the end of mine. He thumbed through *The Merchant* picking the location of words that read 'Nothing to report'. He started the message with his codename, added his comment, and then followed with the message from Falconbridge. He transmitted the long string of numbers and colons per his steady routine, then promptly packed everything away before extinguishing his candle.

As he drew into bed, he thought again of Catherine.

It had been nearly three years since he'd last seen her. A heavy guilt pressed upon him as he struggled to see her face in his mind. Before he was shipped off on his first assignment with SOE, he'd left all personal belongings, including a photograph of her, packed into a few boxes that were dispatched to his uncle's home in Bristol. He'd taken one last, long look at her photo and tucked it away in a box. Now, despite imagining her calm voice in his head, he could not make out her face.

He called up a memory that had been locked away in the recesses of his mind. On an unusually clear and warm April afternoon in the days before he'd joined SOE, he'd met Catherine in Hyde Park for a picnic lunch. She kneeled before him on a red blanket spread out on the grass in a clearing surrounded by primeval trees.

"You need to make up your mind Richard," she'd said.

"I just wish I knew what the right answer was. If I do nothing, I'll certainly be drafted into the Army."

"Perhaps you can become an officer, after all, you have gone to college."

"But dear, the thought of the Army is simply dreadful. That's how my father died you know. Besides, I'm sure college has nothing to do with it. Only privileged men become officers, it's always been that way."

Catherine leaned back upon the blanket. "I turned in my registration you know. It's very likely I'll be called up, unless—", she threw a curt smile at him.

"Yes, yes, my dear. I promise we'll get married soon;

I just feel so uncertain about my immediate future I can't bear the thought of being taken away from you."

She opened a basket he had carried from her flat in Belgravia and opened two sandwiches wrapped in wax paper. He remained standing, frantically smoking a cigarette and looking off into the distance.

"Will you please sit down?"

He took one final drag before smashing his cigarette in the grass.

"My cousin Fred went into the Navy, he doesn't even have to leave shore," she said.

"That's because he's a welder. If he didn't know how to use a torch, he wouldn't be in the shipyards, he'd be hull down with three hundred sailors in God only knows what part of the world. That's my problem, I don't have any skills that would keep me here." He sat down and accepted a cucumber sandwich from her. "Can we talk about something else?"

Little did he know, just weeks after that day, he would in fact be called upon to serve, but not by one of the Branches of Armed Service. A former professor, Robert Clayton, had reached out to him—under somewhat false pretenses—using the premise of returning to Cambridge to become a student teacher. When he'd met Clayton at the Metropole Hotel near Trafalgar Square for lunch, their conversation had taken a sudden turn about.

"I know I spoke to you on the telephone about signing up for Graduate studies at Cambridge in order to avoid serving, and that is still an option that I can help arrange if you are interested, but I wanted to tell you about another opportunity."

The young Thorne listened intently.

"A friend of mine, former Professor, alerted me of a new program under the Ministry of Economic Warfare. They're looking for good men."

"Economic Warfare? What in Heaven's name is that?"

Clayton scooted his chair closer to Thorne and dropped his voice just above a whisper. "Among other things, it's using unconventional means to weaken the enemy. Propaganda, sabotage, and other creative methods. This program was originally to fall under the Secret Intelligence Service, have you heard of them before?" Clayton paused studying Thorne's face, sensing an intellectual curiosity behind his youthful eyes.

"What would I be doing? I mean what kind of men are they looking for?"

Clayton continued, "There's all sorts of jobs that need done. The best part is, you wouldn't have to necessarily fight on the front lines."

"What do you mean, 'necessarily'?"

"You'll have to submit to a battery of tests of course, entrance exams, both physical and mental. Depending on how you rank, you might well be assigned to an office here in London. I don't know all the details for sure, but I know they're looking for smart men, well-fit, college-educated. Naturally I thought of you. Graduated cum laude, didn't you?" Richard nodded. "You were on the debate team four years running, and if I recall, you were quite the athlete: boxing club, rowing, track and field. In fact, if I were to say so myself, you're the exact type of candidate they're looking for."

Richard thought about this for several seconds. "Do they have jobs for women too? I'd love to stay in London, but I'd simply die if I remained in England and my fiancée Catherine ended up getting conscripted and sent away into Foreign Service."

"Sure, they have women working for them as well. I suppose we could find out how to get her an interview, but listen, time is of the essence. It's men they need at the moment. If you are interested, all I have to do is make a phone call and set things in motion."

Thorne leapt to a quick decision. If there were an opportunity to help out with the war effort by staying in London, *and maybe a chance to find a role for Catherine too*, he would take it.

"Of course, I'm interested."

"Excellent! Let me take care of everything."

Within a matter of what seemed like only days after that meeting with Clayton, Thorne found himself accepted into the ranks of the newly formed SOE.

"Oh, Richard, that is wonderful news!" Catherine had cried out after he'd shared the news with her. "What will you be doing?"

"I'm not sure what my role will be, all I know is that they're sending me to Guildford for special training in a few weeks." He could not look her in the eye; he already knew then that he was to be trained as an agent of sabotage, and would likely be sent overseas, but he could not break the news to her just yet. If he'd already taken her up on a marriage proposal, he might have been able to request a job in England, but given his academic background, his mental and physical toughness, and unmarried status, he was a shoe-in for spy-training school.

Even now, the pain of her loss threatened to rise up again. He felt that familiar knot in his stomach and blamed himself for her death. He hadn't been there to protect her, he should have married her sooner, he should have told her about spy school. He swallowed hard forcing the truth down inside.

After his acceptance into SOE, before being assigned to Wanborough, he'd telephoned his uncle in Bristol and had asked for an extension of funds. When he'd graduated from Cambridge, he had borrowed money to rent a flat and tide him over until he found a job in London. Nearly three months after that loan, he was flat broke. Despite his uncle's previous suggestions to return to Bristol, he couldn't bear the thought of leaving Catherine in London where she worked in a newspaper office. He shared his recent acceptance into SOE, telling his uncle he'd be working for the Ministry of Economic Warfare as a writer in their documentation department. His uncle knew nothing about the Ministry, nor the made-up position. After his uncle had congratulated him, he'd asked for an additional short-term loan.

"What on earth do you need that kind of money for?" his uncle asked.

"I want to ask Catherine's hand in marriage."

He buried his head in his pillow, but the harder he tried, the more he continued to see Portia in his mind and not Catherine. They had agreed to meet the next morning to further discuss the business about Falconbridge; he sensed she was in danger. *There's something she's holding back, some clue about Falconbridge that has alarmed her.* And then he pondered on her whereabouts at that moment as he lay in the darkness.

I wonder if she's with Stefan now.

He fought back a tang of jealousy while he tossed and turned, reciting words from the unsolved Falconbridge puzzle, blurring images and echoes in his mind of Catherine and Portia, and tried his best to put all of them up on a shelf—but they kept creeping down into his thoughts, and it was many hours before he finally slept.

Chapter Six

I N THE MORNING, THORNE met Portia in the Parish of St. Michael's, located in the Heugem district of Maastricht. Seated in the third bench at the front of the nave—the large main hall of the church which held twenty or more pews—they talked in hushed tones.

"I sent the message as you gave it to me, with the exception of prepending a fore thought signifying that I had no new information to report ahead of his," he said.

She nodded in agreement.

"It will be interesting to see if London acknowledges it with any further questions."

"Maybe you are right, maybe I am worrying about nothing," she said in a quiet voice.

"How long have you been receiving information from Falconbridge; I mean how long before I came into the game?"

She thought about this for a long moment. "There was another agent before you. House Marten was the name Arragon used."

"House Marten? I don't think I've heard that one

before." *Surely, he must be one of Beecher's other agents.* "Go on." He sensed that she was holding back.

"We had a similar method for exchanging messages. It was in the spring when I was instructed by House Marten to start meeting with Falconbridge," she explained. "In the beginning, we met in Bocholtz, do you know it?"

He confirmed with a nod.

"We met once a week. I would ride a bicycle to the train station in the morning; there is a café there where German officers meet. It overlooks the rail station where long strings of cattle cars arrive, carrying—", she fell silent, searching for her next words.

"I know. Jews," he added for her.

She nodded looking down at the floor. He thought she whispered something.

"It is awful. The trains sit there for hours on end. You can hear the people crying out for help, begging for water and food. Soldiers whack at their arms and shout obscenities into the rail cars. All the while, the Nazi officers sit at the café in plain view drinking their beer and eating sausages."

He redirected her back to Falconbridge. "And you met him in this café?"

"Yes. I would wait outside on a bench. When he got there, we would go into the café together. He usually paid for something for me to eat."

"How did he get there, did a car bring him, or did he come by train?"

"I am not sure. I would wait outside. Some of the soldiers would ask me questions or offer to take me inside, but I would say no and explained I waited for someone else. Then he would come walking up from the station and the others would leave me alone."

"Is Falconbridge a higher rank than the other officers?"

"I do not know."

"Was he dressed differently?"

"He wears a black uniform, most of the others wore green. I remember his vividly because he wore patches on his collar with skulls on them."

Thorne nodded. *SS,* he said to himself. *No wonder the others did not challenge him for her company.*

"Anything else?"

"Not really, he would talk about the weather or how well the German army was doing in France or Italy. Eventually he would slide a piece of paper under a napkin with his message and then he would leave."

"Did he talk to any of the other officers?"

"Never. He would tell me to wait a few minutes until he was gone and then I would leave."

"You said, 'in the beginning', what did you mean?"

"A couple of months ago, he said it was no longer safe for us to meet there. He suggested we move to Vaals, that's where we meet now, at night."

"Did you ask him why you had to move to Vaals? Why it was no longer safe in Bocholtz?"

"No."

He mulled over everything she had divulged. "I'm sorry for so many questions. I'm just trying to figure this all out."

"It's okay," she whispered.

"The messages you received from Falconbridge; you gave them directly to House Marten?"

"Arragon arranged secret message exchanges, coded similar to ours, but I never met House Marten in person. Except for one time. He approached me after a drop, and asked me to hand deliver a book to Falconbridge."

"What book?"

"I don't know. It was the same size as the one we use, but it was wrapped in paper, I did not see it. I guess I never really thought about it until just now."

"It must have been the key for Falconbridge. Did you ever see House Marten again?"

"No, after that, I only left messages for him, from Falconbridge. But then in the summer—". She looked around the church as if seeking condolence. "In the summer, he was caught by the *Gestapo*. Arragon said he did not live."

Thorne nodded and placed his hand on her shoulder to comfort her. *Poor bastard, another of our boys caught up in the game. If House Marten instructed her to give the key to Falconbridge, then Beecher must've orchestrated it; the master tactician, moving his pawns about.*

While they talked, a few people came and went from the church. They found seats, paused for short prayers, and then left silently. Occasionally, a priest or other member of the church staff appeared from a side room, and walked down the center aisle in the nave, nodding to the various guests. They offered condolences where sought, or simply provided a warm hand shake and a smile, which is all that some seemed to need for comfort.

"The messages always start with his codename Falconbridge," Thorne said. "Headquarters must use that as his marker realizing that any following words come from a different text or different cipher pattern. He must have been instructed to always start with that identifier."

"We have to find his key—that is the only way we will know what he is sending," she suggested.

"Yes, you're right. I don't suppose he carries it on him. If only there was a way to follow him into Germany."

"I am to meet him again tomorrow night. You could come with me."

As she spoke, he was fascinated by her intellect and intuition. Behind her eyes—clear, bright blue he'd noticed by now—her brain was a machine computing details and structuring them into some semblance of order and meaning. She had warmed to him by this time also. Her tone was much more relaxed, more accepting, than that first mysterious meeting in the alleyway when he had called out her codename. When they'd talked in the cellar afterwards, she'd been immediately suspect of his inquiries, even after he'd proven his identity through information only known between them both. She had come across as very cold, and even stand-offish, toward him. He could tell she was interested in a mutual working relationship, nothing more. Yet he'd grown fond of her in the short time since he'd met her.

Then it dawned on him, *you don't even know her real name you silly git!*

He paid little attention to what she said, preoccupied instead by her manner of speech. When she spoke certain syllables, her tongue brushed against her upper teeth. This tiny, unintentional gesture became alluring to him. She paused in her dissection of Falconbridge's methods. "What it is?"

"Madame Larsen," he said in a calm voice. She was taken aback and tilted her head questionably. "Madame Larsen, that's what Mueller called you when he found you. What is your first name Madame Larsen?"

A thick silence filled the space between them. He sensed the slightest tinge of blush in her calm face. She looked around the church, confirming no others were in range to overhear them. "Anna, if you must know." She looked away again, scanning the large hall where they lingered. An elderly couple sat several rows away; the husband thumbed through a bible, talking and distracting his wife, while she scolded him with hushes for his rude manners.

She looked back to Thorne and whispered, "And who are you, Mr. Launcelot?"

"Richard, Richard Thorne." He let out a deep breath. Against his better judgement, he knew he had just crossed the line.

"Well, Mr. Thorne, we should not speak of it again." She brushed off the exchange of names as meaningless, nothing more than a casual introduction, and continued with her previous question about Falconbridge. "Do you agree?"

"Well," he smiled coyly.

What would it hurt to call each other by first name? Anna. What a perfectly simple name.

He smiled again. "Can I at least call you Anna? Portia sounds so, so—". He paused searching for a word.

"I'm talking about Falconbridge," she whispered the last word. "I was saying you should come with me when I meet him. See for yourself. Of course, you wouldn't meet him face to face, but you could watch from a distance. What do you think?"

He regained his composure.

"Yes, that would be a good idea. Maybe we could follow him and see what he is up to, find out where he stays."

"It is much too dangerous. He meets me near a guarded crossing at the border. He comes across, hands me his message, and then returns to Germany. There would be no way to cross at Vaals."

"Yes, I suppose you're right. What about somewhere else? Just north or south of there?"

"No, it is the same. There are bunkers all along the border; the Siegfried Line, you remember? The whole area is covered with soldiers and sentries. I do not like going there myself."

They both sat silently for a few minutes pondering the mysterious German agent. Thorne was convinced she was not telling him everything about Falconbridge.

There must be something she is holding back. In time.

She suddenly sat upright, almost rigid. Just then, three German soldiers entered the church. They talked and laughed as they took up a seat near the older couple, much to their dismay. Thorne hunched forward mimicking the posture of an older man.

"Let's leave, there out the back," he whispered.

The soldiers quieted down and each crossed his chest with his hand marking a symbol of the Cross; they each bowed their heads in silent prayer.

Even the Nazis must have some repentant souls in their ranks.

Anna clutched his arm as they stood, and stepped discreetly from the pew; Thorne continued in his hunched-over gait while she led him away toward a door at the rear of the building. They made their way past an ancient cemetery and headed west toward the river. They did not speak for several minutes but continued on a path away from town, looking back continuously to see if they had been followed. They came to a clearing of trees, and stopped on a high perch overlooking the Meuse, where they stood for several seconds.

"It was beautiful here once," she said breaking their silence.

"I'm sure it was. Are you from Maastricht?"

"No, I grew up near Eindhoven. When the Germans came, my father sent me away with my mother and sister to live with his brother on a farm in the country. We were safe there for a while, but eventually they moved into that area too." She was silent for a brief stretch and he left her to her thoughts. As if she'd lost track of time, she blinked several times and continued, "I came to Maastricht after joining the resistance."

"What made you do it? Why did you join the resistance?" He wanted to pull the words back as soon as he heard them leave his mouth. He sensed a hurt in her face when she turned away from him. The wind gently touched her hair while she looked down at the ground fleetingly, and then she lifted her head up high and was about to speak.

A German motorized boat maneuvered along the river below. "We should go," he said. He helped her over a rough-cut series of rock ledges, holding her hand to guide her up the ragged steps of a path. They cleared a hedgerow that lined this side of the river and found themselves on a paved sidewalk that wound along the edge of town. He wanted to take her hand in his again, but she had let go as soon as they were clear of the rough terrain. They walked in silence for a long while before he stopped her.

"I must return to Gronsveld. I should be receiving a message from London soon," he added looking at his watch. "Where will I meet you tomorrow night?"

"Come to the factory. I will have Arragon arrange a way for us to get to Vaals."

He reached down and held her hand. "Will you be okay? I mean now, heading back to the factory?"

"Yes."

"Come with me to my safe house if you wish. After my message comes, we can walk together to the factory and meet Stefan."

Her head snapped up in surprise. "No, it would be best if you came alone, later."

She's right. It is too dangerous for us to be seen together.

But he also wondered if she merely attempted to maintain her distance from him. "Yes, of course. Be safe Anna." He gently kissed the back of her hand.

"You should go now," she said firmly.

Chapter Seven

THE NEXT NIGHT, THORNE arrived in the shelter of an abandoned warehouse on the outskirts of Vaals. Accompanied by Anna, it was here, just a few blocks from the crossing into Germany, where they would meet Falconbridge. She found a lighted patch of dusty floor where the moon filtered through broken windows and she kneeled on the ground drawing a set of intersecting lines in the dirt which formed a crude map for his benefit.

"You will follow me to here." She drew a squiggly line alongside one of the others. "There is a tall, stone wall there. If you stay on this side and follow it to the end here, there is a large, broken tree. From there, you will see him come to the border crossing." She pointed out the various landmarks in her makeshift map. "He will walk this way; we usually meet here. It is an open area, this intersection, we only meet briefly."

"What about soldiers? How many are here at the crossing?"

"They are usually here, and here. Maybe three or four. There is a guardhouse here, two of them control the gate. Sometimes I see others walking along here,

but never has any approached us when we are here."
She pointed out all of the necessary locations to him.
"Now let us go."

He committed the rough map to memory, she
swept it away with her feet, and he leaned in close
kissing her cheek. "For luck!" he chuckled.

She pulled back into the darkness before he could
see her reaction. "Wait here for one minute." Her voice
was firm.

She slipped out the rear of the warehouse onto a
gravel road. Empty fields surrounded the warehouse to
the south, with a few dark structures barely visible far
off in the distance. She walked calmly down the gravel
road to where it joined a paved road, and promptly
disappeared around a hedge row. He watched all of this
from the back of the warehouse.

He checked his watch, then waited another thirty-
seconds before leaving. He kept to what little shade
there was—a partial moon showed brightly in the
western sky. Back in the direction of Maastricht, five
beams of light danced in circles as searchlights combed
the night sky for Allied planes.

From the paved road, he approached the hedge
row, and was forced to the ground as an approaching
vehicle sped past. He did not get a good look at the
driver of the drab automobile with its blacked-out
lights, but it was undoubtedly a German. No Dutch
civilian would be about at night—not that any had
an operating vehicle or petrol privileges in occupied
territory—but the Germans had also placed a curfew

in effect and everyone knew the deadly consequences should they be discovered.

The night was cool, and except for murky, grey patches on the ground where the moon shown between broken clouds, everything was dark. The search lights continued their silent dance on the horizon. Thorne darted across the road, cut between indistinct buildings, and made for the stone wall where Anna had shown him to hide. He had no trouble finding it; it was a sort of medieval retaining wall holding back a hillock of earth dotted with trees and shrubbery that headed off toward the German countryside.

He followed the old, stone wall toward a huge looming shadow that took shape in front of him. A timeworn and now shattered tree leaned awkwardly away from the wall. Beyond the tree he caught glimpses of artificial light through broken limbs that reached the ground. Voices mumbled indistinctly in the distance; knowing that sound carries a long way on a perfectly still night, he could not judge with any accuracy his proximity to them. He continued along the wall at a cat's pace, pausing occasionally to listen and look behind him. At the moment he reached the tree lurching sadly outward from the shadows, he realized he'd misjudged his distance—laughter was close, somewhere just beyond the shadows.

He found a foothold on a thick branch and climbed to a position where he could sit comfortably. From his vantage point, he saw a tiny building adjacent to the road at a gated crossing. His eyes followed the road to his left to the intersection Anna had pointed out.

He surveyed the entire area, and as she had predicted, two soldiers occupied the border crossing, while two others stood on the Dutch side near the small structure talking and smoking cigarettes. To their backs, he made out the dim shapes of dragon's teeth, the pyramidal concrete fortifications that ran along the breadth of the Siegfried line. A chill went down his spine realizing this was the closest he'd ever been to the German border. He worried about her just then.

What if she is discovered?

He watched the two nearest Germans. One dropped his cigarette to the ground, smashed it with his boot, and began a slow walk toward Thorne's hiding place. The soldier stepped into the obscurity a stone's throw from him and he heard the clear sounds of the man relieving himself just out of sight. The soldier coughed once. Thorne could almost feel the soldier's breath upon his neck where he sat with his back firmly against the tree trunk. The soldier spit into the shadows and returned to the gate. The guards who had been seated within the tiny shack, now stood outside looking toward the German side of the border.

A ghastly apparition had emerged from the dead of night. A pale light from the gatehouse revealed a German officer dressed from head to toe in the black uniform of the SS. He walked up to the border guards, promptly exchanged something with them, then walked nonchalantly around the gate. Two other soldiers raised an arm in his direction, and he continued toward the intersection where Anna waited.

Thorne could not see her but knew she hid

somewhere nearby. *She's a smart girl—she must have some signal that calls her into the open.* Just then, her silhouette appeared out of the gloom along the opposite side of the road.

His brain cried out, *No! They'll see you for sure!* He wanted to yell, create a diversion, anything, but he stayed hidden. The officer waved, not the typical Nazi *Heil Hitler* salute but a casual, familiar greeting as she walked up to him. The two spoke briefly and he handed her something. Thorne's eyes dodged back and forth furtively between their position and the nearest guards. She took the offering and conversed with him before disappearing again into the cool shadows. The entire exchange took less than thirty-seconds. The officer hesitated momentarily, then began his walk back toward the border.

That was it. A simple handoff. No one questioned the officer. How did he pull it off? A bribe to the guards no doubt? They'd grown accustomed to the ceremony, the regular ritual, the normal routine. An officer arrived, provided a gift, and went about some unknown business. Who were they to question the stratagem of the SS?

Falconbridge passed directly across from Thorne. He squinted from his shadowy perch, struggling to make out any detail about the man. In the dim light he could only recognize the outline of the close-cropped, black uniform with a stiff hat, and polished jackboots that glistened in the moonlight. There was something else too, a darkness to his face, but under the current circumstances, he could not be sure.

Just then, a black four-door sedan careened around a curve leading toward the border crossing, this time moving in from his left. As it neared the gatehouse, the driver put the car in a hard and sudden stop; its brakes whined in complaint. The guards, alarmed by the rapid approach, cautiously hailed the car with guns drawn. While they conversed with the driver, a man stepped out of the passenger door onto the causeway. He was not a soldier but a civilian. He impatiently handed his identification to the guards and waited for their approval. The SS officer, Falconbridge, continued walking toward the vehicle and stretched out an arm in a formal salute, which was returned in kind by the civilian.

This time, Thorne clearly heard *Heil Hitler* from the plain-clothed man and a like reply from Falconbridge. The men shook hands and began talking. From his proximity, he only caught a few syllables and occasional words of the civilian's questioning. He noted throughout their rendezvous, the plain-clothed man interrupted their dialogue by clearing his throat, his gravel-like voice sounded sharp and craggy even at this distance. They saluted each other again and the plain-clothed man returned to the automobile. As he walked to his car, Thorne got a brief look at the man's face. Thorne had seen it before, the chiseled jawline, cropped hair, and ice-blue eyes of a certain *Abwehr* officer.

The car backed up, made a turn in the road, and sped off toward the direction of Maastricht. The SS officer calmly walked onwards to the gatehouse, saluted the guards, and vanished beyond the border into the blackness of the German night.

Thorne waited several minutes for the border to return to its previous state; once the guards had taken up their positions and resumed their casual talk, he slipped away into the night and made his way back to the abandoned warehouse where Anna waited for him. Upon entering the empty and derelict building, he instantly feared she had not returned, but he relaxed when she materialized out of the darkened interior showing herself in the moonbeams.

"There you are."

"Yes." The moonlight cast a pale hue on her tender face.

"That was very brave of you. I was nervous as hell waiting for you there." He moved closer to her and saw fear in her eyes. "Did everything go as usual?"

"Yes, he gave me this message." She handed him a folded piece of paper.

"Did he say anything? I thought I heard him talking with you there."

"He told me I should come with him. He said an invasion is coming soon; when the Allies come every-thing will be turned to shit. He said he could keep me safe in Germany."

"Invasion? He said 'invasion'?" She nodded and bowed her head shamefully. "What is it? What else?"

"I didn't tell you before, there was this one other time." Her face contorted and she spoke with closed eyes as if trying not to see the SS man in front of her. "That time when I left after our meeting, I didn't see him follow me. He stopped me there in the darkness. He told me I should come with him, leave the country, but I said no. He put his hand on my shoulder and held me there. He tried to persuade me to go to Germany, and I thought he was going to force me to accompany him."

"Oh, Anna. You should have told me. I wouldn't have let you meet him alone tonight." He reached out to her and pulled her close, and she hugged him.

"Richard, I'm scared of him."

"I will talk to Stefan, convince him to assign someone else."

She shook her head. "It's no use, I've asked him before. The order would have to come from your boss in London."

"That's rubbish. Stefan controls his own people."

She pulled away from him and let out a deep breath. Once she recovered her composure, she said, "We should get out of here."

"Yes, in a moment. Did you see the other man? The one that approached Falconbridge after you spoke with him?"

"No. I rushed back here. Who was it?"

"I believe it was the German who chased you in the city a few weeks ago."

"Lieutenant-Colonel Mueller?"

"That's it."

"What would Mueller be doing here?"

"That's a damn fine question, it would be a most odd coincidence that he showed up here, on this very night. He knows your name, and now it seems he knows your whereabouts."

"But how? Only you and Falconbridge know that I am here this night."

"And you told no one else? What about Stefan?"

"He knows I meet with Falconbridge but has never asked for specifics." Thorne put his knuckles to his lips. In a panic, she hugged him again, "Richard, we must go. What if Mueller finds us?"

"He drove off, before Falconbridge crept back over the border." He held her tight and wanted to kiss her. "I am beginning to think you are right about Falconbridge. He can no longer be trusted."

She broke away from Thorne's grasp. "We need to see Stefan. He will know what to do."

"Yes, perhaps you are right," Thorne said disconcertedly.

Chapter Eight

"I DON'T LIKE THIS ONE BIT," Thorne said bitterly.

"Yes, this does present a bit of a problem," Visser said affirmatively. "If Mueller is onto your man Falconbridge, then he may be wise about Portia and my team here."

"My man? What makes you think Falconbridge is my man?" Thorne snorted.

"Well, indirectly of course. Your boss sent another agent over during the spring and arranged for the meetings between Portia and Falconbridge. Surely you were aware of that."

"Yes, I understand, but please be reassured, I had nothing to do with it." Thorne leaned back in his chair and huffed. "If anything, Beecher was misled into bringing on this man."

"Well, there's no point in arguing who's to blame. We need to find out how much Mueller knows about our operation." Visser shuffled through papers on his desk looking for something.

"What do you suggest?"

"I will speak with Portia. She is our link to

Falconbridge. She'll have to find out how much he knows. Where is she?"

"Haven't you seen her?" Thorne asked in concern. "After we returned from Vaals, I went back to Van Buren's. I thought she would come back here. Is this not where she stays?" He added scornfully.

"Sometimes," Stefan replied indifferently. He scooted back from the table and moved to the door where he summoned one of his lackeys to look for Anna.

"Is it safe for her to continue meeting him? I think you should consider sending someone else."

He turned back to Thorne, "There is no one else, no one else I can trust that is."

"Surely one of these other men you have can handle it."

"Are you telling me how to run my operations Mr. Thorne?"

"Absolutely not. I'm merely suggesting that you consider taking her out of harm's way," he replied stubbornly.

"I'm afraid we're all in harm's way, which is why we are here." He dug out a cigarette from a small case on his table, offered one to Thorne, and lit them both on a single match. "What shall you do next my friend?" he continued in a softer tone.

"Our drop spot has been compromised, and with our doubts about Falconbridge, there's no sense relaying any additional information to London. I think I should return home and discuss this in person with Beecher.

Can you get me into Belgium? There's no chance of getting a plane into Holland."

"It will not be easy."

"How much time do you need? I will radio London tonight and arrange a landing zone. They will be able to confirm where the front is and where it will be safe for extraction."

"Come back tomorrow. Everything will be ready by then."

ANNA LARSEN RESTED IN A DISUSED ROOM, one that was once an office on the second floor of the garment factory looking out over Maastricht. The sky was grey and visibility was limited to less than a mile due to a thick fog that came in the night before. The road in front of the factory was littered with debris discarded by fleeing citizens.

She thought of the man named Richard Thorne who had unexpectedly shown up in her world. He seemed different from the other British agents she had worked with; he seemed to actually care about her well-being, as opposed to the others who had simply looked upon everyone in their paths as a means to an end. She sensed that Thorne was actually interested beyond her work in the resistance.

While he seemed a charming enough man, she had purposely placed a wall between herself and Thorne, or more precisely between herself and her feelings. She had seen too many good men fall into the hands of the Nazis, and feared establishing a relationship with another, only to see him suffer a similar fate. Chances are he would be moving on from her life, and this only increased her resolve to avoid becoming close to him.

The night before, they had agreed to split up by bicycle on their return from Vaals; Anna would ride off first and he would leave five minutes behind her. As she was half way out the door, he had reached for her arm, "Anna, please be careful." It was a gentle, caring touch.

"I would have liked to have seen Maastricht before the War." She was startled and turned to find Thorne entering the room. "One of the boys told me where to find you," he added apologetically. He walked over to the window near her and caught site of a church spire in the low-hanging clouds. "I'm sure it was magnificent once."

"Yes, I suppose so. I have never seen it before the War, but you are right. All of the Netherlands was magnificent once; now I don't know if it will ever be so again." She looked down on a vehicle passing outside her window, its motor rattled the fractured panes of glass in the room. Thorne took note of a string of German troop transports lumbering by upon the avenue in front of the factory, and placed his hand on her shoulder as he leaned into the boxed-frame window to get a better look.

There was a firmness in his grip, yet a warmth about his hand resting there. She wanted to take it in her own but instead she turned from the window to face Thorne and his hand dropped away. "Did you talk to Stefan?" she asked.

"Yes, I told him about our suspicions with Falconbridge and the meeting with Mueller."

"What did he say?"

"I suspect he will talk with you about it directly. He really didn't have anything to go on." He pulled back from the window and looked for a place to sit. She perched on a wooden crate next to the window, but there was nothing else of size in the room for him to rest upon, so he instead paced in the confined space. He removed his floppy hat and rolled it in his hands as he searched for his next words.

"What is it? Is something wrong?"

"Listen Anna," he finally started. "I must leave for a short time. I need to return to London and discuss this Falconbridge matter with my boss. He will know what to do next." He stepped toward another window watching the last of the transports rumble by.

A lump formed in Anna's throat. She wondered if he would return, and if he did, on what other errand he would be assigned when he got back. She finally cleared her throat. "How long will you be away?" She heard the shakiness in her words and stared down at the dusty floor.

Thorne came about to face her, and moved slowly to stand in front of her. "I may be gone a week or more, but I will return soon enough and we will figure out our next move." He again placed his hands tenderly upon her shoulders. "Listen Anna, I want you to be careful while I am away. I do not trust these men we are involved with."

She looked up at him, the moisture in her eyes glimmering in the dull light. "I will be okay. Stefan—".

"I know," he said turning away from her. "Stefan will take care of you."

She stood and grabbed his shoulder, pulling him around to face her again. "It's not like that." She leaned in close and her lips found his in the gloomy surroundings. It was a brief kiss and when he reached to find her body she retreated toward the door. She slipped out of his sight, her silhouette ran along the wall and disappeared around a corner. Thorne knew she was on her way to meet with Stefan, and he was leaving the next night for London.

THE NEXT DAY, THORNE FOUND himself crouching behind a stone wall next to Visser. They hid near a crossroads in the Belgian countryside, just southwest of Maastricht, across the border where the U.S. First Army had liberated the region between Brussels and Liege.

"Why are they just sitting there?"

"Let me see," Visser replied reaching for Thorne's binoculars.

It was here that SOE had agreed to pick up Thorne—otherwise it would not have been possible to secure a landing zone for his extraction from

German-occupied Holland. After Thorne's emergency request had reached Baker Street, a series of messages had passed from SOE, to the War department, to SHAEF headquarters in London, and were eventually relayed to the front, where a Jeep was dispatched to rendezvous with Thorne and bring him behind friendly lines to an extraction point.

"What are they doing now?" He asked as Visser scanned the area where the jeep sat some four hundred meters away.

"The driver and the other soldier have left the Jeep; they are taking cover behind it." Visser moved the field glasses slowly to his right in the direction which the driver had pointed. He handed the glasses back to Thorne. "There in the town, see the church steeple? I think a sniper has them pinned down."

Thorne attempted to zoom in but the left lens had been damaged and would not come into focus; he squinted with his right eye and closed the left in order to clearly view his target. He spotted the church steeple which stood some thirty feet tall. A portion of the old building had been destroyed and the steeple itself had been heavily damaged. Thorne looked upon the backside of the church, and there in the steeple, he spotted the sniper.

"You're right. Now what?"

"We will have to wait and see. It is far too dangerous to move any closer, if the sniper were to spot us, we'd have no cover."

"I could skirt that tree line, and get up within pistol

range. There is a small outbuilding behind the church. If I can get a clear shot—".

"It's no use Richard. It's far too dangerous and we have no way to communicate with the soldiers to let them know you are moving toward their position."

Thorne nodded silently, searching the perimeter of the town for other Germans. He handed the binoculars back to Visser. "I don't see any others, just the lone gunman." They waited for several minutes, the scene before them frozen in a moment of time like a still photograph. Nothing moved, the air was still and for once, it was not raining. It was perfectly calm.

As Visser continued searching the countryside, the silence was disturbed by the hum of an approaching aircraft several thousand feet above them. A black speck took shape and soon Thorne could make out wings and a silver fuselage which now glinted in the sunlight. The plane suddenly banked to its right displaying black and white-stripes on the underside of its wings, as it began a shallow dive toward the small town in front of him. The plane leveled off as it gained speed. *What a thing of beauty!* He could now clearly make out its black and white checkered nose-cone, and a white star set within a blue disc, framed by red and white stripes emblazoned on the rear of the fuselage.

Without warning, four rockets launched in rapid succession from the underside of the American fighter plane. Thorne and Visser watched in amazement as the rockets thrust forward at lighting speed leaving spiraled trails of smoke behind. In the blink of an eye, the church steeple disappeared in a cloud of smoke and showering debris; a thunderous boom reached the two men just seconds later. The allied fighter plane swooped low over the town passing its target then shot upward as it banked towards its original approach vector.

"Brilliant!" Thorne said to Visser who smiled back at him like a schoolboy. "Bloody brilliant!"

"Look," Visser pointed towards the Jeep, which now moved rapidly toward their location. As the Jeep neared the intersection, both Visser and Thorne walked out from behind their wall waving their arms over their heads. The Jeep came to a quick stop, its wheels grabbing at loose gravel as it skidded to a stop.

Thorne approached the driver, his hands still raised. "Richard Thorne, SOE."

"Corporal Davis, United States Army," the driver shouted back. "Hop in."

Thorne turned to Visser. "I'll be back in a week or ten days. See to it that Portia is safe."

Visser dropped his arms and gave him a half-hearted salute. Thorne climbed into the Jeep; the driver made a hasty U-turn and sped past the still smoldering church in the village before promptly depositing Thorne in a wide clearing that had been a pasture before the War. In what seemed like just a matter of seconds, Thorne was greeted by his pilot, and rushed into the back of a waiting aircraft. They were airborne moments later, headed for England.

Chapter Nine

ON BOARD AN EXPRESS TRAIN from the quaint market town of Sandy in Bedfordshire, Thorne read a timetable which showed after brief stops at Biggleswade, Letchworth and Garden City, that he would arrive at London's Paddington Station sometime in the middle of the night.

He looked through a newspaper someone had left in the carriage, but couldn't focus on the words in front of him. His mind thought back to the scrawny man who had confronted him in Maastricht near the Saint Servatius Bridge. Who did he work for? Was he under the employ of Mueller? He was no soldier, he recollected, thinking of the man's gaunt frame. It appeared Falconbridge was in league with Mueller as well, and this frightened him. Anna was in all likelihood in danger; he just hoped Stefan would manage to keep her safe for the next several days until he could return.

Upon arrival at Tempsford airfield, where he'd landed after being shuttled across the English Channel by a Westland Lysander—a short takeoff and landing aircraft used for inserting and retrieving SOE operatives—he'd gathered his uniform and a change of clothes awaiting him in a secured locker. His uniform was in a shambles having been stowed in a wooden crate for several months, and he decided to err on the side of caution by wearing his civilian clothes instead of showing up at Baker Street in an unkempt SOE uniform.

After meeting with the Tempsford Air Marshall who confirmed Thorne's arrival with Baker Street, he'd been allowed a phone call with Beecher and they'd agreed to meet the following morning before noon. He knew he'd have some explaining to do regarding the atypical request for an emergency extraction, but he was convinced the threat of a double agent working in his outfit would be satisfactory justification.

He finally closed the newspaper and tucked it into the seat next to him. He wore a fedora and a dark grey suit—*a regular chap for once*—and let out a deep breath as he leaned back in his seat, pulling the brim of his hat down over his brow, and tried to get some sleep.

THORNE'S TRAIN HAD BEEN delayed for several hours somewhere near Knebworth, and he now shook the sleep out of his mind before he walked east from Paddington Station toward his destination on Baker Street. Autumn was heading on with a cool northerly breeze that added to the dreariness of wartime London. Many of the buildings north of Baker Street in the Marylebone area of London were bombed out piles of rubble, but the streets and sidewalks had been swept clear of any debris allowing him to easily traverse the twelve blocks from the rail station.

With time to kill before his meeting with Beecher, he decided to veer toward Hyde Park which was only a couple blocks over from Baker Street. Thorne came to a standstill as he reached the park boundary; the sight of dozens of colossal anti-aircraft batteries positioned throughout the park appalled him. Heaping piles of sandbags were stacked next to man-made ditches, and in more than one place, shell holes defiled the serenity of the once beautiful park.

What a shame, it was so lovely last time I was here.

Dozens of barrage balloons hovered overhead keeping watch against Hitler's V-1 flying bombs. They did little to stop the buzz bombs as they were nicknamed, which sputtered their way across the London sky all summer long terrorizing the population. In recent days, the frequency of the buzz bombs had dropped off. Thorne knew this was a result of the Allied forces taking out launch pads on the coasts of France and Belgium. He also knew the Royal Air Force had become adept at stopping the majority of the pulse-jet-powered missiles over the English Channel before they could strike home.

He rounded the corner onto Baker Street and passed the remains of an office building that had fallen victim to one of the lucky V-1s. He cursed aloud imagining the horror that had stricken Catherine so many months ago. He skirted a hill of brick and stone that jutted out into his path and continued on to SOE Headquarters located at Number 64.

The six-story office building was flanked by rows of sandbags stacked ten feet high. If the public didn't know it was the address of *Churchill's Secret Army*, they certainly knew it was an important building to say the least—an etched plaque leaned inelegantly against the sandbags and read *Inter Services Research Bureau*.

Thorne dawdled outside of Beecher's office inside Number 64 waiting for his arrival. Beecher's assistant was a young woman named Etta Cole, an attractive redhead in her spritely twenties, who took a particular interest in Thorne's work. Thorne took note of her narrow face which had a certain elfishness to it with her pointed chin and dimpled smile. If only a few years older, he supposed, she might be interesting. When she wasn't asking about his most recent exploits on the other side of the Channel, she loved talking about her dog Pudgy which absolutely bored him to death.

"I see you made it back in one piece," she said over intermittent typing of a memorandum.

"Yes, same as always. Not much to tell really, the usual sneaking around, avoiding Nazi security patrols, cloak and dagger stuff. But I survived. I guess that's all that matters."

"You're so clever. I was just telling Mr. Beecher the other day. I said, he's so clever, I guess that's why he always comes home." Then she realized she'd slipped up. The typewriter came to a hush as her fingers hovered above the keys. Several hundred SOE operatives had never made it home. While he supposed there was a certain cleverness to his work, Thorne knew at the end of the day it was mostly pure luck that kept him alive. Her words hung awkwardly for several seconds.

"Nice flowers," he said, breaking the silence.

"A yank sent those 'round yesterday. I met him at the American Red Cross dance hall. Cute chap, I suppose he was looking for a wife before he went abroad." She giggled, but Thorne only nodded in return.

The typewriter resumed its previous rhythm relieving him from further chit-chat which he considered absolute drivel. He looked at his watch again; only two minutes had elapsed since he'd last checked. A deep sigh inadvertently left his lips and he started to inquire again about Beecher's whereabouts, but footsteps ascending the nearby steps told him of his supervisor's arrival.

Inside his director's paneled office, Thorne assumed a familiar seat in a padded leather chair opposite his chief who roosted behind a wide, mahogany desk. He noted that Beecher smoked thin cigarettes like some European playboy he'd seen once before. *Was it in Brussels?* He pondered on this momentarily, shaking off an offer from Beecher. The cigarettes had a mild flavor and lasted but a fraction of the time of his trusted Chesterfields.

Beecher was at least thirty years senior to Thorne he guessed; *a man from a bygone epoch.* With thinning alabaster hair, sunken cheeks, and grizzled yellow teeth, his skeletal face was the kind that young children found frightening, but Thorne admired in the way a grandson loves a grandfather.

After apologizing for his arrival in civilian clothing, Thorne began his debriefing by reviewing the information he'd gathered on the armies in and around Maastricht. For the past several weeks, fragmented German Panzer units had been streaming into the Netherlands from Belgium and France, driven back by the advancing Allies in their swift pursuit toward Fortress Germany. He confirmed a few questions for Beecher, but overall, his superior seemed only half interested in the information.

"Yes, yes. Very good. We've supplied those details to the strategists. Now what was this urgent business that required your immediate extraction from the field?"

He deliberated on where to begin and started slowly, first recounting his story of rescuing Anna from the undercover German security officer before skimming over his ongoing personal meetings with her. He jumped ahead in time to the most recent rendezvous with Falconbridge.

When Thorne had returned to his room that night, he'd reviewed the note Falconbridge had given her; it was much the same as previous missives, starting with his identification followed by a string of seemingly random words. He had not transmitted this information to Beecher and even now mulled over whether to share it with his boss. Over the course of the next two days—while he had waited for SOE to secure a flight out of Belgium—he had continued to fret over the message Falconbridge had supplied and discussed it in earnest with Stefan. Even more puzzling to both of them was the appearance of Mueller in the black automobile at the meeting place of Anna and Falconbridge. Their speculations eventually led to the same conclusion: Falconbridge was working for the *Abwehr*.

"So, you think Falconbridge is up to something?" Beecher asked indifferently.

"We thought it odd that he reports his intelligence in a different cipher from ours?"

"Nonsense. He's simply using a different schema than yours. You know all the trouble we had over there."

He considered this. That certainly would account for the lack of questioning by Beecher in the messages he'd sent that included Falconbridge's coded messages— Beecher already knew how to decipher them.

"Something is very strange, but I can't put my finger on it. What do you make of the meeting with the *Abwehr* fellow?"

"Could be anything. Perhaps he has a friend in the service or a personal connection of some kind. You're not even sure it's the *Abwehr*, are you?"

"Mostly sure."

"And surely, I must have told you, *SD* took over the functions of *Abwehr* earlier this summer. The *Abwehr* no longer exists."

"What happened to the *Abwehr*?"

"Hitler is paranoid. He's convinced they were behind recent assassination attempts, so he sacked Canaris and moved the entire organization, or what's left of it, under Himmler."

"Ah, I see." This was news to Thorne. "So Falconbridge, I wonder if he's with *SD* then. Why else would he dress in Nazi officer's garb if he weren't with them?"

Beecher looked disinterested and toyed with another cigarette debating on whether to light it.

"Wouldn't he simply meet his friend or find another connection to get into Holland?" Thorne continued. "And if he's a Nazi, or German citizen for that matter, doesn't he already have papers that let him travel freely? He is one of our friendlies, right? I mean, do you think it's possible—".

Oops, too far.

"I have no reason to distrust Falconbridge!" Beecher interjected, his face reddening. "His reports have been sent to SHAEF and verified with our military intelligence. He's been totally reliable, why should we think otherwise? We've been working with him since the early years of the War." He worked himself into a hacking cough. "Before you came on board in fact," he added defensively.

"Well, Portia suspects him anyway, she's the one that knows him best."

Beecher smashed his little cigarette inadvertently against his desk sending pieces of tobacco flying toward Thorne. "Now Richard, listen to me. I want you to forget this business about Falconbridge. There are far more pressing concerns I need to brief you on." He swept the remains over the edge into his waste can.

Thorne checked himself from further debate. If there was one thing anyone could say about him, he was loyal to the bone. He'd never bucked the system, nor over-stepped his limits with his superiors. His obedience could be attributed in part to his strict upbringing. From an early age his father had never tolerated mischief, outcries, back-talk or anything besides *yes sir, no sir*. That had been before the Great War where his father had vanished somewhere in the fields of Flanders leaving the young Thorne not only with a lifelong contempt for Germany, but also with a loss for a role model in his impressionable adolescent years. It had been his uncle who ultimately fulfilled that role and helped shape Thorne into a young man.

"Your work in Holland has been of utmost usefulness to the War Department," Beecher continued. "As you know, we're gearing up for a large-scale operation in the Low Countries. With the success of the landings in Normandy, the Americans are rapidly moving eastward across France and will soon be in southern Germany. They're looking for Monty to provide pressure from the north."

Thorne nodded; *no secrets there*. It matched what he'd gathered from newspapers across the region; *common knowledge*.

"We're perhaps just weeks away from a full assault on Holland in preparation for a final thrust across the Rhine; I haven't got all the details yet, but in fact I think it may be very soon."

"But what about Falconbridge? We must determine what he's up to." Thorne paused, secretly thinking of returning to Anna. He longed to see her again, and even more so, wanted to warn her of the upcoming invasion. *Maybe I can shuttle her out of Holland back to safety here in England.* But he worried she was too ingrained in the resistance and would not leave. "If he's a double agent," he continued, "the entire operation may be in jeopardy!"

"Richard my boy, I thought we settled that matter. Now listen, you relax, take a few days and enjoy yourself in Piccadilly. I don't have all this worked out yet, but I'll have a new assignment for you imminently." The finality in his voice told Thorne he was done. Beecher rose from his desk and walked to the door ushering Thorne out of the office. "If there's nothing else, I have another appointment." They shook hands at the open door.

"There is one thing, I could use new identity papers. The ones I have now, the photo is quite dated."

"So be it. Etta, please contact Photographic and make the arrangements for Richard's papers to be updated. Also, find some time, perhaps Wednesday, for Richard and I to continue our discussion." He turned back to Thorne, "Cheers," and patted him on the shoulder before promptly disappearing into his office.

"So, I guess you'll be on R&R for a few days." She smiled at him provocatively. "If you need a date, you know where to find me." He politely returned a smile noncommittally as she thumbed through a calendar book. "Looks like Wednesday afternoon is wide open. I'll pencil you in first thing after lunch."

He brushed his brow in a salute and proceeded down the hallway toward the stairs.

Chapter Ten

ROUNDING THE CORNER FROM Beecher's office, Thorne nearly collided with another man at the top of the stairwell.

"Beg pardon," Thorne said apologetically.

"Richard?"

"Faulk!" At first, he had not recognized—nor expected—to see an old friend, but gladly reached out with a handshake. Allan Faulk had been classmate to Thorne at SOE training school in Wanborough, but they'd lost contact after Thorne was assigned to Altrincham, southwest of Manchester for parachute training. Faulk was transferred to another training school and that was the last he'd heard of him.

"Damn, it's good to see you!" Thorne added.

"What are you doing here?"

"Still holding it together, just got back from the field."

"Splendid, how long will you be in town then?"

"A few days I suppose, haven't received my new orders. So, what brings you to Baker Street?" Thorne had forgotten how much taller Faulk was than himself, a good four inches, as he looked up into the man's clear grey eyes.

"So many stories, so little time. We should pop off for a pint and catch up before you leave again."

"That'd be just swell, I'm free until Wednesday."

"What are you doing now? I just need to drop some files at the records department."

"Now would be just fine." He followed Faulk in the opposite direction of Beecher's office, and the two men conversed freely within the walls of SOE.

"So, where'd you go after Wanborough? Manchester, I believe?" Faulk asked.

"Yes, that's right. Well, nearly, I was at STS 51 in Cheshire County. And you went on to Hampshire if I recall?"

They entered the records department where several women busily filed paperwork and typed memorandums. They all looked up at the arrival of the two men and Thorne detected more than one sit upright, brush a fallen curl, or straighten a wrinkle in her blouse.

"Good morning, ladies." Faulk smiled, stunning them with his rakish profile.

Quite the charmer.

Thorne thought back to training school with Faulk—his amicable and good-natured personality had been infectious, and had had the immediate effect of winning one over instantly upon first meeting the handsome man. Faulk stopped at a short table and searched through his leather dossier before continuing. The women—apparently disappointed that Faulk had failed to notice any particular one of them—returned to their typewriters, annoyed by the interruption.

"I spent some time in Stodham Park, and then—", he paused reflectively, "—Oxfordshire for a while. Then let's see, off to finishing school at *The House in the Woods*." Faulk pulled a few folders of paperwork out of his case and turned to address the secretary who sat at the front of the office. A brass plate displayed her name: Lucille Cartwright. She was a slim brunette with her hair pulled back in a checkered bow and both men couldn't help take note of her overly-tight blouse.

"Lucille my dear, would you be so kind as to make sure these are returned to their proper location." Faulk handed the files to her, flashing his white teeth in a wide grin.

"Of course, Mr. Faulk." She winked at him with familiarity. "And you were looking for this." She discreetly opened a drawer in her desk and retrieved a bundle of papers. She glanced amongst her coworkers, none of whom took notice of her exchange with Faulk, and casually pushed the stack of papers across her desk.

"Wonderful!" He stuffed them into his case and addressed the women again. "You ladies have a delightful afternoon, cheers!" He waved toward the room and motioned for Thorne to exit the records department ahead of him. They resumed their discussion as they left the Baker Street office and walked north to Dorset Street.

"I spent some time in Paris, working with the local resistance identifying *targets of interest*," Faulk said with a wink. "But I've been back in England since the invasion. What about you?"

"Belgium and Holland. Honestly, I've been in and out of the field so many times the past few years I've lost count; reconnaissance work mostly."

"You must be one of the lucky ones. I heard we lost a lot of good men in section N."

"I suppose. I don't know any of the others of course, but I've heard we had quite a problem there for a while, *Gestapo* posing as operatives, and coercing some of our agents to send false messages and the like. I'm sure you're all too familiar with their interrogation tactics. Very unpleasant business you know."

"Yes, yes." The two men walked on silently for some time, reflecting on their own private experiences and lost companions.

"Say, you're pretty chummy with that girl back there in records," said Thorne.

"Lucille? Yes, quite the looker wouldn't you say?"

"No, I mean, you seem to have a good inside connection with the records department."

"Ah, I suppose so. I was injured in France just before D-Day and reassigned to HQ. Now I oversee a number of operations; mostly coordinating the information that funnels back in from the field, working on various strategies you might say. I frequent the records department for reference on previous operations; it's good to have an ally on the inside if you know what I mean."

They entered a pub on Dorset Street named *The Barley Mow* which had been serving local patrons since

1790. They found a table and each ordered a pint of bitter ale.

"Is there something you're looking for?" Faulk asked.

Thorne surveyed the room. A couple of older men relaxed at the far end of a long bar next to a large jar of pickled eggs, sipping beer and talking quietly. A few other patrons were scattered around the room eating, drinking, and conversing. Out of habit, he took note of a clear path to a rear exit. In an instant, he memorized the layout of the room and watched the bartender undecidedly.

"Relax old boy, you're at home now. What can I do for you?"

Thorne cleared his throat and leaned back in his chair. "You never can tell; ears everywhere you know." He took a long drink from his glass and let out a loud gasp. "I can't tell you how much I've missed that!" He paused for another short sip. "So anyway, have you heard of an agent, goes by the codename Falconbridge?"

"No, I don't believe so."

Thorne leaned forward and lowered his voice. "A German." He glanced again at the bar then back to Faulk. "Works for us though, an odd fellow. Freely crosses over from Germany into Holland, dressed as an SS officer."

"Double agent stuff?"

"Something like that. I'm told he's straight up, but I'm onto something. Just not sure what it is."

"German?" Faulk thought out loud. "Must be one of those we rounded up early on. At least that's one thing Chamberlain did for us. May he rest in peace!" He raised his glass.

Thorne raised his in return and they both took a long swallow. Prime Minister Neville Chamberlain had led Britain through the early months of the War, and though unpopular in his mild-mannered and even controversial approach to German aggression prior to the War, he had made some key decisions prior to his resignation. After declaring war on Germany in September 1939, the British Government had rounded up thousands of foreigners residing in the country, many of whom were German nationals loyal to the Nazi party. When these spies were discovered, they were given the option of turning against Hitler's regime as an alternative to charges of treason and certain death. By all accounts, most of the German spies, turned double agent, were working out quite well for SOE.

"I'll see what I can dig up. Do you have anything else to go on?"

"Just a hunch from my Dutch counterpart. She is suspicious of him, in part because even though he is working for Beecher, we're not clear what his role is. He travels frequently from Aachen, Germany to a small village in the Limburg province named Vaals. That's where he shares messages with my colleague; but we really have no idea what type of information he's providing back to London. It seems he's using a different code from ours."

"Have you asked Beecher about him?"

"Yes, he told me to forget about him; I suppose he's right. There's been many times I didn't know exactly what my own role was in a particular operation, let alone that of the others I worked with."

"Richard, you must trust your instincts. Something has aroused your suspicion with this chap. Can't hurt for me to sniff around and see if I find something."

"That would be capital!" Thorne relaxed.

It's good to be home.

Sitting with a friend and trusted colleague was a refreshing change of pace from constantly watching over one's shoulder Thorne thought.

"How is Catherine?"

The words struck Thorne like a bullet to the heart. Faulk immediately recognized his wounded friend.

"Oh, I'm sorry Richard."

Thorne stared away blankly for just a moment, quite possibly a full minute, he could not be sure. He swallowed hard forcing a knot downward through his chest and took another sip from his glass.

"You're fine, it's just been some time since anyone's asked me about her." He stared into his half empty glass.

After several seconds of silence, Faulk asked, "What happened?"

"Bomb raid. Her flat, well her entire block, was leveled, absolutely devastated. Bloody bastards!" He emptied his glass and let it slam down onto the table top. "It was just after Wanborough. You never knew about it. It was that last weekend when we were all in the process of transferring."

"I'm sorry to hear that."

"It's been what, nearly three years?" Thorne

reflected on that somber time; he'd only had a few days to morn her loss and see her buried in her home town of Hempstead just north of London. Shortly thereafter, he was sent to Altrincham and a series of other training schools, before being deployed to Belgium. He had never truly healed from her loss. Rushed into service for SOE, the past three years had been non-stop sneaking, running, hiding, hunkering down, and fleeing back to England for brief respite, before starting the cycle all over again. *God how I loved that woman.*

"It's a damn shame Richard. She was a fine woman."

Thorne took a deep breath and shifted the discussion away from his past. He preferred to keep it buried deep inside where no one could pry at it. "How about you? Have you got a girl?"

"No, haven't time for that. You know how it is, always on the move these days. Besides, I can't imagine putting a wife through all the worrying. I was abroad for quite some time; no contact, except by radio. I wasn't as lucky as you. Sounds like you get the occasional extraction back home. No sir, I was stationed outside of Paris for nearly two years straight through." He set down his empty pint glass and looked at his watch. "Listen old boy, let's touch base again in a day or two. In the meantime, I'll inquire about your friend Falconbridge. I must be running off, need to see a man about some Churchill business," he added with a wink.

They shook hands and Faulk left the pub. Thorne had nowhere in particular to be, so he ordered another pint and tried his best not to think of Catherine, although her ghost still floated just behind him somewhere in *The Barley Mow.*

Chapter Eleven

THORNE STOOD JUST OUTSIDE the entrance of SOE Headquarters tossing over everything he knew about Falconbridge, which was very little. Trust your instincts, Faulk had told him, but he really had nothing to go on, other than the suspicions of Anna. He should've stayed in Holland and acted on those instincts by following Falconbridge, tracking him to his den, and discovering who the man was. Instead, he'd panicked and run back home to tell Beecher only to be scolded for his juvenile actions.

Thorne stepped into the Baker Street office to escape a sudden, driving rain that swept through Marylebone, sending London citizens scurrying for cover. He found a Victorian-era chair which seemed oddly out of place, and after brief inspection, convinced himself it had been deliberately placed there for just such an occasion as this, although he couldn't fathom why anyone should choose to sit in the foyer of SOE headquarters. Nonetheless, he suddenly felt tired and worn out, and collapsed into the antique chair threatening to shatter the frail piece of furniture.

He lit a cigarette and mulled over the idea of

reaching out to the records department to see if he could discover anything from N Section relating to Falconbridge. He wasn't sure what the protocol was for obtaining files; it probably required a special requisition, signed by Beecher no less. He quickly absconded the idea realizing he hadn't established a rapport with Lucille the gatekeeper, and he certainly didn't have the smile that Faulk had that would let him charm his way around her.

He stared blankly across the corridor at a portrait of a member of the Royal family, perhaps a nineteenth century Duke or Archduke, *some wealthy Lord no doubt.* The intense gaze from the portrait challenged Thorne. Why was he there? What proof did he have about Falconbridge? How dare he barge into these headquarters on unfounded claims, accusing one of his fellow agents of treason! Thorne shook his head, clearing the ludicrous vision and pulled together the strength to stand. He extinguished his cigarette in a bucket of sand and stretched out his arms, yawning as if he'd just risen from a bizarre dream.

"Pardon me," a man called out from behind him. Thorne stood such that he partially barred the man's path to the exit. He turned to see a British officer, rapidly bearing down on him, and instantly recognized him as the Director of SOE, Major General Colin Gubbins.

Gubbins had been with SOE since the early years, but had only been at the helm less than a year. Thorne recalled having met Gubbins at a formal dinner where several SOE heads of department were in attendance including others in the upper echelon of the organization. They had discussed the Battle of Ypres where Gubbins first saw action during the Great War. He stepped aside as Gubbins replied a curt, "Thank you."

Gubbins was nearly at the door when Thorne decided to play his cards. "Excuse me Sir," he called out.

Gubbins stopped in mid-stride and turned to face Thorne. Clearly agitated at the interruption, his toothbrush mustache twitched about. "Yes, what is it?"

He approached Gubbins with an animated salute. "Thorne, Sir. Richard Thorne, Operative, Section N." He eyed the man's chest, decorated with colorful ribbons, and admired the pristine uniform the officer wore.

Gubbins eyed him up and down. "Yes, something I can do for you Thorne?" His deep Scottish voice echoed off the foyer walls.

"Knightsbridge Sir. We attended an anniversary dinner together last year." He stood nearly erect like a soldier at attention.

"Ah yes. Thorne." Gubbins was clearly baffled and struggled to recognize the civilian standing before him. "Good to see you again. Pardon me, but I must be on my way, I'm in a most dreadful hurry."

"Sir, if you have just a moment, I have an issue of awful importance to discuss."

Gubbins hesitated momentarily. "Please take it up with your superior. I'm sure it will make its way to me."

"Well Sir, it's a rather pressing issue."

Gubbins looked at his watch as his mustache

danced about. "I suppose you can ride along with me. My car is waiting just outside. But really, I'm in quite the hurry. This way if you must."

He followed Gubbins outside where a driver held a door open for the Major. The officer dashed into the car and the driver looked curiously at Thorne standing in the rain. "He's with me Fernley," the Scottish voice boomed from within the car. The driver stepped back to allow Thorne into the vehicle.

As the car sped away from the curb, a discomfiting stillness hung inside the car. Thorne was unsure if it were appropriate to speak in front of the driver. Gubbins broke the awkward silence, "Now what is this pressing issue?"

"Are you familiar with and agent named Falconbridge?"

"No, doesn't seem to ring a bell."

Thorne thought he caught the driver's eyes in the rear-view mirror, but Fernley turned away when they met his.

"Falconbridge is an operative, working in Holland," he continued cautiously. Gubbins listened inquisitively. "He provides intelligence from inside Germany which is ultimately passed through me in my regular communications back to HQ." Gubbins nodded. "My resistance counterpart has strong suspicions about this man and wonders about the information he's been supplying us."

Gubbins looked away momentarily as their vehicle came to a stop. A police officer redirected Fernley around an accident that was partially blocking their progress. Fernley maneuvered to the far side of his lane and his left tires bumped up over the curb onto the sidewalk jostling Gubbins and Thorne. Thorne hesitated with what to say next.

"Go on," Gubbins said redirecting his focus back to Thorne.

"I believe this Falconbridge fellow may be a double agent."

Gubbins prodded him onward. "What do you mean, what's this about?"

"I've seen him conversing with a man from the *Abwehr*, or *SD* I mean," he added thinking back to Beecher's update. "After my resistance contact shared her concerns about the man, I decided to get a look myself. I accompanied her to a small town on the German border, and waited there watching him as he came across, dropped off his information, and then headed back into Germany. That's where the *SD* came into the picture." He could see Gubbin's attention was waning. "Well, anyway sir, I'm trying to ascertain how to get more information on this agent, sort of a background check if you will."

"Who do you report to in Section N? Huntley? Gardner?"

"Beecher. Thomas Beecher."

"Have you mentioned this to him?"

"He seemed quite distracted with another objective when we last spoke. I was thinking Sir, with the correct permission that is, if I had access to the records department, I could thoroughly investigate this chap and put something more concrete together for Beecher and our team."

Gubbins eyed him guardedly. After several seconds of contemplation, he huffed and looked away from Thorne. "While it seems highly unusual that we would have operatives working in Germany, it might interest you to know that it is not entirely improbable," Gubbins said. "We have an entire section working on black propaganda; false information designed to dissuade the German citizens about the myth of *Der Furher*. Perhaps this chap Falconbridge is merely associated with one of those operations."

Thorne hadn't considered this. "He may be a Nazi officer. I've seen him once, dressed in full SS officer's regalia and openly conversing with German soldiers." Thorne caught a glimpse of Admiral Nelson's famed statue as their vehicle navigated around a busy Trafalgar Square. Gubbins seemed to take this into consideration as their driver turned onto Whitehall. Thorne watched the marble facades of the colonial buildings pass his window and recognized numerous government buildings, including the old War Office building, and the Ministry of Defense.

"Things are not always what they seem," Gubbins provided after a long silence. The driver turned onto Downing Street and came to rest at number 10, just outside Winston Churchill's residence. "This is the last stop. I'm afraid you'll have to find your way back to Baker Street Thorne."

Both men got out of the car after Fernley opened the door on Gubbin's side. "I wouldn't worry yourself about this. I'll mention it to Colonel Thornley, probably just one of his little projects."

Fernley cleared his throat as the two men stood on the sidewalk chatting. "The Prime Minister Sir," he interrupted.

Gubbins nodded. "Good to see you again Thorne. Perhaps we can pick up on our discussion about Ypres the next time we meet," he added with a smile.

Thorne saluted the Head of SOE who crossed the street escorted by Fernley. They were met at the door of Number 10 by military guards who ushered them inside.

Despite the advice of Gubbins and Beecher to dismiss his concern over Falconbridge, Thorne was more determined than before to unravel the mystery, and against his better judgement, he decided he would find a way to get back to Holland, even if he had to work around Beecher's forthcoming assignment.

ON A DESERTED STREET IN Gronsveld, a black Mercedes 260D pulled over to the side of the road across the street from a bombed-out building. A number of abandoned structures lined the block, but several others were still occupied with small shops and nondescript businesses. Before the War, this must have been a prosperous little community, thought Gerhard Mueller.

"This is fine Gunter," he said to his driver who

promptly parked the sedan and turned off the engine. Mueller watched a specific building farther down the block. Before the War, number 410 had been a cozy book shop, but since the occupation, a closed sign had hung on the door. The storefront windows were now dusty, cracked, and hastily patched in a few places; they showed a nearly empty shop with few offerings scattered haphazardly among its dusty shelves.

Appearances can be deciving, he reflected; Mueller's informant had reported a steady flow of patrons visiting the shop. He left his driver and walked down the sidewalk opposite the book store where he stopped at a newsstand and bought a paper. Ignoring the headlines regarding the latest on the War, he feigned interest in its contents while he watched the store over the edge of the newspaper.

The apartments above the book shop appeared to be mostly occupied. He'd seen movement inside the shop, but no one came or entered through the front door. A neighboring doorway to the store appeared to be the common entrance for the residents who lived next door. The street was abandoned when he folded the newspaper under his left arm and crossed to the shop. Inside the dirty windows, he saw a woman rise from a desk and withdraw beyond a curtain into a back room. He stepped over to the neighboring doorway and tested the handle; locked. He moved back to the book store and gestured toward the parked automobile signaling Gunter to join him.

Confirming his assumption, the door to the book shop was unlocked, and he stepped inside without waiting for his driver. The door creaked in objection to his entrance sending notice of his arrival to the shopkeeper. From the back room, he heard a woman's voice call out, "We're closed."

There was no one else in the shop, nor did he hear anyone besides the woman working in the back room. He closed the door and began carefully examining the mostly barren shelves that held a mere handful of books. As he did so, he ran his gloved finger through a layer of dust. He inspected the floor in front of another door on the side wall noticing that several footprints had come and gone from it. He sauntered over to a long counter with empty glass shelves searching for clues, when the woman reappeared from behind the curtain.

"I'm sorry Sir, we are closed—".

He slowly spun on his heels to face the middle-aged woman. Her eyes widened just perceptibly as she took notice of his uniform. He removed his black leather gloves indolently and stuffed them into his coat pockets.

"I am not interested in books Madame Abels." He noticed her reaction had grown increasingly worried. He enjoyed intimidation.

The woman stammered. "I don't understand."

He looked around the room showing little concern for the woman.

"The apartments upstairs, are you taking boarders?"

"I'm sorry, but there are no vacancies at this time."

"Oh, but you are the landlady?"

"No, my neighbor, *Meneer* Van Buren, oversees the apartments."

He walked closer toward the woman who backed away slightly to keep her distance. He judged her movements as scared and overly cautious. He leaned around her to get a better look toward the curtain.

"What is back there?"

"Is there something I can help you with? I will be happy to get in touch with *Meneer* Van Buren for you."

He looked away from the woman, adjusted his tie, and as he turned back to face her, he followed her gaze to the Nazi patches on his lapel and saw fear in her eyes. "Why are there so many footprints coming and going from that doorway?"

The woman shuffled to his right, just beyond his stare, and said apologetically, "The tenants who live upstairs."

"Why do they not use the entrance from the street?"

"Their front door is stuck. After the bombings, it jarred many of our buildings. Most windows and doors no longer open." She reached for a broom leaning against the back wall. "I'm going to have to ask you to leave."

"Am I interrupting something?" His croupy voice hung in the air.

Just then the door creaked open again and he heard footsteps enter. Without turning around, he smiled, seeing the reaction on her face—he knew that Gunter, his protégé, also dressed in the uniform of the *SD*, was standing behind him.

"I do hope not. You see, I have many more questions for you."

Chapter Twelve

A MILITARY STAFF CAR came to a stop outside of 64 Baker Street. The driver jumped out and trotted to the opposite side of the vehicle and opened the rear passenger door on the four-door sedan. Major-General Colin Gubbins exited the car carrying a leather briefcase and ducked out of the rain, entering SOE headquarters below the arched entrance formed by sandbags. He saluted a guard near the front entrance but did not stop for formal inspection. Inside the foyer, he headed purposefully toward an open flight of stairs, tucking his officer's hat under his left arm as he raced ahead in determination. From the staircase he caught a glimpse of Thomas Beecher heading for the exit.

"Beecher?" he said getting the other man's attention. "What are you doing here? I thought your section moved over to Norgeby House?"

"Good morning, Sir. Yes, I do have an office in Norgeby House, but I retained my desk here as well. I have so many connections, as you know, here at headquarters."

"That seems a bit frivolous, don't you think? Norgeby House is only a few hundred meters up the street. I'd like for you to clear out your desk here at your earliest convenience. We're making room for another expansion."

"Of course. I will start making the arrangements."

"Listen, that isn't important at the moment. I was going to send you a memo, but now that I've bumped into you, let me pester you with something if you don't mind."

"No Sir. Was just popping out for tea. What can I assist you with?" Beecher said in a submissive tone.

"Does the name Falconbridge mean anything to you?" He paused as Beecher shrugged his shoulders. "The name of an operation, or perhaps one of our agents?"

Beecher shook his head, "No sir. Can't recall that I've heard that one before. Is it something you'd like me to look into?"

With one foot on the first landing of the steps, Gubbins tapped his finger on the handrail while his mustache fluttered under his large nose. "Hmm. I was thinking this was one of your projects. Are you sure it doesn't ring a bell?" Light reflected off his high forehead as Gubbins hung there ominously.

"Well, come to think of it, I daresay I do recall that name. If memory serves me correctly, I believe he was an agent of ours in Germany. It's coming back to me now. I fear he ran afoul of the *Gestapo* or some such luck. I didn't get a full report, but through the briefings of a few operatives that had worked with him, they pieced together his disappearance. 'Tis a shame, he was a good resource."

"How long ago was this?"

"It's been some time." A frown stretched across Beecher's ancient face, as he tilted his head to the side. "Seems like maybe, in the spring, or could've been late last year even."

Gubbins' right eyebrow shot upward in an awkward arch. "It seems his capture by the Nazis would be something of utmost concern. What if the *Gestapo* whittled away at him until he revealed something about his true purpose?"

"If I recall, and I will look into the records on it promptly, he was killed before they had a chance to interrogate him. The crafty bugger tried to escape as they were transporting him. Gunned down in the streets I believe."

"Well, you just do that. Please find out if there are any records on Falconbridge. I'll check with Johnson or Colby as well. Perhaps it's in one of their sections." He turned and continued up the stairs at a brisk pace. "Good day Beecher," he called down from the top of the stairs.

"And good day to you sir," Beecher added. He hung there at the bottom of the steps until Gubbins was out of sight. "That was odd," he said aloud.

A passing cleaning woman looked toward Beecher. "Beg pardon Sir?"

Beecher smiled at the woman. "Nothing, 'tis nothing my child."

OBERSTURMFUHRER MUELLER sat in a cafe in Maastricht with one of his deputies, Corporal Sturmer, an overweight, middle-aged man whose uniform appeared two sizes too small. As he leaned over into a plate a food, the buttons threatened to pop from the front of the corporal's jacket.

"Sit up, and button your collar," Mueller scolded. He glanced at his watch again for the tenth time since their arrival, and used the last swallow from his third cup of *ersatz* coffee to wash down a white tablet he'd pulled from a red and blue container labeled *Pervitin*. The substitute was bitter and lacked caffeine but he had grown used to its flavor and tolerated it in conjunction with some form of pastry. The amphetamine pill would more than compensate for the lack of caffeine, and his mind subconsciously craved the rush that would soon follow.

He tapped his foot impatiently while he waited for the arrival of a German officer whom his informant had provided as a possible liaison to the Dutch resistance conspirator Anna Larsen. Fifteen minutes after the time of their scheduled meeting, an officer dressed in the black uniform of the SS, walked into the cafe.

"*Guter Tag, Oberstleutnant.* Thank you for agreeing to meet with me. Won't you please join us." Mueller attempted not to look directly into the man's face. A black eye patch covered his right eye adding to his already malefic countenance and instead Mueller looked deliberately to the officer's mouth as he addressed him.

SS Officer Karl Hartmann showed the Nazi salute and took a chair across the table from Mueller. He ignored Sturmer who did not look up at his arrival. Hartmann removed his black officer's hat and placed it on the table facing Mueller. The death's head skull on the front of the hat stared perniciously up at Mueller.

"I apologize for causing you alarm the other night. You see it was quite urgent." Mueller did not introduce Sturmer, who continued shoveling warm potatoes into his mouth, and who paid no attention to Hartmann's inquiring gestures. Instead, Mueller shifted uncomfortably in his *SD* officer's uniform. After the capture of Madame Abels earlier that morning, he had considered changing out of his uniform, but then decided to wear it for this particular occasion, if nothing else, to provide an heir of authority as he questioned Hartmann. He hoped to get this matter with Hartmann out of the way as quickly as possible so that he could return for a thorough interrogation of Madame Abels before another *SD* officer, or the *Gestapo*, started questioning her. He nervously glanced at his watch and continued, "As I mentioned, I am looking for a woman, a Dutch resistance agent. I have information suggesting you might know her." He thought back on the details provided by his informant and decided to go right after him. "I believe you have met this woman before."

A waitress came to the table. "Something I can bring you?" she asked Hartmann.

"Hofbrau." She nodded and walked away. He flippantly added, "What is her name? I have many contacts in the Low Countries."

"Yes, I am aware of that. I thought I shared her

name with you when we met before in Vaals, no? Anna Larsen, do you recall?"

"Maybe. It was late and I was quite surprised when you stopped me."

"Do you know her?" He inadvertently stared into Hartmann's single black eye and quickly averted his gaze.

Hartmann thought about this. "No, I don't think so. But I do not always know the *true* names of my contacts. In my line of work, we prefer to play charades."

"Yes. I am fully aware of your *line* of business *Oberstleutnant*," Mueller added coldly. He flirted with the idea that the tip from his informant—he had proven reliable in the past and had always provided palpable information—may have been incorrect about Hartmann, but the thought was only fleeting. He convinced himself, he must be lying. "If you are not telling me the truth it could mean serious consequences."

The waitress returned with Hartmann's beer. He thanked her and took a long draw leaving foam to rest on his upper lip.

"I am not worried about your consequences. I suspect *Brigadefuhrer* Schallenberg is not worried about them either." He used the tip of his tongue to wipe the foam away with a deliberate slowness, letting Mueller worry about the Deputy who now oversaw *Abwehr's* functions within the *SD*.

"This woman has been meeting with a British agent operating in and around Maastricht. As you know, the Allies are preparing for an invasion soon. I fear the two of them are working on a shrewd plan to aid the invasion. I wonder what Schallenberg would think if it was reported that you are also working with her?"

"Yes, I wonder. It's too bad we can't keep track of these *Britische spione* running all over the place." The German word spy stung Mueller.

"You are not helping yourself Oberst. Hartmann. You know it would raise no eyebrows if you were taken in under mistaken identity. Mix-ups *do* happen occasionally, you know."

"You've got nothing on me. If you have any questions, I suggest you check with Schallenberg."

"I shall do that. As soon as I'm back in the office, I guarantee you, he will be hearing from me." He looked directly into the raven black circle that was Hartmann's left eye, throwing discretion aside.

"Is there anything else Oberst. Mueller?" Hartmann grabbed his hat. As he placed it on his head forcefully, he adjusted the back side and pulled down firmly on the brim as if reminding Mueller of the meaning of the skull above his brow.

"Get out of my sight," Mueller's voice crackled.

Hartmann pushed out his chair as he stood. He took another long draw of beer, set his empty mug down forcibly, and left the café.

"Do you believe his insolence? I should have taken him in myself," Mueller growled. Sturmer, oblivious to the imputation and aspersion in Mueller's dialog with Hartmann, continued gorging himself on sausages and potatoes while Mueller fumed.

IN A LUXURIOUS OFFICE, on the fifth floor of the Bank of England, a white-haired man stood in a window looking down upon the courtyard in the center of the complex. Four mulberry trees near the middle of the garden had already lost most of their leaves, and the grassy areas framed by marble walkways had faded from their once vibrant emerald hues as autumn approached. The office door opened and an attendant announced an entering guest as Mr. Turner.

"Please, have a seat Mr. Turner," the white-haired man said. As instructed, the younger man found a seat at a table in the center of the room. The older man continued, "Thank you for meeting me here, I have other business to attend to this afternoon that keeps me from Baker Street, so I do hope I didn't inconvenience you."

"No bother sir." He looked around the room taking in the palatial décor of the office.

The older man took a seat across from him. "Now, let's get right down to business. I have a special task for you Mr. Turner, I am sending you to Holland." He reached down to a leather dossier and pulled several documents from the case. "I have here your identity papers and local currency. There are also food vouchers and a travel visa. You will see an address there; that is a safe house where you will stay."

The older man waited, studying the younger man while he sorted through the paperwork. He was a prime specimen of SOE, in his early twenties and rakishly handsome, almost too handsome for the clandestine errand about to fall in his lap.

"Have you been to the Low Countries before?"

"Yes sir. It was in '43. Belgium. Spring of that year to be precise."

"And what was the nature of your previous visit?"

"Uh, well let's see." The young man folded his hands across his lap. "I was dispatched to *remove* a certain Nazi officer from power."

"I see. And how did you go about this removal?" He watched Turner adjust his tie and shift nervously in his seat. "It's all right," he said reassuringly, "I have seen your files. I'd just like to hear about the operation in your own words," he added with a grin that showed his yellowed and crooked teeth.

"Understood." Turner dropped his shoulders and sank back into his chair. "It was in Rotterdam. I went in by Lizzie, nothing unusual, reconnoitered with the locals who provided harboring for a week or so while I waited for the signal. The officer in question, a General Wolfe, was flying in from Berlin, I didn't get the purpose of his visit in my briefing, simply his identity and the specifics of his whereabouts."

The older man circled hawk-like around the room listening to the younger man's story.

Turner lost sight of the venerable man who floated somewhere behind him. He continued nervously, "On the night of his arrival, a Mercedes brought him from the nearby airfield to the city centre, a hotel there had been converted into a *Wehrmacht* command center. I was already there when he arrived."

The elder man came into sight, closer than before. "And how did you do it? What was your method?"

Turner took a deep breath. "I wore a German officer's uniform, a Colonel. When his car arrived at the hotel, I met him at the edge of a curved driveway. I approached the vehicle just as his driver opened the passenger door, gave a Nazi salute and called out his name. I even clicked my boot heels together." He paused in reflection and blinked several times. "He looked up at me in surprise as he climbed out of the car. '*Ya, Oberst?*' he asked. '*Oberstleutnant* Hunter', I said. That was the codename I used." Turner lingered. "And then I shot him. I shot him in the head, and shot his driver, and took the car. Two blocks away, I pulled into a garage where the resistance waited. I discarded the uniform and they shuttled me to a field an hour south of there where I was extracted just after midnight."

The older man stood in front of Turner, eyeing him with an impish grin. He supposed he could easily pass for a German. "So, you speak German then?" Turner nodded. "*Was ist die Entfernung von Rotterdam nach Berlin?*" the older man asked.

"*Etwa sechshundert meter*," Turner replied in fluent German.

He had no idea if Berlin was actually six hundred meters from Rotterdam, but was impressed that the younger man had not hesitated in speaking German. He switched to Dutch with his next question. "Have you spent much time in Nederland?"

Turned smiled, "I have visited on numerous trips

before the war. Just business," he replied in fluent Dutch.

"Very good. Well hopefully things haven't changed too much since your last visit," the white-haired man continued, resuming his questioning in English. He paced around the room, and finally stopped near the window where Turner had first seen him. "Now, for the task at hand. I want you to locate a Dutch resistance agent. She uses the code name Portia. We fear she may be a double-agent working with the Nazis. Mr. Van Buren, the owner of the house where you will be staying, can make the necessary connections for you with the resistance in Maastricht. You should have no problem finding agent Portia in short time. I want you to establish a rapport with her; you can use the premise that you are replacing another SOE agent she had worked with recently."

Turner nodded, absorbing the information. "What's the agent's name sir? The one I am to be replacing?"

"Launcelot is his code name. Tell her he was captured or killed, or something of that sort. Do whatever it takes to convince her that you are picking up where he left off. You must gain her trust. She has a contact that she meets on a regular basis, a chap she's identified as Falconbridge in her messages. He's a German spy. In any case, you must convince her to tell you where she meets him; only she knows his true identity and where he resides."

The white-haired man traipsed across the room to a book case, and stopped there with his back facing Turner.

"I understand Sir." He tried to catch sight of what the older man was searching for on the bookshelves. He considered asking the venerable man if he needed assistance, but he quickly turned upon him as if sensing the younger man's probing eyes.

"Good. Once you find Falconbridge, you can eliminate Portia as you see fit. Falconbridge is our real man." He heard Turner shift uncomfortably in his chair and waited for his instructions to sink in. Finally, he turned back to the younger man, "When you've discovered his whereabouts, I will send further instructions on how to engage him. I don't want you revealing yourself to Falconbridge without my orders. Do you understand?" He waited for a curt nod. "Very good. My assistant has taken care of all the arrangements for you. She'll tell you when you leave. She has also taken care of all the provisions you'll need; radio, weapons, etcetera."

The younger man sat passively.

"From this point forward, you will use the name Blackbird when addressing this operation in all of your communications. As long as you start your messages with that word, they will find their way to me. Do you have any questions?"

"No sir."

"You're dismissed." Before Turner was completely out of the room, the elder man already had the Bakelite receiver of a telephone in his hands. Seeing Turner close the door behind him as he departed, he barked out at the operator on the phone, "Get me COHQ, extension

One Eleven." Within moments a dry voice answered from the other end.

"It's done."

"Well, how did that go?"

"About as well as could be expected. He's got all the information he needs."

"Can he be trusted?"

"I believe so. There was a certain spark in his eye; thinks he's on a mission to find a double-agent." The white-haired man smiled and catching a glimpse of himself in a mirror above the fireplace, he adjusted his expression as if his associate might sense his elation. "Once he has given my message to Falconbridge, I will in turn have him eliminated."

"Perfect." There was a short pause as a clinking of ice cubes in an empty highball glass filled the hush on the line. "What about Thorne? He knows too much."

"Yes, well I hadn't accounted for that."

"Do you think he could be convinced to join us?"

"No chance. He's too moralistic, simply incorruptible."

"That is too bad. Then we need to get him out of the picture altogether."

"I have a man after him now."

"If he's killed in London, it could cause a considerable mess."

"Yes, I suppose so. We certainly don't need Scotland Yard or SIS muddling things up. Do you have any suggestions?"

"An accident abroad would not draw any attention."

Chapter Thirteen

"THANK YOU FOR STOPPING BY," Thorne said to his friend Malcom MacLaren who entered his room at the Grand Central Hotel. "Certainly. It was good to hear from you, but I must admit, I didn't really understand what it is you want to discuss with me."

Thorne closed the door behind MacLaren and secured the lock. "Have a seat, I'll explain everything. Can I fetch you a drink?"

"Absolutely! I'm parched from the walk over." The hefty Scotsman took a seat and attempted to smooth his rain dampened hair, but the reddish-brown locks refused to submit.

Thorne poured two glasses of Scotch, and handed one to MacLaren. He also handed the familiar burgundy-colored, hardbound book to his friend.

MacLaren stared at its gold letters: *Shakespeare. The Merchant of Venice. Purcell and Somers.* MacLaren looked up questioningly.

Thorne pulled up a chair opposite from MacLaren. "I remembered back in school that you were quite the Shakespeare enthusiast."

"That's right, what of it?"

"Are you familiar with this one?"

"Of course, it's one of his best. Right up there with *MacBeth, Hamlet, King Lear.*" He paused seeing Thorne's blank face. "You've not heard of those?"

"Yes, yes. But what of this one, you've read it then?"

"I wrote an essay predicated on it, *Evocation of the Reader's Sympathy—*". He spoke the last words proudly with a dramatic flair that fell flat on the floor.

"So, you're intimately familiar with its characters?"

MacLaren took a long drink as he examined Thorne's copy. "I thought you wanted to catch up on old times, not debate the merits of Shakespeare and his characters. What are you about anyway?"

"A puzzle of sorts." Thorne blushed perceptively and rubbed at his ear. He had in fact invited his friend to meet with him under false pretenses, hoping to find some clue about Falconbridge, some link between the fictional character and the German man, and he knew MacLaren was his only hope.

"Where did you get this anyway?"

"It doesn't matter." Thorne finished the last of his drink and refilled his glass, along with MacLaren's which had been empty before his own. He set the bottle back on the floor next to his chair and leaned forward with his elbows on his knees. "I want to learn more about one of the characters. I didn't see him listed in the section titled *Character Interpretation.* Nor was there mention of him in the list of *Dramatis Personae* at the beginning of the play."

"What's this fellow's name you'd be after?"

"Falconbridge."

"Hooyah!" MacLaren exclaimed in a laughter. "He's no major character, I can tell you that. He's one of six possible suitors of Portia." Thorne opened his mouth, but nothing came out. "You have read this have you not?" MacLaren asked trenchantly.

"Read? Well, you could say I use it more or less for reference."

"Come now. You could knock this small task out in one night," he added, waving the book in front of Thorne.

Thorne leaned in. "Someday I'll get around to it, but for now, what can you tell me about Falconbridge?"

MacLaren thumbed through the text, scanning line by line, searching for the first mention of Falconbridge. There was a brief appearance of the character's name, introduced in one paragraph of dialogue between Portia and her lady-in-waiting Nerissa. MacLaren shook his empty glass in the air while keeping his head buried in the book. As he read a specific passage two or three times successively to himself, Thorne refilled his glass and watched in anticipation.

MacLaren acknowledged his refilled cup as he spoke out loud, paraphrasing the passage he'd just read. "And what of the man named Falconbridge, the English baron? I have nothing to say for him, he does not understand me, nor I him. He dresses oddly, with clothes from Italy and France, and a cap from Germany." His words disappeared into the silence of the room and nothing came back to him in response.

He closed the lid of the book in frustration and stared at Thorne.

"What, that's it then? There's nothing more?"

"Laddie, I'm afraid that's the only mention of your friend Falconbridge."

"So, what does it mean? What was that part about he dresses oddly?"

MacLaren took a large swallow from his glass. "It simply means Portia has no interest in the loon. Her friend is throwing out names of possible suitors, but this gent with his poor choice of clothing and inability to communicate with her, is of no importance."

Thorne pinched his lower lip, considering MacLaren's explanation. There must be some reason Beecher chose that name for the German agent, he thought. All of the other names in his operation—Portia, Launcelot, Arragon—came directly from the list of major characters. So why not give the German a code name from the same lot? Why not Lorenzo, Antonio, or Leonardo? He knew the names had no real significance, they were simply used as reference points in the key, but he could not get at the logic behind Beecher's naming of his agents. He reached for the bottle and realized it was nearly empty.

"Malcom my friend, what do you say we go down to the pub and finish getting pissed?"

EXITING THE GRAND CENTRAL the next morning, Richard Thorne stopped just outside of the entrance, surveying the block in both directions. The luxury hotel just west of the Baker Street tube station, had been requisitioned by the military and was used to temporarily put-up service men that had returned from active duty. He'd breakfasted with a downed airman, just back from France, and most anxious to share his story with someone. After bailing out of a burning plane, he'd landed in occupied France behind enemy lines. Even though there was a familiarity to the airmen's circumstances, Thorne reveled in his story as the airman detailed his three-week adventure with French underground partisans who moved him about the countryside from farmhouse to farmhouse, before arranging his extraction by plane.

Stepping out from under the broad awning in front of the hotel, Thorne glanced skyward at a squadron of British Halifax bombers headed south, and thought of the airman. "Best of luck mates," he murmured, then watched the planes disappear beyond a backdrop of grey and brown buildings that made up the London horizon.

He headed directly to Beecher's office only to learn from Etta that his boss was away and had cancelled all of his appointments for the remainder of the week.

"But I heard him specifically say to meet today, you even penciled me in."

"I know dear, these things happen. I never know whether he'll be here, over at Norgeby House, or one of a dozen other places."

"Well, did he leave any instructions? Anything I'm supposed to be doing?"

"I'm afraid not."

Thorne was destined for another few days of down time which left an empty feeling in the pit of his stomach, and with no friends or family in London, the thought of repeating the last three days sent him into a kind of mild depression. Thorne was not one to idle. He desperately longed to return to Holland to resume his original undertaking, or if that was no longer needed by the War Department, then he wished to follow up on Falconbridge.

"There is the matter about getting a new photo," Etta added

He'd completely forgotten. "Ah, yes. Where exactly is that?"

"Trevor Square, you remember?"

"Ah, right." He had a vague recollection of the four-story buildings in Knightsbridge surrounded by black wrought iron fence, but the name Trevor Square instantly recalled the unsavory memory of having to sit through numerous poses, wearing different bits of attire while someone applied mascara or rouge for various photo takes, and he now suddenly dreaded his task.

"Seeing how you have some free time on your hands, how would you like to come around for dinner tonight? I'm sure Pudgy would love the company." She smiled evocatively at him.

He stared blankly at her, searching for an

excuse—*anything to avoid a night alone with her and that damned dog.*

"I thank you kindly for the invitation Miss Cole, however I ran into an old friend just yesterday who invited me to his home near St. Albans." *Hmmm, she's not buying it.* "His wife has only recently had a new baby you see, and he was extremely pressed upon me coming over for a visit." She turned away from him and rolled a fresh piece of paper into the cylinder of her typewriter. "I'm not sure what Mr. Beecher has in store for me yet," he continued, "so of course I had to accept the offer. I do apologize. Certainly, we can work something out in the near future."

She looked away from him in contempt and began stabbing at the keys on her typewriter.

He instantly recovered, "Etta my dear. Once I've had a chance to meet with Beecher, I promise we'll meet up for dinner before I head off on my next assignment." He hoped that would appease her for the time being, but sensed it had not. He leaned in toward her, pulling her closest arm to him, and kissed the back of her hand. As he did so, a handwritten note lying next to her telephone caught his eye. She stealthily pulled her hand away from him and snagged the note from his view in the same motion, then shooed him out of her office as if he were a bothersome child interfering with his mother's chores.

He spent the rest of the day wandering about the city like a tourist with no agenda, no one to see, nothing whatsoever to do until his meeting again with Beecher. He walked down from Baker Street and spent the afternoon strolling about Piccadilly Circus—now overrun with American GI's who hung about their beloved American Red Cross service club.

Talk about an invasion.

Chapter Fourteen

RICHARD THORNE WAS LOST; not lost in location—he knew his way around London like the back of his hand—but lost without purpose. He found himself seated on a bench outside Charing Cross station along the Strand. Thorne hated these periods of idleness and audibly let out a vacuous yawn. He glanced up toward the fluted, granite column where Admiral Nelson stood vigilant watch over the citizens of London; their hero stared resolutely from his perch in Trafalgar Square, as if Bonaparte himself might suddenly come marching down Whitehall.

At the base of *Nelson's Column*, images of British battleships and aircraft carriers had been pasted above the words "Britain's Sea Power is yours–Help to maintain it with savings." He heard a distinct rumbling far off in the distance, an all too familiar humming in the air. Within a minute, the skies overhead were abuzz with a squadron of B-17 Bombers in formation, headed for someplace in Europe. He counted at least thirty planes. The vibration of the powerful turbo-charged Wright engines pushing the Flying Fortresses was overwhelming.

If ever England needed a hero, it was now.

Thorne idled there watching the resilient people of London going about their business in firm defiance—or perhaps stolid denial—of the war lingering on around them. On this typically somber afternoon, he abandoned thoughts of Anna and Catherine, and instead worked over the missing clues to the puzzle named Falconbridge.

He simply did not have enough information to go on, nothing more than a hunch. As he mulled it over, he continued to hear Beecher's voice echoing in the chambers of his mind. "Forget this business about Falconbridge," Beecher had said with a glare in his eyes. It wasn't a direct order of course, but close enough that Thorne would have followed as if ordered to march into hell itself.

Yet, here he sat pondering the mystery. If Falconbridge were a double agent, and was selling England short, and especially if he was working with the Nazis, he deserved nothing less than hanging. *Bloody traitor!* But then he wondered whom he was actually working for. It would have to be someone with enough authority to coordinate the whole thing, he speculated. *Power and corruption always seem to go hand in hand.*

As he daydreamed, staring at nothing in particular, chewing on the bitter tasting reality he believed he'd uncovered, the hair on the back of his neck stood up. His senses snapped out of the detestable quandary and he suddenly had the unmistakable feeling he was being watched.

He remained motionless except for his keen eyes

that swept the semi-circle view in front of him from right to left. Far off to his left, he detected the culprit of his uneasiness; a man dressed in a charcoal grey suit stood at the bus stop just meters away from the bench where he sat. He looked in Thorne's general direction but from this angle Thorne could not be sure of the man's exact point of focus. He casually leaned back with a stretch, then snapped his head in the direction of the stranger. Caught in a gawking moment, the man looked away down the Strand, and then checked his watch.

As the stranger turned away; Thorne popped up from his bench alongside a number of passersby and walked away from the bus stop to mix in with the general commotion of the crowd. He stopped at a cross street and looked back at the bus stop where the man still stood unmoving.

Just my imagination perhaps.

Thorne crossed the Strand onto Duncannon Street, and walked alongside St. Martin-in-the-Fields, the English Anglican church on the northeast corner of Trafalgar Square. He looked back toward Charing Cross as a red, double-decker bus arrived at the stop where the stranger still waited. The bus parked in front of a queue of citizens, including the man, and blocked them from Thorne's view.

Merging into a crowd of people gathered in the courtyard that was Trafalgar Square, just in front of the National Gallery, Thorne veered off to his left, pausing beneath a statue of King George IV mounted on his horse. He scanned the throngs of people all along Trafalgar Square, and Duncannon Street from where he had just come, but did not see the man from Charing Cross.

After several minutes, and convinced of a bad case of nerves, he decided to press on, but just then, he again caught sight of the man dressed in grey coming his way from Duncannon. He kneeled next to King George's statue tying his shoe and buying time. He removed his hat and coat, and rolled them into a bundle under his arm, then counted to three before making a mad dash to the south side of Trafalgar Square.

Weaving briskly between people as he went, he ducked into the circular stairwell that marked the entrance to the Charing Cross underground station. The stairwell opened into a long corridor full of benches that were used as cots and resting places for citizens forced into the tube tunnels during air raids. Thorne wove through the maze of benches, excusing himself as he pushed past other Londoners. He ducked to the side of the corridor behind a supporting wall and watched the stairwell opening for his pursuer. When he saw the man reach the bottom of the steps, he pulled back behind the wall and examined a door behind him. It was unlocked and opened into a dimly lit room stuffed to the ceiling with crates of foodstuffs and other necessities to support the citizens holed up during an air raid. He turned back to see the man from Charing Cross standing a few paces from the end of the wall with his back to Thorne. His head swiveled back and forth as he searched for Thorne in the crowd of tube passengers.

Thorne caught the man off guard by grabbing his coat at the shoulders dragging him backwards into the supply room. The man twisted about as Thorne tried to secure a hold on him. In a flurry of thrashing arms from both men, each managed to land glancing blows against the other. Thorne fell back against a stack of crates when his feet tripped over a small box behind him. His adversary took advantage of Thorne's precarious stance, and pinned him against the crates pressing his forearm against Thorne's chest. With his free hand, he pulled a pistol from his coat and swiftly raised it towards Thorne's forehead.

In a flash, Thorne managed to block the pistol from taking aim, and in the process of shoving the man's firearm to the side, the barrel of the pistol caught Thorne just above his right eye with a sharp stinging blow. Thorne's right arm shot upwards dislodging the pistol which clattered on the floor somewhere in the room. Thorne pushed off the crates at his back and with all his might executed a well-practiced take down which sent the man sprawling toward the door. In an inexplicable maneuver, the man awkwardly stumbled backwards simultaneously opening and closing the door behind him as he fumbled outward into the corridor packed full of tube passengers.

Thorne dashed to the door, but to his dismay, as he exited the supply room into the crowd of stunned onlookers, he realized the man had vanished. He quickly turned toward his left and sprinted by other travelers as he rushed to the ticket windows. He handed a ticket he'd purchased earlier in the day at the Baker Street station to an attendant who stamped it and handed it back to him. Rushing to catch a waiting train that was about to depart, he nudged his way into the center of a crowded car and grabbed a handrail as the doors closed behind him.

The train lurched into motion headed northbound on the Bakerloo line. As the underground train rumbled along, he scanned the passengers in his car for any that matched the build of his would-be assailant. A woman across from him flashed a look of concern as she glanced upwards at Thorne's forehead. It was then that he felt a trickle of blood running down his right temple. She offered him a handkerchief which he pressed firmly against a knot forming above his brow.

Within minutes, Thorne departed the underground at Piccadilly and lost himself in the throngs of U.S. servicemen massed around the West End service clubs. With no further sign of the man from Charing Cross, he put on his hat and coat, and skirted the crowds of soldiers—and countless prostitutes that hung around them like flies drawn to cattle—before making his way off Piccadilly onto Glasshouse Street. There, he located a pub named *Leicester Arms,* just a few blocks away from the noisy crowds in Piccadilly. It was busy, but at least the majority of patrons appeared to be either British soldiers or British citizens.

I'm just not in the mood for Yanks today.

There were no empty tables—Thorne had to squeeze in at the bar—and after ordering a steak and kidney pie, and a pint of beer, he relaxed and searched his pockets for a Chesterfield, but could not find one on his person.

"Need a fag? I 'appen to 'ave an extra one mate."

Thorne turned to address a British sailor on his right. "I would greatly appreciate it," he said reaching out to take the offered cigarette from the burly man.

"No bother," the sailor replied in a thick cockney dialect. He offered Thorne a match. "So, what's your story?"

"Beg your pardon?"

"Look around mate. Most everyone here is in the service. I seen you come in like a fox runnin' from the hounds, and I says to me'self, now that's odd."

"I'm with the Ministry of Defense if you must know. I simply popped in here to steer clear of the bloody yanks."

The sailor took a drink of beer. "Name's George Abbott. Midshipman, HMS Foley." He switched a cigarette from his right to his left, and extended a large hand to Thorne.

"Pleased to meet you." He shook the seaman's rough, calloused hand. "Thorne, Richard Thorne," he added with a nod.

"Ministry of Defense, I see," the sailor said, winking in acknowledgement of the timeworn euphemism. "*Ministry of Ungentlemanly Warfare,* more like it. Your secret's safe with Georgie."

"No, nothing like that. Just ordinary work supporting the War effort." Thorne inadvertently inhaled the saturated odor of alcohol as the sailor leaned in closer.

George winked again and continued in a hushed voice, "I see, and wot about that then?" he said pointing to Thorne's forehead.

"Just a little mishap in the tube," Thorne said as he grabbed a napkin from the bar and dabbed it gingerly against his brow.

The bartender brought Thorne his pie. He poked at it with a fork letting out clouds of steam, and sucked in the luscious aroma in a long, savory moment before finally taking a bite. "So, George, what about you? How do you find yourself in London?"

"Shore leave, t'night's our last night, then we're off to the North Sea, fishin' for U-Boats. Most of the boys come to town to kick and prance, and get pissed, but I says, I just want a swell pint and a place to rest me bones."

"Well, good for you."

"Trust me, a rocking boat come morning after a good night of piss up is no place for me!"

You seem to be doing a pretty good job getting pissed, Thorne thought.

After an hour and a few pints of beer, compliments of Midshipman George Abbott, he began to grow rather fond of his new found friend. "Say, you're a pretty decent chap. Here's to the Navy." He raised his glass.

"To the Navy!" George responded, and they each took a long draw.

"And here's to the King."

"To the King!" Another long swallow followed. "And to the Queen," George added.

"To the Queen!"

This went on for several rounds, toasting to the health of Churchill, the Army, the Royal Air Force, and The Ministry of Defense, until they ran out of important people to toast. After a long pause of contemplative silence by both men, Thorne interrupted, "The best of luck to you George Abbott, I'm afraid I must be off now." He paid his tab and shook the sailor's hand once again.

"I wouldn't be in such a hurry to shove off." The sailor stopped Thorne, grasping his forearm.

"Why is that?"

"Earlier, when you first came in, I noticed a chap pop in right after you, looking around, like 'e were searchin' for someone gone to ground."

"And what chap would that be?"

"A wiry lookin' bloke." Abbott's eyes darted behind Thorne and back again.

"And he's back now?" Thorne asked without turning around.

George nodded. "Must be that tube mishap you mentioned."

"What's he about now?"

"Looking around. Now he's talking to a waiter."

Thorne hunkered down on his stool, attempting to change the shape of his frame.

"Now e's just standin' there, waitin' by the door."

"Do you know a way out besides the front door?"

"That door there leads through the kitchen and out the back. If you want to make a go of it, I'll make sure your friend doesn't follow."

Thorne nodded and shook George's hand one last time. He casually slipped from his bar stool and moved parallel to the bar, keeping his back facing the front door. With one eye on George, he waited for the sailor's nod and turned to the kitchen. He ducked through a set of swinging doors and clung to the back of one of them, peering into the larger room. The wiry man stood in the dim light of the entryway. Thorne could not be sure it was the same man who had followed him from Charing Cross, but when he broke from his post near the front door and shot toward the kitchen there was no mistaking his identity.

George intercepted the man with a jovial laugh, "Who have we here?" He put his arm around the thin man's shoulder and redirected him from the kitchen to a table of sailors. "Look here boys, you'll never guess who I found."

The confused man was quickly surrounded with sophomoric camaraderie and despite his best efforts, the sailors would not let him leave their table. Thorne was about to break for a rear door through the kitchen, but as he turned, a large, aproned man barred his way. With fists on his hips, the apparent cook, glared at Thorne.

"Was just looking for the loo."

The large man did not move.

"I suppose I took a wrong turn," Thorne said backing out of the kitchen. He made a beeline for the front door while George and his friends kept the thin man's attention occupied. He found his way back to the Piccadilly tube station and boarded the next train bound for Baker Street.

Chapter Fifteen

THORNE MOVED NORTH ALONG Baker Street, crossing at George Street, when he was hailed by a familiar voice.

"Richard!"

The shout came from across the street, where Faulk stood waving him down. With a series of hand signals, they acknowledged to meet at the next corner, just one block south of SOE headquarters.

"I wasn't expecting to see you quite so soon," Thorne said.

"Nor I," Faulk added with a grin. "I thought you'd be back in the field by now."

"My orders haven't come through yet. I've just been larking about town on holiday. Have you come up with anything on this Falconbridge chap yet?"

"Sorry Richard, haven't had a chance to start digging into it, I've a few other pressing matters at the moment."

"Of course. Well, I've made up my mind anyhow. I need to get back to Holland and alert the underground team there so they can root out this bugger. Do you think you can help me get a lift out of Tempsford?"

Faulk, taken aback by the request, stammered to find his words. "Tempsford? That would take quite a bit of finagling to arrange something like that. What about Beecher? He should be able to make it happen."

"He's cancelled all of his appointments for the week; I can't locate him at the moment. If I could just pop over and rendezvous with my friends, together we may be able to find out more about this Nazi spy. I can find my way back by the end of the week; Beecher would be none the wiser."

"Richard, isn't that stepping out of bounds?"

"I've got nothing else going on. Hell, I wasn't even supposed to be back in London yet anyway. Do you know anyone, someone who could help arrange it?"

Stopped on the sidewalk outside of a haberdashery, Faulk looked around the street cautiously, lost in contemplation. Suddenly aware of their proximity to 64 Baker Street, he started, then stopped, several times. Finally, he put together his thoughts. "I may be able to pull this off, but let's not discuss it here Richard. Where are you staying?"

"The Grand."

"I will meet you there later this evening—let me make a few calls."

"Perfect, I have some other business to wrap up at Photographic in Knightsbridge. I'll wait back at the Grand when I am finished."

The two men shook hands; Thorne released Faulk's firm grip and felt the warmth of his friend's hand slip from his grasp. He stood watching blankly as Faulk hailed a taxi, and disappeared into the bustling traffic of midday London.

JUST TO THE NORTH OF HARROD'S department store that sits on Brompton Road in the century's old Knightsbridge area of London, there is a section of row houses on Trevor Street, where in Number Two and Number Three, SOE had set up offices under the Photographic and Make-up Section, titled XVc.

Later that day, Thorne approached Trevor Square from the north side, having skirted *The Serpentine*— the forty-acre lake on the western most edge of Hyde Park—and crossed Carriage Drive into Knightsbridge.

Now I remember, he thought, as he strolled onto Trevor Place. The four-story homes all wore the same facade; the first levels were composed of white stone, then two floors of brown brick above that, and a fourth upper floor of shingled roofs and protruding dormers topped off the row houses. He entered Number Three, identified himself to a receptionist who verified his name on a register, and he was asked to take a seat in the waiting area.

A few minutes later, a pencil-thin man with an equally pencil-thin mustache, entered the waiting area and called out, "Mr. Thorne," the way a porter might call out into a lobby full of passengers in a crowded rail station. Thorne took notice of the man's pre-War era jacket, which differed from the toned-down 'utility suit' that most Englishmen wore these days. His coat was of longer cut, with elegant buttons, and touted a silk handkerchief stuffed in the breast pocket. Sizing up the man, Thorne immediately speculated to himself, *must be a shirt lifter.*

He followed the flamboyant man into a side room, where a camera faced a white sheet draped against the back wall. A rack of clothing hung on the opposite wall; different outfits for various SOE agents and their possible environs. Thorne knew that SOE had recruited many of its photographers and make-up specialists from the movie industry, and supposed much of the attire was borrowed from their movie sets.

"So, what shall it be today, Gary Cooper? Humphrey Bogart? Or maybe something more refined like John Sutton?" The fancy man held his chin as he sized up Thorne.

"Just plain Richard Thorne if you please."

"Well, where are you going *just-plain-Richard-Thorne*? It's ok, you can tell me; we're all part of SOE." He dug through a series of men's jackets sorting out his favorites.

"I'm with Section N. Something simple, maybe that grey overcoat there."

"This old thing? How boorish," he said with a hint of pretentiousness, handing over the old coat. Thorne tried it on; a little baggy, but that would do good to cover up any discrepancies in his weight listed on future identification papers.

"And what are we doing with the hair and face? Maybe a mustache?"

"Just as is, if you please."

"That's no fun. Section N you say?" He considered this after Thorne's confirmation. "I hear there's a terrible food shortage in much of Europe. Let me apply a little shade to your cheeks, something like this. And let me see if I can hide this nasty bump." He handed Thorne a mirror.

When the photographer was done using his thumb to apply dark smudges of make-up on Thorne's cheeks, he looked in the mirror and was amazed at what a difference he saw.

I look as if I haven't eaten in days; ten, maybe twenty stone lighter for sure!

Thorne was seated in front of a white backdrop where the man took several photos of him, each time adjusting a set of lights on the opposite side of the room, applying differing smears of makeup to his face, and tossing Thorne's hair to and fro in various images.

"Ok plain Mr. Thorne, we're all done."

"Can you do something about my uniform?" he said handing the man a duffle bag. "It's quite the hodge-podge and in complete disarray."

The man looked at Thorne in aggravation. "I'll telephone Baker Street when everything is ready."

"Thank you. Say, I do recall last time I was here, there was another room where I can get re-equipped for my upcoming assignment?"

"Sorry, but that's Number Two. You're in Number Three, Photographic."

AT THE TRAIN STATION in Maastricht, a Black Mercedes pulled into the parking lot. Soldiers ushered dispirited refugees from arriving trains and directed them away from the station. Gerhard Mueller exited the Mercedes, proceeded directly to an SS officer dressed in black standing on a platform overseeing the arrival of the refugees, and saluted as he showed his police badge to the SS man.

"Good afternoon, Major."

The officer nodded, barely acknowledging the credentials, while he suspiciously scrutinized Mueller's civilian clothes with his dark eyes.

"Major, I am looking for two spies," He produced a photo and handed it to the SS officer. "Have you seen this woman?"

The SS man shook his head in a negative response. "What makes you think she is coming here?" he asked coldly. His mask-like face with its high cheek bones and penetrating beady eyes taunted Mueller.

"I've been tracking her for several days. She is accompanied by a British man, also a spy. Her name is Anna Larsen." He handed the officer several posters that displayed the woman's picture and pointed out detailed information about her. There was a man's face too—a smaller depiction—with a few of his details listed next to hers. "Please have your men post these flyers and be on the lookout for them both."

The officer took the posters and tucked them under his arm. "We will find your missing spies," he said as he turned back to the crowded platform.

"Do you mind if I look around?"

The SS officer looked back to Mueller and started to say something but stopped. He looked away again as a soldier prodded an elderly man near them. "Help yourself," he finally said condescendingly over his shoulder.

Mueller skirted a line of refugees inspecting each of them earnestly. He looked upon the saddened eyes of woman and children, and the tired, long faces of the weary older men and women in the line. They were shuffled along like cattle in single file while German soldiers inspected their papers. Occasionally someone was pulled aside, an SS man would go through their belongings while badgering them with questions.

Mueller stopped one of the soldiers. "Where did this train arrive from?" The soldier merely shrugged his shoulders and continued examining identification papers. *Insolent swine.* It did not matter, checking the train station was merely a hunch. His flyers were already being distributed amongst the soldiers; if Anna Larsen and her accomplice were attempting to leave Maastricht, he would find out, one way or another.

THORNE CHECKED OUT OF Trevor Square with a satchel of men's clothing; he'd hand-picked the best of the lot to match those which most resembled attire he'd recently seen in the Low Countries. He hefted the pouch across his shoulder and made his way back through Hyde Park, purposely taking a different path to avoid further memories of Catherine. He bypassed more artillery guns, and walked near a long ditch where women worked feverishly to fill large canvas sacks with dirt as they made sandbags for protecting London buildings.

He stopped to watch an auxiliary fire drill team working in a field where they practiced rolling out hoses and attaching them to hydrants; all the while their supervisor timed their efforts. It was at that moment; he had the same hair-raising feeling he'd had at Charing Cross. *Is someone watching me?* He continued beyond the fire team and took a divergent path that took him into an area open on all sides. He passed a few gleeful children running and skipping down the path, an uneasy woman pushed a stroller, and a preoccupied, teenaged couple held hands. He stopped in the middle of the great expanse and checked his watch, then looked up toward the sky. In both feigned efforts, he stole glances around the immediate area.

I see him.

Thorne moved along the walkway to a place where the path split again into different directions and this time chose a course that cut through a thicket of crowded trees and bushes. Several feet into the pathway, he looked behind him and did not see anyone. He tossed his satchel behind a round, thorny bush and dove to the opposite side of the path behind a broad tree, huddling there, waiting and watching for his follower.

Within seconds, a man dressed in a dark overcoat approached guardedly, searching. The man slowed his pace and continued looking backwards and forwards along the path. As he neared, Thorne readied himself for the right opportunity, then leapt like a panther from his cover, pouncing on top of the man and knocking him to the ground.

He hovered over the prone man looking down at him ominously. In that brief second, he sized up his opponent. Without a weapon, Thorne kept the man pinned to the ground and was convinced that with his larger stature he could handle the lean man.

The man cowered below him, "Please don't hurt me!"

"Who are you working for?"

"I don't know what you're talking about."

Thorne jabbed his knee into the man's skeletal frame. "I said who are you working for?"

"No one. No one, I swear. I am just out for a stroll." The man's voice was frail, but had a certain trait, a demeanor of over confidence that Thorne had heard before. He reached inside the scrawny man's coat and pulled out a stiletto. Carefully standing up, he grabbed the man up by the collar, yanking him to his feet.

Just then, a constable rounded the corner, saw Thorne clutching his victim, and blew hard into a whistle. Thorne released the man's collar, hid the stiletto in his sleeve, and waited as the bobby ran up to them with a black club extended in his right hand.

"Hear now, hear now! What's this about?"

"This man has been following me," Thorne said.

"I've never seen him before. I swear." The frail

man, inched closer to the policeman, putting distance between himself and Thorne.

"Are you hurt?" the constable asked the trembling man.

"No, just scared the Dickens out of me."

The constable eyed Thorne suspiciously.

I better play it safe.

"Listen, I'm sorry officer, I must be a little on edge." He addressed the small man. "Can we call it a case of mistaken identity?" He reached out a hand to the man who hunkered behind the constable.

"Well, I guess it could happen to anyone," he said as Thorne gripped his hand forcibly. The constable turned to face the small man, and asked again, "Are you sure this bloke didn't 'arm you in any way?"

Thorne released the man's hand, giving him a knowing look.

"No sir, just a bit shaken up. I must run now." The man turned and fled up the pathway.

"Listen mate, you can't be jumping strangers like that. I 'ave a mind to run you in," he said shaking his baton in Thorne's face.

"Yes sir. I assure you; it won't happen again." He waited as the bobby stood with arms on his hips contemplating Thorne's fate. "If you'd like, I can come back to the station with you." Thorne looked around purposefully and lowered his voice. "I'm with V Section. A quick phone call to St. James's will confirm my identity." He looked back and forth again. "Of course, there's some paper work to fill out while they get things cleared up. Just the standard forms, you see."

"V section you say?"

"Yes, yes," Thorne added, bringing his index finger to his lips.

The constable considered his afternoon schedule; his shift ended within the hour. He reconciled with Thorne, "No need for that now. Good day to you sir."

Thorne gave a half-hearted salute and turned walking in the opposite direction as he felt the constable's eyes upon his back, trailing him until he was well out of sight. Thorne was half way across Hyde Park before he realized he'd forgotten his bag of clothing, and he spent the next hour backtracking to find the exact spot where he had ditched it.

Chapter Sixteen

I T WAS THE NEXT DAY BEFORE Faulk could get all the paperwork in order with the Liaison team at Tempsford granting Thorne a drop into Holland. Thorne was shuttled from the Grand Central Hotel to Tempsford Hall, the great country house outside of Sandy where he was routinely equipped with the essentials needed for working in the Low Countries. Because a prearranged drop zone and landing committee could not be coordinated in such short time—both necessities for landing a Lysander in occupied territory—Faulk had instead arranged for Thorne to be dropped by parachute from an Albemarle twin-engine bomber.

Outside Tempsford Hall, Thorne enjoyed a cigarette and awaited orders for the time of his departure. An olive drab car came rushing up the long drive toward the manor house, interrupting Thorne's moment of respite, and as it jolted to a quick stop in front of him, the passenger door flew open abruptly with an offensive groan that was accompanied by the crunch of gravel beneath the car's tires. Even before the passenger stepped fully out of the auto, he heard a familiar voice call out, "I found your man!"

Thorne rose to meet Allan Faulk and the two men moved away from the main entrance to a grassy area framed by two sets of large bay windows.

"You mean Falconbridge?" Thorne watched as two Tempsford staffers exited the main entrance and proceeded in the opposite direction.

"Yes, it seems he's funded by someone named Blackbird. Have you heard that name before?"

"No."

"I found there are—I should say were—records showing Blackbird has funded a Swiss bank account on numerous occasions with instructions to convert Pounds to Deutschmarks as requested by Falconbridge. And I'm not talking a weekly salary, but thousands of pounds over the course of several deposits."

"What do you mean *were*?" Thorne asked.

"I had Lucille do some digging. She recalled the name Falconbridge and searched through a number of files looking for the name. In talking with one of the other girls who also remembered the name, they tied it together with Blackbird. Anyway, long story short, there are no specific files on Blackbird or Falconbridge—they have all been ordered destroyed."

"Destroyed? By whom?" Thorne smashed out his cigarette in the grass and subconsciously began digging through his pockets for another.

"That's just it, no one recalls the details. It seems one of the girls remembers having typed up some handwritten memos a while back, and there is another girl who worked in finance—well, none of that matters. What I could dig up was a connection between the two. You find out who Blackbird is and you'll find out what Falconbridge is up to."

Thorne, ever-cautious, stared up at an open window on the second story of the manor house, and continued in a hushed voice, "When were they destroyed?"

"They couldn't recall exactly when; a few months back perhaps. The girls work with so many files on a daily basis, they're not sure. But they did say it was odd to have something destroyed instead of simply marked classified and shipped to archives."

Thorne considered this, and nodded to Faulk indicating they should take a short walk around the property. He couldn't grasp the situation in front of him without saying it aloud. As if reading it for the first time, he slowly laid out what he thought Faulk was implying.

"So, Blackbird is funding Falconbridge, through a Swiss bank account. In return, Falconbridge, a Nazi double agent no doubt, provides information through Portia, to me, which I then relay back to HQ. That doesn't make any sense."

"Who is Portia?"

"My contact in Holland; Dutch resistance. Among other things, she gets information directly from Falconbridge and then passes it on to me. It's supposedly troop strength reports from around the Aachen, Germany area."

"Whomever Blackbird is, he's sure paying a premium for that intelligence."

"But the intelligence goes back to Head of Section N, through Beecher I presume. And what is interesting,

Falconbridge's messages are encoded in a manner in which no one else can read."

"What do you mean?"

"Beecher, myself and Portia all use the same cipher code. However, when we tried to decode the messages from Falconbridge, they don't match with ours." He paused looking upwards upon the towering bows of an ancient oak tree as if seeking its wisdom. "There must be something else that Falconbridge is up to. I have to wonder about the validity of the information he's been giving us. If he's been feeding me false information all along, then we could be putting the planned invasion at risk." He felt the fool for having not paid more attention to the coded information he had received from Anna. If he had been studying those messages and recoding them himself all this time, he might have seen a flaw, a mistake, a clue that would have tipped him off. His heart raced. "How did you find all this out?"

"I didn't say anything before, but I'm with Combined Operations Headquarters now," Faulk said reassuringly.

"What's that?"

"A branch of the War Office. After I returned from France, I requested a transfer from SOE. I wanted something different, hell, anything to keep from going back into the field. The timing was just right. The Normandy invasion was in the works, and well, let's say I had the perfect background for what Combined Ops needed."

"What is it that Combined Ops does?"

"Simply harassing the Germans as best we can."

He gave Thorne that familiar grin, but seeing his concern with the response, he continued, "It's a joint effort between the Navy and the Army. I'm a bit of a consultant, 'Operations Liaison' with SOE."

Faulk allowed Thorne to digest everything he'd dumped on him. After a long silence, he continued, "Richard, I do believe you're right about this Falconbridge chap. He could likely be a double-agent the Nazis are using to throw off our game. We did the same thing you know, prior to the Normandy invasion. Created all kinds of noise, crafted deceptions, dropped false information, anything to dupe the Germans into believing the invasion was taking place somewhere else. I'm guessing your man Falconbridge is doing something similar, and perhaps Blackbird, whomever the bugger is, is working here in London, on the inside helping to derail the entire scheme."

Thorne seemed lost in contemplation.

"I'm not sure what you've uncovered Richard, but you better watch yourself. This might be bigger than you can handle."

"What do you mean?"

"Well, I can't divulge everything, I have my own secrets too," he smiled. "But Blackbird, Falconbridge, hell even you, may just be pawns in a bigger game."

"But none of this makes sense. It's almost as if someone in SOE is working behind the scenes." He paused in step to light another Chesterfield and offered one to Faulk. "And who has the kind of money lying around that you're talking about. No one has access to those kinds of funds."

"There's more you should know. I've uncovered links between the Bank of England and the Swiss Bank, the Bank of International Settlements, which was set up after the Great War as a system for Germany to compensate the Allies. It's possible that money is changing hands beyond the reach of Churchill."

"Changing hands?" Thorne's voice rose in a falsetto pitch, "Between England and—?".

"Yes, Germany. The money from Falconbridge seems to be making its way to an industrial firm in Germany."

"The hell you say. You're not suggesting the King is supporting Hitler's war machine?" His face reddened noticeably. "That's bloody preposterous!"

"No, nothing like that. I'm just saying there is something big going on. As you know, the next invasion in Europe is in the works and may be happening sooner than later. I can't help but wonder if you're correct—it may be in jeopardy from what you've uncovered about Falconbridge and Blackbird. I wish I could give you more to go on, I've probably shared too much. Maybe you can do some digging on your own," Faulk said.

Thorne scratched his head, tossing the new information over in his mind.

"Richard," Faulk said sternly. He lowered his voice, "You've got to find out who Falconbridge is and who he's working for, post-haste."

Thorne looked into the inspirational face of his friend. "I know." He started, then lost his words. As he accepted the truth of the matter, they came to him,

"Allan, I may need your help when I get back from Holland."

Following Faulk's lead, the two men turned and made their way back to the main entrance at Tempsford where Faulk's car waited, now pointed in the opposite direction.

"Of course, Richard, I'll do what I can. Listen, it was great seeing you again." They shook hands. "I've got to run, catching a train to Northampton; official business, you understand. Good luck with this Falconbridge business and do be careful when you go back in the field."

As Faulk's car bolted down the driveway in a cloud of dust, a cold emptiness settled into Thorne's stomach; it was as if everything he had done up to this point in the War had been worthless. Despite his best efforts, and those of the brave men and women working for *Churchill's Secret Army*—let alone the thousands of Allied soldiers fighting abroad—it seemed the outcome of the War was being planned out and financed by some larger power.

Chapter Seventeen

THORNE MET WITH HIS PILOT later that day at the airfield administration building where they discussed various drop areas in rural Holland; the weather had changed recently from clear skies the past several nights, to thickening clouds with no sign of clearing any time soon. Thorne wanted to get as close as possible to Maastricht but realized the risk he was putting the pilot and his crew in. The deeper they flew into the Low Countries, the more they would be exposed to anti-aircraft fire and *Luftwaffe* patrols.

Using a large wall map for reference, the pilot pointed out that the shortest route would have been direct over Antwerp toward Maastricht, but he quickly reported that recent flights along this route had undergone heavy flak and suffered many losses. They agreed to fly over France, using Calais as a reference point. The British 2nd Army under Field Marshal Bernard Montgomery held much of that part of Northern France and although it was a longer flight route, it would provide a safer approach before they had to turn left heading due east over Brussels. The Welsh Guards of the British Army had recently liberated the

Belgian capital, so Thorne's pilot suggested a drop zone east by southeast of Brussels, just behind the front lines in the safety of the Allies. Once he met up with Allied field command in the region, Thorne could inquire about the best crossing point somewhere between Brussels and Liege. From there he would be on his own to find his way back to Maastricht.

The Albemarle was more than enough aircraft for a simple one man drop, it normally carried upwards of ten paratroopers at a time. But on short notice, it was all that Faulk could pull together. A number of the twin-engine aircraft had recently been strategically relocated to Tempsford Airfield in preparation for their role in *Operation Market Garden*—they would be dropping an unprecedented number of Canadian and British paratroopers near Arnhem. Thorne's drop would prove good practice for the new navigator in this particular crew.

Thorne was anxious for his reunion with Anna. He guessed it had been nearly a fortnight since he'd last seen her, and wondered if she'd continued to meet with Falconbridge or whether Visser had dispatched her on a different errand. He also wondered if she'd missed him; but then his thoughts turned against him.

What if something has happened to her?

He thought back on the day he'd received the tragic news about Catherine. Even now it seemed like a dream. He had not immediately felt the enormity of it—the shock had taken some time to set in, and even longer to get over. It was many weeks afterwards when he'd been granted leave, prior to his first assignment in Belgium, that it hit him. He was alone that day, walking through an English village where he was stationed awaiting his departure. He broke down and cried. What would he do now if the worst had happened to Anna?

"Ready mate?" His pilot broke his silent reflection.

Once the Albemarle was airborne, Thorne fell asleep. The droning engines lulled him into a restive state and despite his best efforts, his weary body gave in. Something roused him much later. It was dark, but the dim lights inside the hollow body of the plane cast an eerie glow throughout the hollow shell of the fuselage. The flight engineer stuck his head through the doorway from his forward compartment just behind the cockpit. "You doing all right?"

"Yes. How much longer?"

"We're getting ready to make our first bank, and then I'd guess a couple more hours."

He nodded and rested his head against the bulkhead. Thorne was seated in a bunk in the storage compartment located between the Albemarle's wing spars. Originally intended as a crew resting area, it was almost always used for nursing injured crew members during bombing runs. There was nothing to do now but wait, and Thorne's mind fell into puzzle-solving mode sorting through the pieces of the Falconbridge mystery.

Nearly two hours later to the mark, the flight engineer returned and passed Thorne's bunk. He watched the airman navigate the narrow corridor of the fuselage working his way toward the center of the plane. The airman opened an oval hatch in the center of the floor and began checking the parachute connections attached to a bar that ran horizontally above the opening. The engineer summoned Thorne to the doorway and instructed him to begin his routine of getting ready.

Thorne had already donned his *striptease suit*, the baggy, over-sized, camouflaged jumpsuit he wore over his civilian clothing. He also carried a small satchel which contained his trusty Fairbairn-Sikes commando knife, a pistol, a box of ammunition, notepad and pen, and three apples wrapped in an oiled cloth. All of these were stuffed inside the grey overcoat he'd taken from Trevor Square. It seemed a meager amount of gear to take into occupied territory, but given that he planned on returning to London within the week, he was thankful for the minimum compliment he had received.

Thorne fitted himself into the harnesses that secured a parachute pack to his back and attached one of the straps the engineer handed him to the chute—when he left the plane, the strap would automatically open his parachute. This was necessary as the jump from the Albemarle was no piece of cake. He sat sideways at the open hatch with his feet hanging over the edge of the oblong hole. When a red light above his head changed to green, he would launch himself out of the plane. At an altitude of less than six hundred feet, there would be less than ten seconds of hang time once his parachute opened.

The low cloud cover made it difficult to see anything outside the jump door. Even if there had been no clouds, much of the countryside below was intentionally blacked out in fear of night bombings, and what wasn't intentionally blacked out, was permanently blacked out from previous Allied bomb runs. He steadied himself as the Albemarle banked slightly to his left and struggled to look for landmarks between breaks in the clouds before the plane leveled out again.

To distract himself while he waited for his jump signal, he began planning his arrival in Maastricht. If everything worked out, Thorne would land near his target just southwest of the ancient city. Upon landing, he had a practiced routine of removing his parachute, hastily bundling it up, and either burying it or finding a place to hide it. In the worst case, he would simply cut himself free and run away if threatened.

He recalled a particular time when dropped into Belgium; he'd been sighted on his final approach. From several meters in the air, he could hear German soldiers below shouting out warnings. They thought they were being invaded by a large force of paratroopers. Luckily, he'd made a perfectly executed landing that night and was able to immediately free himself of his chute. He'd sought cover in a nearby hedgerow and as he dropped to his stomach, he looked back over his shoulder where the wind had caught his downed chute and lifted it back into the air, blowing it a hundred meters away from his position. This had bought him time to crawl down the length of the hedgerow while German soldiers pursued the drifting parachute.

This incident conjured up yet another time when after hitting the ground, a sudden updraft had caught his still attached chute and threw it into a tree with enough force that he was lifted three meters off the ground and left dangling like a marionette. He'd had to cut himself out of that mess before anyone had come along and found him an easy target. He reflected on a dozen other drops into Europe—each had its own serendipitous glitches—and none had gone by the textbook.

Tonight will surely be no different.

He thought back to his familiar safe houses in and around Maastricht. He had stayed on multiple occasions in the home of a family named Mertens. Greta Mertens, the matron of the family, had been overly hospitable in helping agents, downed pilots, and even Jewish refugees seek temporary shelter by putting them up in the attic of her home. Another nearby family, the Segers, had shown him the same hospitality.

It never ceased to amaze him how these ordinary people had taken it upon themselves to aid partisans, displaced people, and fugitives. It was the burden they had chosen to undertake, their own personal war against the Germans, even if it meant risking their lives. He guessed that many people outside of Europe, certainly most Brits and Yanks, had no concept of what it meant to live in tyranny and occupation.

A significant amount of time must have passed; he snapped to readiness when he overheard the pilot radio back to the flight engineer.

"We're getting close. Captain's going to take us down a bit, see if we can break this cloud cover."

They broke free of the overcast night sky and

Thorne looked down into the inky blackness. It was difficult to make out any features other than varying shades of black and grey signifying towns and structures below him.

"Yes sir, this it. Whenever you're ready."

Thorne disliked jumping from planes, he preferred a decent landing in the Lysander—*the Lizzie* as she was affectionately called by most of his SOE peers. He took a deep breath; *this never seems to get any easier*. He was just about to jump when the plane suddenly lurched up several meters and was engulfed again in clouds. Now instead of inky blackness, a pervasive smoky mist enshrouded everything around him. He heard the engines of the Albemarle drop a note or two in pitch and felt the plane start to roll gently. He counted three to himself, then pushed off the plane.

His stomach heaved in the momentary free fall before the line attached to the plane yanked at him, releasing his parachute with a loud unfurling sound followed by a sharp snap as it came to.

After the initial jerk signifying the break in his momentum, everything went silent, save for the Albemarle which trailed off behind him. Floating quietly on his open chute, he began to make out forms in the approaching land. Trees, buildings, fields, and roads all took shape in the darkness below. He prepared for the terrain rushing up to meet him, but despite his best efforts, he could not judge the distance to the ground until it was nearly too late.

In a split second, he saw the terrain rising up with a silver, shimmering lining that he barely had time to recognize as water, and he was down. He had readied himself for the customary roll he'd learned in training school, however, instead of dropping and rolling on firm land, he landed in a mushy, rain-soaked field of mud. The Germans, in their anticipation of an upcoming invasion, had busted many dikes in the area, flooding the fields and flat lands of Holland. This, combined with continuous rains in September of that year, turned the entire countryside into a swampy mess.

Thorne couldn't help but wonder if anyone had heard the loud splat of his swampy landing. He slipped and struggled to regain his feet several times while he freed his parachute, then leapt onto the still open portion of the bubble which slowly collapsed to the ground. Even though he was safely behind the front lines, he performed the same routine, ditching his parachute, and seeking cover until he could determine his whereabouts.

At least in the mud, it would not be difficult to hide the chute. He hurriedly rolled up the fabric, pressed all of the air out of it, and patted it down so that the majority of the chute was either submerged or thoroughly covered in mud and water. He waited, listening and searching, but it was silent in the immediate vicinity. He began slogging his way through the muddy field toward a black tree line in the distance; it was here that he knelt against a short, fat tree, removed his jumpsuit, and would hide until daylight came. In the dimness of the clouded night, he checked his coat pockets, reassuring himself that his new set of identification papers were still neatly tucked inside of his now mud-caked clothing.

Making his way to the obscurity of the trees, he struggled to account for his gear. He readied his Ballester–Molina .45 caliber pistol, a copy of the U.S. Colt M1911A1. It was much larger and heavier than the Walther PPK he preferred, but it was all that Faulk could secure on short notice.

He came out of the trees at daybreak, his clothes—despite the use of the jumpsuit—had gotten damp and soiled with mud. As the sky turned from onyx to slate with the sun rising somewhere in the distance beyond the clouds, he moved from tree to tree, in a direction he guessed was more or less easterly.

Where are the bloody Yanks?

He eventually made his way to a road where he was able to determine by road signs that he was in the proximity of Bilzen and Hoeselt, an area of Belgium just to the west of Maastricht. He looked around the unfamiliar terrain and momentarily wondered if the signs were correct. He knew of several instances where road signs had been deliberately turned in the wrong facing by the resistance—in many cases by local citizens—in retaliation against the Germans moving about their occupied country. He would have to trust the signs in this instance and chose to head in a general direction toward Maastricht.

As the skies continued to lighten, he looked across the field beyond the crossroads and was quite alarmed to find that what had appeared as a formless, dim patch of trees in the distance just moments earlier, was in actuality a massive fortress named *Alden Biesen*, a sixteenth century castle the Nazis had moved into shortly after their occupation of the Netherlands, and which they now used as a command post and *Gestapo* barracks.

Thorne realized his landing trajectory had taken him not only beyond the safety of the Allies camped behind the front lines, but had also dropped him right over the Nazi fortress before landing in the surrounding fields. He shuddered to think what would have happened had his landing been off by a matter of several meters putting him in immediate proximity of the castle. He also knew this area was heavily occupied by German troops—the front line opposing the Allies—and quickly crossed the road entering into another wooded area, aiming to put as much distance between himself and *Alden Biesen* as he could in the next several minutes.

He continued through the wooded area, keeping the nearby road in sight as he made his way closer to Maastricht. Occasionally he ducked into the brush as a German staff car, or other military vehicle went zooming past, but by midmorning he'd managed to reach the outer limits of Maastricht and the woods began to thin out. He remained hidden as best he could, while more and more German vehicles appeared along the roadways.

LATE IN THE AFTERNOON, Thorne hid from a long line of German troops marching on a path through the wooded area. Once they had moved on, he braved out of the woods into a stretch of fields where he remembered a friendly family that might take him in. As he neared their farmhouse, he saw that the building had been partially destroyed; but whether bombed from above or destroyed by mortar, artillery, or armored shells, he could not say. There was something else strange about the tiny house. As he crept closer, he realized a German machine-gun unit had taken up position in the house. MG42 barrels protruded from gaps in the walls and from behind sandbagged window sills. He cautiously slipped back into the cover of trees and felt a sadness as he tried to recall the various family members that had once lived there.

All in all, the day wore on in miserable fashion, light rain began in the afternoon and by nightfall he was soaked again, and still no closer to finding safe lodging than the night before when he had first fallen into the muddy fields. He used the dusk to his advantage and sought out back alleys, abandoned vehicles, and ruined buildings to hide in, as he made his way into the inner city of Maastricht.

Exhaustion crept up on Thorne, but he trudged on, recognizing various locations in the city that helped him find his way to the basement of the abandoned garment factory. It was here that he sought refuge and reunited with former companions in the Dutch resistance. He immediately sought out Stefan Visser and

Anna Larsen, but no one had seen either in the past several days.

Chapter Eighteen

WELL-FED AND RE-OUTFITTED, Thorne rested at the factory in a primitive room where he slept—nothing more than a confined enclosure that might have been a closet at one time, now separated from the rest of the building by a worn rug hanging from the rafters that served as a door.

Laid out in front of him were all of his effects he'd brought from England. He double checked the magazine of the Ballester-Molina, making sure all seven rounds were loaded, and tucked an additional five bullets into the lining of his floppy hat. He inspected a small corked bottle and counted eight Chesterfields, and half as many wooden matches, resting inside the dry container. He put the bottle next to his commando knife on top of the wool blanket he carried everywhere he went. He kept a small note book that held folded into its pages several one-sheet cipher pages for coding messages with Faulk. Lastly, he set out his identification and travel papers, and a ball point pen which concealed two cyanide pills in the cap.

When there was still no word of Anna's whereabouts after the first day, he left for St. Michael's in

Gronsveld. At the old cathedral, he sat at the same pew where he'd previously met with her, and he said a sort of prayer—it was the type of prayer that someone who had not prayed in a very long time, if ever, made— bargaining with God to return her to him in return for his future devotion.

"You are waiting for her," a soft voice said over his shoulder. He turned to face a clergyman dressed in a black cassock.

"Excuse me?"

"I can see it in your eyes, you are looking for someone you have lost."

Thorne rapidly processed a response. Perhaps this man was sympathetic to the underground, or just the opposite, he may be a Nazi informant. He vaguely recognized the man, but now cursed himself not only for failing to have noted specific details of St. Michael's staff previously, but also for now putting himself in a position to have been noticed by someone.

"If you are referring to my wife, yes, I fear she has been lost. She travelled north a few weeks ago to aid her mother, but she has not returned, and I fear the worst."

"Do not worry *Monsieur*. She will find you again, I can feel it in my heart." The clergyman returned to the pulpit. Reassured that no one else was in the church besides the chaplain, and seeing the man pay him little more attention, he checked his watch to see that nearly an hour had passed.

His thoughts had been muddled by anticipation of reuniting with Anna, but then turned dour as he feared for her safety. He realized he'd spent too much time waiting and needed to be out searching.

Thorne walked away from the church, formulating a plan where he'd return to his former safe house, and then try to arrange transportation to Vaals, and continue his search for Falconbridge by himself. He rounded the corner on the familiar street in Gronsveld where he'd first met Van Buren, and stopped dead in his tracks. Even from the corner some two hundred feet away, he could tell something dire had befallen the once neighborly, city block. The few businesses that had previously been spared from Allied bombings now stood vacant, their windows shattered and showing dark splotches above them where fire and smoke had stained the brick buildings.

The book shop next to Van Buren's apartments was now a hollowed-out ruins. He immediately ascertained that it was not the result of bombs or mortars, but fires set from within. The Nazis had desecrated this street, looted most of the businesses, and destroyed what remained. Several buildings had been painted with the word *Juden,* a clear signal to the people of Gronsveld, particularly the Jews, whom the *Gestapo* suspected as having cooperated with the resistance.

He hastily returned to the garment factory in a sullen mood and wondered if he alone was to blame for the Nazi retaliation on Gronsveld or whether others, including Anna and Stefan, had unknowingly contributed to the retribution against the quiet town. Anticipating his reunion with Anna, his elation was at once deflated as he learned she had come and gone with no indication of when she'd return.

THORNE CROUCHED IN HIS confined refuge in the basement of the garment factory, despondent and depressed. He rested on a cot in the corner of the room and was about to remove his boots when he saw a pair of worn shoes appear at the bottom of the hanging rug that was his door; the shoes stopped just outside his room and waited. He cautiously rose to his feet as the rug moved slightly to one side, and he recognized a voice, "Richard?"

He threw back the rug, "Anna!" They hugged in a deep embrace as he pulled her into the small room. He lowered his voice after the rug fell back into place. "Anna, it's so wonderful to see you!" He drew her close and kissed her hard on the mouth and she did not resist.

She rested her head on his shoulder, her voice soft in his ear, "Oh Richard, I am so happy you have returned. I thought I might never see you again."

He held her tight for several moments before releasing her. When she pulled back, he wiped a tear from her face. "It's okay. I'm here now." Thorne held her hands and stared intently into her face; it was perfect, he had not forgotten a thing. He slowly backed toward the cot, holding her hands and sat down pulling her next to him as his elation faded away.

He spoke to her now with a grim face. "Anna, you

were right about Falconbridge. He's up to no good. The information he's been supplying is not about the German army. He's been sending requests for money to England, and someone back home has been funding the Nazis. You were right all along."

"I knew something was strange about his dispatches," she added with a trace of concern in her voice.

"Yes. We must find out who he is. All I know is that he's working for someone named Blackbird." He paused, focusing on her placid eyes and taking in the beauty of her face. "I've decided, we must try and capture Falconbridge, and force him to tell us who he is, who he's working for. I have friends back in England who can help us bring this thing to a close."

She nodded soberly.

THEY NESTLED FOR A LONG WHILE on the cot sharing sips of tea and eating bites of bread and jam. It was a brief glimpse of what life might be like after the War. Caught up in their reunion, they were a million miles away from the War, the fear, the despair; and it was a perfect moment.

"Richard, I wish this War was over. Do you think it will ever end?"

"Of course, darling. Before long, the Allies shall liberate Holland and drive the Nazis back into Germany". He took a long swallow from a cracked teacup. "We can speed this whole thing up if we can figure out who is behind Falconbridge, and cutoff the flow of money to the Nazis."

"What will you do after the War?"

"I haven't given it much thought. But I know one thing, I'm going to get as far away from this bloody nightmare as I can." He stared blankly for a short spell, exploring the future. "I've always fancied a Cornwall cottage," he finally announced. He saw this meant nothing to her, so he explained. "A small country house, flowers in the garden, perched in a meadow, with a view of the sea in the far-off distance. And a trout stream nearby." She smiled but did not interrupt his vision. He came back to the present then, "And no more lurking about, no more watching over my shoulder." He finished the last of his tea and set the cup on top of his trunk. "And I promise, once we get this Falconbridge business behind us, I'll bring you with me, far away from here."

He felt her hands slip from his, her thoughts focused inward on some other possible future. When her eyes cleared, she came back to him from somewhere far away.

"Do you think we can get some of them to help us?" he said, pointing beyond the rug. He had seen other members of the resistance slip into dens such as his; he knew they were using the basement as a central location to house various members of their group as they scrambled about Holland performing sabotage against their occupiers.

"Yes, we can find someone."

"I'll go with you to Vaals the next time you meet him, except this time we'll be waiting for him. We'll grab him, pull him out of sight somewhere where we can question him."

She nodded in agreement.

"When are you to meet him again?"

"Tomorrow night. We were to meet two days ago, but something went wrong." Thorne listened intently. "Another officer was there ahead of us and got to him before he could meet with me. They talked for a minute, then both of them left. I knew something was wrong and I came back here right away."

"That does sound odd. Do you think he will be there again tomorrow?"

"We shall have to hope so. I have no other way to contact him."

"The last time we were in Vaals, I watched him walk to the intersection where you meet. It was very dark. Do you think you could draw him nearer to the cross street, deeper into the shadows?"

"Probably." She visibly shuddered at the thought.

"The guards at the border crossing, they cannot see us abduct him if we can get him off the street first. We need someone to distract them while I seize him."

"But Richard, it will be dangerous."

"Do not worry dear, I am trained in this sort of thing." His smile did nothing to break her indifference. He wiped another tear from her cheek and pulled her close again, whispering in her ear, "Listen Anna dear, please stay with me tonight. We can figure out this whole mess in the morning."

She rested her head against his shoulder, but he felt a stiffness, a reluctance in her body. Finally, she pulled away.

"A vehicle would be most helpful," he continued. "Go talk to Stefan. Ask for two men."

As she disappeared beyond the rug, Thorne couldn't help but wonder if she were still attached to Visser.

Chapter Nineteen

THORNE LEFT THE GARMENT factory in the late afternoon, accompanied by Anna, an older man named Martin, and a teenaged boy named Lowie. Neither of their new companions spoke English which was fine with Thorne. He spoke fluent Dutch and this would help him stay in character as they masqueraded about Maastricht carrying bundles on their backs dressed as fleeing refugees.

Thorne worried about moving in the daytime. All able-bodied men between the ages of eighteen and forty-five had either been conscripted into the Nazi army, sent off to labor camps and factories in Germany, or were working nearly around the clock at various industries the Nazis used to supply their war machine. There were others of course—Jews, homosexuals, and gypsies— who were not so fortunate.

Thorne knew that he would be a clear suspect if the Germans caught sight of him; he supposed Martin who was in his late sixties would draw no attention, and hoped the boy would be too young to be of interest. Before he'd left the factory, Thorne had smeared ashes upon his cheeks and under his eyes in an attempt to imitate an emaciated and malnourished appearance much like the SOE makeup expert from Photographic had done. He also had Anna strap his left arm in a sling, adding to his ruse.

After they left Maastricht, they joined another group of refugees wandering the roads of Holland. Thorne couldn't help wonder where the group was headed; if they continued along the main road to the east they would soon be in Germany. Anywhere to the west and south, the Nazis occupied France, Belgium, and Luxembourg.

"Where do you suppose these people are going?" he asked Martin, but the older man seemed to not hear, and trudged along wearily with the others.

Throughout the day, military vehicles passed them in both directions. There was no doubt, the Germans were on the move. Thorne supposed they too had rumors of an impending Allied invasion and scrambled resources to key strategic areas where they guessed an attack would come.

When they reached a stretch of road where at last no vehicles approached from either direction, Thorne stopped his team and they split off from the group of refugees they'd accompanied thus far.

"We are near Lemiers." He looked to Martin for confirmation. "We should leave the road behind us and enter Vaals from the west, there'll be less chance of German interference." Martin and Anna both agreed.

They walked along the edge of a stream that Martin called Zieversbeek. It flowed along the perimeter of what was once rolling, green pastures. But since the beginning of the War, the lands had become overgrown and were pock-marked with shell holes, scarred with dirt tracks that crisscrossed the fields, and defiled with the remnants of burned-out vehicles. Dead animal carcasses, which Thorne was quite used to seeing everywhere throughout the Low Countries, also dotted the fields. The entire plain stank of death and ruination. They continued down the creek's edge and crested a low hill where they hoped to find a more uplifting view, but it was more of the same. Death had left a swath of annihilation a mile wide for as far as they could see.

In the distance, a long, two-story building with many windows stretched in front of the edge of a wooded area.

"Martin, do you know what that place is?"

"It was once a mill, but now the Germans occupy it."

Thorne looked closer. "Yes, I see. And by the looks of it, those eighty-eights are fixed on the crossroads there in the distance." He habitually noted the position and surrounding features of the landscape as something to report, a potential target.

For now, they skirted the building, staying well to the east of it along a broken tree line, and soon reached the outskirts of Vaals where they stopped and rested in the shelter of a hedgerow. Martin proceeded into town to establish contact with his local connections and returned a few hours later, taking them to a farm where they could sleep in a hay barn. Once night fell, the farmer brought them fresh milk and a hearty soup which they supped on in the safety of the barn.

"I could not find a vehicle, we will not be able to capture your man," Martin announced pragmatically.

Anna looked to Thorne questioningly.

"We will just have to do without. If we can drag him into a nearby building, we can interrogate him there. It will be risky, but it's our only chance. We'll need to find such a place ahead of time. Let's go now and see if anything has changed since the last time I was there," he said to Anna. "You two rest here, we'll be back shortly."

Thorne weaved through the quiet town, following closely behind Anna step for step. As they lurked about in the dark like stray cats, he was thrilled at watching her work. It reminded him of an earlier time in his childhood, playing night games; some would hide and others, in teams of twos, would search out their companions.

They reached the abandoned warehouse where they had waited weeks before—it was her staging area for her routine meetings with Falconbridge. He wanted to reach out to her, hold her back momentarily, but she was focused on the urgency of their mission. Before he had time to share his thoughts, she stepped out of the warehouse and motioned him to follow her. Anna took him along a different path from his previous visit to Vaals, eventually stopping at a stone building.

"It's there, around the corner where I meet him," she said.

He peered over her shoulder, getting his bearings. It was all there, the guard shack to the east, the wraith-like tree overhanging the stone wall, and the intersection where she met Falconbridge. He surveyed the area in the moonlight.

"Where exactly do you wait for him?"

"There, I stand by that fence. He walks down the far side of the road, and then crosses to meet me there."

He searched for an advantageous place to hide, but there was not much there. A waist-high fence lined the right side of the road, but there were no large obstacles for cover nearby. A cluster of trees across the road would prove too far away to make a swift charge against Falconbridge.

At that moment, a military truck bearing a German cross came lumbering down the road from Maastricht, forcing them to crouch low against the building to avoid its approaching headlights. As the truck came around a slight curve on its approach to the inter-section, its lights shined for just a second on the fence line revealing a cluster of bushes Thorne had not seen before. The truck slowed beyond the intersection and stopped at the guard building to the east. When the motor revved again signaling its movement across the border, they used the opportunity to slip back into the shadows of Vaals.

Back at the barn, they found Martin and Lowie asleep. Thorne urged Anna to join him in another corner of the barn, but she chose to sleep by herself in the loft. He rested in the hay, turning over the abduction of Falconbridge in his mind. How would it work? Could Martin or Lowie make a sufficient distraction to occupy the guards? Would the boy be able to escape? He seemed so young, he had a long life ahead of him, yet he chose to risk it routinely in defiance of the Nazis. How had he become involved in the resistance? Where were his parents?

A snore brought his attention to the far end of the barn. And what of Martin? Was he related to the boy, maybe an uncle or family friend? They shared a bond of some sort, but Thorne could not pinpoint it. All the time he considered the backgrounds of Martin and Lowie, another part of his brain continued analyzing, recalculating, and planning for the abduction of Falconbridge the next night.

AFTER DAYBREAK, THEY REGROUPED at the abandoned warehouse and shared a brief meal, going over their plans while they ate. Thorne drew out a map for his team, using bits of straw, rocks, and other tiny objects as landmarks.

"When it is dark, we'll split up. Anna and I will move to her meeting spot with Falconbridge while you two distract the guards at the border. Once Falconbridge has cleared the border and gets to the meeting point with Anna, that's when you go to work. I need enough of a distraction for the guards so that we can force him out of sight without being seen." Martin and Lowie hung on Thorne's words. "If anything goes wrong, make your way back here, or if you're followed, head directly back to Maastricht. Do not wait for us."

"What if you need help?" Martin asked.

"If we run into any problems with Falconbridge, we'll do the same."

THE MOON WAS BEGINNING to rise when they split into teams of two. Thorne followed Anna to the vicinity where she would meet with Falconbridge, but first they located a disused shed sitting behind a home, which they cleared for the spy's interrogation. Thorne's plan was to confront Falconbridge at gun point, escort him through a back alleyway, and force him into the small structure. They propped the door open with a board and removed a broken section of fence along the alleyway to ease their approach to the shed.

When everything was ready, they returned to the rendezvous point and took up their positions. Thorne scrambled along the ground beside the white fence and huddled next to the fragments of shrubbery he'd seen the night before. He could see Anna waiting across the road near the corner of a building and signaled to her with a wave. There was no way to alert Martin or the boy, nor even a way to know where they were for sure.

Thorne checked his watch; it was time to begin.

Falconbridge arrived at the border on schedule. With the precision of a well-oiled machine, Thorne's partisans went into action. The German spy went through his routine of checking in with the guards before moving forward to meet with Anna. Thorne watched cautiously from the shadows and waited for

Falconbridge to get in position as Anna crept out from her hiding place and walked into the road. She had just stepped out to engage Falconbridge, when the commotion broke out behind them.

A flash of light caught their attention. A German *Kubelwagon* parked across the road from the guard house suddenly burst into flames. Thorne could not fathom how Martin, or most likely the boy, had managed to sneak up within a few meters of the guard house, light the vehicle on fire, and escape without being seen; but the distraction was all he needed. Every soldier within sight scrambled unheedingly to the border gate, watching the vehicle burn with no apparent sense of urgency or recognition of the plot at hand.

Thorne had already snuck within arm's reach of Falconbridge, and there standing behind the man's broad back, he heard his deep voice for the first time as he spoke with Anna. The German turned toward the pandemonium at the border and Thorne jammed the Ballester-Molina into his back.

"Move away from the road. Quickly."

Falconbridge as if he had fully suspected an assailant at his back, stood unfazed by Thorne's command. Thorne kept the barrel pressed hard against the man's spine to discourage him from any hijinks, and grabbed the German's shoulder with his left hand, urging him to step backwards away from the road.

Falconbridge, trained in similar self-defense and all-in fighting tactics as Thorne, swiftly kicked down on Thorne's foot and spun to face him using his left arm to lock around Thorne's right, which jarred the pistol out of the way. For that fraction of a second as Falconbridge turned, Thorne considered pulling the trigger, but his better judgement prevented him from shooting. In the same movement, Falconbridge clawed with his right hand for Thorne's face, but Thorne ducked and rolled to his left, right arm still entwined with the spy, and used his right foot to kick at the inner knee of the German. Falconbridge fell to the ground in agony, still entangled with Thorne, who now stood above him. Thorne got a look into that grim face for the first time, its coal black eye and dark patch taunting him. The man's fall also dislodged Thorne's pistol from his grip; his gun skittered across the pavement out of reach.

In a split-second decision, Thorne had to choose between going for his gun or maintaining his grapple with the fallen spy. Out of the corner of his eye, he saw Anna swiftly scoop up the Ballister-Molina as she dashed across the road. But in that same split second, Falconbridge had managed to free his own pistol and was bringing his arm up to face Thorne.

Thorne caught the right arm of Falconbridge keeping the pistol away from his direction, while the German squirmed along the ground attempting to knock him off balance with his good leg. The German spy was a large man and gave Thorne a challenge. He did not wait for further attacks, nor for the guards to take notice of their struggle in the street, but instead plunged downward landing on top of Falconbridge with both knees.

Unaffected by the pain in his shattered knee, and

apparently resistant to Thorne's weight on his chest, Falconbridge fought with the desperation of a madman. His right hand was still held in check by Thorne, but he thrust his left onto Thorne's neck and took advantage of Thorne's precarious position managing to catch him off balance. Arms still locked on to each other, both men rolled, and Falconbridge was able to get his pistol ever closer to Thorne's face.

As a bird materializes out of thin air at the hands of a magician, so too had Thorne's commando knife appeared from nowhere. He buried it to the hilt into the German's chest. With a short, sharp twisting movement of the blade, he watched the man's coal-black eye go wide, and then felt his body go limp on the ground beneath him.

Anna did not wait for instructions but impulsively rushed to Thorne's side. She fell to her knees and began rummaging through the man's coat pockets; Thorne did the same as he looked back to the border. They hastily gathered a handful of papers and other effects from the German's body. Thorne grabbed Falconbridge under the arms and pulled at the lifeless body, in an effort to drag him from the road. He had barely taken a few steps backwards when a sputtering sound sent a hail of bullets ricocheting off the pavement near his feet. Anna darted out of the street while Thorne dropped Falconbridge facedown where he lay.

A soldier ran toward them, his MP38 submachine gun leveled at his hips. He caught sight of Thorne kneeling at the edge of the road and stopped, squaring his feet, readying another salvo of bullets. A single shot, somewhere close to Thorne, sent the soldier sprawling haphazardly backwards, while the MP38 sprayed a stream of hot lead into the air. The soldier dropped to the street and fell motionless. Jackboots clattered on the pavement as more soldiers advanced on the intersection.

Thorne sprinted away from the street catching up to Anna who had already entered the alleyway that was their escape route. "Excellent shot!" he called out as they ran, and she handed his pistol back to him like a relay runner passes a baton. As they made their way back to the warehouse, they did not hear any sounds of pursuit by other soldiers, but they were none too cautious, and split up, taking different routes back to their rendezvous point.

Thorne arrived first where he found Martin and Lowie waiting, and in between gasping breaths, he cried out, "Great work boys!" He hunched over with his hands on his thighs and caught his breath. "Did anyone follow you?" They both shook their heads confirming they were alone. "Good."

Within seconds, Anna appeared through the doorway.

"This town will be crawling with Germans within the hour, we've got to get back to Maastricht," he said to the others. Their concerned looks showed they realized the same thing. It was too dark to examine the papers and personal effects they had taken from Falconbridge, and it was far too risky to light so much as a candle. It had started to rain. Thorne wished for his team to hole up in the building overnight, but he knew they must leave.

No one argued as they scampered away into the wet night, following more or less the same route they had used by daylight, making their way back to Maastricht.

Chapter Twenty

MUELLER RUSHED TO HIS DESK and shook his last two tablets of *Pervitin* into his palm. He washed the powerful amphetamine down with a gulp of water and took a deep breath. He had just returned from the basement of the Wilhelminasingel house and was now sweating profusely. The collar of his *SD* officer's uniform scratched uncomfortably at his neckline and he cursed out loud.

Normally he did not directly partake in the torture of prisoners, at least not male prisoners. When it came to interrogating female captives however, he favored a hands-on approach. Despite his displeasure, he had been present the last three hours as a captured man in his twenties, a suspected member of the Dutch resistance, had been brutally beaten by one of his *Gestapo* peers Ludwig Steinmann. He had known Steinmann since the twenties when he served as a policeman prior to his appointment in the *Gestapo*. Mueller was furious at Steinmann's barbarous tactics which resulted in the prisoner's death before he could get the essential information he sought.

He finished his glass of water and quickly refilled it to the brim. Nonetheless, he had learned quite a bit of valuable information. A British spy had been operating in and around Maastricht the past several months; this much he already knew. He looked at his notepad. The spy was apparently one of the more clever ones; he had somehow evaded discovery on numerous occasions, having been dropped, and subsequently extracted from the Netherlands, more than once without tipping off the *SD* or *Gestapo*. This infuriated Mueller. He emptied his glass again and slammed it down on the desk shattering the vessel.

An administrative assistant came running into his office. "Is everything okay, *Herr Oberst?*"

"Yes. Get me Worner on the telephone." He stared blankly at his notepad feeling the *Pervitin* kick into action. Several moments later his desk phone rang.

"Yes? Ah, *Herr* Worner. Do you remember that name you gave me recently, *Herr* Hartmann of Aachen? You said he routinely meets with a member of the resistance in the town of Vaals, correct?" He twirled a pencil around in his fingers, watching it spin like a propeller. "Yes, very good. And when do you think they will meet again?" The pencil stopped and snapped between two fingers. "Thank you, *Herr* Worner; I will mention you most favorably in my report to my superiors."

He hung up the phone and summoned his assistant. "Get me a car, urgently."

Mueller opened the top drawer of his desk and retrieved his Walther PPK. His particular model had the *Parteiadler,* the emblem of the Nazi party—an

Eagle holding a wreathed Swastika—embossed on the Bakelite handgrip. He checked to make sure the magazine was full, and placed the gun in his inner breast pocket which he'd had custom tailored to fit the small handgun.

The Walther was his favored weapon. While it only held six rounds of 7.65 mm ammunition, its snub-nosed design and compact size was perfect for concealment. He exited his offices onto the street where a driver stood alongside a Mercedes black four-door sedan. The driver motioned toward the rear door but Mueller stopped him, "I will take this car myself." The driver stepped aside letting him into the driver's side of the vehicle, and the car sped off leaving him at the curb.

Mueller raced through town. The sun had set at least one hour before and he wanted to arrive at Vaals before it was too late. There were no other vehicles about; the road to Vaals was unoccupied and he abruptly accelerated to nearly one hundred kilometers per hour. His tires screeched as he sped around curves, and swerved around destroyed vehicles and other debris that occasionally littered the roadway. He passed through several villages and towns, Margraten, Gulpen, Sinselbeck, and a half dozen others, but paid no attention to them. All he could see in his mind was the meeting place in Vaals, where at the border, a German spy would soon arrive.

For the entire thirty-kilometer trip to Vaals, he could not stop thinking about the broken voice of his prisoner; "Launcelot" echoed hauntingly in his mind. Each time Steinmann had shouted, "Who is the British agent in Maastricht," the prisoner would only reply Launcelot. Steinmann would then deliver another brutal blow from a lead pipe to one of the prisoner's limbs. The prisoner, already suffering from broken fingers and hands during the first wave of persecution, faced the excruciating pain of being hit in the shins and forearms each time he did not answer Steinmann's additional questions.

When Mueller had first entered the interrogation room, the prisoner's face was already a bloody mess. He promptly sent Steinmann away on a false errand, telling the prisoner, "Now you are going to talk with me. Tell me what I need to know, or I will have to summon Major Steinmann again."

The broken man shared limited information. He did not know the British spy's formal name, nor did he know where he was dropped or retrieved. He only knew that he had been in and out of Holland on multiple attempts and was not responsible for sabotage but merely for gathering reconnaissance information. He also knew that the spy regularly worked with a specific woman in the Dutch resistance.

When Steinmann returned to the room the prisoner shared a brief description of the English man, but there was nothing unique about his appearance to make him stand out in Mueller's mind from the dozens of other suspects he routinely rounded up. It was after Mueller had stepped out for a phone call and subsequently returned, that he found Steinmann at work again on the poor soul.

He had hoped to shift his questioning in order

to learn which resistance faction this prisoner was associated with, but upon his return, it was nearly too late. The prisoner, bleeding from multiple bone fractures and on the verge of death would only repeat the name Launcelot to any further questioning.

Suddenly Mueller sat upright in his car. *The British spy!* Could he have been the man that accompanied the bitch that nearly shattered his larynx three weeks earlier? Even now—the pain was gone—his voice still sounded squeaky and frail like some pubescent teenager.

When he'd first set eyes on her that day, he was surprised to see that she was quite attractive. She did not have the qualities of a Jewess, but instead he believed she might even have German stock in her blood. He daydreamed about seeing her naked in the interrogation room. How much fun it would be to have his way with her before Steinmann got to touch her. He assumed the uneducated grunt would also enjoy her just as much once he was finished with her.

The imbecile has no sense of decency.

Mueller's attention was suddenly averted back to the road as he slowed down just outside the town of Vaals; up ahead several military vehicles were at a stop in the middle of the road. He slammed on his brakes at the last second adding the effect of screeching his tires to alarm the soldiers ahead of him. He jumped from his vehicle and proceeded to the driver of the truck sitting in the middle of the road.

As he walked up to the truck, he straightened his officer's hat and projected a displeased mask of frustration to the driver who eyed him curiously in his mirror.

"What is the meaning of this?"

The driver straightened up in trepidation after recognizing Mueller's rank from the patches and epaulets on his collar. "A shell hole is blocking the road ahead, *Obersturmfuhrer*."

Mueller strained his neck to see what was going on ahead of the stalled vehicles but only saw a number of soldiers standing around a hole in the road talking and smoking cigarettes. He furiously stomped back to his car. He forced the vehicle in gear with a lurch and maneuvered the car to the outside of the trucks, passing them with one set of wheels staying on the pavement, and the other dropping into the silt on the extreme edge of the road.

His tires on the right side spun wildly flipping mud into the air but the left tires maintained enough grip on the firm pavement that he was able to control the car and get around the stopped vehicles. He pulled back onto the road just beyond the shell hole and sped off into the darkness.

Mueller glanced at his watch; it was nearly eight o'clock. Acting on the information from his most creditable informant, *Herr* Worner, a German citizen living abroad in the Low Countries since before the War, he was ready to capture both Hartmann and his Dutch accomplice Anna Larsen in action.

It began to rain, but that did not slow him down. The road narrowed considerably and he entered a gentle curve to the right coming into Vaals. He cleared the last building before the border crossing and as he came around the bend, his headlights flashed upon several German soldiers standing in the road.

Now what!

He instantly made out the shape of a body lying amongst them in the intersection where they stood. One of the soldiers waved his arms over his head signaling Mueller to stop. He pulled up to the soldiers, threw his car in park, and looked again at his watch as rain pelted noisily upon the rooftop.

Exiting the vehicle, he shouted, "*Sicherheitsdienst,* step aside!" He did not wish to argue with the corporal before him on his identity or purpose, but merely sidestepped the soldier. He looked down at the body lying in front of his headlights and instantly recognized the black uniform of an SS officer lying face down in a puddle of blood. "What is the meaning of this?"

"He came across the border and was attacked here in the road," the corporal responded.

"When did this happen?'

"Not more than five minutes ago."

Mueller knelt down next to the officer's body and touched the man's shoulder, lifting it slightly to get a better look at his pale face. Hartmann was dead.

BY LATE AFTERNOON THE NEXT DAY, Thorne and his crew had arrived back at the garment factory. He and Anna had split from Martin and Lowie on the edge of the city, and came into the city centre through a series of tunnels along the bank of the Meuse. They returned to Thorne's tiny room and lit a candle so they could examine the possessions of Falconbridge.

Emptying their pockets of everything they had collected, they laid it all on top of the trunk that doubled as Thorne's table and desk. First and foremost, of interest to Thorne was the spy's identification papers. A standard military identification card showed that Falconbridge was a member of the *Schutzstaffel*, the *Waffen* SS, under the name Karl Hartmann, and held the rank of *Oberstleutnant*, Lieutenant-colonel.

Thorne was convinced that this was not Falconbridge's true identity, however Anna produced a personal identification card showing the same name with a matching photograph. Among other effects they took from Hartmann were a package of cigarettes and matches, a tin carton labeled aspirin that held two tablets Thorne believed were suicide pills, a Ruger pistol, several Deutschmarks, and a handwritten note of the same type he usually passed to Anna.

She rummaged through a small pouch. "I also found this."

Thorne's eyes popped wide in disbelief as he looked upon a burgundy-colored, hardbound book: Shakespeare's *Hamlet*. He startled her, grabbing her in a firm hug. "We have the key!"

They quickly cleared Hartmann's effects from the trunk and set about deciphering the coded message he had planned to deliver to her. When they finished,

Thorne lit a cigarette and huddled onto his cot next to Anna. "This is very interesting."

"What does it say?"

"Access denied to records STOP Could not destroy STOP Provide day and time of enemy assault STOP."

Thorne flashed a look of concern at her then glanced back at the message in contemplation.

"What does it mean?" she finally interrupted.

"I'm not sure, but it appears he is aware of the upcoming Allied offensive. I'm afraid our trail here has gone cold. With Hartmann dead, we've no idea where to continue our search for clues."

Anna waited patiently; she watched Thorne's jaw clinch as he worked through what must be done. She interjected again, "What shall we do now?"

"Now that we know Hartmann's identity, I must get back to London; my colleagues there will pick up the investigation." He turned to her; the gravity of the situation now apparent in his eyes. "Anna my dear, it's going to get very nasty here, and in short time. The Allies will be advancing soon. It will not be safe."

Before she could respond, someone called out to Thorne from beyond his room. He jumped up and pulled aside the rug to see one of Visser's partisans. "Yes?"

"We have to move," the man said with urgency. "All of us," he added, looking past Thorne.

"Where are we going?"

"We are joining our comrades in Liege. They have

a strong presence there with little interference from the Germans."

Anna rose from the cot and placed her hand on Thorne's shoulder. "Liege? Why are we leaving Maastricht?" she asked.

"Stefan tells us that some parts of Nederland have already been liberated. The Allies are moving into Antwerp, Breda, and other towns in that area."

"That is wonderful news!" she added.

"Yes, but the German armies are now swiftly moving back to the Rhine. They will arrive here soon to defend Maastricht before withdrawing into Germany."

"Yes of course." This aligned with what Thorne had seen over the past few weeks with the retreat of the German army from Northern France.

"When are we leaving?" Anna asked.

"I heard him say by nightfall we should be gone."

"Where are we to go?" Thorne inquired. He watched others scampering through the hallway beyond his den.

"There is a man in Liege, using the name Leo. We are to rendezvous there; he will help us. I must go." The man rushed away from Thorne's room and the rug fell back into place.

Thorne began gathering his belongings. Inwardly he set aside his concern for the rest of the resistance unit and thought only of getting word back to Faulk confirming Hartmann's identity. He also knew that with Hartmann out of action, it was only a matter of time before Beecher discovered the man named Falconbridge was missing, and realized their little operation was out of business.

"I must get back to London," he said with his back to Anna. He folded his things neatly into a bundle as he spoke.

"Can't you just relay the information by wireless when we get to Liege?"

"I could, however my commander does not know I am here." Puzzled, she stared up at him with uncertainty. "It's rather complicated." He sat down and pulled her alongside him. "When I got back to London, I shared everything we knew at that time with my chief. I told him of our concerns, your suspicions, about Falconbridge. He thought I was chasing a red herring, told me to dismiss it." Thorne reached over and placed his hand atop hers as it rested on her knee. She made no motion to pull away, and he continued, "While my boss was detained with other matters, I spent my days in London mulling over the mystery. I knew I must get back here and discover his true identity. I needed something more to convince my chief of our hunches."

She stared down at his hand upon hers, but said nothing.

He craned his neck forcing her to look him in the eye. "Falconbridge was not the only reason I came back." Their eyes locked. "I was worried about you, worried that he would harm you, or take you back to Germany." He let out a small laugh. "It sounds silly now, but my imagination led me to many conclusions about your safety." His pulse quickened in that moment, and the next words left his mouth before he had fully conceived of them. "Anna, come back to London with me."

She smiled, "I told you; Stefan will take care of me. My duty is here, with him. He will make sure nothing bad happens to me."

A pang of jealously clenched at his gut.

Maybe it is not over between them.

Chapter
Twenty-One

LEAVING ANNA THIS SECOND TIME had been much harder for Thorne than the first. He'd seen a tear in her eye as she ducked out from the rug that separated his space from the rest of the factory, and he'd sat there for several minutes on the cot, her warmth still evident on the blanket next to him. Thorne finally clinched up the blanket in his fist, and knew at that moment he had crossed the line—crossed over from professional to personal in his relationship with Anna Larsen—and he cursed himself for it. He knew that he was in love with her.

While he couldn't be entirely certain of her status with Stefan, he knew she was entirely devoted to him, or at least to his cause. The move to Liege would be risky for Stefan's crew, but each and every member of that clandestine team was adept at evading the Germans and there was no reason to believe they couldn't accomplish the feat at hand. The German army was in disarray in their retreat back to the Fatherland and was far too busy fleeing the advancing Allied front to be bothered with rounding up anyone in their midst. He also knew the resistance had an unseen network of communication lines, and pathways that ran right under the Germans' noses, and with a spot of luck, Stefan's team would slip right past them.

It was one of these paths in the underground network that he had used to cross over the Axis front seeking the protection of the Allies somewhere west of Liege near the Hoegaarden region. After being shuttled through numerous Allied command posts in the Flanders region, he was finally able to arrange a lift aboard a cargo plane headed back to an RAF airbase in the vicinity of Brighton. It had been a long thirty-six hours of jostling rides in the backs of Jeeps and cargo trucks, as he was shuttled across the English countryside, but Thorne eventually made his way back to the Grand Central Hotel.

From the lobby he attempted to reach Allan Faulk, leaving messages with the various branches of Military Intelligence that he knew how to reach; in the end, there was nothing to do but wait for Faulk to find him. He settled in for a long nap after reaching out to Baker Street to determine his next appointment with Beecher.

In the morning, he found messages waiting for him at the front desk from both Beecher and Faulk. He was to be in Beecher's office later that morning, but first he wanted to place a call to a number Faulk had left.

The telephone earpiece blurted out a shrill buzz as he awaited someone to answer the extension. It took three calls during the hour before he finally got through.

"Faulk here."

"Allan, it's Richard. Can we meet?"

"Afraid not, I'm tied up with something for the next few days, but this is a secure line. I take it you made it back to London in one piece?"

"Yes, I've got the identity of our man. Can I share that here?"

"Yes, we're safe on this connection." There was a brief silence, then, "Go on."

"His name is Karl Hartmann, Karl with a K and two Ns in Hartmann. That's from his SS identification papers. Does that name mean anything?"

"No, but I will take it and see where it leads. Anything else?"

"Yes, I've got his key and was able to decipher his last message."

"What did it say?"

"He could not get access to destroy some records, no details, but he also requested the day and time of the Allied offensive. Not sure it gives us much, but simply another piece of evidence in the larger schema."

There was a long silence on the other end, finally Faulk said, "Yes."

"I'm on my way to meet Beecher, perhaps we can discuss this at a later time?"

"No Richard, time is of the essence. Listen closely, here's what you must do. There is a man named Pasteger, a Belgian underground sympathizer, he will be able to get you into Germany. In Aachen, there is a factory, the German firm I mentioned. You must get inside the Englebert Tire factory; find any evidence there linking Blackbird to Hartmann and the Swiss

Banks. Everything points to Englebert as the source behind your mystery."

The line was quiet again as Thorne repeated everything back to himself. "Where do I find this Pasteger?"

"He heads up an underground faction in the town of Liege, are you familiar with it?"

Odd coincidence.

"Yes, I know where it is."

"Good. Go to the church of St. Walburge. You should be safe there until you locate him. And Richard, this is getting very dangerous. Our prying around has ruffled some feathers. Use all caution until you link up with Pasteger. I'm afraid there's nothing else I can do for you at the moment."

"I see. Thank you again Allan. I'm sorry to put you in this compromising position."

"Richard. I must go now. Be careful."

"Shall I contact you when I get to Belgium?" Thorne asked, but the line had already gone silent.

"AH, RICHARD MY BOY, PLEASE do sit down." Thorne assumed his usual position in the padded leather chair across the desk from his boss and waited for Beecher to go through his routine with his thin cigarettes. Still fixated on the Blackbird mystery, Thorne contemplated how to get back to Belgium before his next assignment. Surely with the identification of Hartmann, Faulk could help in putting the puzzle together of how the Nazi spy tied into SOE and the mysterious operation.

Beecher lit a cigarette and leaned back in his chair, his face blank of emotion. Thorne stared into Beecher's clear eyes, but could not read anything in them; there was no hint at his thoughts about Thorne's whereabouts the past week. An awkward silence hung between them as Thorne waited for Beecher to make the first move.

"I do hope you're feeling refreshed, and I must apologize for the delay. Urgent business, which affects you I must say." Thorne waved off an offer of a cigarette. "I have something a little extraordinary for you, and if it gives you any peace of mind, it will keep you out of the line of fire," Beecher added.

Thorne shifted uncomfortably. *Here it comes.*

"I have a bit of a diplomatic operation for you in Stockholm; there's still an element of danger which I know you crave."

He stared blankly back at Beecher. *Stockholm?* He'd planned on asking to be dropped into Belgium, but now Beecher was sending him nearly fifteen hundred kilometers away; *away from Anna.* Beecher slid a file toward Thorne forcing him to interact.

"*Operation Bridford.* You can study the details before your departure. Under command of Sir George Binney, Royal Naval Reserve, sort of a piratical chap if you ask me. He organized the shipping of large quantities of ball bearings out †of Sweden, a blockade-running operation. Sweden is still claiming neutrality and all indications show they are leaning toward our side with the War turning against the Hun," he grinned.

Thorne browsed through the paperwork, letting Beecher see his unhappiness.

"I'd like you to pick up where he left off, he was planning a new operation to ship arms into Denmark to assist the Danish resistance." Thorne thumbed through various documents, struggling to grasp the meaning behind it all. Beecher waited for him to look up. "You could probably even finagle a portion of the munitions to be delivered to your *friends* in Holland." Thorne assumed he'd added this as an attempt to further sway him in favor of the plan. Of course, he knew he had no other option. A direct order was enough to send him on his way, but he sensed Beecher wanted to gain his trust.

"What happened to Binney?"

"Recovering from a heart attack, poor chap. You'll find all the contact information in the dossier. You'll be reporting to the British Ligation in Stockholm. We need you to finish the negotiations and arrange the shipping. Binney has done all the heavy lifting. He's got a small fleet of boats—motorized gun boats, or MGBs as they call them—all lined up. You simply swoop in, make the deal with the Swedish Government and receive all the credit for completing what he could not. Of course, you'll be under direct regional control of the Embassy, so if they have any other tasks for you, you're obligated to assist as they see fit."

"I don't understand why you're sending me. I don't have experience in negotiations or diplomacy. Why isn't the Swedish section sending one of their own agents?"

"You were recommended as one of our top

operatives. It was coincidental that you were back in London at this time. I met with the other section heads and your name was well favored among the various candidates." Beecher rose from his desk and sauntered around the room playing with his cigarette while Thorne absorbed the details. He circled behind Thorne and placed a hand on his shoulder. "I must admit, I did boast about your past accomplishments which may have had some influence."

Something doesn't feel right. There was something personal here, a punitory nature to the assignment. "Let me guess, there's no one else available," he said coldly.

"True," Beecher hesitated. He shifted back to his chair. "But it is also true that your reputation weighed heavily in the decision process."

Trapped. He gave in. "When do I start?"

"Etta is already working on the arrangements. I suppose a day or two at the latest."

"But I have unfinished business in Holland. I need to get back." He stopped himself and avoided Beecher's glaring eyes by looking down at the Bridford documents.

"I hope you aren't still thinking about this Falconbridge business. Besides, it seems like the timeline for invasion of the Low Countries has moved up. I can't risk having you right in the middle of that onslaught, it's far too dangerous to send you back at this juncture."

Thorne bit his lower lip and decided to force his hand. He looked up pleadingly to Beecher, "But I've uncovered new information. I believe I may be able to link the German agent back to an operation, or operative, named Blackbird. Major Gubbins suggests that Colonel Thornley might have additional insight, whether it relates to the German section that is." He stopped himself at the sight of Beecher's grimacing face; *overplayed again.*

Beecher's eyes narrowed; his face tightened around the edges. "I told you to forget about Falconbridge." His voice took on a tone Thorne had never heard before. "You needn't be digging around in something that is already buried." After a short but awkward pause, anger building, he continued, "I can't believe you went around me, and to Gubbins no less!" His face reddened and his voice grew louder. "This is tantamount to insubordination!" He stood behind his desk, leaning forward on both hands, and towered over Thorne. His next words came out slowly and deliberately, "I can ruin you." Thorne was taken aback by the threat, and shrunk back in his chair.

And then of a sudden, it was as if Beecher's demon had left the room and the kind-hearted, grandfatherly man returned from afar. He swiveled to face the window and combed his wispy hair back with his long fingers letting out a long breath, "I'm doing you a favor here. There will be no more discussion about Falconbridge," he said in his normal tone.

Thorne started to reply in affirmation, but hesitated. He was stunned at the sudden outrage that came seemingly from nowhere and had vanished just as quickly.

Beecher continued looking out his office window. "Best of luck in Sweden Richard, and Godspeed."

He left Beecher's office in shock.

"What's the matter with you? You look as if you've seen a ghost?"

Thorne cleared his thoughts and turned to Etta as if seeing her for the first time. "Oh, nothing."

"I've just about got everything in order."

"Very good. Tempsford as usual?"

"Of course. No direct flights out of London my dear," she smirked.

He looked back, confirming that Beecher's door was firmly closed, and continued in a hushed voice, "Do you suppose there's a way to get a message to Belgium for me?" As soon as he asked it, he knew she would not be able to help.

"Yes, let me put you right through," she said sarcastically. "Honestly, you think I can do anything."

"Well, you are the best my dear." His smile fell flat on the floor. He knew of no agents in Belgium that might be connected directly to Visser's organization. Even if he did, he would have to find someone in the Baker Street radio division to get a coded message through, but that was no use; the recipient needed to be on the air at the correct time in order to receive the message and with Visser's team on the move, it was simply too difficult a task to coordinate in such a short time. *There's no going for it now.* "So what have you got for me?"

She handed him a piece of paper. "I jotted down the connection points between here and Stockholm. It will take a few days, considering the distance and all," she added apologetically.

"Don't suppose I could divert through Belgium?" *If she can arrange a drop, I can find Anna in Liege, let her pick up the trail with Pasteger while I get on with this Stockholm business.* "I can work with my connections to arrange an extraction and secondary drop into Denmark, then find passage to Sweden, or maybe you can help from there?"

Etta simply looked at him with disbelief. In the end there was no chance—it was much too complicated, there were too many logistics, not enough time, and it was far too risky based on the wrath of Beecher.

"What is it with Belgium? Mr. Beecher mentions nothing about Belgium."

"Unfinished business."

"Yes, like your unfinished business here. I'm not forgetting about dinner. I'm holding you to that when you get back." She handed him his travel orders, ignoring further pleas. He knew there was nothing else to be done and by the end of the day he was off to Sweden.

Chapter
Twenty-Two

FOUR DAYS LATER, THORNE FOUND himself walking beneath the arch that led into old town Stockholm. His guide Anders, a man at least ten years younger than himself, had met him at the Stockholm train station and offered to escort him to the British Ligation offices in the Town between the Bridges—the local name for the medieval inner city of Stockholm. The old town seemed aglow; its Gothic buildings brilliantly reflected the high latitude sun in hues of amber, marigold, and mahogany. As they walked down cobbled streets and narrow alleyways that curved around the island city, Anders seemed to twitch about with a jitteriness and timidity that suggested he was being followed—which made Thorne all too uneasy himself—but they finally arrived uneventfully at a nondescript, black door on a narrow side street.

Thorne was exhausted. He'd flown at night from Tempsford airfield by Westland Lysander and arrived in Gothenburg, Sweden, some nine hundred odd kilometers from London, about the maximum range for the liaison aircraft, but he had slept very little on the noisy plane. Changing planes to a Swedish air force de Havilland Dragonfly—a twin engine biplane built before the War—offered no additional comfort. He enjoyed a brief lay over in Orebro during refueling where he slept in the backseat of the open canopy plane before continuing on to Broma airfield outside of Stockholm. It was there that Anders had met him.

Thorne dared not think of how little sleep he'd actually gotten these past few days, but anxiously awaited a warm bed upon his arrival to Stockholm. Instead, Anders had rushed him into a waiting car where they travelled on rough roads fringing greater Stockholm, and eventually they reached the edge of the old city and finished their journey by foot.

At the British Embassy, Anders introduced him to various staff members on the Empire's payroll, before escorting him to a nearby hotel where arrangements had been made for his extended stay. He checked into a room and looked forward to a long nap, however, as soon as he'd put his belongings away, a knock on the door turned out to be Anders who rushed him away to a clothier across the river *Riddarfjarden* where Thorne was to be outfitted for a societal gathering the following evening.

He had not purchased new clothing in many months, having relied on SOE to supply the local clothing for his assignments. Now he felt awkward as a Swedish tailor measured his shoulders, arms, and inseam for a fitted suit, his required regalia for a formal black-tie affair.

After a grueling day spent with Anders getting to

know the locale, he ravenously craved sleep and despite it still being light outside in the late evening due to their extreme latitude in Stockholm, he found the single bed in his hotel room a hearty reassurance, and fell into a deep slumber—probably deeper than he had had in months, if not years—and did not wake until late the following afternoon.

Anders had arranged a car to pick up Thorne and deliver him to the *Riddarhuset*, the House of Knights. It was a 17th-century mansion once used by the Swedish Parliament which now served as a meeting place for the House of Nobility. Anders had attempted to educate Thorne on the structure and workings of the Swedish Government the day before, but in his exhaustion, he had retained little of the information. As he exited the vehicle, he was promptly met by Anders who escorted him through the foyer of the palatial building.

"Welcome Mr. Thorne. I trust you are doing well?"

"Just fine, and you Sir?"

"Good, very good." Anders said with a sudden jerking tick that caused Thorne to survey his surroundings, but then he decided the poor chap must suffer from some nervous condition.

They hastened to the rear of the manor house and ascended a wide set of steps leading up to a grand ballroom.

"Now Mr. Thorne if you please, I will take you around and make a few introductions for you. We will keep our distance at first, but feel free to mingle with anyone once I have pointed out the most important attendees."

"What about the Royals? You mentioned there'd be a few here I should rub elbows with?"

"Ah, yes," Anders replied rubbing his chin. "I think I should make a formal introduction there."

The men were stopped just outside the ballroom by two guards dressed in bright blue and yellow military regalia. After Anders shared their invitations and identifications, they were allowed to enter the ballroom where Thorne estimated at least one hundred guests in attendance, clustered throughout the immense space in groups of threes and fours, immersed in lively discourse. He was astonished at the sight of hundreds of coats of arms neatly displayed on the walls of the cavernous room. Grandiose chandeliers gave the room a warm glow, and a cacophony of conversation threatened to drown out a quartet of orchestral musicians who played a medley that no one particularly paid attention too.

Baroque, I never cared for baroque.

They were served glasses of champagne by one of a handful of attendants that entered and exited the room from a set of double doors adjacent to the main entrance. Thorne noticed other doors placed at regular intervals in the side walls, and straight across from his position, the back wall of the room was composed of floor to ceiling windows with a wide set of doors in the middle that opened onto a balcony.

"Now let us see who we have. That man there is the Minister of Defense, Jansson," Anders looked around the room casually. "Over there, Engstrom, Finance Minister I believe. You met Ogleby yesterday," he pointed out a familiar face Thorne had seen at the British office.

"And what about the tall blond?" Thorne asked, pointing to a young woman dressed in a cobalt-blue gown. *She's absolutely stunning.*

"Ah yes, in due time. That is Duchess Bergman."

The Duchess wore an elegantly cut dress which set off her blond hair and ice-blue eyes. She wore a brilliant necklace of white and blue gems that Thorne could not identify, and her long arms were adorned with alabaster silk gloves that extended from her hands to her elbows.

This might be interesting yet.

Anders made introductions to a dozen others, potential financial backers and armchair adventurers, who reveled in the thought of partaking in the 'war effort'. When he'd finally been introduced to the Duchess, he'd awkwardly said, "We look forward to your continued support of the War." His fear of over-stepping foreign protocol had led to a bumbling but brief interaction and he was left standing at the side of the room as she departed with other dignitaries who summoned her away from him.

He wasn't sure if he was to openly discuss the shipping of the arms or if he should wait for a proper introduction to the people in charge, whoever the hell they were. In his review of *Operation Bridford*, there were no details on *how* the deals were made, just straight-forward, after the fact details of the outcomes of Binney's mission. As he sauntered around the room, he bypassed groups of people, uncomfortable mingling or interjecting himself into their discussions. He was truly a fish out of water.

They forgot to teach me about hobnobbing back at Wanborough.

He thought back to his initial training manual at spy school and recalled a passage instructing agents, "Be inconspicuous, avoid all limelight by being an average citizen in appearance and conduct, especially when it comes to drink and women." But on this occasion, he used his true identify and in fact, the first few introductions he'd made had set off alarm bells inside his head, causing quite a bit of anxiety.

He awkwardly approached a group of men engaged in animated discussion about hunting—this he surmised by the way the man at the center of attention held his arms up as if shooting birds—but as he neared the group of jubilant men, he realized they were not speaking English, and abruptly turned away from them. He made his way around the spacious room in its entirety, and having failed to engage in a single direct interaction with anyone in particular, he chose instead to deliberately disengage, and waved toward an attendant to replenish his drink.

A long table was laid out with meats, cheeses, and breads. Little towers of desert pastries and tiny candies were surrounded by floral decorations.

Such extravagance, surely these people know there is a war going on.

He sampled a few bites and was studying a thick cracker-like piece of bread when he heard a man's voice address him. An English man dressed in a white dinner jacket and bowtie approached him—he thought for a moment that he'd committed a major faux pas by sampling the food in front of him.

"Thorne, I believe?" the man said with an extended hand.

He gripped his hand firmly in return, "Yes, Richard Thorne, Ministry of Economic Defense."

The stranger ran his left finger down the length of his nose adding an almost imperceptible wink, then stuffed his left hand into his coat pocket leaving his thumb exposed.

"Brian Reynolds," he responded haughtily. "They told me you'd be arriving shortly, but I had no idea this soon." He recognized the name as belonging to one of the staffers working closely with Binney's operation. "Have you any word on George's health?"

"Recovering from what I understand." Thorne finished his glass of champagne and handed it off to an attendant. He gladly accepted a full glass in return as his eyes circled the room scanning the guests. Satisfied that no one had shown any interest in either of them he continued, "This is somewhat new to me, I must admit, but I'm glad to assist however I can." He attempted to appease Reynolds who was clearly identified in Beecher's dossier as the number-two man of this operation. "So, tell me, how does this work? Do we rub elbows here with the hoi polloi, then meet later with the real head of operations?"

"Honestly, I am entirely unclear as to why you're here," Reynolds replied curtly without showing amusement for Thorne's attempt at humor.

"I beg your pardon. You are Sir Bryan Reynolds, correct?" Reynolds nodded in affirmation. "I was instructed to assist with your efforts here." Thorne examined the man who cast an air of royalty and pretentiousness that made him feel uneasy.

"I'm afraid you've been had old boy. I've just about got everything all tied up," Reynolds continued in a firm tone.

That's odd.

Perhaps this man was not whom he said he was, although his features matched a brief description and photo he'd seen in the Binney files.

"Ah, well, I'm not so sure what I'm doing here myself. Is there somewhere we can talk privately?"

The two men walked to the end of the table, and made their way through the set of doors that opened onto the balcony. The horizon was aglow with the setting sun which danced off the Gothic rooftops of surrounding buildings. Even though they were out of immediate earshot of other guests, he continued in a hushed voice, "I was informed we are working on arrangements for a special shipment of arms to our Danish allies."

"That's correct. I have that all taken care of. In fact," he glanced at his watch, "in just a mere three hours, the first boat will be on its way."

"Ah, I see. And how many shipments will there be?" He felt Reynolds' probing eyes assessing his character. He'd done the same thing dozens of times in his line of work, sizing up the man in front of him, deciding which side he was on, judging whether he was telling the truth, looking for any suspicion that would tip him off to friend or foe. He must have passed Reynolds' sniff test.

"Well, that depends on how things go. You're familiar with our last operation I take it?"

He nodded in affirmation, "*Bridford*, yes."

"We had quite the go of it in the *Skagerrak*—all this maneuvering at night, outrunning German U-boats and such—quite the undertaking you know. I've got a different game in mind this time. A little more clandestine you might say."

As other guests approached the balcony, they moved back inside to an area of the ballroom where seats were arranged two by two. Reynolds shared the details of his plan whereby he'd arranged for the weapons and ammunition to be loaded in unmarked crates and delivered by truck to a nearby port. Unlike *Operation Bridford*, which was a shorter route directly from the western edge of Sweden through the *Skagerrak* and into Denmark, he chose a longer path of distribution for this effort.

"The Baltic Sea has been mostly cleared of the German Navy and by mixing our cargo with that of merchant ships already engaged in commerce in this region, we'll slip the shipments into Koge Bay on the eastern edge of Denmark without their notice," Reynolds explained. "Danish resistance has already been engaged to assist in the offloading of the cargo with local boats working in the bay."

Thorne shared his vague instructions from Beecher and the two men discussed his previous operations.

Reynolds explained that since the political machinations had already been set in motion, now all they had to do was simply deliver. Furthermore, he suggested that Thorne's expertise in covert operations and reconnaissance would be helpful with engaging the Danish resistance.

"I'm thinking you're much better suited to coordinate the handling of the cargo, getting it into Denmark and such. I've already got a man overseeing the loading of the arms."

The two men parted company with Thorne receiving instruction on the time and location of where the shipment was to be loaded onto a merchant vessel waiting in Kvarnholmen. With his mission in hand, he retreated to the buffet table waiving off another glass of champagne. He realized then that with no specific terms set out by Beecher on the duration of his assignment in Stockholm, the sooner he could get this operation over with, the sooner he could get back to chasing the Blackbird mystery.

He sampled a delicious piece of fish and followed it with a sweet pastry before guiltily turning away from the buffet table. He decided to leave the event.

As he descended the wide stairs out of the ballroom, he was abruptly intercepted by a short, balding man dressed in a wrinkled and worn suit. The man spoke urgently in a hushed manner.

"Mr. Thorne. You are in danger here. Please come with me."

Chapter
Twenty-Three

I N THE FOYER OF THE HOUSE OF NOBILITY, Thorne was led to a side chamber where the short man introduced himself. "My name is Axel Sveinsson, I'm with the Ligation."

Thorne eyed the distraught man suspiciously.

"I received a message from Faulk." He pushed small round eyeglasses upwards against the bridge of his nose.

"Faulk? How do you know Faulk?"

"The message wasn't directly from him, but one of his team members working here in Sweden."

Thorne studied Sveinsson. The man spoke nervously with a trace of an accent that could easily be taken for one of a dozen dialects in northern Europe.

"Listen, we don't have time for my background now." He looked out the open doorway into the foyer, then closed the door, satisfied that no one was nearby. "We intercepted a message to the German Embassy here in Stockholm. It seems they've taken a dislike to you; they want you out of the picture. The whole thing has been orchestrated by someone named Blackbird."

Thorne froze.

Blackbird.

How could Blackbird of known he was in Sweden? Besides Faulk and Gubbins, he had not mentioned the name Blackbird to anyone else. Blackbird must have someone working inside SOE, someone with access to the movement of agents, or records of their operations.

The file clerks.

They are the only others who would know that he and Faulk had been digging around for information about Falconbridge. His mind went into lightning motion replaying all the encounters he'd had in the past few weeks. He momentarily forgot about Sveinsson and his commitment to Reynolds.

"We must go now, for your safety. In front of the house, I spotted two men waiting in an automobile. We should find another way out."

Thorne sprang into action. He opened the door and scanned the foyer for potential exits, and surveyed the staircase that led back up to the ballroom. He wished for a weapon of some sort but saw nothing of use around him. He didn't trust Sveinsson and did not wait for the short man to follow. Instead, he moved at breakneck pace cutting across the foyer, entering another set of doors, and leaving Sveinsson to scamper hastily behind him. They passed through a series of lavish meeting rooms and eventually came to a service corridor that led to a rear exit.

The hallway was well lit, but Thorne could not find a switch to douse the lights. He slowly opened an exterior door a fraction of an inch and looked out upon a well-manicured garden behind the house.

"Wait here for my signal." He left Sveinsson inside the lighted hallway and surged forward in one swift movement, opening the door wide enough to squeeze through, and fleetly shutting it behind him. He rolled laterally to a standing position with his back against the wall of the house and hugged the shadows until his eyes could adjust to the darkening night.

Low-cut hedges lined a series of sidewalks framing a grassy area where an alabaster statue rose up from the middle of the courtyard perched on a tall pedestal. Thorne could see nothing out of the ordinary, there was no one in sight, but he supposed someone could be lurking in one of a dozen concealed locations.

Convinced the garden was clear, he lightly tapped on the door signaling Sveinsson to join him. Thorne looked along the length of the building seeking to regain his bearings while Sveinsson removed his eyeglasses, rubbing them on his jacket as his eyes adjusted to the dark. To their right, fifty paces away, the alley opened onto a well-lit street; to their left, it disappeared further into a lightless ingress between two other buildings.

As if sensing a decision at hand, Sveinsson offered, "This way." He motioned to their left. "They will be waiting back there."

Thorne looked back toward the lit street, and in agreement, followed Sveinsson tentatively into the darkness for several steps. They hugged opposite sides of the walkway, each peering into the surrounding shade for signs of danger. Sveinsson pointed toward a direction that would lead them out of the garden, and they shifted to their right, continuing into a darkened maze of crisscrossing sidewalks and hedgerows.

Both men ducked for cover as a gunshot from somewhere behind them echoed off the walls of the surrounding buildings. A figure ran toward them from the direction of the house. Thorne watched the approaching silhouette closely and waited cat-like to pounce as the runner closed in, but a loud bang from behind him sent their pursuer tumbling head over heels flat onto the pavement. He snapped his head around to see Sveinsson in a crouched position pointing a smoking pistol from the shadows where he hid.

Tires squealed somewhere in the immediate vicinity of the house but neither Thorne nor Sveinsson waited to determine their origin. They sprinted into a narrow gap between buildings which opened onto another series of alleyways, sloping upwards and angling away from the House of Knights which sat at river level. As they ran, he looked skyward in an effort to find the moon, or a familiar star, but he was hopelessly lost in the canyons created by the closeness of the surrounding buildings.

Ahead of them now, car lights shown in their faces and a motor revved from behind the blaring light. They shielded their eyes with their hands and turned to their immediate left onto a bordering street. Ten or fifteen paces forward, they turned again to their right, running down a parallel course to the street they had just left.

Tires screeched again which they assumed belonged to the same vehicle. The side-street on which they ran opened into a wide area that overlooked a part of the river. Thorne guessed they had gone in circles around the neighborhood and were now on the west side of the Royal House by his best estimate. They slid to a stop at the corner of the street seeking shelter against the edge of a building, from here he peered around the corner to his right, and saw a car come shooting in reverse from the parallel street where they'd been just moments before.

The car skidded to a stop and two men leapt from the vehicle running in their direction where they squatted low to the ground, concealed behind the corner. Thorne listened closely as the footsteps approached their position and in a perfectly timed execution, he burst from the shadows tackling one of his pursuers.

The man fell hard to the pavement with a low grunt and dropped a handgun which danced across the cobblestones. Thorne was on top of the man who lay sprawled out in an awkward position—unmoving having hit his head in the fall. Again, the same loud bang came from behind him as Sveinsson shot the second pursuer.

He motioned to Sveinsson and they ran toward the idling car and jumped inside; Thorne took the wheel while Sveinsson plunged into the passenger seat. He wasted no time and sped away from the House of Knights while Sveinsson gave him directions into the south district of the city. After several turns using side streets to move away from Old Town, Sveinsson reassured him that no vehicles pursued them, and he directed Thorne to a warehouse where he stopped in front of a set of wide doors, dimming the car's headlights while they waited.

Sveinsson disappeared into the warehouse for several anxious moments while Thorne, car still idling, looked in all directions for approaching vehicles which did not come. The doors opened inward and Sveinsson motioned him forward. Once inside, he turned off the ignition and stood next to the car awaiting further instruction.

Two men talked in Swedish with Sveinsson, pointing at the car intermittently. Several times Sveinsson pointed to Thorne, and finally one of the men got inside the car while the other took Sveinsson and Thorne to an office, and closed the door behind them.

"Emil and his brother Edwin will take care of the automobile. We need to get you out of those clothes and into something more discreet," Sveinsson said.

Thorne looked around the office while one of the brothers stood waiting for orders. A clock showed it was nearly midnight; he was to meet with Reynold's team at one o'clock. "How far is Kvarnholmen?" he asked.

Sveinsson spoke to the Swede and the young man left the room. He opened a locked file cabinet and went to the bottom drawer where he removed a wooden box from underneath a pile of paperwork in the back of the drawer.

"It is not far. I assume you have some unfinished business to take care of." He opened the box which contained various identification booklets and personal papers, and laid them out on the desk. "We can't have you running around using your true name, the Germans will have their secret police looking for you."

"If I can get back to the hotel and get my things—".

"It's no use. The Germans have either searched your room and already taken everything, or they are headed there now. It will be too dangerous. I will send someone to gather your belongings when it is safe."

"I need to be in Kvarnholmen in less than an hour, near the docks," Thorne replied.

Sveinsson considered this for a moment. One of the brothers returned carrying a bundle of clothing. Sveinsson unfurled the bundle, a suit of workman's coveralls, and held it up near Thorne.

"It may be a little short, but I think it will do." He handed a pair of boots to Thorne and turned back to the desk looking at identification papers. "Let's try this."

Thorne looked at the name on the documents: Erik Johnsson, machinist, age thirty-three. Surprisingly a photo on the identity card looked somewhat similar to himself.

"I think we can get you to your appointment on time," Sveinsson added with a smile.

"I can't thank you enough."

He took off his dinner jacket and shoes, and looked down at his clean white shirt. He turned to the Swede man standing alongside Sveinsson and slowly reached out with both hands, palms up. The youth responded questioningly by showing Thorne both of his hands. He grabbed the young man by the wrists and rubbed the workman's dirty hands up and down the front of his shirt, soiling the pristine evening wear. The Swede grinned as he understood what Thorne was about and after Thorne let go of his hands, he reached up to Thorne's clean white collar and rubbed it between his oiled fingers.

Thorne got into the coveralls and slipped on the boots to the approving eye of Sveinsson. As he followed Sveinsson out of the office, he rubbed his hand along a dusty shelf and rubbed it around his clean-shaven face and intentionally disheveled his hair.

I wonder what the Duchess would think of me now.

"Emil will drive you to Kvarnholmen," Sveinsson said. The three men stood next to a truck on the opposite end of the warehouse. "When you are finished with your business, I trust you can find your way back here." He handed Thorne a piece of paper that looked like an invoice or delivery form. It had the name of the warehouse and address printed in bold letters across the top with handwriting in the bottom section. "In the meantime, I will look for a way to convince the German Embassy that you were killed tonight." He looked back across the warehouse to the car. "Crashed into the river should do nicely."

Thorne still wasn't sure about Sveinsson. What if he were working for the Germans? Emil could simply deliver him right into the hands of the waiting Nazis. He decided to test him on his background.

"How do the Germans know I am here?"

"As I mentioned, we intercepted a Nazi communique; it was received by one of our agents in

Gothenburg, and then wired by teletype to our office. It read something to the effect that you have been targeted for assassination by the Nazis. The directive came from someone named Blackbird—I assume that means something to you?"

Thorne nodded. *What if Sveinsson is working for Blackbird?* He chose to dig further.

"And you say you know Faulk?"

Sveinsson realized he was being challenged. "I first met Faulk in Hampshire; security training. He was dispatched to northern France while I stayed at Baker Street. I worked on creating false papers, propaganda, and the like for the Swedish Section. I later began working here in Stockholm, preliminary work for our friend Sir George. I have direct communications with Faulk and his staff from time to time." He paused. "Are there any other questions I can answer to convince you we're on the same team?"

"Just being cautious, you know how it is." Thorne was satisfied with Sveinsson's response.

There is enough there to link him to Faulk.

"Oh, one more thing. Do you have a way to get a message to the resistance in Belgium?" He watched as Sveinsson thought it through.

"I cannot see how."

"Me either, but I thought it was worth a shot."

They shook hands as Thorne climbed into the passenger seat of the truck with Emil; they left the warehouse after Sveinsson gave Emil instructions for delivering him to Kvarnholmen.

After several minutes of driving through the

winding streets of Sodermalm—the south district of Stockholm linked to the city by a series of bridges—they crossed over to the island Kvarnholmen. Emil turned onto an unlit gravel road that went along the waterside and stopped where the road took a sharp turn headed back into the central part of the island.

"Here, you walk," the Swede pointed toward a feature in the distance that Thorne assumed was the dock area.

"*Tack*," he thanked Emil in Swedish.

"*Valkommen*." In broken English he added, "Be careful."

Chapter
Twenty-Four

THORNE FOUND A NARROW PATH amongst the knee-high reeds and grasses skirting the shore line where Emil had pointed. The moonlight illuminated Waldemar's Bay where distant lights from the opposite shore flickered and glistened on the water. Despite his best efforts to move silently, his feet crunched on loose pebbles and stones much to his dismay. The path rounded a bend, and there jutting out into the water, stood a long pier with several boats moored in the darkness.

At the foot of the dock, a small structure sat juxtaposed against the backdrop of masts dancing in the moonlight. Thorne tactfully approached two men who stood outside the shack talking and smoking cigarettes, and waved at them making it clear that he had no hostile intentions.

After an awkward conversation in broken English, Thorne was able to convince them he was looking for a man named Nyberg. They escorted him to a fishing boat tied half way down the long pier where Thorne was amateurishly searched by one of the men who patted him down along the length of his coveralls, and convinced he was not armed, he was allowed to step onto the craft.

Thorne's quick assessment told him the boat was not seaworthy and perhaps only served as a rendezvous point for this circumspect mission. He was taken to the wheelhouse where he was introduced to Nyberg, a gruff looking, stumpy man of the sea. He wore a scar across his left cheek, hidden in part by a stubbly beard, and deep creases in his jowls.

"Reynolds sent me. He said I could assist with security." He handed his identification papers to Nyberg who eyed him suspiciously.

Nyberg smoked a short pipe that smelled of sweet, pungent Turkish tobacco. "What do you know about tonight?" he asked with skepticism in his voice.

"Reynolds filled me in on the details. A shipment is to arrive by truck. You are loading it onto a boat and transferring it to Denmark." Nyberg handed the papers back to him.

"You come to me with nothing, yet you are supposed to help with security?" As he spoke, foul, acrid smoke left his mouth and hit Thorne in the face contemptuously.

"I have worked in Copenhagen before. I can help with the transfer of cargo to the fishing boats." He saw that Nyberg was still unsure. "I have done this type of work before."

Nyberg looked at him diffidently and removed his cap scratching at his bald head. "I wasn't planning on any passengers." Nyberg finally offered him a cigarette.

"You can wait over there; Reynolds will be here later." He turned away from Thorne and resumed looking over a set of maps laid out on the console before him.

Thorne looked out onto the adjoining harbor at the boats tossing in the breeze. Down the length of the pier, he saw a few boats tethered with ropes, and near the end of the pier, a much larger vessel was docked. After two puffs on the stale cigarette, he tossed it into the water, found a seat among some crates stacked near Nyberg's office, and plopped down fuming in frustration while he waited for Reynolds to arrive with further instruction.

What the bloody hell is going on?

Beecher had sent him to help arrange the financing and procurement of arms, "finish the negotiations," he'd said, but Reynolds already had that tied up. Surely there was a mix up in Beecher's orders.

Or perhaps I simply arrived too late.

Reynolds had said rather matter of factly, "I'm afraid you've been had old boy." Had he not received word from Beecher that Thorne was on his way? And what about Sveinsson?

Should I have trusted him?

He had willingly helped him escape. Escape from who, *Gestapo*? Blackbird's minions? Nor had Sveinsson attempted to interfere with his getting to the docks for Reynolds' errand. Yet, something about the little man worried him. Sveinsson was expecting him to return after his work was done here, but he'd already made up his mind.

I'm getting the hell out of here.

He moved from Nyberg's boat to the edge of the pier. Thorne decided at that moment to get to Denmark, establish contact with his network of underground agents, and figure out a way to get back to Holland or Belgium. He didn't like undermining Beecher and worried there'd be hell to pay once his chief found out he'd disobeyed his orders. All he could hope for now was that Beecher would buy into an elaborate story of why he had to urgently leave Sweden, and how he coincidentally ended up back in Holland.

There'll be time for that later.

His thoughts were disturbed when he heard the sound of approaching vehicles. Three trucks rumbled toward him in low gear threatening to dislodge the pier from its supports. As if reading his mind, the drivers passed Thorne, slowing their vehicles, and crawled the remaining length of the pier where they finally came to a standstill alongside the large boat.

He deliberated on whether to wait for Reynolds or take matters into his own hands. Nyberg was still in the wheel house of his makeshift office, his attention focused on his maps, and no one else was nearby. Men and boys began unloading the trucks and stacked several cartons and crates next to the boat at the end of the pier.

Time to move.

Hoping to avoid attention, he crowded alongside the boat which towered above him by at least three meters. A hoist was moved into position and the crates were lifted onto the deck of the boat into the waiting hands of crew members who stowed them away. At one point, something mechanical failed with the hoist and the men shouted back and forth at each other from the pier to the boat and back again to an operator somewhere out of sight. While this commotion was going on, Thorne sauntered leisurely to a separate gangplank set out at the rear of the boat and managed to board without anyone's notice. He found a place to hide beneath a tarpaulin on the bow of the boat while the hoist resumed lifting crates off the pier.

Thorne stayed hidden beneath the tarp while crewmen loaded the cartons of arms and munitions into the ship's hold. He intended to temporarily avert any questions to his identity, and avoid probable denial for his request to travel to Denmark, and instead decided he would eventually reveal himself once the boat was well out of port. He succumbed to a disturbed sleep while the enterprise of loading the secret cargo continued long into the night.

THEY HAD BEEN AT SEA MANY hours before Thorne was discovered by a crewman and taken to Captain Olsen. Olsen was the antithesis of Nyberg, unlike the surly seaman, he carried himself with an air of authority much like a naval officer. He was a tall man, clean shaven, and wore a cream-colored, wool sweater. His blonde hair stuck out beneath the edges of his captain's hat, proclaiming his Scandinavian heritage.

In the wheelhouse, Thorne claimed innocence and

explained his presence as merely a mix-up in communications, suggesting that Nyberg should have arranged his passage. He made it obvious that he was involved in the scheme from the get go, but he couldn't explain his behavior in stowing aboard beneath the tarpaulin instead of reporting directly for service.

Much to the dismay of the captain, and the mistrust of the first mate who'd discovered him, he was allowed to remain on board. However, Olsen made it clear, he would be treated as one of the crew and was fully expected to pull his weight.

Thorne was initially sent below deck to meet with the head mechanic, but after it became clear that Thorne had no basic comprehension of marine engines, nor any skill or inclination of any such device, he was sent back to the first mate who assigned him as lookout after a lengthy interview about his background and skills.

He was thankful that most of the crewmen spoke English, and guessed that the crew of this vessel—named *Ambergris* he eventually learned—had served in merchant marine duty before they were summoned into this covert operation. One crew member, Felix Nilsson who had a game leg—a prosthetic wooden limb attached below the knee that earned him the nickname Woody—took a particular fondness to Thorne. The short stumpy seaman spent many hours escorting Thorne around the boat and explaining the details of her make and origin.

Thorne learned that *Ambergris* was a Motorized Gun Boat—MGB he recalled from details in the

Operation Bridford files—which had been obtained from the British Royal Navy. He also learned that the MGBs supplied to Sweden had been altered from their original design with extra holds incorporated for hauling cargo, and had been retrofitted with other changes to the bridge structure which involved moving it toward the rear of the ship along with crew quarters, galley, radio room and the wheelhouse.

Woody eagerly shared more knowledge about the ship, much of which, including displacement, draught, and other nautical terminology, Thorne did not fully comprehend. Nonetheless, it was apparent that he was aboard a heavily modified boat, purpose-built with the intention of outrunning Nazi submarines and other like craft. Woody pointed out machine guns placed both fore and aft that had been concealed with tarpaulins and surrounded with stacks of wooden crates to give the appearance of cargo stowed above decks.

Bad weather plagued *Ambergris* from the start. A deep fog had set in on the inner stretches of the Baltic Sea. Due to their clandestine mission, Captain Olsen had refused to move into the central corridor of the Sea, but instead chose to stay within a mile or less of Sweden's shoreline. However, this hampered their speed; *Ambergris* drudged along slowly beneath a sullen sky with low hanging clouds, as the captain and his crew labored over nautical charts to avoid troublesome shallows, hidden rocks, and submerged ledges.

Thorne watched the black water flow past the hull, and noted on more than one occasion a gull or other seabird flying low alongside the boat, eventually outpacing *Ambergris* and her sluggish progress. The seas roughened that first night causing Thorne to succumb to seasickness for several hours; he was forced to stay below deck until he was finally able to tolerate the motion of the vessel. When he gained his feet, he was posted atop the wheelhouse, perched on a wooden crate where he hoped to get a view of their course and act as lookout while *Ambergris* crept along the Swedish coast, rising and falling in an ugly swell.

Instead, he could see no more than a quarter mile distant in any direction. He made out flotsam and jetsam floating hazardously past the vessel and hoped they would not hit anything of danger. Beyond the debris, within close range, he could only make out endless waves and white caps destined to batter *Ambergris* mercilessly as his seasickness threatened to return.

By the third night out from Stockholm, the seas had calmed but the fog refused to relent. Thorne learned from his fellow shipmates that they were approaching the southern tip of Sweden, an area of the Baltic still frequented by German patrol boats and submarines, and this night would prove to be no different.

At first, Thorne thought he had imagined a dark spot somewhere in the distance off the port bow; possibly a shadow or maybe a trick of the mind. When he looked directly toward it, he could not see it, but out of his peripheral sight, he was sure something was there. Eventually the dull spot took shape and he could just make out a round light in the distance.

He leapt down from atop the wheelhouse making

to alert the captain, but by the time he'd reached the bridge, *Ambergris* was already slowing and it was apparent that Captain Olsen and his crew had seen the same light. Within seconds, *Ambergris* had stopped her forward progress altogether. Creeping out of the fog and rocking in the swell, another boat moved in on their position. He couldn't understand why *Ambergris* didn't try to outrun them, *that's what the MGBs were designed to do!* He assumed it was beyond his understanding and there must be a logical reason the captain had chosen this tactic.

A foamy wake pressed ahead of the bow of the other ship and the sound of her rumbling engines soon became clear. A spotlight burst out of the fog beaming directly onto the port side of *Ambergris* accompanied by a voice that squawked out across the water—the caller's voice, thin and boxy over the broadcast system, but the accent completely clear—demanding her to prepare for boarding.

The *Ambergris'* crew came pouring out of her lower decks like rats out of a sinking barrel and they frantically lined up in a ragged formation along her decks where Thorne joined his crew mates. As the strange vessel pulled alongside, there was no mistaking her identity—a Nazi flag flew at her helm and black crosses adorned the sides of the bridge. Two large single-barreled guns, one fore and one aft, were aimed at *Ambergris,* and two sets of double-barreled anti-aircraft guns were also leveled at the Swedish MGB.

Thorne supposed that had there been no fog, and had *Ambergris* caught sight of her predator earlier, she might have had a chance to outrun the Nazi patrol boat. But now it was useless to attempt a face-to-face fight as *Ambergris* was outgunned. He learned from a crew member next to him that the Swedish versions of MGBs had been stripped down for speed, her small compliment of two 20mm machine guns was far less than her original outfitting and offered no resistance to the Nazi gunboat staring down at her.

With German precision, the patrol boat came along side *Ambergris* with a slight nudge and Nazi sailors hurriedly secured the two ships together with grappling hooks and ropes. Other sailors armed with MP38 submachine guns took aim at the crew of *Ambergris,* while a short gangplank was slid into position between the two boats.

Two Nazi officers came across followed by a few soldiers sporting their weapons. By this time, Captain Olsen was standing beside his first mate in front of his crew. Thorne stood several feet away from where the two captains stood eyeing each other ominously. Woody hung by on his left and whispered just audibly the Swedish equivalent of, "Fucking Nazis."

The Nazi captain spoke to Olsen, "What ship is this?"

"Free merchant *Ambergris,* Captain Olsen at your service." He flashed a weak *Heil Hitler* salute.

The Nazi acknowledged him with a similar wave. "*Kapitan* Schermer," he responded. "And what is your business in these waters *Kapitan* Olsen?"

"Cargo sir. We are destined for Wismar."

"Wismar? I fear you have not heard the latest news;

Wismar has been nearly destroyed by Allied bombers. The port is out of service."

A Nazi sailor approached the two captains. "Ship's log *mein Kapitan*."

Thorne shot a quick glance at the Nazi captain's shadowed face as he thumbed through the log book. "I do not see any reference to Wismar here. What are you transporting to Wismar?"

"Ball bearings destined for your German factories."

Schermer eyed him suspiciously. "If you are not telling the truth *Kapitan* Olsen, I will be forced to treat you as a saboteur at the least."

The Nazis began systematically checking the identification of each of the *Ambergris* sailors, asking their name and rank, and pressing them for identification papers. Many of the crew did not carry paperwork, so the Nazis began sorting the men into two groups, those with identification and those without. Thorne carried his papers that Sveinsson had provided and was questioned no further after his name matched his ID card.

While the interrogation of the crew took place, Captain Olsen and his first mate were isolated from the remainder of the crew and kept under watch of two soldiers. Meanwhile, Schermer and other members of his crew went below deck to search the holds of *Ambergris*. Olsen was summoned below within a matter of minutes.

Woody turned to Thorne, "They've found him out." Thorne did not speak but nodded in agreement.

Another crew member spoke in a low voice to his

mate and the German sailor watching them shouted, "There is to be no talking!"

They waited for several anxious minutes before the Nazis finally came back on deck, forcing Olsen along by prodding him with a gun in the back. The crew of *Ambergris* saw their captain had been roughed up; his left eye was swollen shut and blood trickled from the corner of his mouth. He limped slightly as he walked back toward his awaiting crew. Schermer came on deck at last, his demeanor much more severe than before, and he addressed everyone present.

"This man is a liar and a saboteur. This ship is not carrying ball bearings, but is running armaments." The Nazi officer was furious. After several seconds, he took a deep breath. "I am feeling very benevolent today, so I am going to give you an opportunity to redeem yourselves. Anyone who wants to come forward and share the details of your subversive mission, please do so now. You will be treated fairly."

He waited, inspecting the Swedish crewmen, but only received averted gazes as he looked upon them. A gull squawked from somewhere nearby breaking the extended silence. "Very well. I shall show you no mercy."

Just then, one of the Swedes lurched forward crying out in German, "*Mein Kapitan.* These men are enemies of the German State and are illegally providing weapons and ammunitions to our enemies."

The German officer charged toward the man. "Name?"

"Dahlberg." He stood erect while his crew mates

eyed him in disbelief, and scowled at the man whom they'd believed was their Swedish comrade, now that his true colors had been revealed.

The officer continued in German, *"Bist du Deutscher?"*

"Jawohl Kapitan!"

"Very good *Herr* Dahlberg." The officer turned back to his crew and shouted several orders sending *Kriegsmarine* sailors running on board *Ambergris* and down into her holds. Schermer escorted Dahlberg to his ship while the *Ambergris* crew stood for more than an hour watching the Germans offload crate by crate onto their boat. Finally, Schermer returned to the side of his ship and shouted to the captives aboard *Ambergris*.

"Had the circumstances been different, perhaps clear weather, I would have undoubtedly blown your vessel to smithereens. But to your good fortune, I am going to spare pity upon you."

The *Ambergris* crew whispered amongst themselves.

"Silence! I have detained your illicit cargo, but I cannot spare any of my crew to transport your vessel back to Germany, so it must be destroyed." He paused to let this sink in with the despondent Swedish crew. "However, as I said before, I am in a most benevolent mood today. I shall allow your crew to abandon ship and use your lifeboats to return to Sweden."

The German sailors forced the *Ambergris* crew into several life boats and ushered them off toward Swedish shores. When the Swedes were approximately a quarter mile away, they heard three muffled explosions and looked back toward *Ambergris* as the ship erupted in a ball of flames. Smoke and fire mushroomed upwards into the fog shrouded skies.

The crew paddled their lifeboats in haste, all the while watching their ship burn in the distance. Another spout of flames leapt upwards and the hull of the ship listed to starboard and sank into the murky sea. The German ship was no longer in sight. Instead, a dark smear of smoke—a stain hanging against the foggy sky—was all that remained.

For several hours the *Ambergris* crew labored against the sea, taking turns every thirty minutes paddling in shifts, and as the skies darkened, they began to see dotted lights on the distant shoreline. They arrived on a pebbled strand of beach at dusk and dispatched a patrol inland to determine their whereabouts.

All of the lifeboats were pulled out of the Baltic Sea and after a headcount was taken, the first mate confirmed all were present. The inland crew returned and confirmed to Captain Olsen their arrival near Ystad on the southern coast of Sweden. The captain ordered his men into formation to march into town where the exhausted seamen were allowed to rest in a square courtyard while he and his first mate went to secure lodging.

An hour later, the crew was allowed to take up shelter in a former casino after Captain Olson had made arrangements with the town's mayor for their safe layover. He found Thorne bunking with the rest of the crewmen and pulled him aside. "We have failed our mission and I must return to Stockholm. You are welcome to remain with us if you wish."

"Thank you, Captain, but as you now know I have business elsewhere. Can you tell me where we are?"

Captain Olsen summoned one of the sailors to bring a map and he laid it on a table in front of Thorne, drawing a circle around Ystad with his finger. "We are here, not more than fifty kilometers from Copenhagen."

Thorne's face brightened at this news.

"How can I help you Mr. Thorne?"

Chapter
Twenty-Five

A WHITE-HAIRED MAN CROSSED Threadneedle Street in central London, advancing on the imperial facade of the Bank of England. He passed through an arched portico that sat at ground level beneath a row of Roman columns that supported a roofline nearly seven stories tall. Although the building was scarcely two decades old, it appeared as antediluvian as any of London's oldest edifices. He entered through two brass doors that led into the front hall. With purpose, he hurried past a security guard with a familiar wave and diverted to one of the first-floor parlors named the Ante-room.

As he entered, he paid no attention to the 18th century décor some considered garish and ostentatious; his venerable features blended in with the ambience of the room as if he were part of its furnishings. He closed the double doors at the far end of the room and settled into a cream-colored chair next to a marble fireplace. From a silver case in his coat pocket, he removed a thin cigarette and lit it using a book of matches he found on a table next to his chair.

Within moments two men dressed in double-breasted, dark blue military uniforms entered the room and closed the doors behind them. On their shoulders, a tombstone patch consisting of a Tommy gun, an eagle, and a stockless anchor, etched in red threading announced the men as members of the Combined Operations unit of the War Office. The younger of the two, was a short pudgy man in his mid-twenties with rosy cheeks. His eyes blinked excitedly from behind a pair of round eyeglasses. His apparent superior—a handsome man at least ten years his senior—led the way into the room in apparent recognition of the elder man waiting for them.

The older man rose from his chair, accepting a handshake from the taller of the two arriving men.

"Thomas, good to see you again," the tall man said, turning to present his colleague. "Braxton, this is Thomas Beecher, SOE." Beecher took small puffs from his thin cigarette and returned to his posh chair as the other men maneuvered furniture around the fireplace taking a seat opposite of him. "What is this urgent business that you phoned about Mr. Beecher?"

"Something has run afoul with my agent in Holland." Beecher, wary of the identity of Braxton, spoke cautiously in front of him.

"Are you talking about Thorne?" the tall man asked.

"No, no. I've got a plan to get him out of the way. I've sent a new man to Maastricht to track down Hartmann, but now I fear he's run into complications," Beecher said. He looked again apprehensively at Braxton as he revealed this information.

"I see. And Thorne, you're sure he's out of the way?"

"Yes, I've dispatched him to Stockholm. I've already reached out to the German Ligation to have him disposed of."

"Stockholm? Why not the North Pole?" the tall man added sarcastically.

"Trust me, were that an option, I would've taken it. I was stumped in finding somewhere to dispatch him, somewhere far away and out of our hair, but then this unfinished business came up with Binney. You recall the operation I told you about, *Bridford*?"

"Yes of course, and you're certain they've eliminated Thorne?"

"By some stroke of fate, they found his car at the bottom of a river a few days after my orders went through to the German office."

"Could be a trick, let's make sure there's nothing they can pin on us."

Beecher looked at Braxton again apprehensively.

The tall man escorted Braxton to the door. "If you please, I'll be with you shortly."

When the door was closed, Beecher started again, "Listen, I must take things into my own hands. I'm leaving for Germany—".

"Thomas, aren't you getting a little old for this espionage game? Maybe you should find another trusted agent."

"We've lost too many good agents and there simply isn't time. I must get to Aachen before the Americans cross over into Germany. Patton's racing across the Lowlands at breakneck speed; you know as well as I do what will happen if they come across any records at Englebert."

"I thought you ordered your man, Hartmann that is, to destroy everything?"

"I never received his confirmation. He'd always followed up with an immediate response passed back through Thorne." He fumbled with his thin cigarette as the taller man eyed him with uncertainty. "I pulled Thorne out when he began meddling in the whole ordeal," he explained, "and now my new man has been running around trying to make contact with the underground cronies Thorne ran with in order to find Hartmann. But it seems he's gotten himself snagged up with the *Gestapo*. I've received no messages from either of them in several days."

"It might take a little more time for your man to establish contact; assuming the *Gestapo* haven't terminated him already. I could reach out to our *SD* contact in Amsterdam, have him find out in which *Gestapo* office your man is being held."

"We haven't time. I've learned Monty's moving forward with *Operation Market Garden*; it's only a matter of days before the Allies drop into Holland, targeting Aachen as their gateway into Germany." Beecher rubbed at the back of his neck and looked away. "I've been rethinking our agreement; I'm ready to get out now."

"Thomas, don't be a fool. We have a chance to reap so much more; enough to cover our tracks so that no one will ever be able to find us after the War."

"I'm good with what we've gained thus far. The

longer we wait, the more risk we have of Hitler taking it all."

"You convinced me it was out of his reach. Is it safe? I don't want this whole undertaking to blow over only to find out after the War that our funds are locked down."

"Yes, it's safe. I just worry that someone from Threadneedle or the *Reichstag* will uncover our enterprise."

"Thomas. I need your assurance that our money is safe."

"Once I get situated, I will figure out where to transfer the money. Perhaps through South America."

"Where will you go?"

"I will get to Aachen and make sure nothing is left behind. Once this mess with Hartmann is cleaned up, I suppose I'll make my way to Geneva until the War is over."

"Do as you see fit Thomas, but I must warn you, once you leave England, you will no longer be under my protection."

"Yes, I know."

THORNE WAS ESCORTED BY an Ystad townsman and driven to the Swedish town of Malmo situated across the Oresund Strait between Sweden and Denmark. He thanked his driver and pushed on through the town toward the waterfront. As he neared the water, he crossed *Ribersborgsstranden* and *Limhamnsvagen* along the waterfront, and advanced toward a pier where he spotted a ferry boat that shuttled passengers between the two countries.

Having no means to secure passage, he at first attempted to speak with several passersby, asking for help, but was shunned by all he spoke to. He decided to try a ticket agent at the end of the pier. Thorne approached a podium where the man stood, and waited for Swedish citizens to purchase their tickets and move on. When no one remained in queue, he approached the attendant. "*Pratar du Engelska?*" he asked.

"*Ja.*"

"Ah very good. Please sir, I am English and here by misfortune. I need to cross over to Copenhagen. Is there any way—".

He was cut short by the attendant. "Sorry I cannot help you. Please go away." Despite his protests and begging he was dismissed by the agent.

Thorne walked toward the shoreline and looked for another method to cross the strait. He had judged from Olsen's map that Copenhagen was not more than five kilometers away, but the thought of rowing that distance in a tiny craft was too daunting of a task for his weary body. He realized at that moment that he had not eaten since the previous morning; he'd been in such an urgent need of departure on this day that he'd left his crewmates in Ystad without breakfast. Now he regretted that decision.

He walked along the shore until he reached an area where several small fishing boats were moored at a long, narrow dock. From there, he hung about the dock indiscreetly, nodding at a few local fishermen who passed. At his first clear chance, he hopped aboard one of the boats, but his initial search showed the vessel had been stowed for some time and was empty of petrol and other provisions. He hurriedly jumped back onto the dock and advanced further down the short pier looking for another worthy craft.

After checking several other boats, he came across a skiff with an outboard motor that had fuel in its tank. He also found a loaf of bread and three bottles of beer tucked in a narrow chest on board. He managed to start the engine, quickly unsecured her harness to the dock, and idled out into a causeway where he drifted on a stuttering motor toward the strait between Denmark and Sweden.

As the boat glided away without drawing attention, he quickly pried open a bottle of beer and devoured a huge chunk of bread. He maneuvered the craft into a stiff wind and managed to make his way toward the distant shore of Copenhagen.

Nearing the Danish shoreline, he came upon a wall of bracken, boulders, and rough-cut stones, and turned the craft parallel to the sea wall where he continued for a few hundred meters without finding a dock or landing pier. He finally decided to cut the engine and let the small boat drift upon the rocks. Using a loop of rope to make a crude lasso, he secured the boat to one of the boulders, then stuffed what was left of the loaf of bread into his overalls along with one remaining bottle of beer.

Thorne searched for anything else of use aboard the craft, finding a tool box with a hammer, screwdriver and wrench. He took the wrench, nearly as long as his forearm and put that in his pocket. He then retrieved a bottle opener, a filet knife and a rain jacket—the only other items of possible use—and scrambled up the rocky seawall headed into the industrial district of Copenhagen that he was vaguely familiar with.

In the warehouse quarter, he donned the rain jacket and passed a few German soldiers who paid no attention to him.

That was too close for comfort.

He turned onto an unfamiliar street that wound through a section of commercial buildings, and encountered another soldier. Thorne immediately looked away from the German as he started across the road.

"You there," the soldier ordered in Danish.

Thorne looked around but no one else was nearby.

"You, wait," the German shouted again, sprinting across the road.

"*Ja*," Thorne finally called out as the soldier ran up to him.

"What are you doing?"

"*Ja*," was all Thorne could come up with at the moment. He sized up the soldier and could not surmise why he hadn't unharnessed his rifle from his shoulder, but it gave him the advantage.

"Where are you going?"

"*Ja*." Thorne nodded his head in an exaggerated fashion.

"Let me see your papers."

Thorne smiled at the soldier.

"Papers!" the soldier shouted in German.

Thorne deliberately fumbled through his pockets, and when he did not immediately produce identification, the impatient soldier started to un-shoulder his rifle; Thorne made his move. In a nimble, yet sudden movement, he pulled the long wrench from his pocket, and with a back hand strike hit the soldier across the side of his face with the jaw of the wrench. He cringed as the heavy tool smashed the man's cheek bone knocking a few teeth loose.

The young German fell sideways, unconscious before he hit the pavement. Thorne tucked the wrench back into his overalls and dashed away from the fallen soldier. He ducked into a warehouse startling a woman who worked in a cramped office at the front of the building. He summoned what little Danish he could recall and conversed with her briefly.

"I am looking for a man named Sorenson. He is helpful, how do you say, at aiding—", he searched for the correct Danish word, "refugees? *Allierede? Engelska?*"

He saw her eyes brighten and she replied, "Wait please." She disappeared into the warehouse where he could see other men working. He backed away from the front of the building, moving further into the office where she had been typing. A messy desk full of paperwork revealed nothing about the nature of the business. A few minutes later she returned with another man.

"How can I help you?" he asked in Danish.

"Do you speak English?" When the man nodded

in agreement, he continued, "I am looking for Emil Sorenson. I have worked with him before." He could detect suspicion in the man's face. Two hefty men appeared just outside the office; their demeanor made it apparent they did not trust him, and their posture showed their readiness to cause bodily injury if needed. Thorne fumbled with the crude fishing knife in his pocket.

"What is your name?" the first man asked.

Thorne had been using the name Erik Johnsson for several days now with his Swedish comrades. He produced his identification to the man and continued after giving the same name, "I have come from Stockholm and need to get into the Low Countries. Sorenson has helped me before."

"I'm sorry to inform you, but Sorenson is dead."

Chapter
Twenty-Six

A FTER NIGHTFALL, THORNE WAS taken to a house on the outskirts of Copenhagen where he met the local Danish resistance leader William Moller. Moller was a short, stocky man who spoke with a conviction that Thorne interpreted as all business. He was able to convince Moller of his true identity as a British agent and gain his support, and although Thorne made it clear that his main objective was to return to Belgium, Moller convinced him it was far too risky—it required multiple border crossings through Denmark, Germany, Belgium, or Holland where he faced questioning and additional scrutiny of his identity papers throughout the tenuous trip.

Another option Moller offered was to cross Denmark to the west, and then by boat, head toward Amsterdam, Antwerp, or one of a dozen other seaports heavily occupied by the Germans. In the end, they both agreed there was no safe or expeditious way back to Belgium except by airdrop which needed coordination by SOE. Moller had previously arranged retrieval of downed British pilots in Denmark by escorting them to the western coast where SOE operatives working in the area coordinated the communication and extraction with someone on British soil. They settled on this as Thorne's best option for getting safely out of Denmark.

"How quickly can you get me out?"

"It will take a few days of hard travel. You better rest here tonight," Moller said reassuringly.

Thorne did not argue when he was shown a room where he could take a hot bath and rest while Moller and his colleagues started planning his escape from Denmark. Before he fell asleep, he lie awake for many long minutes contemplating his situation. If Beecher discovered he was no longer in Sweden, he would be considered in breach of duty and faced removal from SOE should Beecher decide to press the issue. Considering Beecher's wrath during their last bout, the outcome could be worse.

Treason.

He knew the routine for extraction from Holland and Belgium, and assumed it was the same in Denmark. For the most part, the pilots flying in did not know what they faced. They were told to fly to a specific location and look for a lighted signal from the ground marking their landing zone. They seldom knew whom they were extracting or under what purpose. Upon arrival back in England, Thorne would meet a member of the Air Liaison Section for a face-to-face debriefing at the local airfield; SOE headquarters would be notified shortly thereafter of his arrival.

It would be a bit of a trick to convince the local air marshal of his identity and reach out to Faulk directly, instead of contacting Beecher under normal protocol. His chicanery in England would of course depend entirely on his safe passage across Denmark, which Moller had assured him was no piece of cake. All of these concerns crisscrossed his mind as he weighed the various risks of every step in his path back to London. He finally fell into a deep sleep.

The next morning, one of Moller's assistants woke him with a tray of pastries and coffee, as well as a fresh set of travel clothes in the style of the Danish civilians.

"Good morning. I trust you rested well," said Moller entering the room.

"Yes, thank you." He ravenously devoured a sweet roll. "Are we leaving today?"

"Yes. I have new papers for you." He handed him a stack of cards and forms. "I won't lie, this will not be easy."

Thorne studied his new identity. Among the paperwork was a medical release document. "What's this?"

"You will be escorted as a wounded patient. We will dress you with bandages to disguise your face. I will be your physician escorting you to your home village—I can think of no better way to explain why we would be traveling westward."

"And the airlift?"

"There is a British airman hiding near the coast. One of your agents named Quicksilver is working on arrangements. With any luck, we will meet up with him tonight or tomorrow morning. We'll find out more when we reach Holstebro, that is our destination."

Thorne was bandaged as Moller had explained, his head and hands wrapped in white strips of cloth and his face and hands dirtied with burnt cork. His clothing was given a going over with a pair of scissors producing holes and torn seams that gave him an overall disheveled appearance. He left Copenhagen with Moller by car—a small black vehicle that was hastily fashioned to resemble an ambulance with red crosses painted on each of its doors. For the first part of their day, they moved against traffic; German soldiers and vehicles moved eastward toward Copenhagen.

They were stopped a few times at checkpoints but heedlessly waived onward with no concerns. Moving into the western portion of Denmark, Thorne stared out of his window at long lines of refugees and citizens who packed their belongings by cart, or simply carried what they could on their backs. Just before nightfall, they reached a rural village and diverted from the main roads using rural paths, until they came upon a farm that Moller recognized.

They left their car at a gate and cautiously approached the barn as Moller called out for the owner. They were met by the farmer's family, who directed them to take their car to the rear of the barn, where it was hastily covered with a large tarpaulin before they were led to a cellar to hide. Nearing darkness, Thorne remained alone in the cellar where he studied his documents by candlelight, while Moller left to make arrangements for their next connection. Thorne wanted to remove the bandages which itched at his face, but knew they were his only chance of averting suspicion about an identity photo that hardly matched up with him.

Thorne made up a cot with several blankets stacked upon a pallet in the corner of the cellar, and tried to comfort himself while lying there imagining his reunion with Anna.

Moller returned a short while later obviously in distress. "We must leave now; *Gestapo* are in the area."

"Wouldn't we be better off waiting here until they pass?"

"No, they have been searching farms and homes nearby, clearly looking for someone. If they find us, they will take us without question."

The two men left immediately and walked along the rear edge of the farmstead, against the broken silhouette of a tree line that stood pale and grey in the waning daylight. They moved at an aggressive pace covering a kilometer in a matter of a few minutes, and as they looked back toward the barn in the distance, they could make out two sets of headlights that were not there before.

Moller guided Thorne into a narrow line of woods where they discovered a dry creek bed running in a northerly direction from their original course. They ran, ducking broken limbs and leaping over fallen branches. Several minutes passed before they paused, breathing heavily, waiting and listening intently for pursuers. The horizon was barely identifiable as a pale, lavender glow giving them a general sense of their intended path.

Moller motioned him onward but then immediately froze. The two men listened warily against a gentle breeze. Intermittently between the crackling of rustling leaves, they heard the unmistakable sound of dogs barking.

"It sounds like they are that way," Thorne said pointing off to the right of the direction they had come, but as they listened again, they could not be sure.

Moller decided to move out of the creek bed to their immediate left where the trees thinned out and from here, they skirted the tree line for several more meters, using the rising moon to guide them. The baying dogs followed somewhere behind them but they could not be sure of their proximity. As they kept more or less parallel to the trees and the dry creek within, they came to the end of the tree line where a man-made reservoir glimmered in the faint moonlight.

Moller instructed Thorne to enter the water up to his ankles hoping to throw the pursuing dogs off their scent. They splashed awkwardly in the frigid water as they skirted the eastern edge of the reservoir, but it soon became apparent, the barking hounds were getting closer. There was no use staying in the water now, they needed to put distance between themselves and their hunters. They hastily climbed a bank of rock and bramble to the top of a dam along one side of the reservoir, squatting there to take in their surroundings.

The barking grew louder by the moment coming from the general direction where they had first come out of the woods.

A few shaded buildings dotted an otherwise barren field on the opposite side of the reservoir, several hundred meters away by their guess. Down the back side of the dam, they saw clusters of trees and bushes but could see no secure hiding place.

"Can you swim?" asked Moller.

"Barely."

As the sound of the baying dogs grew louder, they saw flashlights moving through the thin trees in the distance.

"Let's go," Moller said leading them onward. They hustled down the backside of the dam to where the ground leveled off and continued running through a desolate field weaving between thorny briars and clusters of decimated trees as they went. Thorne found a pathway where vehicles had recently passed; wide tracks had flattened the terrain which allowed them to run faster. They stole occasional glances toward the reservoir but did not see anything. Reaching a small group of destroyed outbuildings, they looked for shelter in the ruins, finally ducking into a small farm building where they waited.

"Where are we?" asked Thorne.

"I'm not entirely sure. We will have to wait until daybreak."

The men huddled in the gloomy shelter, clearing debris so they might rest in a seated position. Their sleepless night passed painstakingly keeping them on edge. Occasionally a dog barked far off in the distance. Sometime in the middle of the night, a fleet of vehicles passed within meters of their position as they anxiously awaited their discovery, but the German army swiftly passed in the hours before dawn. Every sound caused fright as they supposed their pursuers had found their tracks—this continued until the sky finally began to change from black, to grey, to shades of pink and orange.

Moller eventually stood up and went to the doorway; he looked outside for several long moments, assessing their whereabouts. Thorne arose, and after relieving himself in a corner of the shaded building, joined Moller at the doorstep.

"Town is that way, but so are the Germans. If we head that way instead," Moller added, pointing to a dark spot on the horizon, "we may be able to make it before the sun rises, but we must hurry!" They took off at a jog through the field as the skies continued to brighten, and made for a building off in the distance. Half way there, they came across a road intersecting the field and paused again while Moller got his bearings.

"Listen!" Off in the distance a train whistle sounded. "If we can make it to the tracks, they will lead us to Holstebro."

Walking at a brisk pace, they followed the paved road until the sun crested the horizon at their backs. A firm line formed across the landscape marking the railroad grade and they hastened to the tracks as the sun fell upon their shoulders. A train's headlight rounded a bend just meters down the track ahead of them. The approaching train huffed and hobbled toward a patch of rubble where they crouched, hiding as best they could. The locomotive chugged along the tracks shaking the ground as it passed their position and Thorne took note of several flat cars hauling German tanks.

Thorne couldn't help wonder if there wasn't a way to

derail the train, but he fought off the urge and instead held his position until the last of the train cars passed. Once the train became a drab blotch in the distance, they rose to follow the rails northward.

"This is Holstebro," Moller pointed out when they neared several buildings and houses. He looked Thorne up and down with a smile. "I guess you are no longer injured." Thorne felt his forehead and realized his bandages had come dislodged at some time during the night. Likewise, his previously bandaged hands were now nothing more than a mess of rags bunched around his wrists. He shed the scraps of cloth as they forged onward.

They left the railroad tracks and sought the lower elevation alongside the roadbed. In a half crouching movement, they sprinted toward the town, hoping their silhouettes would not stand out against the backdrop of dawn. Reaching a cluster of buildings on the edge of town, Moller led them across another set of tracks to a rail yard; an abandoned box car hunched on the ground, its axles and wheels gone. Two men waited there and acknowledged Moller in recognition.

"You got my message?" Moller asked the apparent leader of the men.

"I did indeed," he said in perfect English spoken with a Welsh accent. He reached out a hand to Thorne, "Quicksilver at your service. We will wait until nightfall and then we'll be on our way. I suppose you're ready to get home."

"Yes, but at the moment I am quite famished and half mad with thirst."

Thorne rested inside the box car, the provisional headquarters for the resistance group operating in Holstebro. The man named Quicksilver gave him a canteen of water, a loaf of bread, and some hard cheese. The other man did not speak. Moller soon parted ways, wishing Thorne the best of luck, and after he was gone, Quicksilver reintroduced himself simply as Brown. They remained inside the rail car until darkness had settled in, and eventually left their hiding spot when Brown signaled it was time to go.

Circumventing the outlying buildings and houses of Holstebro, they kept to a paved road southwest of town. It was lined with thin trees that cast narrow shadows in the moonlight, and after a few kilometers, Brown turned off into a lightly wooded area covered with scrub trees. They made their way through the bramble to a long, narrow clearing and waited amongst the bracken and bushes at its edge.

Brown leaned over to Thorne in a whisper. "We'll wait here for a plane. Once it arrives—".

He was cut short by Thorne, "I've done this before. What time do we expect the flight?"

"It will be some time now. We are waiting for another passenger."

A few hours passed while they sat in the darkness, each man alone in his thoughts, when Thorne noticed a flicker of light across the clearing. After a second flash sparked on and off, he pointed it out to Brown.

"That's them. Let's go."

They darted across the clear patch of land, slipping into the trees on the other side where three shaded figures awaited them. Brown ran forward to converse with someone, and after a series of whispers, one of them disappeared leaving the others hunched near the ground. Thorne cautiously approached and could just make out Brown sitting next to another person.

"This is your traveling mate," Brown whispered. "Thorne, meet Harding, RAF." The two men shook hands and it was apparent that Harding was injured, he could not move easily. "This is going to be touch and go," Brown continued. "Once the plane is on the ground and has come to a stop, you'll run out first and tell the pilot to wait while I bring Harding. Once we get him onboard, I'll give the signal and the pilot will start moving."

Thorne watched as small lanterns were lit in the clearing. Someone else must have assisted their man, because two more lights appeared several meters apart from each other almost simultaneously. From the obscurity where he hid, he watched the torchlights bounce around in the darkness before settling into a position more or less forming a large letter L on the dew-laden ground. The lights would designate the landing zone for the incoming flight.

Just moments later, as if on cue, he heard the familiar sound of the radial engine of an approaching Lizzie. The matte-black aircraft appeared as a dark blotch against the sky, and cut its engine as it floated downward on a mere hum. The plane dropped effort-lessly over a short line of trees, pounced on the far end of the clearing, and raced toward Thorne's position before slowing just in front of him. The pilot immediately revved the engine and spun the plane around.

This is the most critical moment.

If the Germans had not seen the Lysander yet, they certainly would hear its motor if they were anywhere within a kilometer. Thorne sprinted to the plane which had a fixed ladder on the left side just behind the wings. He grabbed onto the ladder, opened the sliding hatch window to the rear cockpit, and yelled forward to the pilot alerting him to hold steady a little longer. The seconds ticked away while the plane waited for its final passenger. Originally designed to carry one passenger in the rear cockpit, the Lysander Mk III was modified to accommodate two SOE operatives, albeit uncomfortably, but Thorne had never ridden with a second passenger before tonight.

Brown came staggering along with Harding who limped awkwardly, arm draped over Brown's shoulder. Harding grabbed onto the ladder, favoring his good leg to secure a foothold, and Thorne gripped his arms and pulled the injured man upward. Harding let his game leg drape while the good one pushed on the rungs of the ladder. It was an awkward go of it—Harding climbing in head first with his legs dangling outside— and Brown finally signaling the pilot to start the roll down the rough airstrip.

Thorne helped Harding jostle into a seated position, with much effort and discomfort to the RAF pilot, but as the plane lifted off, they were both seated in the rear cockpit, side by side facing aft, and he managed to slide the canopy forward to a closed position. The entire landing process when well-rehearsed could take less than a minute, but Thorne estimated they had spent considerably more time on the ground struggling with their wounded comrade.

The plane lunged skyward drunkenly as its huge 870 horsepower radial piston engine roared to life and fought against the increased weight from its passengers. The Lysander climbed rapidly to a few thousand feet and continued gaining altitude. Tipped off by the approach and takeoff, nearby German troops began searching for the aircraft with huge spotlights that lit up one by one seeking out their prey.

None of their beams found the Lysander, leaving German antiaircraft guns to search by shooting randomly toward the sound of the plane. Tracers jutted up from the ground and Thorne thought he heard more than one bullet hit the fuselage of the plane, but he quickly convinced himself the Germans must have missed as the plane continued effortlessly on its course. Still, he watched in fear, and the tracers and searchlights circled endlessly probing the night sky. Peering over the edge of the canopy, he could at last make out the edge of Denmark a few kilometers distant as the plane raced toward the North Sea.

He breathed a sigh of relief when they crossed the last stretch of land they would see for the next five hundred kilometers and sank back into his seat, practically on top of Harding, the tracers and searchlights now sought other targets in the distant night sky.

"Are you doing all right?"

"Yes. God bless you sir," said Harding.

Chapter
Twenty-Seven

THE LYSANDER TOUCHED DOWN before daybreak at Tempsford Royal Air Force station, perhaps the most secret airbase in all of England. The citizens who lived in the surrounding village of Sandy, about fifty miles north of London, were completely aware of the existence of the 'secret' RAF airfield.

No one was fooled by a sign suspiciously marking a side road as Gibraltar Farm—a place no one could recall having heard of prior to 1940. Nor had anyone been tipped off by gossiping employees working at Tempsford Hall, a country manor house SOE used as an assembly point for pilots and agents going into the field. Instead, shortly after it was put into service, the locals became aware of the true purpose of Gibraltar Farm with the coming and going of RAF planes at all hours of the day, particularly those returning in the pre-dawn hours of the night.

Thorne was all too familiar with Tempsford, having used the airfield on previous occasions under the assistance of Group Captain Sir Edward Hedley Fielden who oversaw 138 Squadron of the RAF. Once his plane came to a halt after taxiing to the main hanger at the aerodrome, the pilot rushed inside to find help for Harding while Thorne did his best to help the injured airman out of the rear of the plane.

A group of airmen assisted the wounded crewman and escorted him to their living quarters. Thorne, mostly ignored by the crew, walked into the familiar administrative office of RAF Tempsford. With any luck, he hoped Fielden would not be on duty at this early hour, and as he entered the office, he relaxed when he determined the head officer had not yet arrived. Instead, a junior officer—a young man barely out of his teens—greeted him from behind an oak desk stacked with log books, maps, and other paperwork.

"Good morning. I understand you're with SOE?"

"Yes Sir. Richard Thorne, Sir." Thorne saluted the officer attempting to mollify the youthful man. "Sir, I'm reporting for duty back to Allan Faulk with SOE, special assignment. He's aware of my return, and there will be no need to contact him. If you can kindly show me where I may find transport back to London, I'll be on my way." Thorne had rehearsed this line the last hour of his flight.

"Nonsense. Standard protocol you know. I must contact SOE immediately and notify them of your safe arrival."

"Sir, that's fine, but I highly doubt they will acknowledge my whereabouts. You see Sir, I was on *special* assignment." The officer eyed him with skepticism. "*More* special than normal Sir."

"Well, just the same, I'm sure Baker Street will sort it all out. You're welcome to wait here, or you'll find the airmen's mess two buildings over if you'd like breakfast. We'll get this all cleared up and you'll be on your way in a few hours. Welcome home Thorne."

There was nothing else to it. He hoped at this early hour that any communications with Baker Street would bypass Beecher. He also hoped the officer would reference Faulk if there were any confusion by SOE staff.

Famished, he walked to hanger four where the mess hall adjoined the living quarters at the rear of the building. Thorne ate a full breakfast of sausages, tomatoes, and mushrooms, accompanied by muffins, juice, and coffee. Refreshed and reinvigorated, he dawdled around the aerodrome grounds with famil-iarity. Six enormous hangers surrounded the main runway. At the center of the airfield stood a control tower, and far off to his right, between runway one and two, stood two petrol installations. A large number of bomber aircraft parked in the surrounding fields caught his attention, these he assumed were part of the buildup for the upcoming invasion of the Low Countries.

Thorne looked in on his companion Harding, but was shooed away by an over-watchful nurse who scolded him for interrupting Harding's rest. He eventually made his way back to the office where he found recent copies of newspapers and poured through them for the latest information on the War.

The Junior Officer returned to the waiting area. "Thorne, your phone call is in. This way please." He was taken to a private office where the call was patched through by an operator on the base.

"Hello, Thorne here."

"Richard?" a familiar man's voice asked, failing to hide his astonishment.

"Hello Allan, bet you didn't expect to hear from me."

"No! How did you—or how are you, I should ask first?"

"The usual, a little worn, but holding together I suppose. Listen, I got your message in Stockholm, Sveinsson found me and said Blackbird—".

"Not here. Listen, find your way to the Black Horse pub in Woburn, not far from Bletchley. I will be up that way in a few hours and will meet you there."

"Will do."

"And Richard, it is good to hear your voice, glad you're home safe."

Faulk made sufficient arrangements with the officer in command to allow Thorne's release, and followed through with a call to the Black Horse, securing a room for Thorne with an open tab on SOE. Thorne was shuttled to Woburn by a FANY driver, a woman in the Auxiliary Transport Service assigned to SOE, and as promised, Faulk arrived by private car late in the day. The two friends met alone in the Black Horse pub catching up on the past week.

"At first, I wasn't sure about Sveinsson. He approached me right off saying I was in danger. You know me, I never trust anyone, but eventually he gave me enough information to confirm he was working with you."

"Yes, he's performed a number assignments for me, decent chap. I'm sorry to have alarmed you, but I'm glad he was able to reach you in time."

"Do you think it is true? Has Blackbird really requested my assassination?"

"I'm afraid you've poked your nose in a honey pot and stirred up the bees!"

"Yes, I suppose so. I left it with Sveinsson that I had another assignment to attend to, but I do believe he expected my return to Stockholm. Even now the poor chap must suspect that I am either dead, captured, or still at large."

"I'll patch things up with him."

"And then there's Beecher. He hasn't heard from me in days and I'm not sure what he'll do once he finds out I'm no longer in Sweden. I'm wondering if there's a way you can help keep that under wraps, at least until I get a chance to sort through this whole nasty business with Blackbird."

"Perhaps Sveinsson can get word back from Stockholm. Something simple that looks like you're following your orders?"

"Yes, I think that would work." Thorne finished a pint of beer and wiped his mouth on the back of his hand. "I'm still peeved about this whole affair. It absolutely chafes me to believe someone in London is financing the Nazis. Before the War, they used to hold rallies and demonstrations back at Cambridge; I could never figure out why any loyal subject of the Crown couldn't see through their facade. It was absolutely abominable, pure evil from the get go."

"Richard, there are many things bigger than any one man. I want you to be careful. You're up against something much larger than you think."

"And I intend to bring it to daylight, if I have to deliver it to Churchill myself!"

Faulk stared at him solicitously. Several more seconds passed while Thorne emptied his glass. Faulk finally interjected, "Right. So, you'll be working for me now, at least until we get things sorted out with Beecher. I'll have to get new identification papers and establish a radio frequency for us, you know, get it cleared through Signals Directorate and what not."

"Yes, of course. How can I help? I got these from the underground in Denmark." He handed over his identification papers Moller had forged.

"I doubt these will work; it may just make things that much more dangerous for you. I need a day to get things in order, you can rest here. I doubt anyone will inquire about your business, but if you're pressed and need official orders, you're now using the codename *Centaur*. Anyone gives you a hard time, have them reach me at COHQ."

TWO DAYS LATER, THORNE WAS shuttled across the English Channel in the austere cabin of a Lockheed Hudson RAF aircraft which served in special duties and clandestine operations under No. 161 Squadron from Tempsford. The twin-engine aircraft flew at breakneck speed through the middle of the night and deposited Thorne gingerly on the ground in Allied territory of central Belgium without the perils of a night drop.

Thorne was outfitted with papers and clothing allowing him to travel into Belgium and Germany as an ordinary citizen, and he carried nothing else on him besides a Ballester-Malina pistol tucked into the pockets of a heavy overcoat. Upon his landing, he was promptly introduced to a British rifle regiment captain who ordered his man Lance Corporal Godfrey McIntyre to escort Thorne to a gap in the German lines near the Belgian village of Borgloon, less than ten kilometers outside of Liege.

It was a cloudy morning and although the sun was fully above the horizon, the overcast skies made it difficult to tell precisely what time of day it was. Parked on the outskirts of Liege, a Humber staff car rested on a short rise overlooking a broad valley. Thorne stood in the open-topped vehicle surveying the city from beneath the cover of a grove of trees. Using a pair of field glasses McIntyre had provided, he searched for a specific steeple sticking up out of the vanquished city that was his intended destination, St. Walburge's parish.

"Can a gie ya a haund?" McIntyre said, offering Thorne the use of a field map. Together they quickly located the church and planned Thorne's route into the German-controlled town.

"Can you get me any closer?"

"If I get you any closer Laddie, you'll be ate'n sauerkraut with Hitler 'imself!"

"Thank you kindly for the lift Corporal." Thorne stepped out of the staff car and handed the binoculars to his driver.

"Godspeed to you Mr. Thorne and haste ye back!" The driver backed over the edge of the hillock and made a U-turn on the narrow road on which they'd come.

Thorne could make out movements of vehicles and people within the town, but from this distance, could not tell whether they were civilians or soldiers. He hiked down from the hill and came into Liege, walking in the general direction of the church, and attempted to blend in with other civilians he encountered.

He cut behind buildings, used side streets and alleyways, and all the while checked at every turn for Germans. Thorne was surprised at the number of soldiers he encountered; it seemed an entire battalion had settled into town. After several minutes and a few close calls, he ducked behind a building and waited.

Off in the distance a familiar droning indicated Allied bombers approached somewhere overhead. He glanced upwards but could not see the planes. During his visit to London, he'd read that the Allies now dominated the skies over Europe. Beginning in the middle of 1943, the Allies began using precision bomb runs during daylight in favor of less accurate night bombings. There was still the occasional skirmish with Luftwaffe fighters, but the Allies were willing to take that chance.

Eventually, he came to *Rue Sainte-Walburge*. As he

looked each way down the paved boulevard, he spotted the church steeple, a few blocks down on his right. However, he also noticed a group of soldiers standing between him and his objective. He crossed the road to the opposite side of the intersection and waited in a recessed doorway, contemplating his next step.

Just then, a group of bombers came into view, popping out from behind a blanket of clouds. A wave of dark planes flew overhead in tight formation that reminded him of migratory birds. The soldiers paid no attention to him, nor anyone else walking down the street; their attention was drawn upwards too. One of the soldiers pointed up to the sky. Thorne also looked up to catch sight of other planes swarming around the Flying Fortresses. The Luftwaffe was making a desperate attack on the bomber squadron despite the accompanying Allied escort fighters who broke away to engage them.

He considered pressing on past the soldiers, hoping the dogfight overhead would hold their attention, but it was far too risky; no sense jeopardizing everything when he was this close. He chose a side street and worked his way toward the church by circling around from its far side.

He lurked along a cobbled street which had no alleyways; all of the buildings were attached and adjacent to each other like walls lining a narrow corridor. If he was approached now, there would be no escape unless he could find a business or home with an unlocked door.

He passed a few children who reached out to him

with begging arms, but he ignored their pleas. Overhead the air battle continued as fighters swooped and dived, shooting at each other in acrobatic maneuvers. He moved beyond the children, but one boy decided to follow. Thorne reached another intersection at *Rue Jean Dister*; to his left down this paved road, he could see the church a mere hundred meters away. The boy cried out, "*monsieur, monsieur.*" Thorne dug through his coat pockets looking for anything to appease the boy and showed the boy his empty hands.

Across the way, a man dressed in fine clothing talked to a shop keeper. The boy noisily bawled, "*s'il vous plaît, monsieur, s'il vous plait!*" He again dug into his pockets only to find a loose cigarette which he showed the boy. The boy looked quizzically at the cigarette and then snatched it up and ran down the street.

Thorne turned away in the direction of the church, ignoring a man's voice from across the street calling out in French. The voice yelled out a second time in German, "Halt!"

Bollocks!

In exasperation, he stopped and turned to see the well-dressed man hurrying across the road. *Rue Jean Dister* was much like the other roads in town, lined with close-packed buildings on both sides. Near the church, an angled stone wall, nearly eight feet high flanked the right side of the road. There was no escape. The man rapidly closed the distance between them and stopped a meter distant revealing a badge which Thorne did not immediately recognize. An all too familiar phrase promptly followed. "Papers!"

He produced the required papers and as the officer thumbed through the documents, Thorne sized him up.

A gun on his right hip, beneath his buttoned jacket. Advantage Thorne.

"What is your name?" he asked in French.

Thorne was not fluent in French, but recognized some common phrases and words. As the officer compared the photographs on the identification and work papers to the calm face before him, Thorne decided to go with his cover story.

"I am Dutch. My name is—", he paused momentarily as the officer's attention was drawn to machine gun fire overhead. He'd forgotten the surname on the new credentials Faulk had supplied. He heedlessly scanned his memory replaying his last visit with Faulk. It was no use. He recalled something starting with the letter H and several vowels, mostly A's, so he decided to bluff.

The officer looked back at him. "My name is Franz Haastennton." Even as Thorne spoke it, he knew the surname did not come out right. He repeated again, "Franz Haastadenston." Another attempt to throw off his inquisitor. The officer looked puzzlingly at the papers, but his attention was carelessly averted to the sky once again.

In that moment, both men were distracted and turned their heads toward the whining of a descending aircraft plummeting downwards. A spiral of black smoke crossed the sky overhead and from behind the roofline on their immediate right, a burning aircraft came screaming into view. Both men panicked as it collided with a building not more than fifty paces nearby.

The officer dove for cover along the edge of a wall, while Thorne instinctively ducked where he stood and covered his head as a shower of glass and rubble was thrown his way from an intense explosion. Both men looked in awe upon pieces of a Luftwaffe fuselage that protruded from the upper floor of a two-story flat which was quickly engulfed in flames.

Thorne used the diversion to his advantage and took off down *Rue Jean Dister.* Several screeching children ran from the burning building followed by three panic-stricken women, but he did not stop to help them. He reached the Church of St. Walburge, its steeple towering overhead, and looked back to see the policeman herding the women and children together away from the flaming ruins of their home.

Thorne ascended a set of stone steps that led to the entrance of the church and entered a foyer-like room where he stood alone panting. Once he caught his breath, he entered the church through a set of colossal, wooden doors.

He walked down the center aisle toward the front of the nave, surveying the cathedral as he went. A woman was seated to his right, her head bowed in prayer beneath the watchful eyes of angels and disciples looking down upon her from ornately decorated stained-glass windows. There was no one else in the main hall.

Thorne took a seat three rows from the altar and

slid toward the middle of the pew. The droning of the bomber squadron outside faded into the distance and a hush fell upon the sanctuary. After several long minutes, a clergyman entered from the right and approached the podium in the pulpit. The man paid no attention to Thorne, but placed a sheaf of loose papers on the lectern and opened a bible. Thorne sat patiently but the clergyman did not seem to notice him.

Seeing the woman leave through the double doors, he rose slowly and approached the altar, calling out in a calm voice, "Padre?" The man looked up from his papers. Thorne looked around to reassure himself no one else was there and continued, "*Parlez-vous anglais?*"

"Yes."

"My name is Richard." He looked around cautiously once again. "I need your help." He lowered his voice to nearly a whisper. "I am seeking a man named Pasteger, do you know him?"

The priest did not immediately respond, but closed his bible and stepped down from his perch to meet Thorne face to face. "And what is an Englishman doing in Liege?"

"Father, please, I am an ally to the resistance," he whispered.

"Please follow me." He took Thorne to a doorway and asked him to sit in a chair just outside an antechamber off the main hall. The ancient artifact, covered in red velvet and adorned in ornate, scrolled woodwork was much more comfortable than the oak pew. Thorne lingered timorously as the minutes passed.

Chapter
Twenty-Eight

"**Y**OU ARE THE ENGLISHMAN?" a curious voice asked over Thorne's shoulder.

Thorne's attention had been glued to two men who had entered the church just moments before; they sat in a pew in the hindmost section of the nave. They had taken no notice of Thorne, but now looked to the front of the church inquisitively when they heard the voice summoning Thorne.

Thorne turned to respond and saw the priest standing erect, his face expressionless, while another, shorter man who had apparently addressed Thorne, stretched a warm, jovial grin across his round face in contrast to the clergyman, and bobbed his head prompting Thorne's response.

Trapped.

Thorne's mind went into action as he speculated on whether the priest had summoned the *Gestapo*, alerting them of his arrival. He instantly formulated a plan of escape. If he tackled the man in front of him knocking the priest aside in the process, he could use the door behind them to find his way to a rear exit. From there, he could not guess his next turn until the opportunity arose.

As if sensing Thorne's calculations, the man continued in fluent English, but spoken with a peculiar inflection, "Do not be alarmed. We are friends here."

The priest interrupted Thorne's deliberation, "What is your name?"

It was now or never—*I must make my move*—yet something prevented him from taking action. A sudden calm overcame him as the priest gave him a reassuring look.

"It's alright my son. You are safe."

As they spoke, the two men from the nave closed the gap and now stood behind Thorne. He realized then, that he had lost his identity papers back in the street when the policeman had confronted him. Once the plane had crashed into the nearby building, Thorne had fled in panic. There was no use now. His opportunity for escape had eluded him and there was no other option but to give in to fate.

"Thorne. Richard Thorne."

"Do you have any identification Mr. Thorne?"

After he replied no, the two men were motioned to search him. As they ran their hands up and down the length of his body, one of them felt the bulge in his armpit signifying a hidden weapon. Expertly, one of them reached into his coat pocket and retrieved the Ballester–Molina pistol and handed it to the man beside the priest.

"How is it that you walked into town without any identification Mr. Thorne?" the priest inquired.

"My papers were taken by a—shall we say—*friendly* officer of Liege."

"So, tell me Mr. Thorne, what are you doing here?" the other man asked.

He looked again into the gentle face of the priest and then back to the man questioning him.

"I'm looking for a man named Pasteger."

"I am Pasteger. How can I help you?"

Thorne considered his options. It was quite plausible that this man was a *Gestapo* officer posing as Pasteger, the man would simply play along to get information out of Thorne. He was trapped; the goons had taken his weapon and it would be difficult for Thorne to break free from his captors under the immediate circumstances.

"How do I know you are Pasteger? Perhaps you already have my papers and have come to arrest me."

"Mr. Thorne. We are not going to get anywhere if you do not put your trust in me. You have come seeking me and here I am. What can I do for you?"

At that moment, two others entered the church. Before Thorne had a good look at the new arrivals, he was ushered—along with the man calling himself Pasteger—into a modest room that served as the priest's office. The priest closed the door behind them, while the others waited outside.

"I can tell you are a cautious man Mr. Thorne. I admire that quality in the men who work with us. Can I get you something? A glass of water, or wine perhaps?"

"No thank you." Although he was famished and

thirsty beyond imagination, he was still leery about this man until he could confirm his identity.

Pasteger poured himself a glass of wine while the priest stood behind him listening to their exchange. "Whenever someone comes looking for me, they generally use a pass phrase, a series of predetermined code words. I am guessing either you weren't given the pass words, which raises my suspicions about your true nature, or else you weren't planning on meeting me directly."

Thorne scanned the priest's office. A wide set of floor-to-ceiling shelves, over-stuffed with books and papers, lined one wall. A desk situated in the center of the room was in neat order. "Both are correct. Allan Faulk, of Combined Ops, sent me. Do you know him?"

"Please have a seat." Just then one of Pasteger's men entered the room from the main hall.

"Those men are asking to see Leo. They said, 'the lion sleeps in black'."

"Ah, now we are getting somewhere. Send them in please." He turned back to Thorne. "You see Mr. Thorne, they knew not only whom to ask for, but what the correct phrase was to let me know I can trust them."

Thorne committed the phrase to memory and continued searching the room for other clues or useful items that would aid his escape. He spotted a letter opener that would prove beneficial if needed, but nothing else that might be used as an impromptu weapon. There were no other exits beyond the solitary door in the small room. Thorne's eyes scanned his surrounding as the questions went on.

"If you recall your history," Pasteger continued, "the Duchy of Brabant was a state in the Holy Roman Empire, and once the heart of the historic Low Countries. The coat of arms for Brabant was emblazoned with a gold lion lying upon a field of black. I'm guessing you know that *Leo* is Latin for Lion, that is my codename." Pasteger sat behind the priest's desk. "You see Thorne, I was liaison officer with the Royal Flying Corps in the Great War. My name is Alexandre Pasteger. I have many friends in Whitehall and a few contacts at Baker Street also. To answer your question, yes, I know of Allan Faulk."

The office door opened again and two strangers were escorted into the room. Thorne instantly recognized the younger of the two; he had seen him around the basement of the garment factory in Maastricht. His mind shifted from escape to discovering the whereabouts of Anna now that the Maastricht resistance circuit had arrived.

Within the hour, Pasteger had informants out searching the streets of Liege for any sign of Anna. With the arrival of Visser's men, Thorne was able to confirm that Pasteger was the same man helping in relocating their operations from Maastricht.

The two men now sat alone in the priest's office sipping tea.

"Now, Mr. Thorne, I can't help but feel there is some other plan at work here. I do not think you were merely tied up with the Dutch resistance by happenstance; you were sent by London you said?" He slid Thorne's pistol across the desk.

Thorne picked up the gun and tucked it into his coat. He wasn't sure how Pasteger could be of help, so he decided to play it straight with the man and see where it led. "That's right. Faulk said you could help me get to Aachen."

"Aachen? Whatever for?"

"There is a factory there. Englebert Tire. Do you know of it?"

Pasteger laughed heartily. "Know of it; yes, I am very familiar with it. It is the largest factory in Aachen." He cleared his throat as he saw the concern on Thorne's face. "What is it you need at Englebert?"

Thorne sipped his tea.

Okay, let's see what else you know.

"There is a connection between a man named Karl Hartmann in Germany and another in London; I only know him by the codename Blackbird." He paused looking for a reaction in Pasteger's round face but there was none. "It seems the man in London has been funding Hartmann, or perhaps Englebert. I don't have it all worked out just yet, but there is definitely some scheme at play. Do you know these names?"

Pasteger grasped his chin, his eyes set in deep thought. "Karl Hartmann yes. Blackbird no."

Thorne waited patiently for details while Pasteger refilled both of their cups with steaming water.

"It's *Englebert Tire and Rubber* to be more precise; Aachen is actually a branch of the main headquarters here in Liege. By coincidence, I used to manage the Aachen plant before the War. When the Nazis took over, I came back to Liege. At one time, I knew many of the top executives there. Hartmann was nothing more than head of security; a wormy little man, always looking for mischief. I seem to remember someone on the Board of Directors; his name escapes me just now, but he was very interested in Hartmann's contrivances."

Thorne listened attentively.

"The Aachen plant was bombed and destroyed by the RAF in the summer of forty-one," Pasteger continued. "But the Germans quickly rebuilt it and resumed production. Originally, Englebert was set up to make bicycle and automotive tires, but later the Nazis converted the factory into a war machine producing not only tires for their vehicles and motorcycles, but also treads for their Panzers, and other goods for their armies." He finally paused, reflecting for some time on his past.

"Do you think I could get into the plant? There must be an office where I can find records, I need proof linking Hartmann to the man in London."

"It will be dangerous. Very dangerous. But it can be done."

"How will you go about getting me into Aachen?"

"Of course, you will need papers." Pasteger took out a notepad from the desk. "Perhaps, I can get you into Englebert as a member of the custodial staff. And then there is the matter of where you will stay while you are in Germany. He scribbled his thoughts in a queer script and penmanship which only he could interpret. I know of a safe house in the Brand district of Aachen. The proprietor's name is Gruber. You should be able to find it easily enough as he will have a Nazi banner in the window, but if you look closely, you will also see he has posted the coat of arms of Brabant that I told you about."

Thorne instantly committed the details to memory. *Brand district. Gruber. Lion on black field.*

"Before you leave, I can provide you a layout of the facility, at least the offices that I was most familiar with before the factory was bombed. I have to assume the basement infrastructure of the main building is still intact. The Nazis set up a telephone exchange in the central part of the plant in an area fabricated with thick, reinforced, concrete walls; that is where you will find the information you are looking for, if they haven't destroyed it yet."

"How much time do I have? The Allies are already advancing into this region."

"Very little, a week or two at best."

Thorne nodded in agreement.

"Perhaps you could wait for the British to liberate Aachen, then you can simply walk into the factory and search at your leisure."

"No, this is of an urgent matter." Thorne knew there was no sense guessing the timing of the offensive into Germany. If anything, it would only delay his access to the information, particularly if the Americans, and not the British, took Englebert.

"It will take a little time to set things in motion; give me a day or two. You will be safe here. I suggest you take your rest; you will need it in the coming days."

AFTER A RESTLESS NIGHT, spent in a secluded room of the church, Thorne learned that Anna had not been located, and Pasteger had also mysteriously disappeared. He stared out a window in the priest's office and finished a cup of tea. A truck rolled into view and parked across the road; two men he recognized as Pasteger's accomplices emerged from the vehicle, and dashed across the road toward the church. Thorne waited and continued watching out the window. A soldier walked past his position but did not see his apparition in the lead glass window, nor had he seen Pasteger's men.

"I'm sure she's all right," the priest said as he entered the office. "She probably sensed some danger and took shelter elsewhere to avoid being followed here."

Thorne turned to face him. "Perhaps you are right. She is a smart girl." He set down his teacup. "Have you heard from Pasteger this morning?"

"No, but I presume he will be here shortly." The priest leaned over his desk and looked through some papers.

"Can the man be trusted?"

"Quite so. Everything he's told you is true. You are in the best care you could expect given the circumstances at hand." Thorne paced the room in agitation. "Please have a seat, worrying about your friend will not help us find her."

Thorne sat across from the priest. "You've been most kind. I sincerely appreciate your help."

The priest smiled at him in return. "We must all work together if we are to defeat the evil lurking across our borders." His smile disappeared in short order and he cleared his throat. "Are you familiar with a British agent using the name Nuthatch?"

"No, I am not privy to codenames used by other agents, except those whom I have been instructed to engage directly."

"I'm sorry to say he has fallen into the hands of the *Gestapo*. One of Pasteger's informants speculates that they will expand their search for you into Belgium. You must leave for Aachen immediately. When Pasteger returns, he will likely move you from here."

"I'm not leaving until Anna arrives."

"She may stay in hiding for a number of days if the *Gestapo* have learned she too is in Belgium. She has likely taken shelter with one of her contacts here in Liege. We will find her, do not worry. As you said, she is a smart girl."

Thorne walked back to the window hoping to see her approaching the church. With the *Gestapo* tightening their search it would be increasingly difficult for him to travel. In fact, he still did not know Pasteger's plan for getting him into Germany. He also had no idea what he would do once he found the information—if he found it at all— in the Englebert factory.

Chapter
Twenty-Nine

THORNE'S DELIBERATION WAS interrupted when a boy rushed into the priest's office. The altar-boy stammered and couldn't find his words, his distress apparent.

"What is it Mathis?" the priest inquired as he rushed to comfort the boy who stood inside the door frame frozen with terror. Thorne followed suit and all three of them peered out the doorway into the main hall.

Two civilian men, well-dressed in neatly pressed suits, had entered the church and were questioning other patrons who had sought refuge in the cathedral. One of the men pointed to a piece of paper as he spoke.

The priest carefully inched the door closed. He turned with a grimaced look, "Mathis. Hurry, take Mr. Thorne into the catacombs and show him the way to the river!" He spun around to Thorne, "Pasteger will find you, do not worry."

The boy dashed to the opposite side of the office and put all his strength against a book case, shoving it aside wide enough to reveal a passageway behind it. Thorne squeezed into the opening behind the boy, and with a quick wave to the priest, he followed the boy down a flight of stone steps that ended in a square tunnel. At the bottom of the steps, the boy retrieved a torch from the nearest wall and fumbled with a box of matches until it was lit. Behind him, the bookshelf slid back into place. Thorne snatched an unlit torch and used the boy's to set his own alight. Its flame sent hissing and popping sounds throughout the narrow passageway.

"*Monsieur*, follow me."

Together they ran through a long tunnel passing a series of murals depicting knights, priests and monks dressed in ceremonial garb. The boy stopped at an intersection and looked back and forth in indecision. He turned right and ran down a long corridor with rough flagstones upon the floor; Thorne followed closely on his heels moving into a wide room with a vaulted ceiling that glowed in patches of amber light from lanterns placed at regular intervals around the room.

Thorne was momentarily awestruck at the size of the room and struggled to visualize how the great expanse had been built below the church and beneath the streets of Liege. The boy took Thorne down an adjoining passage on their right. Thorne paused momentarily in fright; four mummified priests, perched in recessed alcoves cut into the walls, looked upon them through veils of dusty cobwebs. Their sunken eyes stared from within sneering skulls that hid under the tattered remains of priestly robes.

His thoughts turned back to the corridor and he saw two lights bobbing in the distance accompanied by footsteps echoing through the chamber. The boy earnestly waved him onward. Next, they passed several horizontal pockets cut into the stone walls which held the skeletal remains of erstwhile church elders.

A fist-sized piece of wall next to Thorne's face exploded in fragments of rock and dust as a gunshot echoed simultaneously from behind them. The boy turned into a side chamber and tugged at Thorne's sleeve; he followed closely reaching for his pistol. The round chamber they entered had several exits and the boy counted to himself, pointing to each, finally choosing the fourth doorway from their left. The boy's torch sputtered, changing color from yellow to bluish-gold and Thorne handed him his own as the boy moved recklessly down a narrow shaft cut in the stone.

Thorne tossed the spent torch aside, and as they moved forward, he looked to his rear to see reflections of light in the tunnels behind them. The boy suddenly came to a halt; the tunnel ended in a sealed wall of stone. They turned around and retraced their steps to a passageway they had ignored just seconds before and entered another crypt-like antechamber. Hundreds of skulls shoved into square nooks framed a stone plaque set in the wall; its engraved words in Latin made no sense to Thorne. He stood awestruck at the macabre burial site, and it wasn't until the light around him began to fade that he realized the boy had run down an adjoining passage.

He shuffled behind the boy and they crept along

a narrow winding path where the walls changed from smooth, cut stone to rough, chiseled rock. Thorne heard footsteps closing in behind them and crouched firing wildly into the darkness. The footsteps stopped.

The boy moved onwards several paces ahead of him and disappeared around a bend in the tunnel. Thorne ran back to the boy and caught up to him in a twisting space that narrowed to the point where he caught his shoulders on ridges of hand-hewn stone jutting out from the walls.

The footsteps behind started again, shuffling and scraping the rough stone floor somewhere in the gloominess beyond his sight. The boy stopped at another intersection and looked to his left and right in indecision. Thorne stole another glance behind him and saw a glowing light framed like a half moon in the narrow hallway. He fired a warning shot in that direction and the light faded as their pursuers backed off cautiously.

While he watched the fading light of his stalkers, he realized his own light source had suddenly vanished. He turned to follow the boy, but the passage was completely dark; the boy was gone and the warm glow of torchlight had disappeared. He advanced warily, arms outstretched, until he bumped into the cool stone wall ahead of him in the blackness. He had reached an intersection where the boy had stood just seconds before, and now Thorne stood motionless, waiting, listening, and turning his head in all directions. The distant shuffling somewhere behind him started again and his eyes made out a faint glow as his hunters resumed their pursuit.

He diverted into a ragged opening on his left and kept to the edge of the wall using his left hand to feel the rough stone, his right outstretched in front of him still clutching his pistol. His eyes strained to find any source of light—a reflection, a glow, a tiny speck in the distance—but he could see nothing.

Without warning, his legs stopped in place as he bumped into something below his knees. He felt a sharp pain in his shins and toppled forward over an object that stuck out in front of him, landing face down on his hands. His pistol skipped on the stone floor and slid somewhere into the blackness that surrounded him. His hands burned intensely from the prick of several sharp pieces of rock and gravel that ground into his palms. He lay flat on his belly, listening for his followers, but they had also stopped when they heard his fall.

A cool air closed in on him from the darkness, its dry, dusty scent stung his nostrils. He rubbed his palms on his shoulders and reached out across the debris strewn floor in search of his weapon. Behind him the shape of the low wall that had tripped him now stood framed in the darkness by a glowing light coming from beyond. With the light growing in brightness, his hand closed upon the familiar steel of the Ballester–Molina, and he rolled onto his side against the wall where it met the floor. From his prone position, his eyes adjusted to the light source, and then he heard the soft whisper of the boy, "*Monsieur? Monsieur?*"

A shadowy form took shape in the brightening

light as the boy searched the passage. Before he could respond, Thorne saw a second light appear from out of nowhere as the shapes of two figures rapidly descended upon the boy.

In the wane light, he took aim at one of the taller figures and fired. He heard a low grunt. One of the torches fell to the ground followed by the thud of its bearer hitting the passage floor. With the light on the ground and the second suspended in midair, he could just make out the second man's face and feet alongside the smaller frame of the boy. Fearing for the safety of the boy, he took careful aim knowing it was a risky shot and fired toward the man's head. In the dim light, he saw the man's head disappear as his body fell backwards out of sight behind the boy.

He scooted to a seated position against the wall. "Mathis? Are you okay?" The boy came closer and the two were joined again under the sputtering flame of the boy's torchlight.

"This way *monsieur*," the boy, seemingly unphased, said pointing back in the direction he had come. Thorne brushed himself off and followed the boy, stooping briefly to retrieve a fallen torch next to one of the dead men. They hurried past the fallen bodies and the boy led him to a stone stairway that climbed upwards. "This is the way out."

At the top of the steps, the boy struggled with a rusted bolt that held a door firmly in place. Thorne moved the boy aside and used all his strength to slide the bolt just millimeters passed its catch, enough to release the lock. He pulled on an iron ring affixed to the door and it opened inward with a defiant groan.

Beyond the door, he had hoped to find the bright, natural light of the outside world, but instead Thorne looked into a long, featureless corridor that led onward to yet another door. They continued along the tunnel to the second door, bolted much like the first, but it was easily opened by the boy and they rushed headlong into a cavernous room with wooden floors.

A pale, natural light filtered through narrow windows several feet above them. Thorne surveyed the area as best he could and guessed they were in a large storeroom. The boy continued on without hesitation, zigzagging around objects of broken furniture and other unidentifiable refuse and came to a wide door that held a small window looking out into the grey skies of Belgium.

Outside the structure, a truck waited in a narrow alleyway. Two men sat in the cab smoking. As Thorne cautiously emerged from the doorway, one of the men rapped on the frame of the truck signaling a rear canopy flap to open on the side. The familiar face of Pasteger poked out from behind the flap, his head twisting awkwardly like a turtle.

"Come quick!" He motioned them into the bed of the truck where another man crouched with Pasteger. They helped the boy into the truck and Thorne hopped in as the driver started the engine. The vehicle began to roll forward.

"That was close. You are a lucky man Richard Thorne," Pasteger said.

"Business as usual." He could see the side of Pasteger's face was bruised and swollen. "Are you okay?"

"Yes. I'm sorry I could not stop them. Are they still coming?" He peered out the rear canopy.

"No. I took care of them."

"Good, good!" He smiled at the boy nestled against the front of the truck. "You did well today, Mathis!"

They bounced and jostled uncomfortably in the bed of the truck as it rumbled through the streets of Liege. Thorne eyed the other man in the back of the truck and recognized him as one of Pasteger's cohorts. He turned to Pasteger, "Where are we going?"

"There is a rail tunnel that crosses into Germany. It cuts directly through the Scharnhorst Line, part of the Siegfried Wall on the southwest side of Aachen. We will get you to the tracks not far from here. From there, you will go by foot, maybe one mile, and cross the border." Thorne sat across from Pasteger and peeked out the rear canopy to reassure himself they were not being followed.

Thorne held on to the frame of the vehicle as they were jerked around. Guilt weighed heavily upon his mind knowing that he was leaving Anna behind while he pursued his mission. He only hoped that Visser would protect her long enough for his return from Aachen.

"Now listen," Pasteger blurted out. "When you get to Germany, you must make your way to the Brand District as soon as you touch German soil. Everything you need will be at *Herr* Gruber's. I will send a message when it is clear for you to enter Englebert, until then, try to get your bearings and stay clear of German authorities." His head snapped forward in alarm as the truck's brakes squealed in a sudden braking, its tires gritted in loose gravel, and the vehicle came to an abrupt stop.

Pasteger inched his way to the cab of the truck and rapped on the back wall of the cab with four short knocks. A single knock responded and he looked back at Thorne with apparent distress. Firm footsteps crunched in the loose gravel on both sides of the truck, moving from the front of the vehicle toward the back. Thorne hunkered down and motioned for Mathis and Pasteger to do the same. His hand slipped instinctively inside his coat to find his pistol, but he immediately relaxed his grip when the flap was thrown open revealing several German soldiers.

Thorne counted at least four submachine guns aimed into the back of the truck and braced himself for the hot lead that would spit their way. Instead, several tense seconds passed as the soldiers stood rigidly in place, guns at the ready. Another set of footsteps approached from the left side of their vehicle and a *Gestapo* officer came into view.

Chapter Thirty

UPON THEIR CAPTURE, THEY had been yanked from the bed of the truck and promptly searched by the Nazis. They took Thorne's pistol and identification papers, and promptly bound his hands firmly behind his back with a rough rope that burned his wrists. He'd been shoved into the back of a waiting *Gestapo* car along with Pasteger, while Mathis, and the other resistance men were lined up against the side of the truck. Thorne and Pasteger had found themselves momentarily alone, as the Germans stepped from the car to question the other men.

Pasteger swiveled in his seat, "Richard, there is more I didn't tell you. I have learned three things. First it seems the *Gestapo* are after you."

"I've already surmised that much."

"Just before your arrival, I received alarming information. Another British agent who recently dropped outside of Maastricht a few weeks ago was captured. He was looking specifically to meet a member of the Dutch resistance using the name Portia."

Thorne clinched his jaw in response; he saw that Pasteger took note of his dismay. "Yes, that's Anna."

"Apparently this agent has revealed much to the *Gestapo*. They have been searching for a man and woman traveling together. Flyers have been posted throughout the Low Countries with both of your photos."

Thorne nodded and looked over his shoulder, but could not see the Germans. "Yes, what else?"

"Richard," he said sternly. "I'm afraid they have her."

Thorne's heart sank into the pit of his stomach. "We must go back!"

"It is no use," Pasteger said, shaking his head in reaction to Thorne's dismay. "She is on her way to Germany."

"Germany? Why are they taking her there?"

"I can only speculate. The Nazis are in full retreat now. Brussels has been liberated and the Allies are racing toward Liege. I suppose the *Gestapo* is quickly pulling back ahead of their armies."

Thorne dropped his head against his chest and let out a deep gasp before turning back to face Pasteger. "The third thing, what is it?"

"Blackbird. I did not put two and two together until I had some time to think more on it. At first, I did not recognize the name when you mentioned it, but something in the back of my mind kept calling out to me. And then last night, in a dream, it came to me!"

"What? What came to you?"

"*Amsel.* That is the German word for Blackbird. The man I mentioned whom was on the Board of Directors, the one that was very close to Hartmann." Thorne listened intently. "He was our chief correspondent with Britain and secured financing from many sources. He always mentioned a mysterious colleague named *Amsel* who coordinated everything from England. I think he is your man."

"What is this man's name?"

"Tomas Becker." The name did not instantly come to Thorne. Pasteur continued, "He also used the name Thomas Beecher when he travelled abroad."

Amsel! It came to Thorne in a flash just then. That was the word he'd caught a glimpse of from Etta's desk so many days earlier. He suddenly felt sick.

Beecher is Blackbird.

THE *GESTAPO* CAR RACED through the streets of Liege; from the back seat, Thorne caught a glimpse of the steeple of St. Walburge in the distance. He looked at the heads of two German soldiers who rode in the front seat while he searched about the interior of the vehicle planning an escape. He shuddered to think of his companions' fate and hoped it had ended quickly. At the last minute, Pasteger had been pulled from the car and shoved in line with the others.

Now alone in the backseat, Thorne sized up both the officer and the driver in the front of the car; he recognized the insignia on the officer's collar as that of a sergeant. He could not see the driver's rank patches but assumed he was nothing more than an enlisted man. Thorne had at first thought it odd that neither the officer, nor any of the other soldiers, had spoken to either him or Pasteger upon their capture—not that there was any hope of creating a plausible story for their situation—however, when he was separated out from the others, he knew that he'd already been identified.

He looked out the window again as the car came to a stop at a border crossing. The driver rolled down his window and showed a paper to a guard. An unpleasant, pale face of a soldier peered banefully through the window at Thorne; he stuck his tongue out at the soldier, and they were impetuously waved on. As the road surface changed from a rough gravel-like form to that of smoothly paved asphalt, Thorne knew they were now in Germany.

His heart picked up its pace as he thought of what was to come, but he realized it was quite a different fate from that which his captors would surely set upon Pasteger and the other resistance members. The car travelled on a winding road flanked by large pines on both sides. He decided he could not wait until they reached their destination before he took action.

Almost immediately upon entering the car, Thorne had fumbled hopelessly with the rope bindings at his wrists. They were tied so firmly onto each wrist that he could feel his hands going numb from lack of circu- lation. However, he had also discovered that the soldier who had hastily secured him, had carelessly left several inches of space in the rope between his two wrists. He twisted his arms uncomfortably struggling behind his back to add a few more inches of slack to the rope.

After much effort he was able to stretch his hands apart just wide enough to slide the rope under his buttocks, and he now sat upon the rope across the back of his legs.

He looked again at the soldiers in the front seat. The officer looked back at him momentarily, but turned away as he gave directions to his driver. Thorne carefully twisted and turned in his seat, lifting his right leg followed by his left, and slid his hands—still secured by the rope—out from under him to rest on his lap.

In a flash, he slung his arms forward over the front passenger's seat, knocking the officer's hat forward and brought his arms down in a violent jerk causing the rope between his wrists to clasp around the officer's neck. He pulled with all his might and leaned backwards putting the full weight of his body on the rope.

The officer clutched at the rope, but his black leather gloves prevented him from getting a grip on the primitive garrote around his neck. The driver did a double take as his officer flailed about wildly beside him and stepped hard upon the brakes causing everyone in the car to lurch forward.

The momentum of the car's rapid deceleration worked in Thorne's favor by adding additional pressure to his victim's throat. Thorne tightened his stranglehold and leaned to his left jerking the officer's body into the driver. The soldier clumsily lost control of the steering wheel and the car veered across the road and skidded into a ditch. Thorne allowed the weight of the officer to keep pressure on the stranglehold and as the car began to tilt and swerve off the road, he braced for impact all the while keeping the rope taught around his victim's neck.

What happened next, he could not say for sure, but in a brief chaotic moment, the car rolled over onto its side while several things, including all three passengers, flew about wildly inside the vehicle. Thorne was pulled forward by the weight of the officer and thrown clear from his victim as the car hit something solid, stopping the pandemonium inside. He found himself precariously twisted against the side of the car. Still in the backseat, and apparently all in one piece, he instantly took account of every bone in his body.

Miraculously he was not injured. A groan came from one of the Germans. Thorne peered over the front seat and saw the driver hunched awkwardly under the steering wheel with a bloody gash on his forehead. The officer was crumpled next to him, eyes closed, lips foaming and struggling for air. His face was turning blue and his mouth moved queerly like a fish out of water.

Thorne brought his hands over his head and reached toward a section of broken window, using the jagged glass to cut through his ropes. Once his bonds had been broken, he squirmed over the front seat and reached for the Luger still strapped in its holster on the officer's hip. He promptly put a bullet in both of the Germans and looked for a way out of the wrecked vehicle.

He pushed upwards against the passenger door

which now lay above him as the car rested on its side. The door protested but after a firm shove, its bent frame gave way and opened upwards. He tucked the officer's Luger into his pocket and looked around the car for anything else of use. He grabbed a black leather dossier that the German had held moments before and scrambled through the open door of the vehicle. He stood on the pavement in disbelief looking in both directions down the paved road, and reassured that no others were nearby, he ran off into the adjoining woods that lined each side of the road that led to Aachen.

Chapter Thirty-One

RICHARD THORNE WAS IN GERMANY. He had escaped *Gestapo* capture and made his way to the boarding house of *Herr* Gruber in the middle of the night. Even now, he could not believe his good fortune. Once he had identified himself to Gruber, he'd been given a room and was left to go about his business.

As promised, Pasteger had taken care of all the arrangements. Thorne found a neatly tied bundle of clothing waiting for him on his bed. He untied the parcel to find several identification papers and other documents wrapped inside. There were two different outfits, one clearly that of a worker, and the other of an average German citizen. He looked over the papers and determined which were to be used as identification and work permits, and recognized the others as food rations and travel visas.

He's thought of everything.

He hurriedly changed into a set of civilian clothes and donned his new persona; there was no mirror in his room, so he had no idea how convincing his new identity was. All that mattered at the moment was that he now stood on German soil holding the papers he needed to walk about freely, carried enough Deutschmarks and ration coupons to obtain food, and held work papers that would allow him to enter the Englebert Tire and Rubber factory as an employee.

Thorne set about examining the contents of the leather dossier he had taken from the wrecked staff car. He shuffled through various documents, setting aside those that had no immediate meaning, but then his heart stopped as he came upon a letter addressed to all *Gestapo* units in *die Tieflander*; the Low Countries.

The letter had orders for all *Polizei* units to be on the alert for a Dutch woman and English man traveling together, wanted for espionage. The Nazis knew their true names and also had the various false identities they would be traveling under. The instructions for their captors clearly specified to expect their arrival in Liege, and to apprehend both suspects unharmed and return them to Germany. As he read the final lines of the German missive he stiffened in horror. The prisoners were to be taken to Englebert's executive offices.

How did the Nazis know all of this?

He dropped upon his bed with his full weight and looked again through the papers Pasteger had given him. Like a wave crashing upon a rocky shore, the pieces of the Blackbird puzzle fell upon him all at once; when the wave retreated, they lay scattered in front of him. His mind instantly tried to put them all in order: Beecher, Becker, Blackbird, Hartmann, Mueller, Englebert, Shakespeare, Portia, and Falconbridge.

Thorne was stunned. A lump formed at the base

of his gullet as everything became clear. Beecher was behind everything, and even worse, Thorne himself had been right in the middle of the illicit enterprise, relaying information between Beecher and Hartmann. How had he missed it? He slammed his fist into the mattress and took a deep breath.

It can't be true!

Thorne had worked for nearly three years under the employment of Thomas Beecher and would never have suspected him behind such a plot. He was dumbfounded. He thought back on his last meeting with Beecher, the man's face had distorted and turned grotesque as he challenged Thorne with his cruel words 'I can ruin you'. The threat had come out of nowhere, briskly and unexpectedly. Thorne had dismissed it almost immediately once Beecher's normally calm facade had returned.

But now there was no denying that Thomas Beecher was Tomas Becker. Thorne thought it brilliant that he referred to himself in third person as *Amsel* when he moved between Aachen and London; no one would have reason to connect Tomas Becker to his alter identity and certainly no one would be able to link him to Blackbird.

He wished for a way to reach back to Faulk, but knew it was all up to him. He had to get inside Englebert, had to find the proof he needed that would show SOE that an infiltrator had been working within their ranks.

He also had to get into Englebert and rescue Anna.

ANNA LARSEN AWOKE ON a lumpy cot in a poorly lit room that reeked of urine and sweat. She immediately relieved herself in a corner floor drain like dozens of other forlorn souls had done before her. She was stiff and sore from the ride out of Liege. She'd been tossed into the rear of a van, then handcuffed, and barbarically groped and strip-searched by two Nazis before being brought to the prison-like room where she now waited for the inevitable torture that would come.

Other than the initial interrogation on the street where she'd been abducted, none of her captors had spoken to her. She estimated she had been in the room for a few hours, yet no *Gestapo* officer had come to see her, and no one had even checked to see if she was still alive.

She wanted to cry, but years of living under cover with the Dutch resistance had hardened her; she did not know if she was capable of giving into her emotions. She had an ache deep in her gut that came not from physical contact but emanated from her very soul as she now thought of Richard Thorne and wondered whether she would ever see him again. She strongly doubted it, no one came to this place and left again—at least not alive.

Anna had been schooled on the torture process by her mentors. First would come questioning and then, depending on her resolve, the torturing would begin in an attempt to break her. She'd heard of physical abuses ranging from beatings, broken fingers and bones, to a dozen other diabolical means of inflicting pain. Even now she wondered how long she would be able to hold up.

But even as she shuddered to think of the upcoming assault on her body and her mind, she continued to imagine her reunion with Thorne. She had to find a way to escape. She was a tough girl; she knew how to take a punch and how to deal a number of blows in return that would send a man to the ground. If she could find just the briefest opportunity and overpower one of her captors, she might be able to secure a weapon, obtain a disguise, and find a way out.

She must survive. She must escape. She must find her way back to Thorne.

But even now, she had no idea where she was. She guessed she'd been driven for at least an hour after her abduction in Liege and could now be anywhere from Brussels, to Eindhoven, to Dusseldorf, or even Luxembourg. If she were no longer in Belgium, it would be virtually impossible for Stefan and his compatriots to locate her; their reach was limited, and if she were now in Germany as she suspected, no one would be coming for her.

THORNE SPENT THE NEXT few days familiarizing himself with the ancient town of Aachen. Life during wartime in Germany was not so different from that of the occupied territories. Bombed-out buildings smoldered, homeless families drifted from town to town, citizens formed long lines at warehouses and depots where food was distributed, and a general sullenness hung depressingly everywhere he looked. And then there was the Germany Army.

The *Wehrmacht* was building up its defenses, that much was obvious. Squads of infantrymen took up positions in abandoned buildings, set up anti-tank guns at significant crossroads, and blockaded bridges and other key thoroughfares. Half-tracks and troop transport trucks arrived continuously throughout the day depositing fresh soldiers who gathered in formations in the central part of the city.

Thorne traveled as he had in Belgium and Holland, in the disguise of a refugee. He walked with a stick and purposely moved in a hunched-over gait suggesting he was an elderly man. He knew the guise would not pass a close inspection, but hoped it would at least allow him to move about in plain sight at a distance from anyone who took notice.

The Englebert Tire Factory was not difficult to find. It was located in the center of a decimated industrial district to the east of Aachen. With simple instructions from a few citizens, he quickly found the tire plant. It was a massive complex made up of many buildings. Despite the Allies' best efforts to disable the German war machine, the Englebert factory was still under full production in the fall of 1944.

Thorne made several walks around the entire plant, some five hundred meters square, and made note of where soldiers were posted, where employees entered the facility, where workers were allowed to roam, and where they were not.

He familiarized himself with the daily operations of the factory. Trains arrived carrying chemicals and supplies, individual rail cars were offloaded into sidings on one end of the facility. Tires and other products were loaded back onto train cars and trucks on the opposite end of the complex.

German police, the *Werkschutzpolizist*, occupied the factory complex, complete with barracks and training grounds. He recognized the factory and railway police, who's grey uniforms differed from the other police factions who wore shades of light green. The majority of the police officers and guards posted around Englebert were middle-aged men. Thorne made note of the venerable, security staff, deciding how to use their unfit and aging faculties in his favor.

On the eastern side of the plant, employees waited outside gates in between shifts. Factory police inspected work permits and identifications as employees entered at their designated times.

Thorne walked on the north side of the factory complex on his way back to Gruber's. There, just inside the fence, under the watchful eyes of the factory police, workers emptied barrels of refuse into long pits where trash was burned. One worker pushed a barrel on a dolly, and even though the barrel was clearly marked with labels indicating flammable material, he walked dangerously close to one of the smoldering fire pits.

The man accidentally toppled his dolly sending his barrel rolling toward an open flame. A guard posted nearby started yelling "*Dummkopf!*" at the worker. The rolling barrel—some of its flammable contents had spilled and caught fire—crashed into the fence spilling more fuel.

As workmen dampened out flames with shovels, two guards continued to harass the employee who had dropped the barrel. They shouted names and kicked him. At one point, the man was knocked to the ground and he looked toward Thorne who stood beyond the fence watching the entire episode. The man seemed to reach out in a desperate plea, but there was nothing Thorne could do.

Chapter
Thirty-Two

ANNA WAS STRAPPED DOWN in the center of a cold room on a hard, wooden chair, facing a wide window that showed into an adjoining room. Her ankles were bound to the chair by tight ropes, and her arms and wrists were tied to a long pole that stretched out horizontally across the back of the chair. She clinched her fists intermittently to reassure herself that she still had feeling in her hands, but after a long period of sitting in this position, she could no longer tell.

For days—how many she could not be sure—she had waited in her dark cell, waited for her captors to begin their torture, and now she knew it was about to begin. She hung her head and took a deep breath summoning an inner strength for what was to come.

Her head snapped up when a German officer walked into the room alone; she immediately recognized him as Lieutenant-Colonel Gerhard Mueller. He smiled at her and walked circles around her twice before speaking. When he stopped directly in front of her, the toes of his polished, black jackboots rubbed against the insides of her feet, and he bent slowly toward her.

"We meet again Miss Larsen." His breath stank of onions and cigarettes. He stepped back a few feet but continued to study her face. "You're much prettier than the photos I have in your file; and much prettier than I remember from our last visit."

She projected a cold and subdued look telling him he was going to have to work to get answers from her.

"I know all about your operation, I have been following you for many months." He smiled at her, but she continued to stare at him, unwavering from her stolid visage. "I have much information on your subversive activities and the actions of your comrades." He slowly began to circle her chair again.

As he moved out of sight, her eyes darted back and forth looking for him, waiting for him to return to her peripheral sight. After circling three times he stopped behind her; a chill ran down her spine as he stroked her hair.

"But there are a few things you will tell me. A few missing pieces to the puzzle I seek." He clinched her hair and pulled on her head, but then released his grip. She began to perspire and talked to herself. *Be strong. Do not give in.* She reflexively shrank back in her seat as he came around her right side and brushed her cheek with the back of his hand.

He decided to go right for the information he wanted most. "Who is the British agent you are working with?" She did not answer. He waited several seconds. "You are going to tell me what you know." He looked closely into her eyes. "This is not the first time I've sought answers from your type."

She looked away as his face drew closer and she closed her eyes briefly. She took a deep breath and looked back at him staring blankly into his dark eyes.

"If you do not tell me what I want to know, I will be forced to take certain measures, certain *liberties*, to make sure you provide the details I seek." He removed his jacket and laid it on a table in the corner of the room. He turned back to face her and rolled up his sleeves. "I do not want to hurt you."

He walked to her left and stopped. With a sudden and swift movement, he swung the back of his hand and smacked it fiercely into her left cheek. She gasped at first, and then took a deep breath. "But I will do what is necessary."

Her cheek burned where he'd hit her. She stared blankly at the window in front of her, fighting back tears. He slipped behind her again, and locked his hands onto her shoulders, at first gently massaging, then slowly tightening their grip.

"Tell me. Who is he?" His thumbs dug into her spine between her shoulder blades. From behind the window, she saw another man watching her ordeal with a sinister smile across his lips.

She hysterically ran through countless scenarios in her mind, each more horrifying, each leading down a dark path of fear. If she gave him some information, some false lead, it would make things easier. She tried to think of a codename for Thorne. Something that would have no meaning. A word formed in her mind. "Dormouse," she said. "He goes by the name Dormouse." She cursed inwardly as she heard the word leave her mouth.

He released his hands from her shoulders and began to laugh. "Dormouse? That does not sound like a very daunting name for a British spy!" He laughed again and circled back in front of her. "Okay Miss Larsen, I will believe you for now. So where is Dormouse? Where was he going before you were captured?"

"I do not know."

He reached down and put his hand under her chin and raised her head slightly. She clinched her jaw in his hand. "But you must have been going somewhere. The two of you fled Maastricht for Liege. Why did you split up?" When she did not speak, he bent forward and kissed her firmly on the mouth.

His cold, dry lips pressed against hers, but she held firm and did not give him the satisfaction he sought. He released her chin and his hand slipped snake-like down her neck and unbuttoned the first button on her blouse. In the window, the man smiled as his hand inched toward the waist band of his pants. She thought of Thorne momentarily, and imagined him entering the room to pull Mueller away from her. A tear trickled down her cheek; she knew he would not be coming.

THORNE TRIED TO REST IN his bed at Gruber's boarding house. With his reconnaissance work done for the day, his thoughts turned toward the fate of his friends.

He imagined what would have happened to Pasteger and his band of compatriots by now, and reached a quick conclusion; the *Gestapo* would waste no time disposing of the men in the underground movement, but Pasteger would be spared. He would prove valuable to them—the *Gestapo* would likely keep him alive to use as a pawn in their counter-espionage schemes with SOE.

An abrupt knock on the door averted his attention from his horrid thoughts. An envelope slid into his room from under the door, and the retreat of steps beyond the doorway told him the messenger was gone.

He picked up the envelope and inspected its seal looking for signs of tampering, but could not tell whether anyone had opened it. Using his finger, he slipped it under the cover of the envelope and ripped open the top edge. He found a handwritten note folded over another document. The note read, 'Report tomorrow for your assignment at Englebert. Bring the enclosed work order. Ask for Otto Fischer.'

He used a match to burn the handwritten note, dropping its crumbled ashes into a waste basket, and then folded the work order in with his other papers.

Could Pasteger still be alive? He contemplated whether the note was part of the Belgian resistance fighter's well-coordinated plan, but then supposed Pasteger had already made the arrangements prior to his capture in Liege. Nonetheless, he knew it was time to uncover the mystery behind Falconbridge and Blackbird.

AT HIS OFFICE ON BAKER STREET, Thomas Beecher emptied the drawers of the old Mahogany desk where he had spent the past four years. He put matches, pencils, and other loose items into a box Etta had furnished to be taken to his other office at Norgeby house. One item, a German Luger he'd received from one of his agents, went into his personal attaché case.

Etta wrapped softly on the door before entering the room. "Sorry to disturb you Mr. Beecher. A courier is waiting outside; requires your signature. A dispatch from Bletchley Park."

Beecher went outside his office and signed for the letter nodding toward Etta to tip the dispatch boy. As she rummaged through her purse for coins, Beecher opened the letter. The delivery boy left and Etta went back to her task at hand of sealing boxes that would be moved down the street.

"Get me COHQ on the phone, extension One Eleven," Beecher barked after reading the missive. He rushed into his office and slammed the door behind him.

Momentarily, a voice came on the line and he calmly replied, "Yes, it's Beecher."

"He's dead, automobile accident," the voice flatly announced.

After a brief pause, Beecher replied, "A brilliant stroke of luck!"

Chapter
Thirty-Three

HE NEXT MORNING, THORNE made his way back to Englebert. He followed a group of men toward the factory entrance and as they neared the massive complex, others soon joined them from different directions combining into one mass of people headed for the main gate. In the gathering of men, he recognized a familiar face, the trash worker who had dropped the barrel the previous day.

Thorne made his way through the crowd and took up step alongside the shabby man. "*Guter Tag.*"

"Ah, *Guter Tag,*" the spindly man replied, obviously surprised that anyone would speak to him.

Others were immersed in conversation as they walked, so Thorne continued, "I saw you yesterday. When the barrel rolled away from you."

The man nodded and looked down with a frown.

"I would like to catch one of those guards off duty and give him a good kicking," Thorne added.

The thin man looked up and smiled. He spoke German in a broken dialect that Thorne at first could not place. "They do not like me because I am Polish."

"What is your name?"

"Josef."

"I am Nikolas," Thorne said, using the cover name provided by Pasteger. The crowd came to a halt just outside the main entrance as the workers began showing their identification cards to the security police before being permitted inside the factory. He waved goodbye to Josef after the guards inspected his work permits. Thorne watched from a distance as Josef crossed the expansive open ground between buildings and entered a large brick building with the letter K painted above the door.

Thorne found Otto Fischer in the administrative offices and was shown where to check his assignment board every day. He was taken to building B where he was expected to spend most of his time.

While he worked at sweeping floors and cleaning up around the building, he thought constantly of Anna. He also spent a considerable amount of time pondering over ways to get into the administrative building where Pasteger had told him to seek out the records he needed. He desperately wanted to rush in, grab the files, and run back to England with her in tow, but he knew patience was the only way to proceed. He also realized time was working against him. At any moment the American onslaught against the German-held city might begin, and there was no telling what would become of Englebert and its employees. He would have to look for opportunities to get into the administration building safely and without suspicion; he did not want to fail having come so close to his objective.

He'd already learned that access to anywhere within the factory complex was granted to employees by a work assignment card that was issued to them by Fischer. Upon entering any building on the facility, each employee had to show their personal identification and their card justifying their admittance. He thought it should be simple enough to exchange cards with an employee destined for the admin building, but that would take bribing someone out of their card or possibly stealing one from another employee—both options seemed like a good way to tip off the work police to his scheme.

As a member of the janitorial staff, Thorne was allowed to leave building B and had access to a limited number of other buildings, namely the maintenance shed near building B and the trash facility across the complex. Each time he had ventured beyond one of those locations, he was reprimanded for loitering or taking too long between visits.

He considered returning to Fischer's office claiming he had lost his assignment card and hoped a secretary or other member of Fischer's staff might be tricked into giving him a new card for the admin building, but as he thought through this scheme, he assumed his appointment to building B was recorded in a file; it would be difficult to convince someone otherwise. The more likely scenario would be that Fischer himself would either distribute a new building card to him, or reprimand him for losing the card which could jeopardize his future access to the plant. He worked through yet another strategy in his mind that involved overpowering a guard, but came up with too many disadvantages for that option to play out. All of these things played out in his head, over and over, as he pushed a broom, rolled a square rubbish bin around the factory floor, and went to and from his regular duties.

Thorne struggled with the puzzle of gaining access to the administration building, not so much with the task itself, but more with the *why* it was so difficult for him to come up with a plan. He had performed similar feats in the past, was well-trained in the art of espionage and sabotage, and this job was no different from other such affairs. The danger was the same. If caught, he would be treated as a spy. Torture and eventual death were the same outcomes. What was it that was different about his current undertaking?

Focus man, focus!

He thought of Anna, worried about her fate, wondered about her whereabouts, and wished he could see her again. It struck him then. His feelings for her had obscured his concentration on his current job. He had thought about her nearly constantly since their separation in Maastricht. Another line from Shakespeare worked its way to the forefront of his consciousness just then, 'Love is blind, and lovers cannot see the pretty follies that themselves commit'. He was confounded by his current line of thought, as if seeing himself from afar, muddled in a hopeless relationship and foregoing his duty to the Crown.

He had not had feelings—nor any consideration—for another woman since Catherine. It was a subconscious thing which only now came to the surface. He felt her presence hovering over him. Thorne had only met a few other women in recent years but had shown no interest in them personally; his focus had been purely professional. In fact, he now realized how much of a social recluse he'd become. Traveling incognito, keeping relations under the table, he was a shadow, he was a mystery man. No one knew, or even remembered the man named Richard Thorne. He had vanished from existence.

His recent reunion with Allan Faulk had brought the real person back to life. Someone knew his name, someone knew his story, someone cared. And then he fell in love with Anna. *Love?* Was he really in love with her?

"Hello Nikolas," a voice shook him from his thoughts.

He looked up to see Josef approaching.

Josef looked away as a guard passed them giving them both a suspicious glare. "I must go before we get in trouble. I will see you at the gate." He turned to walk away.

"Wait," Thorne said. "Where are you going? I will walk with you. Just let me grab my things."

Thorne pushed a trash cart and carried a broom as he followed Josef toward the tool building. He struck up a conversation with the Pole, inquiring about where Josef was allowed to go, what sort of duties he performed, and what he knew about the coming and going of guards at the facility. Thorne was careful not to reveal too much, he knew that Josef despised the guards that mistreated him, but did not know if he could be trusted.

At the tool shed, Josef put away a bag he carried and checked in with a soldier as he left.

"Let me see your pockets, I don't trust you Polish dog." The soldier roughly patted Josef down and finally pushed him away after finding nothing on him. The soldier spat at Josef's heels as he walked away. "I will be watching you Polish Dog."

Thorne watched from a safe distance.

Josef walked up to him. "The man is always a badger."

"Do not worry about him," Thorne said. "The Nazis have trained him to hate."

"Someday I will give it to him." Josef made a gesture with his fist, lifting it in an upper cut.

Then Thorne had an idea. He needed to win Josef's loyalty unquestionably.

"Is that the same one from yesterday?" Josef nodded confirming the guard's harassment during the barrel mishap. "Wait here."

Thorne walked back to the tool building with purpose and at first the guard paid him no attention, but as he entered the small building the guard followed. Josef waited at a distance to see what Thorne was about. After a few minutes, Thorne appeared in the doorway, wiping sweat from his forehead.

"He won't be bothering you again," Thorne said pragmatically. Josef looked past Thorne in shock and disbelief. "And I wouldn't come near here again for a few days." Thorne grinned as he took up the Pole's boney elbow, directing him away from the tool shed. "Where are you going next?"

"I have to meet Denski over there." He pointed off toward an area where other workers shoveled trash. "Do you know him?"

Thorne shook his head and explained he did not know any other workers, none but Josef. He followed Josef toward the trash pile and as they passed the central administration building, he asked, "Have you ever been in there?"

"Only to get work assignments. I do not work in this building."

"Do you know anyone who does?"

Josef stopped and looked deeply into Thorne's eyes.

This is it, the moment of truth.

After a second, Josef looked away and continued walking, Thorne kept even pace with him.

"I know someone who works in that building. Is there something you need?" He stopped again and turned to Thorne.

"I need to get inside. No trouble. I need access like I am supposed to be there."

Josef thought for a moment. "Okay, I will see you at the gate when we leave."

Thorne left Josef to his work and walked back to building B, all the while considering his approach with Josef. He should have made his intentions clearer instead of leaving it with Josef to coordinate, he should have asked him to arrange a meeting with the person that worked in the admin building. Yet there was something of a spark in Josef's eye, something mischievous, something revengeful that told Thorne he could be trusted. Josef could sense a game at hand, some kind of plot against his tormentors, something he could savor at participating in.

At the end of his shift, Thorne made his way to the entrance gate and loitered without drawing attention to himself. Before long, he recognized the doleful countenance of Josef coming his way, accompanied by another man.

"Josef."

"*Guter Tag mein Freund*," Josef replied, his face noticeably brightening.

Before he could make an introduction, the other man interjected, "Are you Nikolas?"

"Yes, Nickolas Boer," Thorne replied.

No danger yet.

"Josef told me about you," the man grinned. "I am Jan Bulicek."

Thorne, fearing a trick at hand, shook the man's hand. The man motioned him to follow and after clearing security guards at the admittance gate, they walked south away from the factory, in line with other workers leaving the plant.

Thorne looked the man up and down. His round face was covered with a stubbly beard. A bulbous nose protruded from beneath thick, bushy brows, and charcoal-grey circles under the man's eyes showed signs of exhaustion. His dirty hands bespoke of his life as a laborer. He was clearly not German, this Thorne could tell from his accent, but instead the man wore the mask of an immigrant. Eastern European he supposed. Was he working for the *Gestapo*? Was he an informant that Josef had inadvertently tipped off?

"I think I can help you," he continued. "You are looking for entrance into the offices?"

Thorne proceeded cautiously. "Not here," he said quietly as they continued walking not far from other workers. "Can you meet me later?" He impulsively played back images of the city centre in his mind, searching his memory for a neutral meeting place.

No, not neutral.

If this man were with the *Gestapo*, Thorne needed a place where he would have an advantage, an escape route, a way out if things turned against him. He'd seen the man nod affirming his agreement to meet at a later time.

"Seven o'clock. Aachen *Hauptbahnhof.*"

The man smiled and nodded in agreement, then disappeared into the crowd of people followed closely by Josef who waved goodbye.

A policeman positioned near the front gate watched the three men and turned to one of the soldiers who guarded the front gate. "Have you seen that man before?"

"Which one?"

The officer pointed at Thorne, "That man in the grey trousers and dark coat."

"Maybe. They all look the same to me."

ANNA AWOKE IN UTTER DARKNESS. A thin line of white light shown at the bottom of what she presumed was a doorway in front of her. It took a moment for her to adjust to the space around her. At first, she thought she was still in the *Gestapo* cell where she'd been the past several days, but then she recalled having been moved during the night.

She shuddered briefly thinking back upon Mueller's clammy hands groping her, but she shrugged it off, and whispered a thanks that he had not gone any further. Without notice, he had suddenly stopped his interrogation and left the room after someone came to the door. The man behind the window had cowered farther into the recesses of his dark hole.

She had feared she was being held for more questioning, or other nightmares she could hardly imagine, but instead, she'd been cut free from her bonds and promptly ushered out of the building where she was roughly hogtied and loaded into the back of a waiting truck by two armed soldiers.

She knew the *Gestapo* and *Abwehr* had established offices throughout the occupied territories, and also knew from her underground comrades that their prisoners were usually handled in one of two ways— either they were shipped off to a prison camp, or depending on the severity of their crimes, they were swiftly executed on site. She could not figure out why she had been moved, nor why her captors had only questioned her briefly.

When she'd arrived at her present location, it had been night, and now she only vaguely remembered her surroundings. It seemed she had been taken to a building adjoining, or enveloped by, other factory buildings. After the bindings on her feet were cut free, she was pulled out of the truck. The circulation was slow to return to her feet. Barely able to walk into the building on her own, she was dragged up three flights of stairs and prodded through a long-paneled hallway before being put into a small locked room that resembled an empty closet.

She now rested on a hard floor with her back against a wall, and other than the thin line of white light, there was nothing she could see. When she had first been shoved into the confined enclosure, she briefly caught a view of the barren room before the door was shut and locked behind her. In the darkness, she had confirmed there was nothing in the room, not even a light switch on the wall.

Her wrists were still tightly bound and she could not wrench them free. She put her hands in front of her on the floor and managed to push herself up to a standing position where she stretched in the inky blackness. Beyond the door, she heard footsteps walking across a tiled floor. At first, they were merely a feint rhythm echoing somewhere in the distance, but eventually they grew louder and with her ear pressed against the doorway, she saw shadowed movement in the light at her feet.

She moved backwards into the darkness and as the door opened, she turned away from the bright light outside, shielding her eyes in the palms of her hands.

Someone stepped into the room and grabbed her

arm turning her toward the door. She squinted through crossed fingers over her eyes and saw two figures standing in front of her.

"Bring her this way," one man told the other in German.

Chapter
Thirty-Four

THORNE FOUND HIS WAY BACK to Gruber's, all the while stopping and cautiously taking diversionary routes as he left the factory to ensure he was not followed. He still did not trust Bulicek and would take all precaution until he knew the man's intentions. Once he reached Gruber's, he made quick time in gathering his belongings. He changed clothes, swapping his dirtied, work trousers and overcoat for his civilian outfit. He tucked a wad of Deutschmarks inside his coat pocket and stuffed the Luger into the waistline of his pants. He would use either to entice Bulicek should he prove trustworthy ally or duplicitous foe.

Thorne had chosen to meet Bulicek at the *Hauptbahnhof*, the Aachen railway station, a huge building that was always busy with citizens and soldiers. He'd given the man three hours head start—plenty of time for the *Gestapo* to set a trap—perhaps too much of an advantage if in fact Bulicek's loyalty was with the Nazis.

Thorne knew that if the *Gestapo* were onto him,

they could be headed to Gruber's even at this moment. However, if Bulicek was on the level and could arrange access to the administrative office, he knew his mission was nearly complete.

It was time to move. Thorne would succeed and retrieve the information he sought linking Beecher and Hartmann to their detestable scheme, or he would be killed or captured in the attempt. Either way, he would not be returning to Gruber's boarding house.

A knock on the door jarred his attention, he opened the door cautiously to find Gruber waiting in the hallway.

"*Guter Tag.* Is everything okay with your lodgings?"

"Yes. Everything is splendid. *Danke.*" Thorne started to close the door, but Gruber hesitated, then nudged his foot across the threshold.

"Will you be staying long?" Gruber added, as if reciting a script for someone to overhear.

"I have business to attend to and will be leaving soon."

The dwarfish man scuttled into the room and quietly closed the door behind him. "I am sorry to meddle in your affairs," he added handing Thorne a folded letter.

"What's this?"

"A leaflet the Nazi's dropped earlier today; they have ordered an evacuation of the city."

Thorne skimmed through the lengthy missive that suggested among other things that the Allies intended to destroy the Reich and exterminate the people of Germany.

"A few fools such as myself remain, but everyone else is fleeing into the countryside," Gruber explained. "The Americans have the city surrounded and it is only a matter of time before their attack will begin. If you stay, you'll be conscripted. Squads are moving from house to house, pressing old men and boys into action to defend the city."

"I'm not worried about that."

Gruber looked toward the bed where Thorne's clothing was laid out.

"You cannot leave through the front door."

"I understand. Thank you, *Herr* Gruber. Do you have something to write on?"

Thorne jotted down a note—a brief account of his actions and whereabouts in the preceding days—in case he did not make it out of Englebert alive. He handed it to Gruber with instructions to get it to Pasteger in two weeks' time.

As if understanding Thorne's undertaking, Gruber simply nodded. "Take care and good luck to you," he added after a solemn moment. He turned and opened the door an inch, and peered through the gap before writhing through the doorway and closing it silently behind him.

Thorne grabbed up his bundle of clothes and tossed it into a large bush below his second story window. He climbed through the opening and hung by his fingers momentarily before leaping to the ground. He snatched up his clothing and slipped out the backyard of Gruber's, ever-cautious with every step, and made his way toward the *Hauptbanhoff.*

The leaflet Gruber had shown him, had had its intended effect. Everywhere Thorne looked, people—mostly women and children—were in a state of panic and confusion, and wandered aimlessly carting their meager belongings behind them. If nothing else, the Nazi missive had flooded the streets with civilians which would slow the Allied advance into the ancient city.

Thorne skirted his way around the center of town, making for the direction of the Aachen rail station. As he did so, he passed an air-raid shelter where soldiers tried to control a frantic crowd swarming around the entrance. He pulled his hat low over his eyes and unfurled his collar to help shield his face. The leaflet had declared that all men between the ages of sixteen and sixty who were capable of work should remain behind to assist with the deployment of makeshift fortifications and roadblocks. The last thing he needed was to be pressed into a work gang and prevented from accomplishing his mission.

THE COVER FROM THE DARKENED corner where Thomas Beecher lurked obscured his face. With his back against a paneled wall, he waited in a pub named *Northern Belle*, located in the seaside town of Margate, in the County of Kent. The seventeenth century pub sat tucked away on a street near the harbor that faced the Thames Estuary, and here Beecher waited for his contact to notify him when it was time to leave for Germany.

He did not look forward to the harrowing passage across the North Sea and finished another pint of beer giving him the bravado he needed. In a matter of minutes, he would be rowed out in a skiff under cover of night to meet a waiting U-boat that would shuttle him to a wharf in Hamburg, and despite his fear of water, he knew it was the only way to get into Germany under the current circumstances.

Across the room, two fishermen talked with the bartender while at the opposite end of the bar another man was seated by himself reading a newspaper—Beecher watched this man closely. He glanced at his watch wondering when he would give the signal.

Just then, the local constable ducked in from the pouring rain and greeted the bartender. He knew the fishermen by name, and nodded to the man at the end of the bar, as he joined in with the others. If he had seen Beecher, he had not paid particular notice to him.

As if sensing the urgency, the lone man at the bar swigged a shot of Irish whiskey and set his shot glass upside down on the countertop. Having given his signal to Beecher, the man folded his paper, thanked the barkeep and walked out of the *Northern Belle*. Beecher waited a full minute, then exited the pub, pausing only to open an umbrella near the door way.

Within seconds of their departure, the constable—prompted in part by his own curiosity, but also pressed by the suspicions of both the bartender and the local fishermen—followed Beecher out into the rain. It would be the next day before the policeman's body was discovered in a back alley, victim of a knife thrust downward into the top of his shoulder that had severed his left subclavian artery.

Chapter
Thirty-Five

I N THE CENTER OF OLD TOWN Aachen, Thorne walked in the shadows of the skeletal structure that was the *Rathaus*, the historic town hall, which had been bombed nearly a year early. The nearby cathedral—the primary coronation site of Germanic Kings and Holy Roman Emperors during the Middle Ages—had suffered relatively minor damage in comparison. He snaked his way through an array of twisting streets before arriving several minutes later at the Aachen rail station.

The magnificent edifice reminded him of an ancient castle, built in the medieval German style. The stone building, built in the years before the Great War, displayed a huge arched window over its main entryway, with dozens of smaller arched windows and portals lining the front wall. A large clock, framed by recessed notches that looked like arrow slits, hung over the main window, and a large, red Nazi banner draped neatly from the roofline above the clock.

A brattice protruded from the tower-like structure on the far left of the building, and from the viridian green roof line, four conical shapes rose up like miniature watch towers. He knew somewhere behind this splendid medieval veneer, Nazi police and *Gestapo* agents eyed every approaching citizen.

Amber light spilled out from the main doorway where dozens of soldiers and citizens came and went, and he paused to confirm the time on the large clock, ten before seven. In the spacious main hall, a cacophony of voices echoed underneath a vaulted ceiling. More banners hung throughout the structure, each baring the Nazi swastika.

He moved toward the right side of the building where he'd taken note of various side exits from his previous visit. He knew from here, should he need to make a hasty retreat, he had a few options. He had an escape route by foot along a perpendicular street lined with row houses, he had access to departing trains through a wide tunnel that led behind the station, or he could simply blend in with foot traffic leaving the station.

A line of soldiers paraded in front of Thorne and moved into the corridor leading to the covered platforms behind the station. They shuffled by him with their packs of gear as their superior officers barked orders at them. On the opposite end of the terminal, a line of refugees underwent the usual inspection of identification papers and confirmation of their destinations.

Thorne found a row of benches and sat by himself. From here, he kept an eye on people coming in through the main doorway, and also kept a clear view of the main corridor where travelers rushed about beneath the vaulted ceiling.

Just before seven, he caught sight of Bulicek entering the station; he was alone. Thorne instantly moved to the foreigner's position, caught him up by the elbow, and motioned the venerable man to move toward the far side of the enclave, opposite a long tunnel jammed with soldiers lined up against each wall.

"Nice to see you have arrived safely." He released his grip on Bulicek's arm.

"Yes, and I trust the same for you?"

"No capers now," Thorne added. They moved back into the main lobby of the station where Thorne pointed out an empty bench. "We will sit over there. Just know that I am prepared to take any necessary action."

"It is good to know you are a cautious man. No worries from me, I'm no Nazi."

Thorne looked around the enclave, suspecting that eyes watched from everywhere within the building. "Then why are you helping me?"

"You did not make your intentions clear, but it is obvious that you are up to something if you wish to gain access to the offices at Englebert. If I can help create chaos for the Germans, then I am your servant."

"Are you with a resistance group?" He paused as two German officers, railway police dressed in grey uniforms, passed them by, engaged in their own exchange.

Bulicek laughed aloud. "I am too old for such games. But I will tell you I have no love for the Nazis.

They invaded my homeland in Bohemia. I was too old to fight, so I was sent to a factory in Dresden. Later they moved me to Frankfurt, and finally I ended up here in Aachen. I have not seen my family in four years."

Both men waited several seconds before continuing their conversation, all the while watching for signs of their discovery. Thorne started to speak again, but his heart skipped a beat as a *Gestapo* officer rounded the corner, looked in their direction, then sped away on a different errand.

"Let's walk." He helped Bulicek up from the bench and the two men crossed to the other side of the building. They paused at the base of a square column that held one of the ridge lines supporting the vaulted ceiling above.

"What is it you're looking for?" Bulicek asked, confused by Thorne's erratic movements.

"A room in the basement that holds records. I need to get in without suspicion, recover some information, and get out just the same. Can you help?"

"I am familiar with the security there. I can get you into the building, but you will be on your own to find your way to the basement." Bulicek scrunched his bushy eyebrows and stared intently into Thorne's face. "I will likely have to bribe someone to help us."

Thorne sensed the Bohemian testing the waters. "That's not a problem. I can take care of that. Also, I'm looking for a girl, a prisoner. Have you seen anyone like that?"

"No, but if they have her, then she is likely in that building. I can think of nowhere else they would hold someone." He suddenly changed the tone of his voice, speaking in a high, throaty inflection using German, "*Ja, Frankfurt. Zugnummer achtzehn.*"

A German officer passed directly behind Thorne. He repeated to Bulicek, "*Ja, Frankfurt.*" The officer continued on, heedless of their conversation.

"Will you be at the factory tomorrow?" Seeing Thorne nod, he continued, "I will take care of everything."

"Wait here." Thorne walked across the gallery and purchased a newspaper. He thumbed through the paper while standing in front of the newsstand, unsure whether anyone watched his capers. With the sleight of hand of a practiced magician, he slipped a wad of Deutschmarks into the paper and folded it under his arm. He walked back to Bulicek who stood patiently at the column, and handed the paper to him. "You will find what you need in here. Until tomorrow," he added with a tip of his hat.

THE NEXT MORNING, THORNE took up his usual duties sweeping an area of building B. His neck ached, a result of uncomfortable lodgings he'd secured the night before in an abandoned box car. He later arrived at Englebert without harassment from the *Gestapo* or *Werkschutzpolizei*, yet he could not help wondering whether a trap had been set.

He carried the Luger and worried about being

found with it. If it was discovered, there would be no questions, he would be taken away and shot. As soon as he found a secure location, he stowed it away for later retrieval; he would take no chances before he carried out his plan.

Around the middle of the day, he was moving a barrel of rubbish out of building B when he saw Josef. The gaunt man waved frantically and rushed over to his position.

"Jan will meet you inside building C at two o'clock."

"Will you be there too?"

"I will watch out for you there at an open freight door." He looked around cautiously. "Have you heard? They have locked the front gates, no one is to leave."

Thorne had wondered about the large group of employees huddled around the fence near the main gate, now he guessed at the reason for the gathering of workers.

"I must go," Josef said, and then hastily moved away from Thorne.

At precisely two, Thorne went to building C where he saw Josef busily at work replacing a wheel on a dolly in front of an open garage door. Josef nodded as he passed, and just beyond the doorframe, inside a darkened storeroom, he found Bulicek waiting for him. Even in the dim light, he could make out the familiar, warm smile of the Bohemian.

"I have taken care of everything for you. You were very generous."

Thorne hung back, burying himself deeper in the

shadows where Bulicek stood next to a refuse barrel sitting on a small cart.

"Are you sure you have everything in place?"

"Yes. We haven't much time, so listen carefully." Bulicek lifted a layer of papers in the barrel and revealed a badge that read *Hausmeister*, which Thorne recognized as the word for janitor. There was also a work card permitting him into the administrative building. A few rusty tools, and a flashlight also lay amongst the trash. Thorne acknowledged them as Bulicek placed the papers back on top of the hidden items.

"You will enter the building through the main entrance as if you are reporting for regular assignment. Show your identification at the checkpoint. You will be familiar with the officers there, maybe Krause, Hoffman or Dieber. You know them?" Bulicek continued, "Good. They do not know about this, so it is business as usual. Instead of continuing to the administrative area, you will turn into the first hallway on your right. Do you know it?"

Thorne nodded, recording every detail in his mind.

"Wear the badge from that point on. There are stairs that lead down to the telephone exchange. It is located in the central core of the building, just below the offices you are familiar with."

Thorne nodded again and looked over his shoulder to ensure no one approached.

"You will see the sign *Telefonzentrale*. The layout of this floor is the same as the main floor. Walk around the exchange room until you see a door on the far side marked *Renigungspersonel*. In this room for the cleaning employees, you should be alone until the end of the day. From there, go to the far side of the exchange where another set of stairs takes you to the next basement level. Do you understand so far?" Bulicek asked, reaffirming Thorne's comprehension of the directions.

"At the top of the stairs, sits a guard. His name is Meier. You will recognize him by a black mustache like Hitler's. He has been paid to let you proceed. Use the stairs that go down to the power room. *Mashinerraum,*" he repeated slowly. "There is another door there labeled *Speucherebene*, it will take you to the lowest level of the building, the storage area, where you will find the records room." He paused while Thorne digested this information.

He expected him to ask several questions or repeat it back to him; instead, Thorne replied, "Got it."

"From there, I am afraid you will be on your own my friend," Bulicek continued. "I cannot guarantee whom else you will encounter in this building."

To be caught would be fatal. In all his years serving SOE, this was perhaps Thorne's most dangerous mission, and he realized for the first time, his own planning had brought him here, not the orders of Beecher. "I am not sure how I can thank you enough for your help."

"If your errand helps bring about the end of the War, then that is thanks enough. With God's blessing, someday you may find me in Prague after this ordeal. Then my friend, we can share thanks."

A loud cough alerted them to danger—the

predetermined signal from Josef. Thorne wheeled the refuse barrel past an officer approaching the building. He smiled at the officer as he walked by and turned back toward the open garage door. Josef and Bulicek had already vanished.

ANNA WAS DRAGGED INTO a long hallway, paneled in dark wood, and pushed forward by a German soldier who waved a pistol at her threateningly as she stumbled along. They followed a white-haired man in a grey suit that walked ahead of them. The older man stopped at a pair of large doors that opened into a long room with an oak table framed by a dozen or more chairs. The soldier pushed her into the room and closed the door behind them. He took up a position next to the door, standing at attention with his pistol still held firm and ready.

"Please sit down," the older man said. His accent was that of an English man.

As her eyes adjusted to the brightly lit room, she was bewildered by the ambience of the elaborately decorated meeting room. She nudged a chair back from the table with her knee and sat in its soft padded seat, which felt overwhelmingly comfortable after the hard, tiled floor where she'd slept for the last several hours.

She looked over several paintings and photographs of business men lining the walls, and frowned at a familiar Nazi flag positioned in the corner of the room.

The older man drew back a set of curtains, and again she turned her head away as her eyes adjusted to bright sunlight from outdoors.

"Is there anything I can get you?" After seeing her lick at her dry lips, he told the soldier, "Bring a pitcher of water please."

The soldier left the room and closed the door behind him. She looked across the table searching for anything to use as a weapon against the frail man but doubted she could overtake him just now. He stood opposite her next to the window. The soldier returned carrying a beautifully engraved sterling silver tray with an equally exquisite, glass pitcher of water, and for a fleeting moment, she considered tripping him in hopes of grabbing his weapon, but in her present state she decided to wait for a better opportunity. He poured a glass of water and set it in front of her. Using both hands, she cradled the glass and longingly quenched her thirst taking the contents down in one drinking.

"I apologize for your harsh treatment, but you must realize they consider you a spy. It is only at my request that you are still alive."

She licked at her parched lips now that her tongue was moist. "What do you want?"

"Ah, no beating around the bush with you Miss Larsen, or should I call you by the name I am more familiar with, Portia."

Her eyes widened when she heard the name. Her immediate fear was for that of Thorne, he must have been captured and shared her codename. She could only guess at what torture he must have endured in order to have revealed her identity, and a tear formed in the corner of her eye.

"You do not know me, but I feel as though we have met. You may be familiar with the name Blackbird?" He paused letting this hit home. "I know that you are familiar with the name Falconbridge." He continued to watch her reaction.

Her gaze changed to a stone, cold complexion; she was not going to willingly admit to knowing anything he threw at her.

"It was such a shame that he was killed. I will find out what happened in due time. But for now, there is something else I am more interested in. The information you used to get from Falconbridge, did you ever stop to consider its purpose?"

She shook her head in denial. She desperately craved another drink of cool water but was afraid to ask.

"Well, you see, Falconbridge was working for me. So, in a way, you were working for me also."

"I do not work for Nazis."

He smiled back at her cold eyes. "Neither do I. That's the beauty of it. No one really knows whom they are working for sometimes. You may have thought you were working for Stefan, but do you know whom he works for?" Her eyes darted away from him momentarily. Again, she wondered if they had captured Thorne or whether someone else had revealed their names.

"So many people are caught up in worrying about the Allies versus the Axis, good versus evil. That's not what this is about. Someday this war will be over Miss

Larsen and with any luck, we'll both be around to enjoy it. And hopefully your friend Thorne will be around to share that joy with you."

At this, he turned to the soldier, and using German, ordered him to leave the room. When the door closed, he walked over to Anna and pulled a knife from his pocket. She tensed up for what was about to come, but he gracefully reached down and cut her bindings. The ropes fell upon the table as she rubbed her wrists; she kept her eyes on the older man the entire time.

"You see, this is not going to be some *Gestapo* torture, this is simply a conversation between employer and employee. Perhaps you've heard Thorne mention my name, Thomas Beecher?" When she showed no reaction, his anger flared. "Trust me, I could have let these bootlickers have their way with you long before I got here. This could be a totally different situation right now if not for my influence."

"What is it you want from me?"

"We'll get to that in a moment. But first, let me gain your trust." He walked behind her to a door.

As she turned to see what he was doing, she now noticed several doors along the wall at her back. He opened one of them and reached inside turning on a light switch.

"This is where you'll be staying. No more rough conditions. You cannot leave, be assured there are armed men throughout this building, but while you are here, you may at least be comfortable."

He motioned for her to go into the room.

She slowly rose from her chair, mostly out of

curiosity, and sidestepped to a point where she could look into the doorway. She saw a lavish room with opulent furnishings, floral wallpaper, and velvet curtains. He stepped back from the doorway seeing her hesitance to enter.

"You'll find a bath at your disposal and all the comforts of luxury. Once you have settled in, I will have them bring you something to eat." He walked across the long room toward an oval table that held crystal bottles and fine glassware. He opened one of them and poured two glasses of a dark liquor.

"Here, please enjoy this Brandy, it will put you at ease." When she declined, he set the glass on the long table and took a sip from his own. "You're going to be here for a while, so you might as well relax and take advantage of my hospitality before I change my mind."

"Why are you keeping me?"

"When was the last time you saw Thorne?"

"I don't know. It has been hard to keep track of time the way your men have kept me locked away in dark places."

"Was it in Maastricht? I know he used to meet you there."

She decided to play along and see how far this would go. "No, the *Gestapo* were looking for us. We moved to Brussels."

"Brussels? But they picked you up in Liege. When were you in Brussels?"

"We were moving to Brussels but then changed our plans," she added in an attempt to throw him off.

"I doubt you were headed to Brussels. The Americans have already liberated much of Belgium."

She looked away, camouflaging her lie.

"Perhaps if you'd gone to Brussels, you wouldn't be here now," he chuckled. "But back to Thorne, did he accompany you to Liege?"

"We went our separate ways. It was too difficult to travel together," she added reluctantly.

"Where was he going?"

"I don't know."

Why the questions about Thorne? Maybe he is alive! Her heart beat faster in anticipation.

"I do hope you didn't have a spat."

"Spat?"

"A fight. Did he break up with you?"

"Break up? No, we were just traveling together, nothing else."

"I hope he's not in danger. You see, I lost contact with him when he returned to Holland. He's usually very thorough about staying in touch." He watched her walk over to the window and look out upon the factory grounds. "As you can see, there is nowhere for you to run. You are in Germany now. Every soldier in this complex will be on alert watching for you. As long as you stay here—in your adjoining apartment that is—you will be safe."

She looked up at him and immediately looked back out the window.

"When the time comes, I can get you safely out of here. If you agree to behave yourself and cooperate with me, I will make it as pleasant as possible."

Tears suddenly streamed down her cheeks uncontrollably.

"Are we in agreement?"

She nodded reluctantly.

Chapter
Thirty-Six

THORNE RECITED EVERYTHING to himself that Bulicek had shared about the administration building. He visualized every turn that he was familiar with, and tried to imagine those he was not. Bulicek hadn't specifically noted the time of day for the operation, but it was clear from his mention of the familiar guards' names that he assumed Thorne would enter by day.

Thorne had no intention of walking into the file room during the middle of the day; he knew a staff of Nazis worked around the clock, but assumed fewer employees were on duty in the middle of the night, but with the recent lock down of the factory complex, he could no longer be sure of anything. He also doubted whether he could gain entrance through the front door without a reasonable explanation.

He decided to take a chance and search for a different entrance he could use at night. It had been dark for nearly three hours when he slipped from concealment behind the tool shed to a hedgerow that framed the administrative building. He was on the south side of the building watching the entrances in his view, taking note of whom he saw within the building, and watching who was coming and going, when a truck approached and stopped near the side door.

Two soldiers jumped out of the back of the canvas covered truck. He ducked and watched through a thicket of foliage and twisted branches to see what they were about. He couldn't be sure, but thought a third person came out of the truck as another set of feet showed briefly. When the truck pulled away, it momentarily blocked his view of the soldiers, when it moved out of the way, he could see the side door to Englebert was errantly left slightly ajar, however the soldiers were nowhere in sight.

Grasping the opportunity, he rushed from the darkness and made for the door. He clipped on the janitorial badge as he stepped inside a long, well-lit tunnel that was empty; the soldiers had already moved on by the time he made entrance. From the location of the door, he knew he was one level below the main floor.

Thorne rushed through the corridor, passing several unmarked doors and halted at an intersection with another hallway. He guessed he had walked all the way to the central part of the building; a sign confirmed the central telephone exchange room lie just ahead. He walked around the corner with purpose but saw no one in either direction; he knew he must find the supply room before someone questioned him on his business.

He carried with him a small canvas bag which held the few tools and other items Bulicek had given him. As he recalled Bulicek's directions, he turned left in front of the telephone room and continued toward another corner at the far end of the hallway. Bulicek had failed to tell him that there were windowed doors that gave access to the phone exchange. As he passed each door, he looked inside; several workers busily transferred calls by plugging and unplugging black wires on switch boards that surrounded them. None of them took notice of him.

He came to the door marked *Renigungspersonel.* Two soldiers walked in his direction from the far end of the passageway, but neither paid him attention as he opened the door and entered the supply room.

It was a crowded room lined with shelves full of cleaning supplies. He grabbed an empty bucket and emptied his tool bag into the bottom, covering the screwdriver, the rusted pair of pliers, and the flashlight Bulicek had given him with rags. Looking over the various cleaning supplies, he discovered a square can that contained a stringent alcohol-based chemical he was not familiar with, but he guessed from the strong fumes that its contents were highly flammable. He tucked the can into the bucket and scanned the shelves for anything else of use. A box of matches and a candle made their way into the tin pail. Lastly, he pulled the Luger from inside his overalls and checked the magazine, it held five bullets. He tucked it back where he could agilely retrieve it when needed.

As he left the room, bucket in one hand and mop in the other, he headed to the far end of the telephone room and turned again to his right looking for the stairway that led down to the next level. He heedlessly descended the stairs and stopped just before the bottom. From there, he could see a guard desk just beyond the doorway, but it looked as if no one was there. He scampered out of the doorway and bypassed the desk, moving into the next stairwell.

As he took his first step down, he paused considering the soldiers from the truck he'd seen just minutes earlier. He replayed the scene in his mind.

I should've risked a better look!

There was something about the movement of the soldiers; the first two jumped out freely but they had to assist a third.

A prisoner?

Then his heart sank in his chest.

Anna!

His mind raced wildly through a dozen scenarios, each supposing that she could be here now. He stood frozen in deliberation. Finally, he took a deep breath and forced himself to put her out of his mind.

Get the records first.

In the brief moment while he agonized over her predicament, a squadron of soldiers shuffled past the open doorway where he hovered and passed his location. He waited a few seconds until their footsteps faded out of range before proceeding down the stairs to the next level. Just as Bulicek had promised, there was another door leading to a stairwell to his immediate right.

So far so good.

He rounded the corner and made his way to the

lowest level of the Englebert building. At the bottom of the steps he stopped, invoking his practiced routine. *One, two, three.* He slowly exited the stairway into a dimly lit hallway and found the records room.

He sighed in relief when he found no one else in the room. It was lined with rows of file cabinets and he quickly crossed the room to a door on the far side which opened into a closet that had boxes stacked against its back wall. *A good place to hide if someone happens along.* He left the closet door ajar and returned to the main doorway where he peered out again into the empty hallway. Ever cautious, he set to work devising a simple trap in case someone arrived in the middle of his errand.

Thorne took the tools from the bucket and transferred them to his pockets, and left the rags which he'd soaked in cleaning chemical in the bottom of the bucket. He removed the lid from the cleaning fluid can and positioned it so that when the door opened inward, it would knock the can over spilling its contents. He also placed the mop in a position in which it would also fall with the opening of the door and tip the bucket over in the same place as the can.

Next, he melted the end of the candle creating a puddle of wax in the lid of the can, and pushed the end of the candle into the wax. As it cooled, he tested it out. The lid made an excellent base for the candle and he placed it in a position on the floor so that it too would fall into the spilled chemicals. He lit the candle and stood back surveying his work. The trap would make enough diversion for him to run to the closet to hide.

It was not the best plan, but he was confident it would buy him time in case he was discovered.

Finally, he set to carrying out his task. He opened drawers thumbing through file folders and envelopes; much of the information appeared to be records of shipping details. Older documents dated prior to 1938 showed the factory had produced tires and rubber goods, but as he turned to files labeled in more recent years, they showed the factory output had shifted to strictly military output—truck tires, tank tracks, and even army boot soles were the majority of goods produced at Englebert during the War.

He turned to another set of cabinets finding still more documents regarding the ordering of supplies and raw materials. He pulled a file that showed a steel, ball bearing order from Sweden in 1942, and chemicals received from overseas in South America. He laid these aside starting a pile of documents that had relevant information. He shifted his attention to a cabinet on the far side of the room, and as soon as he looked upon its contents, he guessed he was in the right location.

Many of the folders were labeled in bold red letters *Vertraulich*—these files were meant to be confidential—but why the cabinet was not locked, he could not guess. He thumbed through the contents and found what he was looking for; a stack of records showed transfers of funds through the Reichsbank to BIS, the bank in Switzerland Faulk had mentioned. As he rummaged through the files, it was clear that this was the evidence he needed showing how money flowed from the Bank of England, to BIS, and back to Englebert.

He retrieved several documents that showed the money trail, but there were no names in the records; he needed something that linked Beecher and Hartmann to Englebert. Returning to the first row of cabinets, he searched for something that had piqued his curiosity. The bottom drawer contained a history of the executives of Englebert and other personnel. He looked through the files and found they were ordered by year, and contained the names of the Board of Directors and Senior Management within Englebert. In multiple places he found the name Tomas Becker.

That's it!

While he knew Beecher's given name was Thomas, he also knew it was not a common man's name in Germany; he could recall having seen the spelling Tomas used in other surrounding countries, including the Netherlands, the Baltics and many others, but never in Germany. He continued searching the files until he found a folder that contained photographs and names of the company officers. There, on a page from 1941, was a photo of Tomas J. Becker; this was what Thorne needed. He assumed Faulk already had a means to tie Beecher to Blackbird, and with the photo of Beecher seated on the Board of Englebert, along with the records of funding, he hoped there was enough evidence for Faulk to link everything together. The only thing missing was Hartmann.

Pasteger had said that Hartmann served as head of security at one time. Thorne wished for a watch—he guessed he'd already been in the file room for several long minutes, he could not be sure how much more time he had. He sped up his search. Looking back in the personnel files that listed various positions of employees, he hunted for the title *Sicherheit*, the German word for security, but could not find it; nor had he seen the name Hartmann in the previous files. He closed the file cabinet and reconsidered where Hartmann's records would be.

Scanning the labels of each file cabinet and drawer in slow motion, he finally came to the end. The last drawer in alphabetical order contained files W through Z; in this drawer, he located a folder labeled *Werkschutzpolizist*, Factory Police.

Thank God for German efficiency!

In the folder Thorne read lists of various officers and their titles, including one Karl Hartmann, *Brigadefuhrer;* he pulled these pages and added them to his stack.

He carried the papers to a table in the center of the room, and carefully sorted through them to see if he had everything he needed. He grouped them into smaller piles, walking through the process in his head. Hartmann would request funding from Beecher, the money would then move between the Bank of England to BIS, some of the cash was funneled to the Reichsbank, while the rest was transferred to other firms in Scandinavia and South America where raw materials were shipped back to Germany and made their way to Englebert.

He decided he had enough evidence to put together a story that Faulk or others in SOE could use as evidence against the scheme. He looked around the room for a container to conceal the files in. He could no longer use the bucket; the soaked rags had left a pool of chemical in the bottom that would ruin the documents, so he returned to the storage room and searched for an empty box, but each seemed too bulky to easily carry without causing suspicion.

On a shelf he found an open gunny sack with a single sling. It did not have buttons, nor a way to close the bag, but he decided to use it and carry the strap over his shoulder while tucking the bag under his arm.

He had everything he needed. He only had to find a way out of Englebert without being caught.

Chapter
Thirty-Seven

THORNE LURKED THROUGH THE TUNNELS of the lowest levels of Englebert's administration building, cautiously retracing his steps. He scaled the risers in an empty stairwell, focused on how to eliminate any threat he might encounter. He carried the bucket, now full of soaked rags—before leaving the file room he'd emptied the chemical contents onto them—along with a mop, and kept the satchel with the evidence against Beecher tucked closely under his arm.

He longed for his FairBairn-Sikes fighting knife or Ballester–Molina Faulk had given him, but the Luger with five bullets would have to do.

As he considered his options, where he might encounter roadblocks and how to remove each, something else gnawed at the back of his mind. *Where was Anna?* He was not prepared for a rescue mission, not by himself, and certainly the information linking Beecher to Englebert was of far greater importance. Or was it? He deliberated on what he was really after.

He intuitively felt that the plot he'd uncovered

would help unravel a larger funding scheme of some sort. It was critical that he escape Englebert alive with the documents in hand, without them, there was no other proof directly linking Beecher to the scheme. If he could relay the information back to Faulk and MI5, and interrupt the flow of funds to Englebert, and possibly other German factories, it would be a slight distraction at best to Hitler's war machine, but perhaps there were other clues that would shed light on something larger at work behind the curtain of war.

Unsure of Anna's whereabouts, he hadn't formulated a plan for rescuing her, nor accounted for what he would do if he came across her. He paused at the top of the steps. What if she were still downstairs? He tried to put her out of his mind.

Focus man, focus!

The task before him was clear.

Get out of Englebert alive, get the documents back to England!

Looking out of the stairway onto a sign that read Machine Room, he counted slowly in his head. Thorne tried desperately to fight off the adrenaline fueling his system. His immediate impulse was to run, flee, get away as quick as possible, yet some other rationale part of his brain sought calm, and forced him to slow his pace. As he started toward the stairway exit, he heard a low gruff signaling someone close by. He inched out of the stairwell and immediately turned toward his right making for the doorway that led up and out of the lower levels.

"You there. Wait a minute," a firm German voice

came from behind him. He stopped, and in a slow motion turned on his heels to face a hefty soldier who stood up from the previously empty desk. There was no one else in the corridor. The soldier walked over to him—by the lack of mustache, Thorne realized this was not Meier, but a different man.

"Where are you coming from?"

"I was cleaning downstairs as I was told," he replied in German, imitating a foreign accent.

"Who gave you orders to clean down there?"

Thorne looked dumfounded; he did not know the names of the cleaning staff nor superiors he supposedly worked for. As he searched for a name to throw out, "Schmidt," was the first that came to mind.

"Let me see your identification and work orders."

Thorne set his bucket down and went into action. In a swift upward movement, he thrust the handle of the mop toward the guard catching him with the blunt point of the handle in the soft underside of his chin. The unexpected blow sent the heavyset man reeling backwards, cursing through clenched teeth. Before he had a chance to respond to the blow, Thorne rushed the guard who stood hunched over clasping his chin in both hands and stomping his foot on the floor.

The guard's eyes widened as he saw Thorne leap for him; he did not have time to recognize a long steel blade as that of a screwdriver, he only saw Thorne's fist plunge the steel into his throat. He fell back against the wall, clutching the screwdriver with both hands, and made gurgling sounds in his throat as blood poured down the front of his uniform.

Thorne let go of the mop handle as soon as it had hit its mark, and now reached inside his overalls pulling the Luger from concealment. He held the gun against the soldier's chest intending for a quick kill to the heart, but the gun jammed and would not fire. He slammed the pistol into the side of the man's head, silencing the wounded guard, who slid down the wall to rest at the foot of the floor. Thorne stuffed the useless weapon back into his pockets.

The screwdriver fell to the floor, expelled by the flow of blood from the dying guard which oozed across the smooth, tiled floor. He struggled to drag the unconscious heavyset man behind the desk and was just able to dump the body out of sight. The mop proved useless in his attempt to wipe up the pool of blood; it simply created crimson streaks across the tiled floor in his effort to conceal his crime. He finally tossed the mop behind the desk on top of the guard who would be dead shortly.

Thorne's heart pounded in his chest, threatening to leap from his body. He dashed into the adjacent stairwell and took the steps two at a time as he sprinted upwards. Now time worked against him—it wouldn't be long before someone discovered the guard and sounded an alarm. He came out of the stairwell in the same fashion as before, immediately turning to his right where he moved as swiftly as he could without running. He glided past the telephone exchange room and found his way back to the supply closet.

He started to close the door, but as he stepped inside the supply room, he saw traces of blood from his boots throughout the hallway. Gasping in deep breaths, he gathered up loose rags and began thoroughly wiping down his feet and hands. He reached for a can of paint, dabbing it over splotches of blood spattered down the front of his work clothes and searched the room for anything else to aid his escape. He took up a push broom leaning against the wall, twirled it in his hands loosening the handle, and pulled the shaft from the broom head. He then placed the bristled end into the bucket and tucked the makeshift staff under his right arm.

He took another deep breath, concentrating on the remainder of his escape. He would leave the room, move to the right, then turn left at the end of the hall. From there he would pass the telephone exchange and continue on into the narrow passageway which exited the building. Once through the outer door, he would make for the line of shrubs some twenty meters distant, then finally work his way back to building B, where he would figure out how to get out of Englebert.

But what about Anna you fool?

Thorne knew that once he left the building, and Englebert for that matter, there would be no turning back—if he were to rescue Anna, he had to do it now or never. He would have to stash Beecher's paper trail and search for her post haste; there was no other option. He decided to hide the papers in the bushes just beyond the entrance and then resume his search for her.

Convinced he had a plan laid out, he exited the supply room. No one had apparently discovered his handy work downstairs yet. He stepped over streaks of blood in the hallway and moved to the end of the corridor, but as he rounded the corner, two men approached from the opposite end of the hall. The older of the two wore civilian clothing, the younger was dressed in a soldier's uniform. Thorne crouched to tie his boot lace, shielding his face from the two men.

They stopped in the middle of the passageway, near the exit tunnel. It was then that Thorne recognized a voice speaking German.

"Very well. I shall return shortly. See to it the woman is unmolested," the older man said to the soldier.

Beecher!

He recognized the familiar voice and stole a glance to confirm his suspicion, he looked just in time to see his SOE superior leave the passage into the adjoining exit hallway. The soldier shot a puzzled glance at Thorne. Thorne grabbed the broom head and set to work as if putting the broom back together. The soldier ignored him and turned away in the opposite direction.

Thorne momentarily considered running after Beecher in hopes of overtaking him and forcing him to tell the whereabouts of Anna, but he chose instead to search for her himself.

Chapter Thirty-Eight

THORNE RACED TO THE END of the hall where the soldier disappeared beyond the opposite side of the telephone exchange room. Around the corner, he did not see the man, but looked upon an open doorway at the stairwell across from the telephone exchange. This is where Bulicek had instructed him to enter the lower levels of Englebert.

In reverse order from Bulicek's directions, he hurriedly climbed the steps to the main floor. Exiting the stairwell in front of the administrative offices which were now a bustle with workers coming and going, he caught sight of a clock that showed it was nearly six o'clock in the morning.

Good God!

His night errand had taken considerably longer than he realized—what had seemed like only a matter of an hour or so, had in fact taken Thorne more than three hours to accomplish.

An open staircase ascended to a short landing above him; the soldier had just made the top of the steps and stepped through a doorway disappearing into the second-floor offices. Thorne had no choice but to follow in hopes the soldier would lead him to Anna.

Workers crowded the office space—with the front gates of the Englebert complex locked, many sought an explanation from their supervisors while others simply sought shelter inside the building. Thorne swept through the mass of employees and made for the stairs. He hastily withdrew into the second story of Englebert where he found himself in a long room lined with several rows of desks. To his right, a door noiselessly drew shut; he rushed over and opened it in time to see the soldier vanish into another corridor. He darted into the long hallway and came to the end of the passage where he peered around a wall to see the soldier move up a wide set of carpeted stairs just beyond his grasp.

The décor here rapidly changed from neat and efficient, simple white walls and tiled floors, to luxurious paneled walls and marbled floors. As he approached the stairs, he froze—a portrait of Hitler glared down with menacing dark eyes from the top of the stairway. Half way up, the stairway took a bend to the left, and there on the landing, the soldier paused beneath the portrait. He lit a cigarette and saluted Hitler before passing out of sight toward the top of the steps.

Thorne set his broom down and pulled the Luger from his overalls. He released the magazine and freed a jammed bullet; the cartridge was dented rendering it useless.

And then there were four.

He crept up the carpeted stairs, pistol in hand, ready to face what lie ahead. At the top of the stairs, he pressed himself against a smooth, paneled wall and listened for sounds around the corner. *Nothing*. He poked his head around the corner and popped it back without being seen. In that short glimpse, he'd seen the soldier standing outside a set of doors, fumbling with his keys at the far end of a wide corridor, fringed on the right by curtained windows overlooking the Englebert complex. He did not hesitate any longer than needed.

Thorne exited the staircase with pistol held firm and closed the distance to the soldier who had not seen him yet. He ordered the man to hold steady during his approach. Judging by Thorne's appearance, the soldier assumed Thorne was an amateur with a gun. He dodged to his left, knocking a small table on end, and reached for his own pistol as he leapt for cover. Thorne wasted no time and took a hasty shot at his moving target; the man grunted in response as he scampered behind the table. Blood splatter on the wall confirmed Thorne had hit his mark, but ever-cautious, he thought back on his training in that instant, recalling the 'two-shot' rule. An SOE instructor's voice echoed in the recesses of his brain, "You must kill your man. One shot may kill him but it is better to be absolutely certain by putting two shots in him."

Thorne did not seek cover. His target was firmly in his sights, and convinced the table provided no shielding, he fired another round. He inched his way over to the edge of the table, gun held in check, and confirmed the soldier was out of action. As a precaution, he picked up the man's gun and pocketed it.

Next, Thorne rushed to the double doors, fearing

the pop, pop from his Luger may have alerted someone. He cowered low behind one door, gently pushing the other open. When nothing happened, he chanced a look into the room. He gazed into an elaborately decorated meeting room where sunlight struggled to penetrate thick curtains drawn tight on the right-hand wall. An eerie, blue radiance from that wane light hovered over everything in the room.

Opposite the curtains, several doors lined the wall; the middle door stood ajar. Silently with the stealth of a serpent and with pistol extended in front of him, he crept to the open door. Everything was dead silent in the room and he wondered if he had been led astray by the soldier he'd followed, yet something drove him forward.

He peered through the open doorway into a room furnished like the penthouse of a luxurious hotel. A bed jutted out from behind an interior wall a few meters inside the room. He tiptoed into the room, listening, searching. His eyes fell upon the disheveled bed; its ruffled sheets and blankets draped haphazardly onto the floor.

Something alerted him to an unnatural shape beneath the blankets at the foot of the bed. In a moment of panic, he rushed to pull the covers back, convinced he could detect the outline of an arm or a leg. With gun pointed toward the heap, he gingerly pulled the covering away, fearing what he might find underneath.

With a start, the bundled heap came alive; a tiny, bare foot kicked out of the covers. In the same motion, the blankets flew away revealing a woman in silk pajamas thrusting a knife forward in warning.

"Anna!"

She tossed the knife aside as he dropped into her outstretched arms in instant recognition. They held each other there, kneeling on the floor, and she hugged him with all her might as if to never let go.

"Anna my dear, I am sorry it took me so long to find you, are you alright?"

"Yes, yes," she replied through tears, but could not get out her next words.

"My darling, I'm here now. I have everything here I need to solve the Blackbird conspiracy," he said, patting the gunny sack under his arm. He set the satchel at the foot of the bed and laid the Luger next to it. He kissed her longingly for several seconds before she let out a gasp and rested her head on his shoulder. He helped her up from the floor, holding her outstretched hands in his own.

"Oh Richard. I thought you were dead. I thought you would never come—", her voice changed pitch in mid-sentence.

From behind him, a familiar voice broke their intimate reunion.

"Thorne, old boy. Beecher always said you were the clever one."

Thorne appallingly turned to face Allan Faulk who held a gun aimed at the two lovers.

Chapter Thirty-Nine

OUTSIDE THE ENGLEBERT COMPLEX, a black Mercedes came to a halt at the main entrance. Gerhard Mueller had driven through the pre-dawn hours after receiving a phone call in the middle of the night ordering him to Englebert. To his surprise, the gatehouse was empty. He ducked under the striped pole blocking the entrance to the factory and walked inside the perimeter of the factory grounds, confused at the disarray within.

Several meters behind the gatehouse, hordes of factory workers were kept at bay by a handful of armed guards. Beyond them, soldiers ran to and fro, setting up crude barricades and defenses. It was utter chaos. Workers ran from buildings on the far side of the factory grounds while soldiers and vehicles scurried about seemingly in all directions at once. He marched around the crowd inside the gate and moved toward a group of officers huddled far off to his right. Dressed in his *SD* uniform, he intended to get to the meaning of the commotion.

ANNA HELD THORNE'S SHOULDERS as she tried to hide behind his stocky frame. He felt something hard press into the small of his back signaling that she had picked up his pistol from the bed. Faulk looked haggard and worn since he'd last seen him. In an instant, Thorne recognized the missing piece to his puzzle.

Beecher isn't Blackbird, it's been Faulk all along!

Everything fell into place all at once: the chance meeting with Faulk outside Beecher's office, Faulk's shock to hear him on the telephone upon his return from Sweden, and his all too eager assistance in sending Thorne to Englebert. He guessed then that Faulk must have supplied the *Gestapo* with everything they needed to capture both him and Anna.

"Step away from the girl." Faulk motioned Thorne sideways with his gun. Thorne side-stepped away from Anna; his hands raised in surrender. "Now turn around. That's a good chap, walk backwards to me."

Thorne hesitantly took a step backwards.

One.

He shot a glance to Anna; their eyes locked briefly. He hoped his message transcended the space between them; *don't do anything foolish.* She lowered her hands behind her back innocently, looking at that moment like a schoolgirl having been scolded by her headmaster. Thorne took another step toward Faulk.

Two.

"Don't move," he heard Faulk command across his shoulder as Anna started to sit upon the bed.

"You're staying right where you are until I dispose of your friend." Thorne paused momentarily as Faulk continued, "If you're lucky, you will be able to see his execution just outside your window; the Nazis will surely assume he is a spy."

"And what do the Nazis do to traitors?" Thorne asked.

"Handsomely now, nice and easy," Faulk said ignoring his questions and urging Thorne to resume his exit from the room.

"All of Britain must be on to you by now," Thorne said. "We know about your scheme. Blackbird, Falconbridge, monies transferred behind closed doors, your relations with *der Furher*."

Three.

He took another step backwards continuing his repartee, "Even as we speak, Gubbins is sending teams of operatives into Aachen. For you didn't leave such a clean trail when you fled England." He could not see Faulk but hoped to exasperate him into confessing.

"Why should any of that concern me? I am safe here in my homeland. Even His Majesty could not touch me now."

"I can only imagine the expression on your face when I telephoned from Tempsford."

Four.

His left foot slid silently backwards.

"Beecher was furious when I stumbled upon his little scheme." Thorne forged ahead. "He tried to send me away, but I was too clever for him. When I showed up—back from the dead—you decided to take matters into your own hands. When your cronies couldn't rub me out in London, you decided to send me back into the fray, hoping I'd land right in the hands of the Nazis."

"You haven't the slightest idea. It was Beecher who wanted you out of the picture. But now he's turned coward and run off. He didn't have the courage to see it through."

"Just tell me this," Thorne continued, buying time. "How many agents did you eliminate along the way? Nuthatch? House Marten? Were there others?"

"Shut up," Faulk's cold, harsh voice barked in return. "I've had enough of your nonsense; you are going nowhere with your ploy. That's it, slowly, keep coming."

Five.

Faulk's feet shuffled across the floor in unison with his own.

"I'll be back for you later," he said over Richard's shoulder, obviously intended for Anna.

Thorne gauged the distance to Faulk estimating where he might be standing. If he performed a well-executed reverse somersault, he might take Faulk down in the process.

Too risky.

He would surely be shot as he rolled toward the man. Perhaps a swift turn and rushing onslaught; he might take a bullet, but he'd seen Anna's proficiency with handling a gun, she might get off a lucky shot. All of these thoughts crossed Thorne's mind in a split second. He knew that he could not leave the boardroom with Faulk or there would be no chance of escape for him or Anna.

Chapter Forty

ON A DISTANT HILL, FIVE HUNDRED meters to the north of the Englebert complex, a private in the U.S. 1st Infantry division calmly exhaled and locked onto his target. Through the scope mounted on his 1902 Springfield rifle, he spotted a Nazi officer walking across the paved entryway to the Englebert factory.

The Nazi walked at a steady pace; the sniper was able to keep him in sight. With the slightest effort, his finger pulled back on the trigger of the Springfield releasing a .30 caliber bullet into the air at 2,800 feet per second. The experienced sniper had already made the necessary allowance for the distance knowing the bullet would travel in an arc toward its intended target. He had been waiting for a target of opportunity and was overjoyed the instant the German officer had appeared in his sights.

In a perfect shot, the marksman watched a red cloud of mist erupt around where the Nazi officer's head had been, sending his flailing body tumbling to the ground. The assault on Englebert Tire and Rubber by the XIX Corps of the U.S. First Army had begun.

THORNE TOOK ANOTHER STEP backwards, *six*, and calculated his next move.

Unexpectedly, a siren sounded somewhere deep within the building, instantly followed by another closer in proximity, and yet others outside of the building. Had someone discovered his earlier capers and were just now sounding an alarm?

"Stop right there."

He judged by Faulk's tone that he was also surprised at the sound. With klaxons blaring wildly throughout the complex, Thorne heard a faint thundering boom. He listened intently. There it was again, somewhere in the distance. He stood framed in the doorway of the apartment with Faulk somewhere behind him in the boardroom.

Thorne watched Faulk's shadow skirt across the room; he took a chance and turned his head slightly to catch a glimpse of Faulk on the opposite side of the table, moving toward the curtained windows. Faulk's pistol was still leveled in Thorne's general direction, but his head was diverted to something outside. Anna leapt from the bed and ran behind the wall also seeing her opportunity at hand.

Another succession of booms erupted, closer this time. Thorne acted quick. He dove to the floor, scurrying for cover beneath the broad table in the meeting room.

"You fool!" Faulk shouted, and fired in Thorne's direction.

Chapter
Forty-One

THORNE LAY MOTIONLESS. A muffled boom shook the building again, this time very close, and he knew then what it was, artillery. Light reflected across the table onto the back wall casting an inset luminous square of yellow upon one of the portraits. He looked up to see Beecher's face bathed in yellow sunlight in one of the photographs hanging above him.

A shadow moved in the room and Thorne looked back under the table. Faulk's lower body was pointed in his direction, his gun gripped with white-knuckled fear, while he searched the room. Thorne also saw the pajama-bottomed legs belonging to Anna delicately creep from the far-right side of the room toward Faulk.

No! Thorne's brain shouted out, but he remained silent locked in a frozen moment of time. He saw her bare feet tiptoeing closer, closer, just a few steps from Faulk, whose attention must still have been diverted to the windows. And then in a reminiscent moment, he saw her arm crash downwards into Faulk's forearm, knocking his gun away.

Faulk yelped in pain at the surprise attack, but used his good arm to shove Anna away from him. Thorne lost sight of her then, but from the sound of her silk pajamas swishing above him on the table top, he guessed she had fallen onto the long table and slid across its smooth surface. In that confused moment, he heard a gunshot, and time stood still. For a never-ending second nothing moved, no one made a sound. Then slowly, Faulk crumpled to the floor like a puppet dropped by its master.

Thorne jumped up from under the table in an effort to reach Anna, but in those brief seconds from when he'd dived under the table, to the last when she took Faulk down, he had not realized he'd also been hit. A burning flame now shot through his left shoulder and he slouched onto the table.

"Richard! You've been hit!"

He braced himself up with his right arm and looked upon the dark stain forming over the front of his chest. He took a deep breath. "I think I'm okay."

She slipped over the edge of the table and rushed to him, quickly inspecting his shoulder. She blurted out, "Oh dear, let me get something to stop the bleeding," and dashed into the open apartment door before he could stop her. He stood propped against the table watching droplets of his blood pool on its surface. Small arms fire erupted outside the building and he wanted to get to the window to see what was afoot. Instead, he waited while she rummaged around in her room. *Hurry.* He started to call to her, but then a recognizable voice interrupted everything.

"You've certainly made a mess of things." Beecher stood framed in the doorway of the boardroom.

Thorne lethargically lifted his head and let out a deep sigh. "If it isn't the fox returned to the hen house." His breath came in short deep gasps.

Beecher smiled at him through grizzled, yellow teeth. "It is most unfortunate that you had to return just now Richard. You see, I'd presumed you were already dead. I'm afraid your arrival will not be as well received by my friends." He glanced around the room and dropped the smile; his next words came out coarsely, reminding Thorne of the day Beecher had scolded him about Falconbridge. "Was that really necessary?" He pointed to Faulk's body.

Where is she?

Thorne waited. Beecher too must have thought the same question at that moment; his attention turned from Thorne to the open apartment door. Beecher cautiously took a step toward the open door; he must not have carried a weapon as he probed the room looking for something to protect himself with. Beecher knelt down and popped back up with Faulk's pistol in his hand. He fumbled with the gun checking its readiness. In that second, a shadow crept along the floor at the open doorway but Thorne was not sure whether Beecher saw it.

"Why Thomas? Tell me why," he cried out in an effort to stall the elderly man. Beecher ignored his pleas and tiptoed closer to the open door. "My uncle always spoke so highly of you." Beecher took another silent step. Outside, machine gun fire sounded nearby.

The klaxons continued to blare within the Englebert complex. "But I suppose that was because he didn't know you were a Nazi."

Thorne felt a sudden exhaustion plunge upon him and he fell back into a chair. He spoke drunkenly, "I always looked up to you." He laughed out loud, thinking suddenly of a passage from *The Merchant of Venice.* "All that glitters is not gold," he managed to get out with a short cough.

Beecher snickered, then made his way toward Anna's room, his pistol wavering between Thorne and the open doorway. He kept one eye on the open door and the other on the SOE agent who now slouched onto the long table hopelessly dying in his chair.

And then the boardroom exploded.

Chapter
Forty-Two

S HARDS OF GLASS, BRICK, AND OTHER debris, showered the board room as the windows were blown in from a massive explosion outside the building. Thorne's hearing went deaf and he shielded his head from falling debris. Another explosion rocked the room, this time he did not hear it but felt the impact. He fell to the floor and scrambled across the floor gouging his hands on broken glass. His ruse—portraying the brink of death—had fooled Beecher just long enough to buy more time for Anna. He had waited expectantly for a gunshot or some other sign that she was on the offensive, but it never came.

Instead, he now rolled across the floor, looked under the table in the direction of Beecher, and saw the man lying prone next to a portion of brick wall. Azure curtains floated on unseen winds and sunlight shone on Beecher's face. His bottom jaw was gone, only a bloody mass of teeth and bone remained, and above the ragged opening, dark eyes stared blankly from their inset sockets. Thorne hadn't thought it possible, but

Beecher's head appeared even more skull-like than ever before.

Thorne tried to get up. His thoughts shifted to Anna's safety. He put his left leg under him and went to stand, but as soon as his weight transferred to his right, a hot pain shot upwards from his thigh and he collapsed into scattered debris. His hearing returned in waves—the silence in his head replaced by a loud ringing in his ears. Machine gun fire sputtered somewhere nearby. Other small arms fire crackled and popped outside the gaping hole in the wall.

"Richard!" Anna's muffled voice cut through the pandemonium of gunfire and blaring sirens. He felt her touch just before another explosion shook the building, dropping wreckage from the ceiling. "We must get out of here." She pulled at him, lifting his right arm over her shoulder and pushed with her legs trying to lift his heavy body.

He saw all of this from his awkward position on the ground. Laying on his side, he saw her tender feet, now scratched and bloodied from the chaos in the room, the satchel with the Blackbird documents tucked under her arm, showers of dust, smoke and other riffraff flying around the air, and Beecher's death stare haunting him from across the room.

He attempted to prop himself up but fell again as she tried desperately to lift him. He managed to get his good leg in position to help her and draped himself heavily upon her lithe frame. His blood dribbled onto her pajamas and he thought at that moment, what a shame he had defiled her beauty. "I'm sorry," was all he could get out in between gasps.

She more or less dragged him toward the door of the boardroom while he steadied himself on the edge of the solid table as he moved. An entire section of curtain was suddenly ripped from the wall and fell upon Beecher's body. Thorne said a silent prayer knowing that Anna would not have to see the grotesque face under the blue shroud.

As they struggled to leave the room, Thorne looked out the row of windows, now devoid of their glass, surveying the factory grounds. Men and women ran wildly seeking shelter in buildings while soldiers poured out of the same buildings shooting wildly into the distance. The entire scene was one of chaos and frenzy, absolute pandemonium. Civilians were mowed down in gunfire as they tried to find safety, while German soldiers huddled behind crates, damaged vehicles, and broken walls, taking up defensive positions against unseen attackers.

Anna pulled Thorne through the double doors into the paneled corridor where the soldier lay dead behind the table. From a cavernous opening in the wall, Thorne could now see a line of olive-green tanks positioned on the outskirts of the factory grounds, firing into the German positions and decimating the defenders.

And then another portion of the wall exploded between them, blocking the stairwell that was their escape, and they both fell to their knees. He reached out to hold her as she tugged at his sleeve dragging him toward her. For a moment he thought she pulled him closer, but then in horror, he saw spatters of blood across her face and midsection. He feared she was already gone, her hands clutched in a death grip onto his sleeve, as she slipped away from him to the ground. He looked into her calm face; she was an amazing woman.

She could be magnificent under any other circumstance.

The klaxons blared, the booming boomed, the gunfire grew louder, and the light grew dim as Thorne fell into unconsciousness.

Chapter
Forty-Three

AS THORNE CLIMBED OUT OF the depths of sleep, several unfamiliar sounds surrounded him; his mind struggled to determine his whereabouts. In the dream-like miasma that clouded his brain, he heard the rumble of a Jeep, moans from someone nearby, and a dozen other sounds he could not identify. He opened his eyes gently to look upon a green tarpaulin or canvas awning above his head. Sunlight filtered through the fabric casting an unnatural, chartreuse radiance upon everything. He heard himself breathing heavily as he turned his head to the side; someone lay next to him on a cot, heavily bandaged and in obvious pain.

He tried to prop himself up to get a better view of his surroundings but a sharp pain caused him to wince and lay back down.

"Easy there partner. You've had a rough go of it." A uniformed soldier knelt next to him. A white armband displayed a red cross. The soldier inspected Thorne's bandages.

"Where am I?" His voice sounded frail to his own ears.

"You sir, are under the protection of the U.S. First Infantry; the Big Red One," he said pointing to a patch on his shoulder.

"How did I get here?" Thorne asked looking into the freckled face of the young man.

"Well, we haven't pieced it all together yet. You're British. That much you told us when we found you. But we haven't been able to figure out what the heck you were doing in the midst of that German factory."

"I'm Richard Thorne. SOE Operative." He could see this meant nothing to the young man. "I'm a British agent."

"Well Mr. Thorne, you better just save all of that for the boys in G5. That's our Military Intelligence unit. They'll be most interested to learn all about you."

"What about the girl I was with?"

"Sir, I don't know nothin' about no girl. I'll ask around." Thorne laid his head back and closed his eyes fighting off sleep. The last thing he heard was, "Now you just rest up. We'll get this all sorted out when you're feelin' better."

Before he dozed off, he felt a warmth flowing through his body, something the medic had administered. He opened his eyes briefly once again and laughed aloud.

"What is it?"

"Your name," he said pointing to the soldier's left breast pocket. "It's Becker."

Chapter
Forty-Four

THORNE SAT UPRIGHT WITH GREAT effort and tucked a pillow behind his lower back in an attempt to ease the discomfort of the rigid hospital bed he was restricted to. The sun shone across central London and filtered through a window illuminating a clock on the wall. Its second hand annoyingly counted out the minuscule increments of his boredom in loud ticks that pricked at his senses. The sun also fell upon a locked wooden box that rested on a table near his bed.

A nurse appeared from behind a privacy screen. "How are we feeling today?"

"I keep telling you, I'm feeling just grand. I'm ready to get up and about."

"Doctor's orders," she replied handing him a glass of water and two pills.

"Where did that come from?" He pointed to the box and downed his medicine with a loud gulp.

"That arrived this morning, your personal effects returned from the Army." She dug in her apron pockets producing a tiny brass key, and set the box on his lap.

As she left him alone, he unlocked the box and set about taking inventory of his remaining possessions.

Personal effects? What could they have sent me?

He removed his forged identity papers and set them aside. Next, he pulled out a rusted set of pliers and the flashlight he'd carried in his pockets at Englebert, and set them on the bed next to him. He picked up a little cardboard box labeled Remington that he had never seen before and discovered that it was empty except for two cigarettes. All of these belongings had been placed in the box, on top of the floppy work cap that he had worn in Aachen.

There was nothing else in the box.

Then, as he began to put everything back, he noticed a piece of paper sticking out from under the cap. He pulled it out, slowly unfolded it, and read the words, "My dearest Richard." He moved the box to the bed stand and rushed back into the letter with both eager anticipation and cautious trepidation. As he read, he heard Anna's voice in his mind,

> "I hope you can see it in your heart to forgive me for leaving without saying goodbye. I will always cherish the time we spent together; your courage and compassion helped me get through those difficult days, and I am eternally grateful to you for rescuing me from the filthy hands of the Nazis.

> "I am going back to Nederland in search of my family, even now my mother and sister have probably returned home. I will use my

connections to discover the whereabouts of my father. I have no more to offer Stefan and his organization. My duty now lies in reuniting my family."

He looked away from the letter and let out a deep sigh. A coldness welled up from deep inside—the same feeling he got when he used to think about Catherine. Before his return to London, he had confirmed that Anna was alive and had come to visit him while he lay comatose in a morphine-induced sleep. She had left the satchel full of evidence against Beecher, which he later relayed to G5, with their promise to get it to SOE headquarters in London. He had hoped she would return again, but when the Americans were forced to pull back from the Aachen region, he too was transported towards the rear of their lines, boarded onto a medical ship, and eventually taken back to England.

He had given his time with Anna considerable thought in the days immediately after his return to London. With Catherine, he'd spent many months courting her, building a solid relationship. In Anna's case, he had only known her for a very brief time, and questioned whether he was really in love or if it was something else. He knew that when two people—often complete strangers—find themselves in a harrowing situation for even a short duration, they form a special bond, a certain relationship, bound by their shared experience. He wondered if he had actually loved her, or whether he was simply drawn to her through their mutual happenstance.

After a long reflective pause, he returned to the letter,

"Someday, when all has returned to normal, and there once again is goodness in the world, perhaps we shall see each other again. I will forever remember you in my dreams and prayers. Sincerely, Anna."

His arm fell to his side, dangling over the edge of the bed, the letter still clutched in his fist. He pressed his head back into his pillow and resisted the urge to cry. He closed his eyes and swallowed hard; a drowsiness over took him as his medication kicked in, and his thoughts drifted off into a dreamless sleep, while the tick of the clock echoed in the corridors of his mind.

Chapter
Forty-Five

A FEW DAYS LATER, AFTER HIS RELEASE from the Central Hospital in London, Thorne checked into the Grand Central Hotel in Marylebone. There, under strict doctor's orders, and no longer medicated, he was to remain for a few weeks while he recuperated and settled back into his new life. But he still had no clue what that would be.

Thorne lounged in a comfortable chair sipping a glass of Scotch while he did what he did best—weighed all of his options at hand, considered every angle—all the while pondering his next move. He relished in the joy of thinking through a strategy without being rushed; there was no immediacy or danger involved, just pure and simple leisure allowing him plenty of time to create his plot. This concept was new to him; he was used to decisions made under fire, in the heat of the moment. He savored the lack of pressure now.

Thorne finally announced triumphantly, "Rook to Queen's Knight Four." His opponent sat across from him and let out an audible *Humpf!* as Thorne moved his chess piece. Less than a minute had transpired since his opponent's last move.

Thorne looked across the vast lobby of the splendid Hotel where dozens of servicemen loitered in small groups, talking and smoking cigarettes. Some recuperated such as himself, others simply took leave from active duty and awaited further assignment. Beyond a marble water fountain surrounded by ferns and floral bouquets, he caught sight of a middle-aged man dressed in tweed talking to a woman behind the central registration desk.

She pointed in his general direction and the man turned scrutinizing each face in the room. Thorne in turn looked over his left shoulder in an effort to see if the man had caught the attention of another guest, and winced in pain as he did so. He leaned back taking another sip of his Scotch, massaging his shoulder as the man descended upon him.

"Richard Thorne?"

"Yes."

"Newbury, Arthur Newbury." The man reached down and shook his hand. Thorne, impassive to Newbury's introduction, eyed his opponent across the table suspiciously. The man made a move for his own Knight, but then pulled his hand back to his knee at the last second.

"Thorne, I'd like a word with you," Newbury looked toward Thorne's opponent who showed no notice of his arrival. "In private, if you please."

"I'm kind of in the middle of something, you see."

Newbury furled his brow. "Um, yes of course."

"It's okay. We can talk here."

Newbury scrunched his brow even further, and squinted at the other man in conjecture.

"It's all right, Walker can't hear. Took a shell just feet away from his foxhole. How he survived is a wonder, but he lost his hearing." Walker reached again toward the chess board and swiftly withdrew his hand.

"Make up your mind, you silly arse!" Walker did not look up, nor pay any attention to Thorne. "See? Pull up a chair."

Newbury crowded in close proximity to Thorne, placed an umbrella across his lap, and laid his derby on top of it. He scanned the room and cleared his throat. His hands crimped at the brim of his hat nervously. "Well, Mr. Thorne. It seems you're quite the hero—".

"I'll have to stop you right there. We go easy on the hero bit around here. Look around, every one of these men is a hero. They've all sacrificed something."

"Yes, I see. Well, you certainly have made an impression upon certain people with your actions overseas." Thorne sipped from his glass. "In fact, I hear you are to be highly decorated."

He placed his drink on the table next to the chess board. "Mr. Newbury, let's not beat around the bush. What can I do for you?"

"I've come from Military Intelligence, Secret Service." He said the last two words in a near whisper. Thorne looked at Newbury with both supposition and aggravation, and started to speak when Walker finally moved his bishop diagonally two spaces.

"I hear you're recovering quite well. Gunshots

can be a nasty business," Newbury added as he leaned forward with apparent interest in their game. Thorne was unimpressed by the well-dressed man, regardless of his branch of service. Newbury's brow compressed again. "Thorne, I'm going to lay it on the table. You're being transferred from SOE to SIS."

Thorne sat back. He took another drink.

"This came directly from Gubbins—no more adventures abroad—you'll be working for us in St. James'." Thorne showed no reaction. "As soon as you're fit that is."

Thorne took a deep breath and reflected on everything that had happened in the past sixty days. It had been a shear stroke of luck that the U.S. Army had advanced into the Aachen-Stolberg area on the very same day that he had made his foray into Englebert's administrative offices. He was aware only by rumor that they had been closing in. Having lost contact with SOE in the final days of his self-appointed mission, he had not been given official warning to avoid the area.

The Allies had hemmed the Germans into the ancient city forcing the Mayor of Aachen to order an immediate evacuation of the city, which in turn caused a mass exodus of people flooding the outskirts of Aachen. The U.S. Army began their assault on the city, including targeting buildings of strategic importance such as Englebert. In the same effort, and in one fell swoop, the Yanks had inadvertently eliminated both of Thorne's adversaries in the same stunning blow. This he learned from Gubbins upon his return to London.

He pondered the loss of Faulk. They had not been

close by any means, but upon their meeting in Baker Street so many weeks ago, Thorne felt as if he had renewed a lost friendship, and looked to his alliance with Faulk like a younger sibling looks up to an older brother. He had completely failed to notice Faulk's involvement in the Blackbird conspiracy, and spent several hours during the past few weeks rethinking their conversations during the whole affair.

Gubbins had revealed that Allen Faulk was the name of a British man missing since the 1936 Olympic Games held in Berlin. He'd also confirmed Faulk's true identity as that of Reinhold Franke, a known Nazi sympathizer prior to the War. However, he could not account for—or perhaps was reluctant to share the truth about—how Faulk had escaped expulsion from England in those early years, nor how Faulk had infiltrated SOE.

And then there was Beecher. Again, Thorne had failed to pick up on any clues hinting at Beecher's involvement in the Englebert funding scheme. He passed this off as a matter of his remoteness. For each face-to-face encounter he had had with Beecher, there were far more instances where their only communication had been via encrypted messages relayed by radio. Beecher's queer obsession with Shakespeare, and his insistence on using the sixteenth century texts in their coding scheme, had only further muddled their correspondence. There would have been no way for him to have pieced together Beecher's involvement. Oddly enough, the few clues he had received about Beecher came from Faulk, in an attempt to throw him off, and to keep Faulk from coming under Thorne's suspicion.

When he reflected upon the entire Blackbird conspiracy, and his unwitting role as a pawn in the game, he felt a certain betrayal; not only a betrayal of trust in his superiors and cohorts, but a betrayal of confidence in the overarching forces at work behind the scenes. His contempt for the system was further exasperated when Gubbins refused to divulge any additional information about the funding scheme, nor would he confirm whether Thorne's efforts had in fact contributed to the unraveling of a larger contrivance at work.

Thorne had checked the newspapers daily, bypassing stories covering the movements of Monty's armies and the Allied advance into Germany, and instead scoured the papers in hopes of finding headlines proclaiming the Bank of England's involvement in a global conspiracy to fund post-war Europe. There were no such stories.

He lamented for his colleagues in the various resistance factions in the countries he had worked in. He pictured Moller in Denmark, Stefan, Martin and Lowie in Holland, Sveinsson in Sweden, and countless other faces that he could no longer put names to. He struggled to put meaning behind the millions of other resolute individuals throughout the world doing their part on the front lines, behinds the scenes, or on the home front fighting against tyranny and oppression. He agonized over the fact that all of these people across the globe were caught up in something outside of their control.

All of these thoughts came to him in the weeks of recovery, and just prior to Newbury's arrival, Thorne had convinced himself that he was okay with it all; in some strange form of acceptance, he had buried everything, just like the pain he hid for Catherine and Anna.

While all of these feelings rose again to the surface just now, Newbury continued to ramble on about Thorne's skill as an undercover operative and the needs of Great Britain after the War. Thorne only half-listened to Newbury's proposition for engagement in SIS and his plea to join forces with MI6 in combating the rising threat of the Communist party.

Thorne took in Newbury's ramblings in one ear and parked the information on one side of a T-diagram, a sort of ledger in his mind. On the other side, he placed his desire to get away from it all. On opposite sides of the diagram, he listed the threats and dangers, the subversion and deception, and the sorrow and heavy heartedness that he had known the past few years.

In the brief stretch of time while Newbury spoke, Thorne computed a peculiar formula in his brain, weighing each feeling and emotion against its opposite characteristic, and formed a general conclusion. Each and every person on the planet is wrapped up in a larger community than themselves, each has a role to play in the greater society in which they exist. Even though they may not always understand that role, and even though they like to think of themselves as totally autonomous, seeking out their own destinies, in the end it's all part of the human condition, trying to discover oneself, attempting to assimilate meaning to all of one's experiences, and aspiring to define a sense of purpose.

At that moment, Thorne knew there was no other life that he wished to live. He coveted the chance for adventure, thrived at the hint of danger, relished in the threat of discovery, and savored the notion of working in isolation. He knew that he was a model candidate for that life style. Richard Thorne was a British Spy. Whether working abroad or at home, he lived to serve the Crown. He knew that whether working for SOE, MI5, MI6 or any other covert agency, in any such avocation, he could be happy.

As if suddenly coming out of a foggy dream, he ardently responded to Newbury, "When do I start?"

The End

Historical Note

In late September 1944, the United States First Army, under the leadership of General Courtney Hodges, advanced on Aachen, Germany. The 1st Infantry division—*the Big Red One*—moved in from the north, the 9th Infantry division took up a flanking position more or less in the center, and the 4th Infantry Division closed in from the south. The first battle of Aachen was about to begin.

Belton Y. Cooper describes the ordeal from the perspective of an ordinance officer in the 3rd Armored Division in his book *Death Traps, the Survival of an American Armored Division in World War II.* Cooper takes the reader into action as his unit sweeps through Normandy and into Germany, in the eleven months after D-Day leading up to V-E Day in April 1945.

Completely surrounded during the initial onslaught, General Gerhard von Schwerin, the German Officer in command of German troops in the beleaguered city, was given the option of surrender when approached by an emissary of U.S. Officers under white flag truce. He refused, and so began the onslaught of artillery and shelling of the ancient city.

A few days after the battle began it was all over—the Americans took over the city—Cooper's maintenance battalion moved into the Englebert Tire and Rubber Factory, finding it a perfect location to set up shop for repair of their armored vehicles.

Although the Germans would launch a counter attack pushing the Americans out of Aachen a few months later, I chose the first Allied onslaught as the pivotal ending for Richard Thorne's story. I placed him in the Netherlands in the days preceding *Operation Market Garden,* and set him on a course that led him to Englebert as he searched for the final clues about the mystery behind Blackbird.

When Cooper's outfit returned to Aachen in February 1945, they again chose to take up position in the Englebert factory. Cooper tells how he and a colleague explored the storage rooms in the basement of Englebert, and eventually came across confidential files which detailed correspondence between English firms and Englebert executives both prior to, and continuing on into the early years of the War—he and his colleagues were astonished to learn that business continued as usual throughout the War. This was the basis for my story.

I too pondered on how this relation could continue as war raged on in Europe and elsewhere, and decided to lay out a method in which clandestine communications might take place between the two countries at a time when it would have been difficult to have any normal correspondence through mail, telephone, or other means.

I set about devising the scheme between Blackbird

and Falconbridge—wholly fictitious—and developed my story on how such an occurrence could take place.

While SOE operatives were fully operational in the Netherlands and Belgium throughout the War, I took definite liberties as I moved Richard Thorne around between Europe and England, but hope I have presented one plausible scenario of how this type of nefarious business may have transpired during wartime in World War II.

About the Author

TED BOLERJACK has been writing historical fiction, poetry, sword and sorcery, and adventure stories since high school. The Blackbird Conspiracy is his debut novel. When not sitting behind his writing desk, he is often found studying jazz and playing the upright bass, or playing Table Top Roleplaying Games in a weekly game session with friends. Ted lives in rural Kansas with his wife Danielle, three dogs, and two horses.

Visit Ted's website: http://www.tedbolerjack.com

www.ingramcontent.com/pod-product-compliance
Lightning Source LLC
Chambersburg PA
CBHW062109290726

48975CB00001B/163